The Irish Connection

By

H. J. Sage

The Irish Connection

A Novel

By

Henry J. Sage

This novel is a work of fiction based on the author's imagination. Any resemblance to actual persons living or dead is coincidental. References to real persons mentioned in the novel are obvious.

ISBN 978-0-578-12548-0

Cover graphic adapted from original image of Molly Malone Statue, Grafton Street, Dublin, by Francis Tyers via Wikimedia Commons.

Rear cover image from *l'Université Paris Descartes*

Published by Sage American History
10509 Old Colchester Road
Lorton, Virginia 22079
www.theirishconection.org

Acknowledgements

I would like to express my deep appreciation to the friends who have taken time to read and comment on this book. Each of them saw it as a work in progress and offered timely suggestions and comments. Their support made the task infinitely easier.

Cammie Liddle read the entire manuscript through twice and carefully edited it for typos and other errors. She has a very keen eye for detail, and her expert scrutiny was invaluable. Jacqueline Wells followed the story as it was developing and offered meaningful commentary, especially concerning the personal relationships within the novel. Her sensitivity to the interaction of the family members resulted in a much stronger narrative. Carol Coose also applied her professional expertise in making suggestions pointing out errors. Her enthusiasm for the story was welcome indeed. Joanne Foster, also a writer and professional editor, offered valuable suggestions about strategies for approaching the construction of the original story. Her insights helped move the project forward at a brisk pace.

I would also like to mention and thank Chet Liddle and Jim Foster, who put up with my grousing and agonizing during our regular lunches as the work was in progress.

Finally, I must thank my wife Nancy and my daughter Jennifer Lian, who kept me on task and offered suggestions and commentary about the plot. Jennifer's expertise as a graphic designer also helped immensely with the layout of the book. Their loving support made the challenging job much more agreeable. The book is dedicated to them, with my deepest love.

Molly Malone

In Dublin's Fair City
Where the girls are so pretty
I first set my eyes on sweet Molly Malone
As she wheeled her wheel barrow
Through streets broad and narrow
Crying cockles and mussels alive, alive o!

Alive, alive o!, alive, alive o!
Crying cockles and mussels alive, alive o!

She was a fishmonger
But sure 'twas no wonder
For so were her father and mother before
And they each wheeled their barrow
Through streets broad and narrow
Crying cockles and mussels alive, alive o!

Alive, alive o!, alive, alive o!
Crying cockles and mussels alive, alive o!

She died of a fever
And no one could save her
And that was the end of sweet Molly Malone
But her ghost wheels her barrow
Through streets broad and narrow
Crying cockles and mussels alive, alive o!

Alive, alive o!, alive, alive o!
Crying cockles and mussels alive, alive o!

Words by James Yorkston, 1884

Prologue

Congressman Kellan Maguire picked up the private line in his office that was restricted to close friends, colleagues and family.

"Kellan, it's Jordan. What are you doing?"

"Oh, you know, the usual—drafting legislation, answering mail from constituents, learning how to speak Hungarian and practicing the fiddle."

"I didn't think you were very busy," said Senator Jordan Montgomery. "How about meeting me in the Senate dining room in about ten minutes?"

"Sure. What's up?"

"Tell you when I see you."

Kellan buzzed for Jean Slater, his Chief of Staff. "Jean, I'm going out for a while. Do I have anything important going on this afternoon?"

"You have a House Democratic Campaign Committee meeting at 3 o'clock. I can cover that for you."

"I should be back by then. If I'm not, you go ahead and I'll catch up."

"Who was that on the phone a couple of minutes ago? Anything I should know about?"

"Jordan Montgomery. Apparently I'm going to have lunch with him."

"Montgomery, wow! What do you suppose he wants?"

"You know, we're old friends from when we grew up together in Boston. He probably wants to discuss how to get New York Democrats to vote for him in the election. You know, something simple like that."

"I know you guys are friends, but lunch with the future president? Must be important. Well, have fun."

Jean's enthusiasm over Kellan's luncheon appointment was understandable. At the recently completed Republican National Convention, Jordan Montgomery, second term senator from Massachusetts, had won the nomination of his party for president of the United States. He had gone into the convention ahead in delegates, but had not quite overcome the challenges of his two strongest opponents. Nebraska Governor Samuel White had won several of the early primaries, but had faded. Senator Rafael Mendez of Arizona had run a strong third in the early primaries and had come in second twice in the later going.

Jordan Montgomery was nominated on the second ballot when Senator Mendez, who stood third in the race, withdrew his candidacy and asked his delegates to vote for his fellow Senator. Although the primary campaigns had been spirited, Governor White had quickly congratulated Senator Montgomery and promised his support. Apparent unity had been achieved. And now the Republican nominee had summoned the Congressman from the 19th District of New York.

Kellan Maguire and Jordan Montgomery had been friends long before either of them had run for office. They both were alumni of Boston College, though several years apart. Once they began to practice law, their paths often crossed, as their law firms both dealt in the same legal area. They had regular contact in courtrooms in Boston on opposing sides of their clients' cases. During the course of those sessions, they would often work together to reach settlements on behalf of their respective parties. They became close friends and often shared tickets to Celtics and Red Sox games. Kellan's sister Mary had also roomed with Jordan's wife Shelley in college, taking the friendship a step closer as the two families spent time together.

A graduate of Harvard Law School, Jordan had given up the practice of law to run for the Massachusetts House of Representatives, where he served several years before winning a seat in the United States Congress. After one term in the House, he won a seat as the junior Senator from Massachusetts. When Kellan followed Jordan into politics, Jordan acted as a mentor for Kellan during his first campaign for the House of Representatives.

Kellan had spoken with Jordan several times during and after the Republican convention, to wish him luck after an unsuccessful first ballot, and to congratulate him on his victory. Although they were members of different parties, the senator and the congressman had worked together closely on legislative matters based on their common legal experience.

In his most private moments, Kellan had contemplated the idea of running for president himself. Although known as an effective legislator, he was still too young and inexperienced, in political terms, and Jordan Montgomery was the only person with whom he had shared those thoughts. As Kellan headed for the Senate dining room, he could only speculate that Jordan wanted his help during the coming campaign, and had invited his old friend for that purpose. Still, Kellan was not so sure; he was dying to know what was really up, and he quickened his pace. He was directed to a table in a far corner of the dining room where Jordan Montgomery was waiting. On his way to the table Kellan noticed a Secret Service agent standing near the door.

Kellan and Jordan shook hands, and Kellan took a seat. "So I finally have a chance to congratulate you in person," he said. "I never had a doubt that you would win."

"When the first ballot didn't go the way we hoped, I have to admit I got a little nervous. White went down fighting." Jordan smiled and shook his head. "It was a good match."

Kellan could see that the flush of victory had not yet faded; he was pleased for Jordan. "So, my friend, what can I do for you?"

Jordan Montgomery leaned forward and placed his elbows on the table. Whatever was coming, Kellan saw that it was a matter of some import. "Kell, I've given this a lot of thought and I have made up my mind. You and I have known each other for a long time, and frankly, there's no one I trust more in this town than you. I want you to run with me for vice president."

Kellan was stunned. He leaned back in his chair and stared at Jordan. He thought carefully before responding. "Jordan, seriously, I am humbled and honored. But ..."

"Stop right there. I'll hear you out, but I want you to know that I have considered all the 'buts,' and I'm sure I know what your reservations would be. But"—he emphasized the word—"I don't care. You and I have worked too closely for me not to have considered you. Having done that, I've made up my mind. Besides,"—he smiled here—"you're from New York, and I need those votes!"

"Jordan, there are so many things—I hardly know where to begin. Not the least of those is the fact that I'm a Democrat."

"Yeah, and half the people in this town, especially the Democrats, think you're in the wrong party."

"Maybe so, but the people in my district elected me as a Democrat."

"Right. And come January, you won't be representing them anymore. You'll be helping me finish what you and I started right here. We've both been working toward the same end."

"That's true, I grant you. But Christ, Jordan, I know others have changed parties in the past, but I might have a hard time doing that."

"Nobody says you have to."

5

"God, Jordan, when was the last time that happened? Must've been way back when John Calhoun ran for vice president under John Quincy Adams and then under Andrew Jackson and got elected both times. From there on it was party tickets all away."

"I'd be lying if I said I didn't think there was risk involved, and I'll admit, it took some heavy-duty persuading by Bob Reynolds to get it past the guys on the RNC. But I've talked it over with some of the party bigwigs, and with a few exceptions, they think it's doable. You have a superb reputation. In less than three full terms you have sponsored or co-sponsored some very important legislation. You serve on two of the most powerful committees, two powerful subcommittees, and you're a workhorse. On top of that, in your spare time you wrote a best-selling book." Kellan was shaking his head.

"Shoot, Kell, you know the traditional view of the vice presidency—presiding over the Senate and going to ladies' lunches. Let me tell you, my friend, that's not what I have in mind. You and I have worked together on some important stuff, and I'd want you to be in the middle of it straight through."

"When did you first mention it to Bob?" Kellan asked.

"Toward the end of the primaries, when it looked as if I had a chance."

"What did he say?"

Jordan laughed. "He said, 'You gotta be kidding me.' But then he went and looked into your record, what you've done here in Congress, and he was impressed. You sold yourself."

Kellan paused and took a sip of water. If Bob Reynolds, chairman of the Republican National Committee was on board, he thought, then it very well could work. A waiter approached the table, but Jordan waved him away. "How many people know about this?"

"As I said, a few RNC bigwigs, a few members of my staff, and a few of my close friends in the Senate, including a couple on your side of the aisle. They're all sworn to secrecy until you make up your mind."

"It sounds like you're giving me a choice."

"Hey, there's no way I can force you, but believe me, I'll be real disappointed if you decline."

"There's some other stuff that might come up—you know about all that."

"The Irish stuff."

"Yeah, the Irish connection—Fiona for starters, and then there's Kathleen. She's got some stuff in her background that's still tender ground for a lot of people."

"I'm willing to take a chance on that."

Kellan shook his head, took a deep breath and looked up across the table at his friend. "When do you need an answer?"

Jordan Montgomery looked at his watch and smiled. "It's about 1:30. Shall we say by dinnertime?"

Kellan smiled and shook his head again. "Give me at least until tomorrow morning. We may both be committing political suicide, and it would behoove us to think it over carefully."

"I already have, and I've made up my mind. You're my man."

Kellan stood up and offered his hand to Jordan. They hadn't bothered to order anything to eat, but neither of them was thinking of food. "I'll get back to you as soon as I can. I just need a little time to catch my breath."

"Call me later this evening so I can twist your arm some more. And keep this under your hat unless you decide to say yes, which I know you're going to do."

Kellan smiled, nodded, and headed back for his office. He decided to skip the Democratic Campaign Committee meeting.

Part I

Ireland Forever

Thirty Years Earlier

Dublin

Kellan Maguire was tired. He had been studying well past midnight. He stood up from his desk in the carrel in the great library and stretched both his arms over his head. He brought his hands down and rubbed his face, yawned, then started walking down the corridor toward the Great Hall. It was early in the day, and there were few patrons in the magnificent old building. He had spent many hundreds of hours here during the last three and a half years, but he still enjoyed strolling through the corridors, looking up at the high, arched ceilings, breathing in the smell of thousands of old books, many with leather covers, along with the faint smell of wax from the polished tables and desks and partly, he was sure, from the years and years when candles provided the only illumination in these vast caverns where centuries of knowledge were stored.

He turned the corner and walked toward the reference desk, expecting to find her at her accustomed station. He stole up behind her quietly, put his hands on her shoulders and kissed her on the neck. She spun around and said, "Mr. Maguire, what do you think you are doing?" Her tone was mock angry, but her eyes were smiling. "I've told you not to be kissing me in the library!" she said.

He looked around but saw no one. "We're all alone," he said. "There's no one who can see us."

She glanced around, noticed that there was indeed no one in sight, and kissed him quickly on the lips. "Now I'll thank you to leave me alone; I've work to be doing."

"I have something I want to tell you that I think will be interesting. What time are you finished?" he said.

"The usual, five o'clock. Why don't you join me at that time?"

"I've got something to celebrate. Where would you like to go?"

She smiled at him again, her eyes bright with anticipation. "So it's to be a celebration, is it? Why don't you let me think it over. Meet me here at five, and sure I'll be ready to celebrate with you." She kissed him again quickly. "Now off with you."

He returned her smile, nodded and went back to his work space, closed his book and went back to his rooms for a nap. At five o'clock she was waiting for him at her desk. "So, where are we going?" he asked.

"Have you been to The Pig's Ear lately? It's just up on Nassau Street." Moira said.

"I've been there a few times. It sounds good to me."

"Well then that's it," she said. "Come on, then, we'll be off."

They walked out of the library and across the broad campus to the Nassau Street gate. They walked to the end of the block, crossed and entered The Pig's Ear, one of Dublin's many pubs. They sat down at a table, and a waiter approached. "Moira, Darlin', how are you? I haven't seen you for a while."

"Fine, thank you, Dylan, and yourself?"

"Oh, I'm lovely, Darlin', and who's your handsome friend?"

"This is Kellan Maguire," Moira said.

"Pleased to meet you, Dylan," said Kellan. He shook hands with the waiter.

"You sound like a Yank," said Dylan. "You must be a student, running around with a librarian." Kellan smiled and nodded. "Well, what'll it be, a couple of pints?"

"That will be fine, Dylan," said Moira.

Dylan brought their drinks and Kellan held up his glass for a toast. "To progress," he said.

"To progress," said Moira, and she touched her glass to his. "And what progress have you made today?"

"My law degree has been completed," he said. "They have reviewed my exam and thesis, everything is done, and now all I have to finish is my economics studies. I would think that by next March or April, everything will be done, and I'll be getting ready to go back to the States."

Moira smiled and said, "That's wonderful, Kellan. So you have decided after all that you won't be staying with us here in Ireland?"

Kellan detected a note of sadness in her tone, which he had expected. "I'd love to, but I have family back home, and the law firm where my father was a partner is expecting me to come and work for them. That's been my plan all along, and although I would love to stay here longer, I miss my country—my other country, I should say." He smiled, and Moira laughed.

10

"Yes, you've become a regular Irishman," she said. "You even have a bit of a brogue." He laughed and shook his head.

As he told Moira, Kellan had completed most of his course of study in law the previous spring, and that work was finally accepted, his Doctor of Laws degree earned. Now he was working toward completion of his master's degree in international economics. The law firm in Boston he hoped to join specialized in international law and business. His fellowship had ended after three years, but he had elected to stay on for an extra year at his own expense. He had managed the latter with what he had saved and by working in the warehouse of a Dublin paper company loading boxes into lorries and helping process orders. He still had enough to get by; according to his rough calculation, if he lived modestly, he would almost make it until time to return to the United States. Of course he still had to think about paying for his passage by ship or air, but he had time to plan for that.

Kellan's father Edward had died during his son's last year in college and left his wife with a trust that provided for her living expenses. Nora Maguire had been in poor health herself for several years, and, except for brief jobs before she was married to Kellan's father, had never worked a day for most of her life. As a partner in the Boston law firm of Phillips, Shannon and Steinberg—the firm Kellan hoped to join—Edward Maguire had made a good living. He had put three children through college, purchased a nice house in the Boston suburbs, and had invested, though not too wisely. At the time of his retirement he was able to provide for his family comfortably and planned to continue as a part-time consultant to his firm. Unfortunately, he had developed a fondness for the ponies, and some of those investments turned out to be disappointing. Like many gamblers, he thought he could recoup his losses at the track, with predictable results. In any case, all his plans ended with his premature death from a heart attack, and what was left of his estate had been spread fairly thinly among Kellan's mother and two siblings, Edward Junior and Mary Maguire.

Kellan had used the residue of his inheritance to finance his last year in Dublin, but those funds had dwindled. So he had worked part time to make ends meet. His mother would be able to help him with the fare for his journey home, but he hated to ask her for anything beyond that. Always resourceful, he knew he could survive, but it would take some doing.

Kellan had begun to become acquainted with Moira Connolly the previous spring when she had been promoted to the position of head

11

reference librarian at the historic Trinity College library, where he had spent countless hours since arriving in Dublin. He had sought her help from time to time, and as she got to know him better, she became more and more helpful to him in his studies. Of course, as part of her duties she assisted other students, but as their friendship grew, she was particularly attentive to Kellan.

Moira and Kellan had shared a few drinks from time to time at the pubs near Trinity College, and he had grown fond of her. Then one evening she had invited him to walk with her to her apartment, and he kissed her good night. On his next visit, she invited him in for a cup of tea. He sat down next to her on the couch and put his arm around her. She turned her face to him for his kiss and closed her eyes. She welcomed his embraces, but did not allow him to go too far. "I'm a good Catholic girl," she had said. "I can't allow myself to get carried away, as lovely as that might be." And so they would talk, often well into the evening, and he found her to be a wonderful conversation companion. And when he kissed her, she kissed him back, her lips parted, warming to his touch.

As Kellan's feelings for Moira intensified, he found himself very much wishing that their romance could go further, but he respected her wishes, just as he had grown to respect so much that was part of Irish culture. It was, after all the culture from which his family had come, and whose roots he felt very deeply himself, especially after more than three years in the Irish capital. Now he was aware that she hoped that her future might be tied to his, and he wondered if he were ready to take that step.

He loved everything about her, her voice, her looks—she was a classic Irish beauty, with dark blonde hair, blue eyes, beautiful white skin, and a full figure—and especially her mind. Her intellect was razor-sharp, and her sense of anticipating his needs truly astounding. From their frequent conversations, she was aware of his academic interests, and every so often she would stop by the table where he was working and place a book at his elbow. "You might be finding this interesting," she would often say, and most of the time it was indeed something that he found useful. It was almost mystical, the way she anticipated his needs. And now, here he was telling her that he was going back to the United States.

Dylan approached and asked whether they might like another Guinness. "I'll take a cup of tea," Moira said, and Kellan asked for the same. "You've been at your studies for a long time," she said to Kellan. "I surely admire your diligence. You haven't been back to America since you got here, have you?" He shook his head. "Your family certainly must miss you."

"My brother and sister were here last summer. Mom doesn't travel much—she hasn't been well for the last year or so."

Moira nodded, then looked at him and smiled. "Well, mister full of surprises, I've got something to ask you," she said. "I have a few days of holiday coming this weekend, and I'm going home to see my family. I've told them about you, and they're full of wanting to meet you. Could you spare a couple of days from your studies and come with me to visit them? I'd really enjoy having you get to know my father and mother. Besides, I have a younger brother and sister who are dying to meet my American friend," she said. "They'll be thrilled, and so will Mum and Dad. Now that your law degree is finished and you have only your economics to complete, I should think you could afford a day or two off."

"That sounds very inviting," he said. "I'd love to meet your family; you've told me so much about them, I feel as though I already know them. And I can sure use a break."

"Wonderful. It will be a treat for my whole family. The Irish always loved Americans, but many of us don't get to meet one very often, except perhaps in passing."

He laughed. "Half the people in America are Irish," he said, and she joined in the laugh.

"Well then it's settled. I'll be leaving this coming Friday on the train, and if you can come with me, that would be wonderful. It's about a three-hour train trip to Mallow, where I live. It's on the main line between here and Cork, so there are plenty of trains."

"That sounds fine to me," he said. "I can easily spare the time, and a train ride to Mallow sounds like fun."

Kellan met Moira at Kings Bridge station at nine thirty on Friday morning, and they boarded a train bound for Cork. As they rolled along through the green Irish countryside toward Mallow, they chatted casually. Moira told Kellan more about the life of her family. The Connollys had owned a farm for several generations, and it was finally starting to be a profitable enterprise. Moira's father Patrick and her older brother Brendan had hired two young men to assist them, and between the two of them and their workers they had turned their operation into a model of efficiency. They had a comfortable house on the farm, and Brendan and his wife Deirdre owned a second house about a quarter of a mile away on the same

13

property. They were planning to expand the original home to accommodate the entire family, but that was some time in the future.

"Some years ago they added a room onto the rear of the house where a young man who worked for us could stay," Moira said. "He eventually got married, and his wife moved in with him, so we were crowded for a while, you could say. But the room isn't very big, and when she got pregnant they had to find a place of their own. But the room is still there—it's where you'll be staying."

"I'm sure it will be comfortable, though I was hoping I'd be staying in your room," he said with a smile.

"With me in my room? Hold your tongue, or I'll be taking back my invitation!" she said. But she laughed.

At the Mallow railroad station Moira waved to a taxi driver. "Frank, can you take us home?" she called.

"Miss Moira, how are you, Darlin'? It's so lovely to see you back home." Frank opened the cab door for them. "And who is your friend?" Moira introduced Kellan to Frank the taxi driver, and they got into the cab and headed for the Connolly farm. "Patrick asked me to keep an eye out for you," said Frank as they drove. "Sure he'll be glad to see you—and your American friend!"

Moira's family treated Kellan like a long-lost brother. Her father, Patrick, shook his hand vigorously and gripped his shoulder firmly at the same time, his face all pleasure. Moira's mother, Elizabeth, "Libby," took both of his hands and seemed about to kiss him, though she restrained herself, even as she bubbled over with enthusiastic greetings. Moira's older brother, Brendan, shook Kellan's hand firmly and introduced his wife, Deirdre; they had been married less than a year. Moira's younger sister, Molly, giggled as she was introduced to Kellan, her eyes sparkling with enthusiasm. Kevin, the youngest of the Connolly clan, was only the slightest bit reticent in the face of all the enthusiasm of the rest of his family.

Kellan was shown to the comfortable room in the back part of the house that Moira had mentioned. He placed his bag on a chair, removed his coat, and looked out of a small window. He could see a barn and a broad expanse of pasture; in the open area beyond the barn he saw some cows, and on the other side of the fence sheep were grazing. He lingered over the view for a few moments, then joined the family in the living room.

14

Molly began pestering Kellan with questions about everything American, ranging from movie stars and popular music to his opinion of the president of the United States, who had visited Ireland the previous summer. Patrick Connolly evoked responses from Kellan on American economic and political events, revealing, Kellan thought, a depth of knowledge he found impressive if not surprising. Libby Connolly seemed equally well informed about the shape of the current American landscape, and Kellan soon became aware to his embarrassment that Moira's family was perhaps more attuned to goings-on in his native country than Kellan himself was. He had, after all, been away from his country for almost four years, and at times America had seemed very far away.

He found the experience with the Connolly family relaxing and invigorating at the same time. He had rarely been in such a warm and hospitable environment in a family setting such as this, although he had a number of friendly relationships with fellow students and professors at the University. But as they joked and laughed and told stories, he found himself drawn to the Connollys. Moira stayed close to him, occasionally reaching out to touch his hand. On his second day with the family Patrick Connolly showed Kellan around the outbuildings of the farm, pointing out where his property abutted that owned by his son. There was no question that the family was prospering, though Kellan could see from the state of the equipment and the buildings that they could not be called wealthy by any means. That they were comfortable was clear; that their condition was modest was also obvious. Nothing he saw or heard told him that they were content with their lot; they seemed to anticipate continued prosperity rather than betraying feelings of outright yearning for more than they already had.

The meals prepared by Libby Connolly consisted of staples of the Irish diet, each meal featuring a variety of potato dishes, vegetables and meats. The gathering around each table was noisy and animated, as the younger ones especially continued to pester Kellan for information about what seemed to be the mystical land across the sea that Kellan called home.

The weekend flew by, and as Kellan and Moira sat at the breakfast table on Monday morning before leaving for the train, Patrick Connolly said to Kellan, "So, I hear you'll be leaving for the States come next spring. That's a lovely thing for you, and we surely wish you all the best in your law career back in Boston. Moira has told us so much about it that we feel as though we know you better than we ought to, for only having seen you for two days. But it has been a pleasure to have you with us, and I do hope you will return before you leave." He turned to Moira. "Moira, Darlin', see to it that you bring this young man back to see us again. It has been a real pleasure to have him here."

"I will, Dad, I promise." She smiled at Kellan and reached for his hand.

"Sure it has been fine having you among us," echoed Libby Connolly. She had fussed over Kellan from the moment he and Moira arrived, making sure that he had everything he needed and that his room was comfortable. And she made a point of asking him far too often whether he might be hungry and would like a bite to eat, or perhaps something to drink. It was Irish hospitality at its warmest, and Kellan thoroughly enjoyed it.

When they arrived back in Dublin, Kellan rode the bus with Moira back to her apartment. "Why don't you come up for a bit," she said. "My friend Kathleen said she would be back from visiting her aunt in Belfast. I've told you about her, but you haven't met her yet. I think she would like to see if you really exist!"

"The pleasure would be all mine," said Kellan. He had heard about this rather strange friend of Moira's named Kathleen, but he had not yet made her acquaintance. Moira talked about her a great deal, and Kellan had become curious and looked forward to the meeting. Kathleen's aunt in Belfast had apparently raised her for much of her life, although Moira had said she was born and raised in Cork, not far from Mallow. In fact, Moira had said that she and Kathleen first met on a train going from Dublin to Cork; they had hit it off so quickly that they arranged to take the same train on their return to Dublin. Kathleen also had another connection with Belfast that Kellan was vaguely aware of, apparently a young man with whom she was involved, but Kellan knew little about that. In any case, he welcomed the chance to get to know Moira's best friend.

Kellan took Moira's bag for her as they climbed the three flights of stairs to her apartment. Moira tried the door and found it open. "Kathleen must be here," she said.

Moira's apartment was small, modestly furnished and neatly kept. The windows looked toward the south, and from the windows he could see the River Liffey and skyline of the busy city. As they entered, he noticed a woman seated at a table in the kitchen smoking a cigarette. She stood up and came into the room and looked curiously at Kellan. "Hello, I'm

Kathleen Morrissey." She held out her hand—her grip was quick and firm. "You must be Moira's American friend, Kellan," she said.

Kellan was surprised that she knew his name. She was tall, slender, and had classic Irish looks—copper colored hair, green eyes, and very white, smooth skin. She was striking looking, on the edge of being stunningly beautiful, but there was a hardness in her look. Something in the way she said 'American' gave him pause.

"Well, I am an American." He waited for a reaction, but saw none. "And I'd like to think I'm Moira's friend." He smiled at Moira, and she returned his smile, but she glanced at Kathleen.

Kathleen gave a quick, humorless smile. "Well, there's nothing wrong with being an American, as long as you think straight. I understand your name is Maguire, so I'm supposing that you do."

"I certainly hope so," he said.

"Most Irish-Americans understand what's going on here and appreciate who we are," she said easily. "But many do not, and that's a shame."

"Now Kathleen, there's no need for getting into politics right off the bat," said Moira. "Kellan knows a lot about Irish history; after all, he's been at Trinity for over three years, and he has studied a great deal about our colorful past." She spoke in a light tone, obviously hoping to keep the conversation on comfortable ground. She had mentioned to Kellan that Kathleen, although apparently not an active participant in any overt political activity, had very strong feelings and was ever ready to challenge people who didn't seem to understand what she felt to be a serious issue, one of which all good Irish people should be constantly aware. In common parlance, it was called "the troubles."

"Why don't we have a cup of tea?" said Moira. She started for the small kitchen-dining area, turned to Kellan and said, "You can stay for a while, can't you?"

"Sure, I can stay for a bit," Kellan said. "I have a seminar to attend tomorrow, but I don't have anything else today."

"So, Kellan, you've been studying history have you?"

"Actually I've been studying international law and economics," said Kellan. "I'm hoping to go into the international law field when I go back to the States."

"Well, it would be very nice if international law could do a better job in the future than they have in the past. A great deal of the world just stood

17

by and watched the British trample on us for centuries without lifting a finger to help. But that's all gone, and we can forget about it for now, but they still have their foot on our necks, and we have to throw it off."

"I'm sure Kellan agrees with you," said Moira. "But it's a very delicate issue, I think you'll have to admit. The Irish people certainly value their freedom, but not necessarily at the cost of violence."

"The only way to meet violence is with violence," said Kathleen. "The violence is what has been visited upon us by the British for generations; but there is a price, I admit."

"Well, I'm sure you two will have further opportunities to discuss Irish politics and other heavy matters, why don't we just relax and enjoy the fine day and talk of more pleasant things?" Moira kept her voice light, and she did not seem to be at all upset with Kathleen. Kellan was, however, pleased that she had steered the conversation away, as it was apparent that Kathleen was not ready to take lightly anything that challenged her basic feelings.

"So what else have you been studying besides economics and the law?" asked Kathleen. "I hope you've had a chance to study our literature. You know the finest English in the world is spoken in Dublin; that's something of a cliché, but I find it's true. English is such a lovely language, and the Irish have managed to put their own shine on it, as I'm sure you'll agree."

"Yes, I can see that," Kellan said. "Studying nothing but law and economics can be a huge grind at times, and I've always enjoyed Irish literature. I took a course on the Celtic Revival at Boston College, as well as other classes that dealt with Irish literature. Of course, I'll have to admit that Shakespeare is not that bad either."

Kathleen laughed. "Yes, as the Brits go, old William was not so bad, I guess," she said. "So you've gone beyond just Joyce, Yeats and Oscar Wilde. Have you read Patrick Pearse?"

Kellan smiled. The home of Patrick Pearse, for which the street was named, was right across from Trinity College, and he had passed it many times. "I've heard of him. He was part of the Easter Rebellion in 1916. I'm not sure I've read any of his work."

"Oh, you should. He was a true revolutionary writer."

The conversation wandered from Irish literature and history and other topics for some time, with Moira seeming to adopt a position of monitor for the conversation as she looked back and forth between Kellan and

18

Kathleen, whose conversation had become quite animated, though friendly. Kathleen asked him questions about America, the American political system, whether he was a Democrat or Republican, and she asked his opinion on some of America's political leaders. It became apparent to Kellan right away that Kathleen was very well-versed in the ins and outs of American political life, as she named Senators and Congressman from various parts of the country and seemed to be familiar with some of their ideas.

"You seem to be quite familiar with American culture," Kellan said. "Have you ever been there?"

"No," Kathleen said, "but I would like to go there someday. I'm not quite ready yet; there's too much to be done here in Ireland. But maybe when I'm getting ready to grow old and sit around on somebody's porch in a rocking chair, I'll be ready to go to America." Kellan and Moira laughed.

The time flew by, and eventually Kellan rose and said, "Well I'd best be getting back to my rooms. I want to go over some things before the seminar tomorrow and not walk in totally unprepared. Kathleen, it has been wonderful to meet you." He held out his hand and Kathleen gripped it firmly.

She smiled at him. "Well it's a wonderful pleasure to meet you too, Kellan. I know how Moira feels about you, so I'm very pleased to get to know you. I'll probably be here for a while since Moira and I live together much of the time. I'm sure I'll see you again, and I look forward to it."

A few days later Kellan and Moira sat in a pub enjoying a cup of tea. "Kathleen really enjoyed meeting you," Moira said. "That was quite a discussion you two had. She tends not to think much of Americans, but you're all right as far as she's concerned."

"Well, I'm glad I was able to pass muster. What does she have against Americans?" He asked.

"Oh, she just thinks they're too rich, too self-absorbed, too unconcerned with problems that they ought to pay more attention to. You know, there are problems in the states that kind of get swept under the rug, and Kathleen is tuned into things like that. She's very much against any sort of discrimination or oppression. I guess I don't need to explain any more than that."

"No, that's true. Even in Boston there are problems of discrimination, so it's not only in the South that you find it."

"Well in any case Kathleen surely did enjoy your company."

"I'm glad. She's a very interesting person, and she really seems to value your friendship."

"I think she does. She's had a very difficult life and I've tried to help her sort things out. I think she sees me as kind of a big sister, but in any case we've become very good friends, even though we're not very much alike."

"Well, as they say, opposites sometimes attract."

"So, Mr. Maguire, do you think we're opposites?" Moira asked.

Kellan laughed. "Well, I think we're a lot alike in many ways, but I'm sure we'll find enough opposites to keep us happy."

Now Moira laughed. "So, you said you had something you wanted to talk about?"

"Yeah, I've got a little bit of a problem. You're certainly familiar with it, but it has sort of come up again. I find myself running short of funds, so I'm going to have to go back to work at the paper company. My economics thesis is coming along fine, and I can spare the extra time to put in a few hours a week to make a little money."

"Sure I understand," Moira said. "You know if you're ever in need I can always …"

He held up his hand. "I know you'd be willing to help out, but I couldn't ask that of you. I hope you don't think it's just Yankee pride or something, but I do need to take care of my own finances. And if I keep going the way I'm going now, I won't have enough to make it through till I go back home, let alone pay my way back to Boston. But I'll be okay if I can put in enough hours to keep things going. The only problem is that I won't be able to see you as often since I'll probably be working several evenings a week, or maybe on weekends. Depends on when they want me to help out with shipping and the other stuff in the warehouse."

Moira looked crestfallen, but she tried a smile; it wasn't convincing. "Well, that's unfortunate, but I certainly understand. I do hope you won't abandon me altogether, for I would surely miss seeing you. I do enjoy being with you; I hope you know that."

He instantly realized that she might be misunderstanding his intentions, thinking that he might be trying to back off from their relationship. He reached across the table and took her hand. "Moira, I care a great deal for you. I want to see you as often as I can. I love being with you, please understand that. Your friendship is very important to me and I want nothing bad to happen to it. But I'll be more comfortable with you if

I'm at least solvent enough that I don't have to worry about where my next cup of tea is coming from."

"Oh, you'll always be able to get a cup of tea at my place," she said and she laughed. She seemed to relax a bit. "I'm glad you have strong feelings for me, as you put it."

"Moira, I love you. You know that." She squeezed his hand, and tears came to her eyes.

"I hope so," she said, "For I surely do love you."

Kellan knocked on the door of the manager's office in the warehouse of the paper company, opened it and stuck his head in. "Seamus, how are you?"

The manager of the warehouse stood up and held out his hand. "Kellan, my lad, by Saint Mary and Joseph, it's good to see you. Are you thinking of coming back to work for a bit?"

Kellan took the manager's hand. "Yeah, I'm a little short of funds; I hope you can find a place for me."

"Well business has been fine, Laddie, and I can always use a strong, hard-working young Yank to give us a boost. I told you when you left, come back any time, and by Gor, here you are. Tell me, are you sick of the books then?"

Kellan laughed. "It gets tiresome at times, but I enjoy my studies. They're moving along nicely, though, and I have some spare time on my hands, so I thought I'd put it to good use. You've been kind enough to hire me in the past, so this is the first place I looked."

"Well, you've come to the right place, all right. We've plenty to do, Lord knows, boxes to move and such. We may even get you out on some deliveries, if you don't mind. Other than that, you can help around the warehouse with sorting and preparing orders for pickup. As I recall, you know your way around, so I won't even have to train you—just put your back to it and go to work."

"That sounds fine, Seamus. I look forward to helping out. When would you like me to start?"

"Well, if you're up for it, Laddie, you can start this afternoon. As a matter of fact, one of my lads is out sick, so I'd be grateful if you could get right to it. There's a lorry out front that needs loading, and a couple of the fellas could use a hand. So if you're ready to go ahead, you can just pitch in and I'll start recording your time."

"Thanks so much, Seamus. I saw Colm and Donal out there, so I'll go dig right in. I really appreciate your taking me on. "

"Not at all, my boy. It's fine to see you again, sure enough."

Kellan actually enjoyed working at the warehouse. He needed the physical challenge of the heavy work; he always worried about sitting in the library too much and not getting enough exercise. The work was hard, but he did it easily, without much strain. He also noticed that when he went back to his studies, his mind seemed sharper and more alive. His body welcomed the exercise in contrast to what had become his custom. It was good for him.

When he was in the library, Kellan made a point of stopping by the reference desk at least once or twice a day to reassure Moira that his feelings had not changed. He would sneak out with her for a quick cup of tea or even a pint once in a while. She was pleased that he seemed to be in such good spirits, and her misgivings about his work schedule had disappeared. She was relaxed, and once again became her friendly, serious but still happy-go-lucky self. From time to time he would ask her about Kathleen, and Moira told him that she had found a job at a publishing house where she had worked before and seemed to be doing quite well. He asked her, "How is that friend of hers doing? I've forgotten his name."

"It's Liam. He's up in Belfast, and I guess she hears from him from time to time. I think he was down here for a few days not long ago, but he didn't come to the apartment. I'm not exactly sure what's going on with those two, except that she knows that he's involved in some business with Sinn Féin and perhaps even the IRA. She doesn't want to get too close to it. She seems to be quite fond of him, but I don't think it's a very deep relationship. We'll have to see as time goes on."

Kellan wished he had not mentioned Kathleen. He had found himself thinking about her, maybe too much; he changed the subject. "My thesis seems to be coming along. I should have a first draft completed fairly soon and will submit it for review. I'll still have to finish a few seminar papers. Sean Levinson, my advisor, keeps my nose to the grindstone, but he's a good man and I've learned a great deal from him. He also thinks very highly of you."

"Sean is a fine man," she said. "When I was taking classes, I always enjoyed his courses. He's a very interesting teacher."

22

December was the rainiest month in Dublin, and as the days grew shorter the skies were frequently overcast, and although the weather rarely got below freezing, there was often a damp chill in the air. Having worked long enough to replenish his bank account, Kellan felt that he could afford to take a break from the warehouse. Seamus agreed that business had leveled off from the peak activity of the fall, and he could get along without Kellan. As before, he invited Kellan to come back any time. "You're a good hard worker, and you've a fine head on your shoulders. Enjoy the holidays, Laddie; perhaps we'll be seeing you after Christmas."

Kellan had saved most of what he had earned, which meant that he could live comfortably at least well into the new year. He put in more time on his thesis, and his focus turned to the examinations ahead. He had always been a good student, even as an undergraduate at Boston College; after all, that was how he had earned his fellowship to Trinity, so his confidence was well placed. He looked forward to successfully completing his studies. Not wanting to take anything for granted, however, he put in longer days in the library.

One evening as he worked until past the dinner hour, he noticed that Moira was still at the reference desk. He closed his books, closed the door to his carrel, and met Moira at the reference desk to walk her home. They went out onto Pearse Street, walked down to the Burgh Quay and across the O'Connell Street Bridge over the River Liffey. They stopped in the middle of the bridge and looked at the lights shining off the river. "I often stand here on my way home," she said. "It makes me think of traveling on a boat to some other land."

"England, you mean?"

"Oh no, I've no desire to visit England—there's too much Irish in my blood." She paused for a few moments. "Too much history." She paused again. "No, like most of the Irish, I dream of going to America one day. Perhaps I shall." She looked at him and leaned in to kiss him. He held her in his arms for a few moments. Then she turned away and leaned on the bridge, and he felt a sadness come over her. He was not sure how to respond.

"I've learned a great deal about Irish history in my time here," he said. "It was spoken of often enough in my family at home. After all, most of my ancestors are Irish also." He looked at her and smiled. "This is my country, too."

She smiled. "As I said, you've even got a bit of a brogue, though no one would mistake you for a native Irishman just yet." He looked at her quizzically. "You've still got a lot of Yankee about you," she said. "But you are surely the nicest American I've met—and a lot of American students have come through the college." She turned, took his hand, and they continued walking across the bridge.

When they got to the apartment, Moira invited him in, and Kathleen was already there. The three of them chatted while Moira brewed a pot of tea. Kathleen was sipping what appeared to be a glass of whiskey. They talked about the coming holidays, and Kellan talked a bit about his job at the paper company, which he had found interesting although not especially challenging. He asked Kathleen how she liked her job at the publishing house.

"Oh it's fine," she said. "I've had some experience with editing before, and they have me working with a few young authors who are trying to get their books published. It's interesting to me as a writer to see how stories and books develop."

"How is your own writing going?" Kellan asked. "Moira tells me you've been working on some articles yourself."

Kathleen smiled. "I've sent a couple off, but have heard nothing yet. It takes time."

"You've been published before, though, am I right?"

"Yes, I actually had a paper published that I wrote when I was still studying up in Belfast. One of my professors put in a word for me. I've had a few others in newspapers."

Kellan held up his teacup. "Here's to success," he said. She reached out with her glass and clinked his cup.

"And Moira tells me you are busy writing your final thesis."

"That's right. Working on the final draft. I'll be glad when it's done."

"You've been in Ireland four years?"

"It doesn't seem that long, but yes—it will be four years in June."

"And then back home."

"That's right." Kellan glanced at Moira, and she smiled, and then she stood up.

"Well, you two can stay up all night talking about your writing, but I'm going to bed."

"Have a good sleep, Moira," said Kathleen. "I won't keep him too late."

Moira walked over to Kellan, leaned down and kissed him on the lips. He smiled up at her, and she ran her hand through his hair. Then she leaned down, hugged and kissed him again. "Sure I'll see you Monday," she said.

As Kellan and Kathleen sat in the kitchen talking, she turned the conversation to his feelings for Moira. "I take it you are rather serious about her, aren't you?" said Kathleen. "You two seem to be very close."

Kellan was a bit put off by the question, and for a moment he couldn't figure out how to answer. Then he said, "Yes I guess we are getting a bit close, but I'm not sure it will last forever."

Kathleen looked surprised. "Oh? I thought you were probably heading for marriage. Was I wrong about that?"

"Well, it's always been a possibility," said Kellan. "But we haven't made any definite plans. I'm going back to the States late next spring for sure, and I'm not sure what I'm going to do. Moira wouldn't come with me unless we were married, and I don't even have a job yet."

"Oh, I think you're very wrong about that. Moira is absolutely crazy about you; she'll be heartbroken if you leave without her."

Kellan thought that over for a moment. "She's not the kind of woman who would go off with someone without a ring on her finger, I don't think."

Kathleen shook her head, but then she said, "You may be right about that. Moira is very religious, though she doesn't make a fuss about it. Still, if you wanted her to go with you, I'd be surprised if she didn't jump at the chance."

"She is religious, and I often go to mass with her. I would find it very difficult to ask her to leave her job and family unless we were married."

"Well, you'll have to sort that out, won't you?" Kathleen said. "I'm not so religious myself, but I certainly respect her expressions of faith. I find that for me trying to believe in some God that I don't really understand is difficult. I was of course raised Catholic, and I do attend mass, though not regularly. I'm just not anywhere near as devout as she is."

"I go to mass fairly regularly," he said "though I have gone more since I met Moira. When I was in college I didn't go that much, but I think that's typical of college students. They tend to fall away while they're trying to figure things out for themselves."

"Well, whatever your faith may or may not be, I hope that you love Moira as much as she loves you. It would be a shame to see her disappointed."

25

Kellan didn't answer for a moment. He realized that if he did not acknowledge his love for Moira, Kathleen would react to that, no telling how. "I do love her. But she deserves to have something solid to look forward to, and at the moment I can't offer that."

"Oh, come on, surely you'll have a splendid job when you go back, what with all your studying. I'm betting that American law firm you talk about would snap you up in a moment."

"As a matter of fact I hope to go back and work for that firm—my father was once a partner there. But I've been away a long time."

"I think you're being far too cautious, Mr. Maguire." Kathleen smiled. "Sure I understand your position; I guess it's a matter of male pride. But I tell you true, I don't want to be around on the day when you tell her you're going off without her. That would be a sad affair."

Kellan shook his head and took a deep breath. "I know," he said. "I'll have to figure something out."

"Would you like a tot of Jameson?" she asked. "That might help you think."

Kellan laughed. "Sure, why not? Might as well be drunk as the way I am."

"Well, I have no intention of getting you drunk," Kathleen said. "No telling what might happen."

Later that evening back in his rooms Kellan found himself thinking about Kathleen. He wondered why she had asked about his relationship with Moira; she had obviously been probing to find out how serious he was, but he was not sure it was for her own reasons, or perhaps Moira had put her up to it. He rejected that notion, however; it just was not like Moira to do something like that.

No, he would have to figure something out. At the same time, he found himself drawn to Kathleen, though she was clearly off limits because of her friendship with Moira. Besides, his feelings for Moira were very strong, and he had given a great deal of thought to the possibility that they might become married. But as he had told Kathleen, he was going back to the states to work as an attorney. It wasn't all that simple.

He had been away for four years, and aside from a few friends he kept in touch with, he would have to start from scratch. He would have to get acquainted with American law and study hard for the bar exam, as not everything he had learned at Trinity would carry over. Building any kind of a relationship under those conditions once he was back in Boston would be a challenge. Still, he wanted to be married. He was in his mid-twenties, and it was time. Having a lovely woman like Moira who was his intellectual equal and a joy to be with was very appealing. But with his shaky finances, it seemed to him improper to propose marriage before he even had the promise of the means to support a wife.

If he and Moira married in Ireland, he would be responsible for her passage back to America as well as his own, and he wasn't sure how he could manage that. He was sure that she had some money set aside, but he could not depend on that to take care of their needs until he started drawing a salary at the firm in Boston. He could go back to the paper factory, but he couldn't earn enough there to make a difference. It was a quandary for him, and as he lay in bed thinking about it, he couldn't help but let his thoughts drift back to the other woman that he was getting to know, Kathleen. She certainly was attractive, and he felt himself drawn to her. She was, however, as he had already concluded, not available to him.

The holidays were approaching, and life at the University began to slow down as students prepared to go off for the Christmas break. As Kellan was talking with Moira at the reference desk, she mentioned going home for the holidays. "When are you leaving?" he asked.

"In a few days," she said. "And I've been wanting to talk to you about that. Could we go out after a while and have a talk? Why don't we go over to O'Neill's and have some dinner?"

The old Victorian pub on Pearse Street was usually festooned with flowers during the warmer months, but on this December evening it was not very crowded. "I've been talking to the family," Moira said, "and they're dying to have me bring you home for the Christmas holidays. I'm guessing that you don't have any other plans?"

"Well I was just going to relax and take a bit of a break. I hadn't really given it much thought, but if you are inviting me to your home, that would be lovely."

"Well then it's settled. I've asked Kathleen to come, but she won't be able, she says. I guess she'll be seeing Liam." She paused for a moment, and he couldn't suppress a momentary feeling of jealousy. "Anyway, everyone will be thrilled to see you again and we can have a few days together to just relax and enjoy the holiday time." Moira went on to talk about how her family celebrated Christmas, and Kellan told her about Christmas in his family as he grew up in the Boston suburbs. After a while she said, "Shall we have something to eat?" He thought for a moment and realized that he had left his wallet back in his rooms. He only carried some loose change in his pocket most of the time. She saw his fishing for his wallet and said, "Let this be my treat."

He blushed, but thanked her. "I'll pay you back," he said.

"Oh, that won't be necessary. Just walk me home later and that will be payment enough."

Kathleen was at the apartment when they arrived. As Moira took off her coat she said, "Kellan is going home with me for Christmas!"

"That's wonderful," said Kathleen. "I'm sorry I can't join you, but Liam said he might be here the day after tomorrow," said Kathleen. "You wouldn't mind if he stayed here a day or two, I suppose, after you've gone home, to be sure."

"No, of course not," said Moira. "You've heard from him then?"

"I got a note from him," said Kathleen. "He said there'll be no goings on during the holidays. He's been up to Belfast meeting with some of the members."

Kellan and Kathleen sat down in the living room. "I'll make us some tea," said Moira as she headed to the kitchen.

Kathleen said, "I'm sure Moira has told you my boyfriend has connections with the IRA." She looked at Kellan with an expression he decided was meant as a challenge.

"It has come up once or twice," Kellan said. "Even though I understand the history behind it, I'm not sure I see where it's going to come out well for the Irish. I can't see the British giving up Ulster, and I doubt most of the Irish people would be willing to go to war over it."

Kathleen glanced at Moira and smiled. She seemed to relax. "Liam hasn't killed anybody, as far as I know," she said, but there was no harshness in her voice. "Not that he wouldn't like to."

Kellan laughed. "There are plenty out there who need killing," he said, trying to keep it light.

Kathleen added in a sharper tone, "Liam's uncle was killed by the British." She shook her head. "The bastards."

"I'm sorry," said Kellan. "That must be hard to take."

"Well, he hasn't taken it well," Kathleen said. "Nothing I can do about that. I'd hate to see him get himself in trouble, but he seems bent on doing that." She shrugged her shoulders. "So, you two are off then," she said, changing the subject, to Moira's apparent relief.

Kathleen didn't seem to be in a mood for conversation and left Kellan and Moira alone. "So, we'll meet at Kings Bridge Station at half ten, day after tomorrow," Moira said at last. After he had put on his coat and was preparing to leave, she grasped both his hands in hers and said, "I'm so glad you're coming."

When Kellan and Moira arrived at the Connolly home in Mallow, it was clear to Kellan that the family had prepared for his visit. Libby told him that his room was all ready and that she had laid out everything that he might need. The two younger children Molly and Kevin were happy to see him again, and Patrick welcomed him almost like a long-lost son. Kellan was warmed by the greetings of the family and was glad that he had decided to come with Moira. As he seated himself in the living room, the conversation again turned to things in the United States and other matters that they thought he might find interesting.

The two younger ones continued to ask Kellan about all sorts of things; Kevin seem particularly interested in American sports, and was curious about the team known as the Boston Celtics. "It's pronounced 'Seltics,'" Kellan said. "I can't tell you why because I don't know."

Kevin smiled and said, "Sounds stupid to me." He had also heard of the fighting Irish of Notre Dame and asked Kellan why he had not gone to college there. Kellan explained that because he was from the Boston area, and because Boston College was a highly regarded Jesuit institution, that's where he had chosen to go to school. His father had also been an alumnus of Boston College, and one of his best friends had gone to BC a couple of years ahead of him and urged Kellan to follow.

"Mum said she was afraid you had gone to a Protestant college," Kevin said.

"I said no such thing," said Libby, who had come into the room. "There are many fine Protestant colleges in America, isn't that right?"

"Sure," said Kellan. "I just decided not to go to one, but not because it might be Protestant. Boston College is a fine school, that's all."

"See, I told you," said Libby to her son, but he was smiling at Kellan.

On Christmas Eve the family bundled up and walked to St. Mary's church. After Mass on Christmas Eve, Moira took Kellan around to the rectory. "I want you to meet Father McGuire," she said. "You two might be related," she added with a laugh.

The priest greeted Kellan warmly and said he had heard about Moira's friend from Patrick Connolly. "I doubt we're closely related," he said to Kellan. "There are lots of McGuires. But I'm sure we'll be seeing more of you."

"That would be nice," said Kellan. "It was a very nice service." Kellan noted that the homily had been about the importance of families, especially during the time of celebrating the birth of Christ.

As Kellan and Moira walked home, Moira slipped her arm through his as she continued to talk about her longing for America, and it suddenly occurred to him that he was being courted. Courted not just by Moira, but by her entire family, perhaps even by Father McGuire. Was the priest's homily aimed at him, perhaps? As he reflected on that subject during the Christmas Day meal, it almost seemed to him as if even Molly and Kevin had been enlisted on the side of the family designed to bring Kellan into the fold.

That he found Moira attractive was beyond doubt. He wanted to marry her. But more and more he came to the realization that the way she looked at him every so often, the way she reached out and touched him, the way she seemed ready to embrace him at almost any moment, conveyed the unmistakable sense that her attraction to him was far more powerful. He began to ask himself if he loved her enough, or perhaps more accurately, if he could really come to love her with the kind of passion necessary to sustain a marriage.

On the evening after Christmas, Moira suggested that the two of them take themselves to a local pub for some holiday cheer, where Moira hoped she might be able to introduce him to some of the friends she had grown up with. The Hibernian was crowded and noisy, and Moira introduced Kellan to several of her acquaintances. All of them, especially the women, looked Kellan up and down carefully to see what it was that Moira had brought home. When she told her friends that Kellan was staying at her home, their attention instantly heightened as they speculated that the relationship was heading for serious territory. Moira did nothing to discourage their joshing; neither did she say anything that embarrassed Kellan, but she was clearly pleased at all the attention he was getting.

Later that evening as they walked home they stopped on the bridge over the River Blackwater and stood quietly side by side, holding hands for a time and watching the water drift beneath the span. Before the silence grew awkward, he took her hand and turned her towards him, placed his other hand on her cheek and kissed her. "I've been waiting for you to do that," she said and kissed him back. She put her arms around his neck and he held her close. The kiss deepened until he began to feel his passion rising. He moved his hands inside her coat and around her back and pulled her closer. He had to tell her once more that he loved her, and at length he did. She shuddered with pleasure and pressed herself closer to him, whispering back that she loved him as well. A group of noisy revelers approaching from the direction of the pub interrupted their embrace. They both laughed, and he put his arm around her and they walked back in the direction of the Connolly household on Meadowlands Road. Everyone in the house was already asleep when they got home, and they took off their coats and sat together on the sofa in the living room. They embraced once more and she warmed to his kisses. He moved one hand toward her breast and she clasped it and pulled it tight against her. "Moira," he said.

She whispered, "Shhhh, I know what you want to say. I would love to come to your room tonight, but we can't do that. We have to wait until we are properly married."

He pulled away from her. "Moira, I do want you to marry me, but we can't do that either right now. I forfeited my passage back to the states when I decided to stay for next year, and right now I don't even know how I'm going to pay for my trip home."

"Are you sure you really want to marry me? I mean, if you don't want to, just say so. You don't have to be making up excuses about money." She backed away and looked at him with an expression that was almost angry.

He gripped both of her shoulders and looked at her intently. "I'm not making excuses. I'm just tired of being almost broke." He kissed her, then held her close and whispered into her ear, "I do love you. Believe me."

"Then let's not talk about money right now," she whispered. "And you shouldn't have bought all those gifts for the family, though it was sweet of you to do it."

"They've been so good to me, how could I not?"

The day before he was going back to Dublin by himself (Moira would stay for a few more days with her family), Patrick Connolly was up early as usual and was out looking after his estate for a few hours. He came back in, took off his outer clothes, fetched a cup of tea from the kitchen and picked up the *Irish Times* that Kevin had brought from the stationer's shop. "Slept well I hope," he said to Kellan pleasantly.

31

Kellan nodded. As Patrick turned his attention to the newspaper, Kellan came to the realization that although Patrick had fussed over him and been very interested in his life doings for the first few days of his visit, he had now settled back and seemed to have accepted Kellan as a more or less permanent fixture. There was no question that the Connolly family was looking upon Kellan as a serious suitor for Moira's hand. The thought gave him pause, and he wondered to himself whether or not his plea of financial shortcomings was indeed the real reason for his hesitance. Moira was lovely—of that he had no doubt. She was more than lovely, in fact, if not strikingly beautiful. A friend from law school with whom he had corresponded had asked about his love life, and he had described Moira as "sort of like a gorgeous Iowa farm girl." Although sturdy looking, she moved gracefully; her blonde hair framed a face that grew more attractive to him every time he saw her.

As he looked at Moira from across the table while they dined, he could easily imagine her at a dinner gathering with members of his father's law firm, which he hoped to join upon his return to America. He would have to figure something out. He realized that he had committed himself to Moira and to her family, and he would have to decide how to resolve the issues that lay before them—and between them. It was also clear that he would have to figure that out before leaving Ireland. Leaving her behind, even with the promise of a future together, he now knew would break her heart. Kathleen had been right.

Moira asked him if he would mind carrying a small bag of gifts for her friends and some other items back to her apartment for her. She gave him an extra key and asked if he would mind just dropping it off. When he got off the train at Kings Bridge Station, it was snowing lightly. He decided to walk back to his apartment. Pedestrians on the street slogged through the wet snow that covered the sidewalks. The strong Atlantic wind had dissipated since crossing from the west coast of Ireland, but it still blew the snow around and made people grab for their hats from time to time. His tiny apartment was chilly, and it seemed empty and forlorn to him, especially after he had spent the better part of a week in a comfortable, cozy, well-appointed home. The emptiness of his living space seemed a metaphor for the emptiness of his life, and he was pained at the thought that he could see no way out of that empty state, at least until he once again was employed at a regular job, hopefully at the Boston law firm where his father had labored for much of his life.

32

He dined at his usual pub that evening, and lingered with a pint of Guinness after he had finished his meal. Dennis, the bartender and waiter who had served him for much of his time in Dublin, walked over to Kellan's table during a quiet moment. "I haven't seen you for a few days," he said.

"I've been visiting a friend in Mallow," he said. "I was well fed and royally entertained," he added.

"Your friend in Mallow—I take it she was of the feminine persuasion?" He smiled. "I trust she kept you nice and warm."

"How did you know, you Irish snoop?"

"You have that look about you," said Dennis. Kellan looked at him quizzically. "You know, you look as if you were mellow in Mallow." He laughed at his own witticism. "Might my friend Kellan be in love?"

"Mellow in Mallow, that's pretty good," said Kellan. "But it's hard to be in love when you're down to your last few Irish pounds. I've got to figure something out."

"I could loan you a couple of shillings if that would help," said Dennis. "But I suspect that wouldn't quite do the trick."

"Not hardly," said Kellan.

"And here we've been thinking all the while that you Yanks must all be rich as Croesus." Kellan smiled and shook his head. "Well, good luck my friend. Can I get you another pint?"

"Why not?" said Kellan. "I might as well be drunk as the way I am."

Dennis was back in a few moments with a pint of Guinness; he placed it in front of Kellan. "This one's on me, my friend. In the New Year, may your right hand always be stretched out in friendship and never in want."

"Cheers," said Kellan. He held up the glass to acknowledge his friend's toast.

The next morning Kellan took Moira's package to her apartment. He started to unlock the door, thought better of it, put the key back into his pocket and knocked. In a few moments Kathleen opened the door. She looked surprised to see him, but also pleased. "Hello. Moira asked me to drop these things off. She'll be back in a couple of days."

"Sure. Just put them there on the table. How about a cup of tea, and you can tell me about your visit to the Connollys?"

"That would be nice."

They were seated at the kitchen table with tea and some biscuits. Kathleen asked him how he enjoyed his stay with Moira's family, and he told her how pleasant it had been. How Patrick and Libby Connolly had treated him with kindness. How Molly and Kevin had peppered him with questions and kept a running conversation for most of his time with the family. How comfortable the family seemed to be, even though he understood that their life was not easy, and that they had to work hard to maintain their standard of living. Kathleen asked him several questions, none of which seemed particularly pointed. Then she asked, "What did you think of Brendan, the heir apparent?"

"You've met him, I take it?"

"Moira has invited me down to visit a few times. You're quite right, they are a lovely family. But Brendan and I don't get along very well." Kellan said nothing, but he waited to see where she would go with her thought.

"Brendan thinks my involvement with what he calls the radical element is unfortunate. I have tried to explain to him how our struggle is necessary to maintain the freedom and dignity that the Irish people deserve. He thinks that if we simply go about our business and don't create a fuss, everything will continue as it has been." She took a long drag on her cigarette and blew the smoke out forcefully. She turned to Kellan with a look that said this was sensitive ground. "The poor man doesn't understand how wrong he is," she said. "He doesn't seem to realize the fucking British still want to take back what we have won from them. He does not understand that everything they've granted to the Irish has been given with a grudge, as if they'd been doing us fucking favors all these years."

Kellan said nothing for a few moments. Then he asked, "There's more to it, though, isn't there?"

Kathleen looked at him with a fierce expression. "You can bet your mother's britches there's more to it. You Yanks think you're all up to snuff because you ended slavery a hundred years ago. But how many Americans realize that Irish people were still enslaved after your Civil War was over? Well, our Civil War is still going on. We need to pay back those British bastards for every lash they've laid on our backs, for every piece of property they've stolen, for every Irish peasant they sent to work on their fancy plantations in the Caribbean. How they couldn't even leave us alone to worship God in our own way. Whether there's a God or not is beside the point; the people have a right to believe what they believe and to be left to their own devotions, for Christ's sake. What do you Americans know about that?"

34

"There are millions of people of Irish descent in America," he said softly. "I think most of them have a sense of Irish history. I know in my family stories were passed down from my great grandparents who came over during the famine. I took a course in Irish history at Boston College and have continued reading about it ever since. That's partly why I chose to come to Dublin, rather than Oxford or Cambridge."

"Well, you made the right choice there," she said. She blew out another stream of smoke with a vengeance. "Were those the only choices you had?"

"I thought about going to Heidelberg," he said.

"And ...?"

"I prefer Irish whiskey to beer, and I don't like sausage." He smiled, and Kathleen glared at him for a moment. Then she relaxed and chuckled.

"I actually enjoy German beer," she said. "And I also prefer Jameson to Guinness." She stood up from the table. "Should I brew more tea?"

"I should be going," he said, though he really didn't want to. He felt as if he would give her an out in case she was growing tired of his company.

She looked at him and smiled. "What's your rush? Moira said your work was close to being finished. Keeping me company for another couple of hours won't kill you, will it?"

And so he stayed, and they talked. They talk about history, language, poetry, why Irish football was superior to American football, and how the golf courses in Ireland were more beautiful than those in England. They got into politics again, but American politics this time, which was not as likely to provoke her stronger feelings. "Are you a Republican or a Democrat?" she asked.

"There are a lot of Irish politicians in my state, and of course they're all Democrats. I try to keep an open mind. I think principle is more important than party."

Moira had said that Kathleen's friend Liam would be visiting, but there was no sign of anyone else in the apartment. He asked her about her friend. She stared at him for a moment and then turned away. "Liam was here for a couple of days," she said. "Sometimes he's ... Sometimes he can be difficult. He's always under a lot of pressure, all of them are. He went back to Belfast with some of his friends, I'm not sure what for. He's a handsome devil, but sometimes he has straw for brains."

"He's in a dangerous business."

She looked at him sharply, then her visage relaxed. "They look into the face of death every time they begin a mission," she said. "Some of his friends have been killed. Others are in prison. He has a great deal of courage."

"I'm sure. There's been a lot of violence, and it seems there will be more. It's a shame that people have to die fighting for what ought to be available to everyone. You certainly know more about it than I do, but sometimes I wonder ..." He paused.

"You wonder if it's worth it?" She took a deep breath and sighed. "Well, I can tell you that Liam thinks it's worth it, and the Irish people are happy to have the IRA do their dirty work for them. Many will come out and condemn the violence, but they don't realize how much has been won by showing the British that we will fight for our rights. Just as you Yanks did a couple of hundred years ago. Nothing comes easy to an oppressed people."

"So much violence. You wonder where it's going to end, or whether it ever will."

They moved on to other subjects, but the conversation had lost some of its flavor. It came to him after a while how long he had been there and how pleasant it had been. Kathleen was very different from Moira, but he could see how they got along so well. He could see that Kathleen would put a spark into Moira's rather placid temperament, while Moira could smooth some of Kathleen's rough edges. But he realized later as he was walking back to his own lonely quarters that Kathleen's attractiveness was enhanced by her fiery nature. When her eyes flashed and she shook her head in sheer anger or frustration over some perceived wrong in the world, she showed a primal kind of beauty, the attractiveness of an animal prowling in the forest. A female wolf she was, an alpha female.

When he stood up to leave, Kathleen followed him to the door and out onto the stairway. As he turned to say goodbye, she put her arms around him, hugged him and said, "You're a good man, Kellan Maguire." She stepped back, smiled, turned and went back into the apartment and closed the door. The feeling of her arms around him had been electric.

Moira was due to come back in two more days. During his three and a half years in Ireland he had lived a carefree life, aside from his studies. He had made friends, both male and female, and he had had relationships with several women, none of which lasted more than a couple of months. The women he had been with had enjoyed his company, and he theirs, but both had always known that their relationship, however passionate, was not going anywhere. Each time he drifted apart from one of his women friends, he eased out of it gradually, and none of the women seemed hurt by his withdrawal. Indeed, two of them had probably been more than ready to end it, once they realized that they had no future with this impecunious American student.

But now his life was suddenly complicated. He was drawn to Moira, he was sure that he could love her passionately, and he knew that he had committed himself to a future with her. His financial embarrassment notwithstanding, he was sure that eventually they would begin to build a life together. But since returning, especially following his brief but intense encounter with Kathleen, the tiny shred of doubt that he had felt, even while in the pleasant surroundings of Moira's home, had begun to nag at him. He didn't like the feeling; thoughts like that made him feel as though he had already betrayed her, even though no harm had been done. Whatever had passed between him and Kathleen was, at least from the outside, perfectly harmless. Whether it was deeper than that he was not sure.

Dublin 2: The Dish with the Fish

Kellan met Moira at Kings Bridge Station and went with her to her apartment. When they were inside he asked her if she wanted her extra key back. "No," she said, "Why don't you keep it. Just in case."

"I had a nice visit with Kathleen," he said, not wanting that to come up later and surprise her. "She's very interesting."

"What did you two talk about?" Moira asked. There was no edge in her voice, and he wondered why he thought there might be. Later he concluded that whatever he had felt at that moment was coming from inside him and not from Moira. He had been stunned by how that brief embrace from her had touched him, but she had closed the door. He could honestly say that there was nothing serious going on between him and Kathleen, and Moira was obviously oblivious to the possibility. At that moment he described their conversation as being about history, literature and other obvious topics. All Moira said was, "She's very smart."

Confident that Kathleen would say nothing to Moira to arouse any concerns, Kellan relaxed. They talked of plans, but could only speculate upon what might be possible. Both were aware that the loose ends in their relationship would be difficult to tie up. Moira remained unfailingly optimistic, however. Kellan noticed that, and her certainty about a favorable turn of events, rather than easing his mind, only heightened his discomfort. He did his best not to show his concerns and steered their conversation to lighter topics, such as his coming final examinations.

Over the next few days he began to prepare for the end of his studies. His thesis was all but complete, and the only remaining classes he would attend were seminars where he would prepare for his written examination. He had already received his doctor of laws and would soon complete his master's degree in economics. He had focused his research on international economic issues in hopes of broadening his background in order to be able to pursue international law. The firm of Phillips, Shannon and Steinberg, which he hoped to join upon returning to the states, had as clients a number of businesses involved in international trade. The firm had a partnership with a firm in London, and attorneys at Phillips, Shannon could generally plan on spending a certain amount of time overseas.

As he weighed his options for completing his time in Ireland, he decided to write to Benjamin Steinberg, son of one of the founding partners of the firm and one of his father's best friends. He began his letter.

Dear Mr. Steinberg,

When you visited our home when I was growing up, I always called you Uncle Ben.' I still hope to join the firm, as we have discussed before, but I'm not sure that's appropriate. In any case I wanted to ask your advice on a couple of matters about my potential placement with the firm once I finish my studies here in Dublin.

The rest of the letter outlined what he had to complete with his academic program, and he refreshed Benjamin Steinberg on the international economic theory that he had studied during the past year. He suggested that working directly in that field might be appropriate, and he hoped for some confirmation that a position with the firm might be available to him.

In no more than the length of time that it took for two letters to cross the Atlantic, he got a response that pleased him. "Dear Kellan," Benjamin Steinberg's letter began, and then continued:

I have always been honored to be considered your uncle, as your father and mother were dear friends. But you are correct in assuming that calling me 'Uncle Ben' within the firm might be awkward for both of us. I realize that you will be a junior member of the firm, but in consideration of our long family friendship, you should feel free to call me 'Ben.'

The remainder of the letter suggested that the partners had already decided to bring Kellan into the firm as an associate, and were looking forward to his commencing as soon as it would be convenient following his return to the states. The last part of the letter was particularly gratifying to Kellan.

As a matter of fact, I will be in London in a few weeks and thought we might sit down to discuss your coming employment with us. I have spoken with your mother and she tells me you are, shall we say, financially challenged at the moment. I had hoped that you might be able to come to London to meet some of our partners there. However, I will be traveling with one of our business clients in their private plane, and I have arranged for them to bring me to Dublin so that we might meet face to face. I hope that will be convenient for you. Please let me know if the dates I am suggesting would be amenable to your schedule.

He closed the letter, "Sincerely and ever fondly, Ben."

The next time he visited with Moira in the library reading room, he told her of Benjamin Steinberg's letter and their forthcoming meeting. "The good news is, it looks as if I do have a job waiting for me." She was obviously excited, and pressed him for his thoughts on what it might mean for their future together, something for which she obviously had high hopes. He reassured her that as soon as he could see his way clear, they would be able to plan a wedding. She took both of his hands and kissed him lightly, glancing around to be sure that they were not being observed. Not that such behavior in the library would be frowned on, but she was, after all, a professional, technically a faculty member, and he was merely a student. They laughed over the rather preposterous notion that they needed to disguise their feelings for each other; all her friends on the library staff had been teasing her, she said. She suggested that they go out for supper, and he could walk her home afterward.

As they walked toward the Temple Bar they came to the corner where the famous statue of Molly Malone stood. Four people were standing in front of it, apparently tourists or visitors to the city. Three were posed in front of the statue and the other was holding a camera taking a picture. Kellan and Moira stopped so as not to interfere with the picture taking. "The dish with the fish," said Kellan with a smile; he had often heard the well-known nickname for the statue. Moira laughed. "It's amazing isn't it," she said. "Of all the beautiful things that we have to see in Ireland, the most famous is Molly and her low-cut blouse."

"Well you have to admit she is rather fetching," said Kellan. Moira laughed and slapped him on the arm. "You men are all alike."

Moira, being aware of Kellan's lack of funds, insisted on paying for dinner. He suspected that she did that to challenge his "Yankee pride," though in a playful manner. "That's very nice of you," he said. "I've been thinking about talking to Seamus about coming back to the warehouse. I saw him recently and he said he would let me know if he needed help. I guess business is slow this time of year."

"You should be concentrating on your coming exam and finishing your papers," she said. She reached across the table and took his hand. "Truly, it's my pleasure to share expenses with you. There's no need for embarrassment; I'm a big girl." Since returning from their visit to Mallow their relationship had changed; she was right; there was no longer any need for embarrassment. They shared a pleasant meal and lingered over tea as they discussed their future.

Back in her apartment Moira suggested they celebrate with a drink. "We've no champagne, but I've got Guinness," she said. He got up from his chair and joined her on the sofa and put his arm around her. As she turned toward him, he kissed her. He still longed for physical intimacy, and she was aware of his urges, but she remained adamant that the consummation of their love would wait until the wedding night. All the same, they embraced each other passionately when alone together, and on more than one occasion their desire threatened to boil over. He appreciated her modesty and her devotion to her Catholic faith, but his frustration remained. She did what she could to ease his pain within the bounds of her modesty. On this evening, however, she let him touch her intimately, perhaps because their prospects for the future seem to be improving. Then the door to the apartment opened and Kathleen came in. Kellan and Moira broke apart quickly, but Kathleen instantly recognized Moira's blushing embarrassment.

"All right, what have you two been up to?" Kathleen said with a smile. "Would you like me to go back out for a while?"

Kellan, just as embarrassed as Moira probably was, said, "No, no, I was just about to leave."

"Oh don't run off," said Kathleen. "If you like, I can just sit here and watch."

"Kathleen!" said Moira. But then she laughed.

"Well, you two do whatever you want," Kathleen said with a smile. "I'm going to have a drink."

Kathleen returned from the kitchen with her Jameson and sat down opposite Kellan and Moira. "So, what's up with you two?"

"Kellan has the promise of a job back in the States," Moira said.

"Ooh, that sounds promising!" She raised her glass. "Sláinte!"

Kellan and Moira raised their glasses. "Cheers," said Kellan, and Moira returned Kathleen's Irish toast.

"I guess you two have much to discuss," said Kathleen. "I'll leave you to it." She retired to the bedroom, winking at Kellan as she left the room.

Benjamin Steinberg was waiting in the lobby of the Fitzwilliam Hotel as Kellan arrived. They shook hands warmly, and Benjamin led Kellan to a small meeting room. "I thought we might have a little chat in private before we went in for lunch," he said. He took some papers from a briefcase and laid them before Kellan on the table. "Here's what we had in mind for you in terms of responsibilities, salary, and so on. Look them over at your leisure, and if you decide to sign, then we'll proceed from there."

Kellan scanned the papers quickly, set them down and looked at Benjamin. "I'll be very interested in going over these closely," he said, "but I have no reservations about joining Phillips, Shannon and Steinberg. I've had no contact with any other firm, nor is it my intention to do so. I would be more than happy to sign this right now."

"Splendid, splendid," said Benjamin. He produced a pen and Kellan appended his signature to the employment agreement. "I was hoping you would say that," said Benjamin.

"I can't imagine that you had any doubts," said Kellan.

"You've been gone a long time, Kellan—almost four years, and a young man can dream up all sorts of things when the whole world is in front of him. I see your mother from time to time and she never stops telling me how much you love Ireland. It occurred to me that you might want to stay here. And now I hear that you might have romantic reasons for staying, perhaps involving a young lady you met at the university?"

Kellan smiled. "I do have someone," he said. "We've been making plans, but of course I'm not in a position to make it formal right away. In fact, I've been trying to figure out how to arrange things for the future. I obviously can't expect her to come back to the States on the promise that we would be married right away. I'm not sure what to do, to be honest."

"I suspected as much," said Benjamin. He drew an envelope from the inside pocket of his jacket and slid across the table. "This is not something we normally do when we take on an associate," he said. "But your case is special. Your father was a valued member of the firm, and we are aware of how matters proceeded once he retired. Unfortunate, but things sometimes happen that way. In any case, this should clarify the situation to your benefit, and perhaps to that of your lady friend."

Kellan picked up the envelope, and Benjamin nodded for him to go ahead and open it. Inside was a check made out to Kellan in Irish pounds, a very handsome sum considering that it would be months before he started earning a salary. "This is more than generous," he said. "I don't know what to say."

Benjamin laughed. "Just say thank you, my boy. And let me congratulate you on your coming plans, both for your marriage—I'm assuming here—and for your agreeing to join the firm. We look forward very much to seeing you repay us with your legal skills, which you no doubt possess in abundance."

As they enjoyed lunch in the sumptuous dining room of the old hotel, Benjamin described for Kellan some of the business transactions they had been conducting on behalf of their clients. One was with a shipping firm in Belfast. "I'll be meeting with a vice president this evening for dinner," he said. "He invited me to meet with him in Belfast, but I've always preferred the charm of Dublin. As a Jew, I have always felt especially welcome in this city, especially since the Lord Mayor of Dublin is himself a Jew. We'd be delighted if you could join us."

"Thank you, but I'm sure you have important things to discuss."

"And you want to go and see your young lady," said Benjamin. He smiled. "*Omnia vincit amor.*" He held up his glass. "To the future, and to love!" He chuckled as Kellan touched Benjamin's glass with his own and said, "Amen!"

On his way back to Trinity Kellan stopped by the office of the Bank of Ireland where he regularly conducted business. He deposited the check in his account and withdrew some cash, more money than he had had in his pocket at any one time since he had first arrived in Ireland. 'Don't spend it all in one place,' he said to himself. He was smiling as he walked out of the bank. He hurried back to the library and went to Moira's usual workstation. "She's not here," said Moira's friend Darcy. "She said she had to go to the shops, and took the rest of the afternoon off." She smiled at Kellan. "You're looking particularly chipper today," she said. "I'm sure Moira will be in first thing in the morning."

When Moira answered the door in response to his knocking, Kellan put on a solemn face. "I've got some news," he said. She had started to embrace him, but stepped back. He broke into a smile. "I've got a job," he said. "I met with one of the partners of my father's law firm this afternoon, and he assured me that I will be hired. In fact, I've already been hired, and better than that, I've already received a check for signing a contract."

Moira looked at him for a moment as if trying to comprehend the meaning of what he had just said. Kathleen walked from the kitchen area and looked at them curiously. "What are you saying?" said Moira. Kellan just smiled. Moira suddenly grasped the meaning of Kellan's words. She put both hands up to her face and her eyes rimmed with tears. She threw her arms around him and held him, laughing and crying at the same time. She backed off and held him at arm's length, then wiped her eyes. "So we can …?" He nodded.

Kathleen walked over and hugged each of them in turn. She kissed Kellan on the cheek. "Congratulations, you two. I'm happy for you both." She hugged Moira again and said somewhat wistfully, "So then, you'll be heading for the States, Lassie."

Kellan produced a bottle of champagne he had brought, and Kathleen got three glasses from a cabinet. When they had finished drinking the toast, Moira sat down, folded her hands in her lap and stared at the floor for a few moments. Then she looked up with a look of near wonderment on her face. "Oh Lord, we've got to make some plans." She looked at Kellan. "You'll be wanting to leave for America as soon as you've finished your studies, I suppose."

"I think they're planning for me to start work by the first of July at the latest."

She nodded her head for a few moments, then looked up with an expression of concern. "We haven't got much time," she said.

Kellan smiled. "That's the good news and the bad news," he said. He raised his glass and offered another toast. "Sláinte!"

Kathleen raised her glass in return and said, "To both of you, and to your journey to America! Sláinte!"

They would be married in April, when his final examinations were complete. They would honeymoon in the west of Ireland for a few days, come back and bid farewell to her family, take a ferry to England and board a liner at Southhampton for the trip across the Atlantic to New York, and from there they would travel to Boston. Moira, flushed with excitement, repeated several times, "Lord, there is so much to do!"

Not long after they had finished the champagne and begun discussing their plans, Kathleen stood and said, "You two have a lot to discuss." She hugged Moira again, turned to Kellan and put her hand on his shoulder, smiled and nodded and went to the bedroom. There was something in her expression that moved Kellan, something of which Moira was unaware—blissfully unaware, it occurred to him. He had seen quite a bit of Kathleen recently, and it was clear that she was attracted to Moira's friend. Kellan found it a bit unsettling but did his best to ignore it.

He had no regrets about his plan for a life with Moira, but suddenly seeing his future mapped out for him after weeks of uncertainty was almost overwhelming. He listened to Moira ramble on about all she had to do, smiling, laughing, agreeing with her plans, even as she changed her mind about the details seemingly dozens of times. They talked long into the night, until she finally said, "Lord, I must sleep on this and let my head clear. It's so exciting!" They were sitting side by side, and she turned and hugged him. "I'm so happy, so very happy," she said.

"So am I."

"I guess we can consider ourselves engaged," she said.

"Yes." Then, embarrassed, he added, "I didn't have time to get you a ring."

"Shhhh. I don't need a ring. I have you." They held each other in a close embrace and kissed warmly. Then she broke away and said, "You'd better get out of here before I change my mind."

Kellan's remaining time in Ireland began to pass at a more rapid pace. He saw Moira almost every day in the reading room. She would come by the table where he was finishing up the last stages of his thesis, put her hands on his shoulders, glance around to see whether anyone was watching, lean down and kiss him on the cheek. He would reach up and place his hand atop hers, look up at her, and she would kiss him again on the lips. Sometimes he would stand up to stretch and walk to her post at her desk or wander around through the shelves to find her. Sometimes, if they were in a remote location and no one was in sight, they would embrace and kiss warmly, sometimes having to break from each other quickly when they heard footsteps approaching. Darcy caught them once and mock-scolded them. "I'm going to report you," she said, and they all laughed.

Moira and Kellan dined together frequently, generally sharing the expense; they both realized that although the check he had received from the firm was generous, they would have expenses before them until he started working regularly. As she had set aside from her income most of what she did not give to her parents, she would bring to the marriage her modest savings, which would ease their financial path in the near future. But they knew they could not afford to be careless.

As the days passed Moira's ardor for Kellan grew warmer, and very real; she told him from time to time how she ached for the consummation of their marriage, which only served to inflame his passions further. He had not been intimate with a woman for a long time. He knew she insisted on waiting, and as the time of the wedding grew nearer, he contented himself with the promise of what was to come.

In the middle of March Kellan turned the final draft of his thesis over to a typist he had hired and began reviewing notes for his final oral examination. He had worked hard at his studies and had always been a superior student. He was confident of his ability to pass all the tests that remained before him without a strain, and being so close to the end and possessing the confidence that had come from years of successful academic work, he felt relaxed and looked forward to his marriage, the voyage home and his new career.

With his growing sense of freedom from daily routine, however, came a growing impatience to be completely together with Moira, which made it difficult to focus on exam preparation. She suggested that they marry in early April, and then he could complete his exams. "That's a good idea," he said, "I'll be more relaxed." She smiled and agreed.

Toward the end of March as the university was preparing to break for the Easter holiday, Kellan found himself free on a Saturday morning and decided to invite Moira to join him for breakfast. Kathleen opened the door to his knock—he never used his key to enter the apartment unless he was sure neither of the women would be there—and looked surprised when she saw him. "Moira's not here," she said and smiled. "Didn't she tell you? She left yesterday afternoon to go home and help her mother with the wedding planning for a couple of days."

He had been immersed in preparing for his exam. "I guess I forgot," he said sheepishly. "We talk so much, and she's so worked up about the wedding, I sometimes lose track of what she's saying." He shook his head and chuckled.

"I know what you mean. She surely is excited," Kathleen said. "It's a bit of fun seeing her other than as her usually placid, staid self. She's a different person since you two have decided to get married, and it's only a few weeks off, thank God." Kellan looked around as if wondering what to do next. "Well don't rush off," said Kathleen. "I could use some company myself."

"I was going to ask Moira to join me for some breakfast," he said. He thought for a moment. "Maybe you'd like to join me."

They were seated at a small pub about a block from the apartment enjoying eggs, sausages, potatoes, toast and tea. Kathleen, who could often seem detached and somewhat aloof, was as relaxed and animated as he had ever seen her. She talked about what she had heard from Liam and the doings of the IRA. She leaned across the table and half whispered to him conspiratorially about some sort of planned demonstration. She was not sure what it was about, and expressed concern that somehow or other it might lead to some sort of violence, which had happened from time to time for much of the history of Ireland. Still, she seemed somewhat detached from the subject, which Kellan found a bit strange.

"Have you heard from Liam lately," he asked.

"Oh, indeed. He wants me to come up to Belfast again, but I can't go now. I love my job, and Moira is going to let me keep the apartment once you two leave. So I'll have to keep working. Besides, I love it here in Dublin, so I'll have to tell him 'no.'"

"Does he want you to live with him?" Kellan asked, sensing that he might have touched an area that was really none of his business. But he wanted to know.

"Oh, no," she laughed. "I'd be staying with my aunt again. I've lived with her off and on for much of my life. Things at my home were ..." She paused. "Difficult."

"I'm sorry," he said. "I didn't mean to pry."

"Don't be sorry," she said. "If Moira hasn't told you already, she'll eventually fill you in on my crazy life."

As if to put those thoughts aside, Kathleen shifted the conversation. She talked about her job in the publishing house as an assistant editor and regaled him with stories of a rather absent-minded, as she put it "half witted" senior editor, with whom she frequently disagreed. Kellan had become aware from what Moira had told him and from talking with Kathleen that she was an accomplished literary figure herself. Two of the essays she had sent off to journals had recently been accepted for publication. "They'll be out before you and Moira leave," she said. "I'll be sure you get a copy of each." Kellan was aware that Kathleen also wrote poetry, some of which he had read and found moving. She had drawn on the writings of some of Ireland's more revolutionary writers for her inspiration.

He continued to be surprised at how conversant Kathleen was with American political issues. She had well thought out opinions on a surprising array of political figures, including congressman and senators who were probably not at all well known by many Americans. She spoke knowledgeably of the American political system, often comparing it unfavorably with the parliamentary system used in most of Europe. "Your president is worse than a king," she said. "They ought to just put a fucking crown on him and be done with it." They both laughed.

"At least they're not born into it," he said. "They have to get themselves elected by the people."

"Yes, but once they're in that palace you call the White House, they get to thinking they can do anything they want. Look at Truman firing that general a while back, for example. What did MacArthur do that was so bad that he deserved to be fired?"

Kellan laughed. "Talk about people who want to be a king," he said. "MacArthur would've done it like Napoleon—putting the crown on his own head. He even made a brief attempt at running for president himself."

"I wasn't aware of that," she said.

"Good Lord," he said, "I've discovered something you don't know! What a surprise."

She laughed and reached for his hand. "Ah, Kellan, dear lad, you'd be amazed at how much I don't know—and how much you don't know about me." He smiled and let that pass, but wondered what was behind it.

The talk turned back to literature. Even as he pursued his legal and economic courses, Kellan had read further into Irish poets and novelists, occasionally dropping in on lectures when a favorite author was being discussed. By now he knew that Kathleen was exceptionally well versed in the subject. They discussed and argued the merits of various poets and their works, quoting lines and referring to poignant passages in the great Irish literary works. They agreed on much, disagreed on much, and their discussion was animated enough to draw the attention of the bartender waiter, who came over as he brought them more tea and asked if they might like to take their brawling outside. He joined in their laughter.

At length Kathleen said, "Come and walk home with me. You haven't anything better to do, have you?" Back in the apartment she produced a bottle of Jameson and took out two glasses. She poured the whiskey into each class and handed one to him "A toast to happiness," she said and downed her whiskey.

Kellan nodded and said, "Hear hear," and emptied his glass. She immediately poured refills and took another sip of hers. Kellan was already relaxed and comfortable, and the whiskey warmed him and loosened his mood further. Kathleen was good company, and he was again painfully conscious of how attracted to her he was. He sensed strongly that she had similar feelings for him. They continued to talk as they sipped the Jameson, and when they emptied their glasses, she refilled them again. She held up her glass and looked at Kellan with what was probably supposed to be a wicked smile. "I love to drink," she said. "It's good for the soul."

"Spoken like a true Irish woman," he said, and reached out with his glass to clink against hers. They tossed off the whiskey, and she refilled their glasses once more. As the whiskey worked on him, he felt himself drifting in a dangerous direction, as if he were in a small boat heading downriver toward a waterfall.

After a while Kathleen got up and walked to the window and leaned on the ledge before it. "Look at those kids," she said. Kellan walked over and stood next to her and looked down where some boys were playing football in an open area. "Moira loves children," she said. "I expect you'll have a large brood." He nodded and smiled but didn't say anything. Kathleen looked at him and he glanced at her, and the look in her eyes had an intensity he had not seen before. She turned her attention back to the boys three stories below. She sighed deeply, and Kellan felt himself moved to place his hand on her shoulder. She inched closer to him, tilted her head and rubbed her cheek against his hand. "You're a good man," she whispered. Mere awareness of the danger he was in, he thought, would not be enough.

Kathleen turned her face to him—she was so close he could feel her breath. He wanted to kiss her, but was afraid of where it might lead. But he did kiss her, and she parted her lips and placed her arms around him, turning toward him and pressing her body into him. Their kiss lasted longer than it should have, and he felt himself wanting her deeply. Then she pushed him away to arm's length. "I shouldn't have done that," she said, "But I just couldn't resist."

"Kathleen ...," he began.

"Shhh, don't say anything." She put her arms around him again. "Oh, Kellan, Kellan, if only ... "

"If only what?" he whispered in her ear.

She stepped back and folded her arms over her chest. "It's just the wrong time for us. Maybe if we had met earlier ..."

He went over to the table and sat down. He looked back at her, and she was staring out the window. She turned and looked over at him and smiled, but there were tears in her eyes.

"I'm sorry," he said. "I shouldn't have kissed you."

"I know. And I shouldn't have let you. It's just not our time—you have Moira, and you love her. I know you love her—I can see it every time you two are together. And believe me, I am happy for her and not jealous. Still ..." She wiped the tears from her face and sat down opposite him. Sanity had returned. She reached across the table and touched him gently. "Look, what's done is done, and we can't undo it. I love Moira, I truly do, perhaps not as much as you, but I would never do anything to hurt her. We'll just have to pretend this never happened; she must never know."

He took her hand and kissed it. "That's not going to be as easy as it sounds," he said. "I may have ..."

She interrupted him, suddenly growing serious. "Listen, for Christ's sake, if you start thinking you've made a bad decision or a wrong choice, forget it." She stood up and paced around the room. "If you ever thought about backing out or letting Moira find out what happened, I swear I would kill you."

"I couldn't do that," he said. "I just know that what I feel for you is very powerful, and it's not going to go away, even if I convince myself it was a mistake."

"Are you sorry you kissed me?" Her tone was demanding.

"No, no. But I can't help but feel ..." His voice trailed off.

"Neither can I, but that's beside the point. We have to do what we have to do. We've got to be strong, and we had better start right now. Next thing you know we will all be down in Mallow and you'll be married, and this will be a distant, pleasant and painful memory. We just have to get from here to there without screwing things up."

"I know. You're right."

"Just stay a while and talk to me," she said. "At least we will always be able to talk."

"We'll always be friends—more than friends. I'm never going to forget you."

"Nor I you. I'll wind up being godmother to your children." She smiled and wiped the tears from her face.

They sat for a long time saying very little. At length he stood and said, "I guess I'd better go."

"Would you like another drink?" She smiled.

"Jesus Christ, no." He shook his head. "It's good I wasn't any drunker."

She stood and walked to the door with him. He turned to her and started to speak, but she put her fingers on his lips. She put her hands on his head and bent it toward her, then kissed him on the forehead. "What a lovely man you are! Now get out of here!"

In keeping with Irish tradition, Kellan stayed in a small inn not far from the Connolly home during the two days before the wedding. Brendan rounded up some of his friends, a few of whom Kellan had already met, and they spent the eve of the wedding in a pub, drinking, joking, laughing, singing some Irish songs until Brendan finally concluded that Kellan did not want to be married with a horrible hangover, and the one he was already constructing would be more than enough to carry him through the day.

Kathleen stood by Moira during the ceremony, and Brendan served as Kellan's best man. The priest said all the right things during his homily, alluding to their coming trip to America, a voyage which had been made by millions of Irish people over more than a century. Libby fought off tears throughout the ceremony, and as she hugged Kellan at the reception at the Connolly home she said, "This is the happiest and saddest day ever. I've got a new son, but I'm losing a daughter. You have to promise me you'll bring her home from time to time."

"Of course I will," said Kellan. "And there's no reason you can't come and visit us in America," he said.

She smiled. "Patrick might not like that," she said. "But he loves you too, and he certainly wants to see Moira happy. Perhaps we both can come over."

"That would be wonderful."

There was whiskey and wine, and there were toasts, and there was dancing, and there was singing, and joking, and handclapping when the bride and groom kissed. After dancing with his bride, Kellan danced with Libby, he danced with Molly, and he danced with Kathleen, the last being a lively jig that they enjoyed, even as her eyes flashed with feeling. The assembled guests laughed as Kevin and Molly put on a show for the happy couple with a poem and a cheerful song originally composed by Moira's younger brother and sister. During a lull in the dancing Kathleen came up to Kellan and Moira, put her arms around both of them and kissed each of them on the cheek. "I love you both," she said. She squeezed Kellan's hand and walked away.

"I'm going to miss her," Moira said.

Kellan answered, "Yes."

Kellan and Moira spent their wedding night in a nearby hotel, to which Patrick had delivered them in a horse-drawn wagon. When they were finally alone in the room together, Kellan noticed that Moira seemed nervous and embarrassed. Though she was obviously happy and excited, her cheeks were flushed. She looked at him with adoring eyes. "I'll just go refresh myself," she said, and she disappeared into the bathroom.

Kellan took off his tie, jacket and shoes and stretched out on the bed. He had waited a long time, and whatever his bride needed to prepare herself, he was more than content to wait. After a few minutes she came out of the bathroom. She had combed out her lovely hair, which flowed down to the middle of her back. She wore a robe that reached to her ankles. It was buttoned down the front, and he was not sure whether she had anything on underneath it. As she walked over to the bed, he sat up and put his feet on the floor. She stood in front of him, leaned down and kissed him warmly. When she stood back up, he reached up and began to unbutton the robe from the top down. She watched with a smile, and her cheeks were still flushed.

It was a long time since he had been with a women he knew was a virgin, and he resolved to be gentle. He stood up and took the robe from her shoulders and tossed it onto a chair, revealing a sheer nightgown. She had nothing on underneath. She looked at him and began to unbutton his shirt. He undid his own belt, stepped out of his trousers, tossed them on top of her robe and stripped off his undershirt and shorts. He put his arms around her and pulled her tight into him, her body now pressing against his with a warmth that he had longed for.

"Are you scared," he asked.

"No, not at all," she said in a voice almost trembling. "It's just that I'm not sure of myself. I want to be everything you want me to be, and I'm not sure how to do that."

"Don't worry," he whispered in her ear, "you couldn't possibly do anything wrong." He kissed her deeply, ran his hands down her back and lifted her gown so that he was touching her bare flesh. He took hold of the gown and pulled it up over her head. Then he took both of her hands, lay back down on the bed and drew her down beside him. "We'll go slowly," he said, "as slowly as you like." She kissed him and ran her hands over his chest and down to his waist and below. He was aroused and ready for her. She lay back and pulled him over on top of her and whispered, "Now, my Darling, right now."

He moved over her and began the act gently, almost hesitantly, but she reached down to his buttocks and pulled him into her sharply. She gave a little gasp and wrapped her arms around him, and as he began to move she matched his movements.

"Oh God," she said, "I hated to make you wait for this. But I'm glad we did, aren't you?" She was breathing heavily.

"It's wonderful now, isn't it?"

"Oh yes, oh yes it is. Wonderful." She matched his movements with fierce intensity, and when they reached a climax, she gasped and whispered, "Oh my God, my God." She caught her breath and said, "Stay inside me, my love." In a few moments she began to laugh lightly. "I knew it would be like this," she said.

Later he lay on his back, her head on his chest. They were quiet—nothing needed to be said. He loved her deeply—no mistake had been made; there were no regrets to be found, even as other memories flicked through his consciousness, more or less against his will. "I'm so happy," she said. "I'm the luckiest girl in the world."

"Me, too," he said, and she laughed again.

"I didn't know you were a girl. And now I'm sure you're not!"

The next morning, back at the Connolly home for breakfast—their honeymoon would be their Atlantic journey back to the states aboard the *Queen Elizabeth*—he sat and watched Moira as she talked animatedly with friends and family, many of whom had remained for an extended celebration, as the couple would soon leave for America. Patrick sat next to Kellan and made it clear how proud and satisfied he was with his new son-in-law. Libby fussed over him, obviously confident that Kellan would take good care of her daughter, and that both her daughter and new son-in-law would always be a part of their lives. Kellan had a new Irish family, a good, warm, loving family. He would celebrate his last weeks in Ireland knowing that he would always have a home here.

He stepped outside to get a breath of fresh air, admiring the green, rolling countryside that stretched away beyond the city. Moments later Kathleen was at his side and he looked and smiled at her. "She's a lucky girl," Kathleen said. "She'll make you very happy."

"I'm sure."

"I'll be leaving shortly to go back to Dublin. I just wanted to let you know that Liam has asked me to come up to Belfast again for a few days. I think I'll take him up on it, and I just wanted to let you know so that you and Moira could share the apartment while I'm gone. How soon are you leaving for the States?"

"Early next month," he said. "I'm anxious to get started with the firm in Boston, but I still have to take my exam and clear my rooms. Then we'll come back here for about a week before we take off. We take the ferry to Liverpool and then board the *Queen Elizabeth* in Southampton."

"Your honeymoon cruise," Kathleen said. She took his hand and turned him towards her. "I don't expect to see you again before you go, but I do hope you will come back and visit us from time to time."

"Perhaps you could visit us in the States," he said.

She nodded, smiled, kissed him on the cheek and said, "You be good to her!"

Moira came out of the house just as Kathleen was leaving. They hugged and said a few words, and Moira came over to Kellan and put her arms around his waist. "She surely likes you," she said. "And I take it you find her company agreeable."

"I do."

"She's clearing out to let us have the apartment until we leave," she said. "But I'm wrapping up work in a week or two and then I'll come back here to pack up. You'll be finished by then?"

"Sure. We can spend our last few days here before we head for England."

She hugged him again. "That will be good. Mum and Dad will like that."

Two weeks after the wedding Moira ended her employment with the University. She was sent off with a farewell gathering at The Pig's Ear, her favorite pub. Her friends, sad at her departure but happy for her recent marriage, fussed over Kellan almost to the point of embarrassing him as they insisted on telling him what a wonderful choice he had made, and how happy they were that Moira had found such a fine young man, even if he was an American and would be taking her away from them. Darcy, who had been at the wedding, led the gathering in a farewell toast to the pair.

Moira's colleagues would miss her, they said over and over, then adding that they would miss Kellan too.

Toward the end of the evening Darcy came up to Kellan and handed him a wrapped package. "You've been with us for a long time," Darcy said. "We were all hoping you'd stay in Ireland." Kellan started to tear open the package, and Darcy nodded. It was a handsome, leather bound volume of Irish poetry. "Please don't forget us," she said with tears in her eyes. Kellan hugged her and whispered his thanks.

Moments later Moira's friend, bartender Dylan, climbed up on a table and gave a loud whistle. "Ladies and gentlemen," Dylan shouted. "To our guests who are not part of this unruly mob here in the front of the pub, I would ask you to join these kind folks in a bit of a toast." He beckoned Kellan and Moira to come over and stand next to the table. "These fine two young people, just recently married, are about to leave for America. Having served both of them with pleasure for a bit of time, I would ask you to join me in wishing our darling Moira and her new American husband Kellan as they prepare to leave us, surely not for good, we hope." He raised his glass and looked down at the two of them.

"Here's to you both, a beautiful pair
On the birthday of your love affair
Here's to the husband and here's to the wife
May yourselves be lovers for the rest of your life!"

The room filled with laughter, applause and shouts of "Safe journey!" and "God go with you!"

Dylan jumped down from the table, kissed Moira and hugged Kellan as the party applauded. Moira did her best to keep smiling through the tears that scarcely stopped until the last of her friends had departed.

The next day Moira packed up her remaining things and took the train home to finish preparing for her longer journey. That afternoon Kellan cleared his small rooms and moved his things to Moira and Kathleen's place, where he would stay until he left to join Moira in Mallow. Kathleen was still in Belfast and would probably not return before he left. He found himself hoping to see her one more time, but put that thought aside.

Kellan arrived at the seminar room on the morning of his final oral examination well before the appointed hour of 9 a.m. If he was mildly nervous, it was only because this would be his last official act at the great university before his leave-taking. He would be facing an examination committee of three. Dr. Padraig Murphy, Dean of the Department of Economics in the School of Social Sciences and Philosophy, would chair the meeting. Dr. Sean Levinson was Kellan's advisor, and Dr. Helmut Schweiger was a visiting professor of economics from the University of Freiburg, who had taken an interest in Kellan's economics thesis.

When the three committee members had assembled and seated themselves at a table across from Kellan, Dr. Murphy opened the session. "Mr. Maguire, I am sure you are acquainted with everybody here, so we will get started without further ado. We are here this morning to discuss with you your thesis, 'The Effects of the Marshall Plan on the Economic Recovery of Central Europe Following the Second World War.' You were requested to submit two additional papers from your work at the University for our review, and you chose to submit four. Your diligence has been noted. I have reviewed your work and am satisfied that you are ready to take this final step in this phase of your education. I would like to ask the other members if they wish to make any introductory remarks."

Sean Levinson spoke. "It has been my pleasure to advise Kellan during his final year of study here in Dublin. I was aware of his work during his previous terms, and he came to us well recommended by the law faculty. I have been impressed by his capacity for work, his diligence, and his imagination. I believe he has explored previously untouched areas of economic theory within the realm of his thesis study, and I look forward to discussing it with him."

Dr. Schweiger followed. "I must say it has been an interesting experience examining the work of an American, who has undertaken a critical study of his country's economic policy with regard to Central Europe, of which my country is a key part. I will say at the outset that I'm not convinced that Mr. Maguire has satisfied my curiosity about the justification for his conclusions, but I am confident that by the end of our discussion I will be further enlightened, if not challenged."

With that the questioning began. As Kellan had anticipated based on conversations with Sean, the first round of questioning was friendly, merely preparing the ground for a more penetrating discussion. As he had also been advised, or perhaps warned, by Sean and his other professors, Dr. Schweiger began to bore in on the subject of American policy as it related to postwar Germany, as the beleaguered nation sought to restore her place among her European neighbors. They went back and forth vigorously, with Sean and Dr. Murphy joining in from time to time, occasionally taking up the challenges of their German colleague, and occasionally supporting Kellan's ideas in a lively exchange.

Kellan was surprised when Dr. Murphy picked up a pocket watch from the table, looked at it and said, "I think it's time for a brief pause. This has been a profitable discussion, and we can probably all use a moment to refresh ourselves." It was 10:30; Kellan could hardly believe that an hour and a half had passed. Dr. Murphy's secretary knocked softly, then entered the room with a tray of cups, a pot of tea, and a plate of biscuits, and placed them on the seminar table. She smiled at the four scholars and excused herself. Kellan excused himself to use the restroom. He ran cold water in the sink and splashed it on his face with both hands several times. He had not slept well, despite his confidence that the effort he had put into his preparation would be sufficient. Although he did not really feel tired, he needed the bracing of cold water. He dried his face and returned to the seminar room, where he poured himself a cup of tea and took a biscuit. He realized that he had not eaten breakfast, so he helped himself to a second.

Dr. Murphy picked up the watch off the seminar table and said, "Well, I suggest we get started once more. This examination was scheduled to last three hours, but I think my colleagues would join me in concluding that Mr. Maguire has acquitted himself admirably, and we may be able to conclude after clearing up any leftover points of discussion. Agreed?" The two other professors nodded in agreement, and they sat down to continue the discussion. Kellan was pleased that rather than challenging his thesis, the remaining questions leaned more towards speculating about what the greater meaning of his ideas might be for the future. It was a friendly give-and-take about possible political and economic decisions facing the European nations and the United States as they sought to strengthen their ties against the continuing threats emanating from the East.

At about 11:30, a lull in the conversation prompted Dr. Murphy to wrap things up. "We would generally retire at this point to take a formal vote, but I think we can dispense with that step. Unless there is any further discussion, I propose that we declare that Mr. Maguire has admirably defended his thesis." He looked at each of the professors who both nodded and offered brief words of assent. "I would also like to comment on the superb quality of Mr. Maguire's writing. I understand from some of his previous studies that he has steeped himself in Irish literature, and I am pleased to say that his command of the English language, which is supposedly spoken more beautifully in Dublin than in any other city of the world, has been enhanced by his stay with us. I understand that Mr. Maguire plans to enter the practice of international law, a calling for which he is well prepared. I would hope, however, that in his pursuit of legal matters he will find time to put his ideas down on paper. I'm sure that as his thinking process matures, he will have much to offer in the way of economic, and I might add legal, theory, and I am confident that many journals both in his country and here in Europe would welcome his contributions." The two other professors again nodded their agreement.

"Well then, this examination is concluded." Dr. Murphy stood, walked around the table and offered his hand to Kellan and said, "Congratulations, sir."

Dr. Schweiger did likewise, adding, "Perhaps you will visit us in Freiburg one day. My colleagues and students would be interested in your ideas."

"That would be my pleasure," Kellan said. "I understand the firm I'm joining will have me focus my attention on European-American matters, so it's quite possible that I will be visiting Germany before long."

Sean Levinson, Kellan's advisor, obviously pleased at the way the examination had gone, shook Kellan's hand and said, "Well, off we go to your favorite pub and I'll be pleased to stand you to a pint and a meal. It will be well deserved."

Of all the friends Kellan had made since coming to Dublin, Sean Levinson stood high on his list of favorites. He was an interesting man, whose Jewish father had left Germany before the First World War and made his way to Ireland. He resumed his studies, which he had begun at the University in Berlin, and eventually married an Irish woman. His embracing of Irish culture had led him to name his firstborn son Sean. Sean had followed his father's scholarly path, had also married a charming Irish woman, whose company Kellan had also enjoyed. Sean had become a favorite professor at the University, especially among the international students. He and his wife Sheila had been unable to attend the wedding in Mallow, but they had invited Kellan and Moira for a celebratory meal after they returned to Dublin. Sean and Sheila had often entertained Kellan and other students, many of them from America, Canada and elsewhere in Europe, at their home. Those occasions had been among Kellan's most pleasant during his time in Ireland.

"You've made quite a name for yourself here," Sean said over lunch. "A lot of you Yanks come over here and spend more hours in the pubs than in the library. But you certainly made the most of your time, and you really impressed people when you decided to take a fourth year on your own." He smiled. "Of course, if you had not done that, you never would have wound up with Moira. She is certainly a charmer."

"I'm going to miss you, Sean," Kellan said. "You've been an enormous help to me, not only in my studies, but as a friend. It's been a long four years, and I was very fortunate to have people who made my stay here less lonely than it might have been. We will have to keep in touch."

"Well if you don't, I'll fly over there and break both your legs," Sean said, and they both laughed. "By the way, what's become of Moira's friend Kathleen? I understand you have been living in their apartment."

"She's got an aunt that she went up to Belfast to stay with. She has a friend up there who apparently has some connection with the IRA, although I don't know much about it."

"I thought she was working at a publishing house here in Dublin."

"She is," said Kellan. "I think she was just getting out of the way so Moira and I could relax during our last few days here—she probably took some editing work with her, but I have no idea what her plans are. From time to time she has mentioned the possibility of marrying Liam, her friend. I'm not sure how that would work out. I just met him once briefly and he seemed very nice, but also very intense."

"If he's involved with the IRA, that's bound to make him tense. My father's family has relatives in Israel, and I have some idea what it's like living in an area of constant conflict. It's hard to make a comfortable life in a situation like that."

"Well, I wish Kathleen well in any case. She's quite a woman," said Kellan. Sean looked at him for a moment as if he might say something in response, but apparently thought better of it. Kellan wondered whether Sean might have been fishing for anything of concern between Kellan and Kathleen, but he was reasonably sure that it could only be idle speculation. He had been very careful.

They parted company, and Sean advised Kellan that all of his papers and certificates would be signed and available the next morning. "You'll be wanting to hang all that stuff on the walls of your office," he said. They shook hands. "Good luck, my friend. May the sun always shine on you and your beautiful bride!"

Kellan packed a trunk full of extra clothes and books and took it to a shipping company for transport home. As he walked to the station to board the train for Mallow, he strolled one last time through the beautiful, grand old library. Feelings of sadness mixed with pride swept over him, and he blinked away a few tears as he left the building for the last time.

Crossing the Sea

Kellan and Moira stood at the railing of the *Queen Elizabeth* and watched the remaining passengers who were still boarding the ship. Their trunk was stowed in the baggage hold, and they had placed their carry-on bags in their cabin. Brendan had accompanied them to Southampton to help with luggage, but more important, to share a last few hours with his sister. When the announcement came for onboard visitors to depart the ship in preparation for sailing, Brendan turned and threw his arms around Moira. They whispered to each other as tears washed down both of their faces. He held her at arm's length and they both nodded as they confirmed promises of the sort that Irish family members had been making to each other for generations. He hugged her once more, stepped back, and Moira wiped her face and smiled through her tears.

Brendan turned to Kellan and grasped him firmly by the shoulders, tears still coursing down his face. Kellan said, "It was wonderful of you to come with us, Brendan."

"I wouldn't have missed it, Laddie. You're a good man, and I know you'll take good care of my dear Moira."

"I will. You know that."

"That I do, and you know that I love you like a brother, which, by Jesus, you are." He wrapped his arms around Kellan in a crushing bear hug and slapped him on the back several times. Then he kissed Kellan on both cheeks, stepped over to Moira, hugged her one more time, and started toward the gangway. Back on the pier, he waved to them as he continued to wipe tears from his face. Moira waved and smiled through her own tears.

Kellan thought about something he had learned during his stay in Ireland, the tradition of the American Wake. For decades the children of Irish families had been forced by economic realities to leave the green island nation in search of a better life. The vast majority headed for America. On the evening before their departure, friends and family would gather as if for a funeral, all being painfully aware that they would probably never see their loved ones again. They were occasions of sadness, even mourning, for in the earlier decades when diseases still plagued many

61

Irish people, the ships in which they were transported to America became known as coffin ships. Thousands of poor Irish people died during the transit to America, and the diseases they carried were considered so dangerous that for a time ships from Ireland bound for the states were no longer permitted to land. Instead, hundreds of ships discharged their Irish emigrants in Canada, and the unfortunate passengers would then by any means possible, sometimes even on foot, make their way south to join relatives in America.

Kellan put his arm around Moira and she rested her head on his shoulder. "I love you," she said. She repeated it, and Kellan whispered, "I know. I know how hard this is, but I promise I will make you happy."

Their cabin class room was small if comfortable—they had been unable to afford first-class passage. As the ship made its way toward the ocean, however, they felt relaxed and happy, looking forward to the coming days of relative peace and inactivity. They stayed on deck along with many of the other passengers until the English shoreline receded into a blurred outline on the horizon. The day was warm, the sea was calm, and the great ship gained speed and rolled gently in the Atlantic swell. "I'd like to rest for a bit," said Moira.

"You must be exhausted. Why don't you take a nap? I'll stay up here for a while and watch for icebergs."

She slapped him playfully across the cheek. "We're not on the bloody *Titanic!*" she said.

The first night passed peacefully, but the next morning the sky was grey, and the broad Atlantic flexed its muscles. Whitecaps appeared, and the motion of the ship grew more pronounced as it plowed through the darkening sea. Moira nibbled at her breakfast, sipped her tea and tried to look pleasant. Kellan could see that she was uncomfortable and was not surprised when she told him she thought she would go back to the cabin and rest.

"I'm told that if you begin to feel seasick, fresh air is a good antidote; I'll save you a place in a deck chair." He walked her back to the cabin, saw that she was comfortable, kissed her and went back up on deck. By midafternoon the ship was in a first-class squall, as rain swept horizontally across the decks, and the pitching of the ship became ever more pronounced. Moira had slept through lunch, and Kellan went back to the cabin to see how she was faring. She was not faring well. "I've been a little sick," she said. Her skin was paler than usual, her discomfort obvious from the cast of her face.

"What about some fresh air?" he said.

She smiled bravely. "Well, why not? I'm not doing very well down here, am I?" They made their way to a deck that was still open, although an announcement had been made that passengers should use caution when exposed to the elements. They sat in deck chairs for a while, and Moira acknowledged that she was feeling somewhat better. But then the ship altered course and the wind shifted enough to bring the rain straight at them. They retreated to the cabin, and Moira lay down again. Kellan left her and went to one of the salons to read.

On the third day out she was feeling rocky enough that Kellan decided they should consult the ship's doctor. Moira was not the only passenger who was exhibiting seasickness, but her symptoms seemed to be somewhat worse than those of the other passengers. She spent about fifteen minutes with the doctor, who came out and spoke to Kellan when he had completed his examination. "I don't think we're in any danger here," he said. Then he smiled, and Kellan looked at him curiously. The doctor continued. "I wouldn't be at all surprised if your young bride is going to present you with a child before you know it. I can't be sure without doing some tests, but I think she's pregnant. Congratulations."

"Did he tell you what he thinks?" Moira was actually smiling again. "Good Lord, morning sickness and seasickness at the same time! No wonder I feel as if I'd been drug around the barn!"

"Did you have any idea?" Kellan asked.

"I thought I might be but I wasn't sure." She shook her head and smiled. "Well, if I'm not, we sure have wasted a lot of effort!" She laughed, and embraced him in a warm hug. "I know we were not planning this so soon, but I can't say I'm sorry. I hope it's all right with you."

"Of course it is. Of course it is."

Dublin did not have any skyscrapers. Kellan and Moira stood on the deck of the ship as the tugs guided her into the pier on Manhattan's West Side near 52nd Street. Moira gazed up at the huge buildings, clearly thrilled to be in New York and thankful that the ship had finally ceased its pitching and rolling. The spire of the Chrysler building on the far side of Manhattan was visible, as was the Empire State building off to her right on Fifth Avenue and 34th Street, not to mention a multitude of other buildings, any one of which would have dwarfed even the tallest buildings in Dublin. She said very little, her eyes wide with wonder as she held her hand over her mouth and shook her head from side to side. "Jesus, Mary and Joseph," she muttered as she gazed at the famous New York skyline.

They had thought about spending a couple of days in New York, but decided that proceeding directly to Boston to begin the process of getting settled at home would take priority. There would be plenty of time to visit New York at a later date. Benjamin Steinberg had sent a telegram that Kellan received before the ship docked saying that a car and driver had been dispatched to pick them up and drive them to Boston. It was a kind gesture, one that Kellan appreciated deeply, as Moira was still somewhat shaky from her first seagoing venture—a very uncomfortable one at that. When they had cleared customs and were in the waiting area, Kellan spied a young man holding up a sign, "Mr. and Mrs. Maguire." The driver helped them retrieve their luggage and assisted Kellan in lifting their heavy trunk into the car.

"What's your name, driver?" said Kellan as the car headed up the Hutchison River Parkway toward Connecticut.

"Daniel Shea," said the driver. "You can call me Dan." Kellan nudged Moira and smiled. Daniel said, "I understand you're just arriving from the old country. Welcome to America."

"Well I was born here," said Kellan, "but Mrs. Maguire is here for the first time."

"Well then, welcome to you, Missus," said Dan. He took off his cap and tipped it in the direction of the back seat.

It was early evening by the time their car pulled up to the hotel in Boston where Ben had seen to it that a room had been reserved for them. On her first night in America in a comfortable hotel room, Moira barely slept. They had enjoyed a quiet meal in the hotel dining room, and Kellan had been surprised at how different the atmosphere seemed from the Dublin pubs. Rather than being friendly and garrulous like the Irish bartenders, waiters and waitresses, the staff in the hotel dining room seemed almost lifeless. Instead of music, there was only the soft drone of people talking as if they were afraid that somebody might overhear. Moira had been subdued and didn't seem to notice the difference, but she was probably tired from the long drive from New York. She had fallen asleep quickly after dinner, but toward midnight she had awakened and sat in the window of their room gazing at the lights, traffic, and buildings of downtown Boston.

"Are you feeling okay?" he asked, sitting up in bed and watching her.

"Oh yes, I'm fine," she said with a smile. "I just can't believe we're finally here!"

Ben had left a message for Kellan to call him at home when they arrived. He told Kellan that the firm would be taking care of their room at the hotel for a week, giving them time to look for an apartment. "We can extend that as needed," Ben had said, and when Kellan protested, he added, "Don't be silly. You've been gone for four years, you haven't got a stick of furniture or a car, and you're going to need some time to get settled. We'll talk about it when you stop by the office." Ben added that Susan Johnson, one of the firm's secretaries, would provide a list of several apartments for rent, but that could wait until they had rested from the trip. "Come in when you get rested up a bit."

"We'll try to come by tomorrow," Kellan said, and Ben replied, "Take your time."

Kellan fell back asleep, waking briefly when Moira came back to bed sometime later. She woke early, and Kellan heard her in the bathroom; her morning sickness, though milder than while they had been aboard ship, was still with her. She came back to bed and snuggled up next to him, kissed him and said, "Now I'm hungry again." She laughed.

"We can go down for breakfast if you like."

"Oh, I'm fine. There's no hurry—I'm not starving." She put her arms around him and drew closer to him. "Let's just stay here for a while."

As they breakfasted in in the hotel dining room later that morning, Moira had regained all of her color and was bubbling with excitement. "I can't believe I'm really here," she said. She reached across the table for Kellan's hand and squeezed it.

"Do you know there are supposed to be more Irish men and women in Boston than there are in Dublin?" he said with a smile. "Many of them live in South Boston."

"Is that where we will be living?" Moira asked.

"No, no," he said. "Southie, as they call it, is a lot like your Northside in Dublin. It has a lot of rough edges. We'll probably be living in one of the close-in suburbs. I'll call Susan later this morning and find out where the apartments are and we can begin looking. I also want to pay my respects at the firm. I want to show you off."

"Oh Lord, I don't feel like being shown off today."

"Nonsense, you look lovely, and they will all be dying to meet you, especially Ben Steinberg. You'll like him."

After breakfast Moira wanted to go out for a short walk, just to take in the surroundings. The cities of the Northeast, from Baltimore to Boston, were well known in Ireland because of their large Irish-American populations. They walked a few blocks and then back to the hotel, as Moira gazed at store windows and looked at people on the sidewalk hustling to jobs or other destinations. She said little, but her eyes took in everything, and she murmured comments about what she was seeing. "Why are they all in such a hurry?" she asked, though she really didn't seem to want an answer.

Kellan just smiled and shook his head. "It's the way we are," he said.

"Are you ready to go and meet the partners?" Kellan asked after they had returned from their stroll. "I think I should pay my respects and introduce you to Ben and some of the others. I probably won't know any of the younger lawyers in the firm. I may remember some of the senior ones who were there with my father." He walked to the window and looked out, but Moira didn't say anything. Then he turned back to her and smiled. "It's been a long time."

Half an hour later Kellan and Moira walked into the reception area of Phillips, Shannon and Steinberg. A nice-looking young woman in her mid-thirties was seated at a reception desk, and Kellan noted from the nameplate on the desk that she was Susan Johnson, who had arranged for the car, the hotel and the coming apartment search. As they approached the desk Susan stood and came around and held out her hands. "You must be Kellan," she said taking both his hands and smiling warmly. She turned to Moira. "And you are no doubt Mrs. Maguire," she said and she took both of Moira's hands. "Even more lovely than I expected!"

"Thank you, Miss Johnson," said Moira, blushing furiously.

"It's Mrs. Johnson actually, but please call me Susan. May I call you Moira?"

As Susan was leading them to Ben Steinberg's office, Moira whispered, "How did she know my name?"

Kellan laughed. "This is a small firm," he said. "They'll be treating you like family in no time."

66

Ben Steinberg proved the point by greeting Kellan with a hearty hug. Then he took both of Moira's hands, kissed her on both cheeks, and said, "Moira! What a wonderful pleasure to finally meet you!"

Moira look surprised, smiled and said, "Thank you Mr. ..." But before she got any further he interrupted her.

"Oh for God's sake, call me Ben," he said and laughed. "Kellan has written so much about you in his letters that I feel as if I'd known you forever." Ben picked up a phone from his desk, punched a button and said, "Ruth, would you tell Mr. Phillips and Mr. Shannon that the Maguires are here. And might we have some coffee?"

Charles Phillips Junior was the son of one of the founding partners. Trim and athletic in appearance, he struck Kellan as looking considerably younger than he had expected. He had joined the firm when Kellan's father was still practicing, and Kellan judged that he must be over sixty. William Shannon, now the senior member of the firm, was approaching eighty, and practiced only part-time, though he was still a strong voice in the management of the firm. The two older men welcomed Kellan and Moira warmly, and they all took seats in the comfortable furniture in Ben's office. Ruth came in with the tray of coffee and cups, and another secretary brought some pastries and placed the tray on a large coffee table in front of the couch and comfortable chairs.

The conversation was amiable, as the partners inquired about Kellan and Moira's journey. They congratulated Kellan on the fine work he had done in Dublin, of which they were obviously aware in some detail, and asked polite questions about how Moira, the newly expectant mother—as one of them noted—was adjusting to her new surroundings. Moira glanced at Kellan, surprised that word of her pregnancy had spread so fast. She had never seemed to Kellan to be the least bit shy, but she was obviously overwhelmed by the attention of these older gentleman, whom she judged to be very important figures in Kellan's new life as an attorney.

After about half an hour of conversation, Ben stood up and said, "We've arranged for a little luncheon in the conference room. Some of the other partners and associates will be joining us." He smiled at Moira. "There won't be any lawyer talk—a couple of the wives will be joining us, including my wife Edna, who's been dying to meet you."

As they waited in the conference-dining room, Kellan said quietly to Moira, "This is probably a little unusual. Newly hired associates usually don't get this kind of treatment, I don't think. It's probably because of my father, and because it's not every new associate who brings an Irish bride into the office."

"They're all so nice," she said, "I'm embarrassed. I'm not used to being fussed over like this."

"Enjoy it, and get used to it," he said. "I remember from my father's time that this is a very friendly firm. I'm going to enjoy working here, and I'm sure that before long you will feel part of the firm as well."

The luncheon was pleasant and relaxed, and after a round of inquiries about how Moira was liking America (she protested that she had only just arrived and had no idea) and how long it would take Kellan to reshape his Boston accent, the conversation soon turned to other things, and Moira could relax. Being that it was early summer in Boston, the talk naturally turned to the Boston Red Sox and their annual quest for a World Series championship. Kellan explained to Moira that he would have to educate her on matters concerning baseball, and promised to take her to Fenway Park to get her properly oriented to that feature of Boston culture.

"I'll never remember all of their names," said Moira as they were leaving.

"Neither will I," said Kellan, "but don't worry. We'll know them all soon enough."

Kellan and Moira had arrived in Boston on Thursday evening. On Friday the two of them had visited the firm, and as they were leaving, Susan provided them with names and numbers for their housing search. Before they left the office Ben informed Kellan that he would be on the payroll starting the following Monday, and let him know that if he needed to draw an advance on his salary, all he had to do was say the word. "I'll be all right for a while," Kellan answered, "but that's nice to know—it gives me a bit of insurance." He also introduced Kellan to the partner with whom he would be working directly, a specialist in international law, Julian Michaels. Julian had not been able to attend the lunch because of an appointment with a client, but he seemed pleased that Kellan would be assisting him for the time being. Ben also told Kellan that the firm understood that he had a lot to do before he and Moira were settled, and they would only expect him to be in the office perhaps half time until they were comfortable.

On Saturday morning Kellan's older brother, Edward Junior, came to the hotel and joined Kellan and Moira for breakfast. Kellan had already spoken on the phone with his brother since arriving, and the other family members were dying to see them. After breakfast Edward drove Kellan and Moira to visit their mother in Shrewsbury. She had sold the family home where the three Maguire children had grown up and had moved into a comfortable apartment. They arrived in time for lunch and were soon joined by Kellan's sister Mary, her husband Tom Wells, and their three-year-old son, Brian. Edward's wife, Eileen, would join them for dinner. Eileen had just completed medical school and was getting started as an intern at a hospital in nearby Worcester.

Kellan was shocked at how much his mother, Nora, had aged in four years. Her hair was completely gray, and her skin looked as thin as paper. She had lost weight and appeared very frail and did not seem to be very steady on her feet. But she embraced Moira warmly, and tears came to her eyes when Moira confirmed that she was really expecting a child. She hugged Kellan and rested her head against his chest and said, "Oh, how I've missed you!"

"I've missed you too, mother," Kellan said. "I'm sorry I wasn't able to get home at all."

"Well, you're here now," she said, smiling.

Mary's son Brian took an immediate shine to Moira, and the family laughed as the little boy pestered her with questions and asked her why she talked funny. Moira said, "Your Uncle Kellan almost learned to talk funny just like me, but he's forgotten it already."

They had a pleasant casual lunch and moved out to the patio behind Nora Maguire's apartment. Mary and Nora engaged Moira in women's talk while Eddie Maguire grilled his little brother about his last year in Ireland and how his studies had turned out. Later in the afternoon Eileen Maguire joined the group and immediately started talking with Moira about her pregnancy, whereupon Edward began to tease his wife. "You've been an MD for three weeks, and you're practicing on her already?" he said.

"Oh, shut up!" Eileen said playfully. Edward had made it clear that he was extremely proud of his wife's achievement. Moira immediately seemed pleased to have someone with whom she could talk about her condition, and their chat soon turned to Moira's describing the illness she had felt aboard ship and whether it might be anything to worry about. Eileen offered words of encouragement. She told Moira that one of her first rotations as an intern would be in maternity.

"Where are you two going to be living?" Eileen looked at Kellan as she asked.

"We're going to start looking tomorrow," Kellan said. "They gave us a couple of addresses in Brookline that look promising."

Eddie had made a reservation at a nice restaurant in Framingham. After they had seated themselves and looked at the menus, Moira once again became the center of attention. But as the meal progressed, the family focused more on the person whom Edward referred to as the "prodigal son." Kellan's brother and sister noted that he had changed during the four years he was in Ireland, and Kellan responded that there should be no surprise in that. After all, he had gone over there to learn and grow. Without referring directly to Nora Maguire, they bored in a bit on Kellan, suggesting that perhaps he should have made an effort to get back and see his mother at least once during his time away. It was obvious that she was failing, and although no one referred to it directly, Kellan picked up the suggestion that his prolonged absence might have contributed to her condition.

Toward the end of the meal Moira whispered to Kellan that she would like to say something to the group, and as they had been chatting noisily since sitting down, she wasn't sure how to proceed. Kellan put his hand on hers, took a knife and tapped on an empty glass. The conversation died, and Kellan said, "Moira would like to say something to all of you."

They turned to Moira, who flushed with embarrassment but then began to speak softly. "I just want to say how happy I am to be here. I can see that Kellan has a wonderful family, as I fully expected. If I seem sad at times, it is only because Kellan has become a part of my family, and I'm sure that I will miss them." Her eyes were filling with tears and her voice threatened to break, but she labored on. "I want you all to know that my family would be thrilled if any of you would visit them on your next trip to Ireland." She smiled. "And I'm sure that all of you are just dying to see our beautiful little country. Thank you for being so kind to me already." She took Kellan's hand and looked at him. "And in a few months your family is going to get a bit larger if all goes well." Smiling, she rested her head on Kellan's shoulder, and the family applauded softly and offered words of hope and affection for their newest member.

By the time Kellan and Moira had been in Boston for two weeks, much had changed. After looking at several apartments, they decided to look for a modest house to rent. A friendly realtor recommended by one of the associates in the firm found them a nice home in a quiet neighborhood in Brookline. They went shopping for furniture, and Kellan's mother had offered some of the pieces that she had placed in storage when she sold the family house and moved into her apartment. Eddie rented a small van and helped Kellan move the furniture to their new home. Eileen mentioned a well-known store in Worcester that sold all kinds of furnishings at modest prices. Eddie drove them out there, and Moira began the process of decorating the home.

Kellan had also purchased a car and told Moira she would have to learn how to drive American style. He found a place that offered driving lessons, even though Moira had driven the family car as well as her father's tractor back in Mallow. But driving in Ireland was not the same as driving in the States. When Kellan picked up Moira after her first lesson, the instructor got out and said with a smile, "Where did you find this lady? She keeps complaining that everybody's driving on the wrong side of the street." It was not long before she felt confident enough to drive around the neighborhood and go shopping in nearby stores. Kellan told her he was sure that before too long she'd be ready to face traffic in downtown Boston, famous for being a challenging city in which to drive.

They found time to do a little sightseeing, and Kellan took her to the old North Church, and then drove her out to Lexington and Concord. Moira had studied history and was excited to see the spots where the Americans had taken their stand against the British, a cause with which her Irish heritage placed her in sympathy. He took her around the campus of Boston College where he had done his undergraduate work, and as they strolled through the library he couldn't help noticing the comparison between his alma mater's facility and the great library of Trinity College in Dublin. Moira was impressed, especially upon recognizing that it was a Catholic college.

Eddie managed to get four good seats at Fenway Park for a game between the Red Sox and the Kansas City Athletics. They were joined by Mary's husband Tom Wells, as Mary stayed home to care for Brian. Kellan and Moira sat between Eddie and Tom, who alternated between explaining the game of baseball to Moira and bringing Kellan up to date on the changes in the major leagues that had occurred since he had gone to Ireland. The old St. Louis Browns were now the Baltimore Orioles, the Philadelphia Athletics had moved to Kansas City, the New York Giants and Brooklyn Dodgers had taken major league baseball to the West Coast. When Moira asked politely if the team on the field before them was thinking about moving, both Eddie and Tom responded forcefully that although the beloved Boston Braves had moved to Milwaukee, the Red Sox were definitely not going anywhere! Thus was Moira's initiation into the sacred tradition of Boston and the Red Sox.

As the third week of their time in America began, Kellan began going into the law firm full-time three days a week and half time on Tuesday and Thursday. Mary saw to it that Moira did not have to spend too many days alone, and she and Moira spent a lot of time with each other. In addition, Moira had quickly become friendly with two of the women who lived nearby in the neighborhood. Although they had not sought any particular neighborhood in terms of its makeup, by a matter of good fortune it turned out that the neighborhood into which they had moved had a distinctive Irish flavor, and when the people who lived nearby learned that their new neighbor had just come from Ireland, Moira found herself making more new friends in the days that followed.

As the summer progressed, Moira settled into a comfortable routine. She had taken to Kellan's family, and they to her, and she had made friends in the neighborhood where they lived. People in stores would overhear her Irish brogue and engage her in conversation from time to time, and one or two friendships developed out of those encounters. Although Kellan was busy learning the practice of law, he was attentive to her, called her at home from his office frequently, and tried to bring work home rather than staying late at the firm. For example, the materials that he was using to study for the Massachusetts bar exam could be read and studied in a space in the corner of their dining room that he had designated as his office, and Moira was happy enough to leave him undisturbed when he was preparing for the exam.

If there was anything in their lives to cause concern, it was that as Moira's pregnancy progressed, she would occasionally feel uncomfortable either from nausea or cramps. She also had some minor bleeding, but the doctor they had engaged, who had taken care of Kellan's family for years, assisted by a young associate who had joined his practice, reassured Moira that there were no serious signs of trouble, but that he would expect to see her regularly.

Realizing that Moira was becoming more comfortable with her surroundings every day, and that she was not often alone, Kellan gradually began to focus more on the practice of law. He promised Moira that he would call her daily. He brought her into the office one afternoon to meet his secretary, Alice Schreiber, so that she would feel comfortable if she needed to call Kellan at work. Alice told Moira that she would be happy to receive calls from her at any time. As Alice was the secretary who also assisted Julian Michaels, she was familiar with the part of the practice in which Kellan would be engaged and proved to be of great assistance in bringing him up to speed.

From their very first night together Moira had been enthusiastically engaged in making love with her husband. She welcomed his kisses and caresses and even found ways to be inventive in her affections. Kellan was surprised at first, but upon reflection he realized that Moira was a mature, intelligent and sophisticated woman who had undoubtedly read and heard a great deal about intimate relations between husbands and wives, or just between men and women. But as the summer wore on and her pregnancy advanced, it became apparent to him that she was beginning to experience some discomfort during the act of making love. He talked to her about it, and she reassured him that it was not terribly uncomfortable, and she did not want him to think she didn't want to make love whenever he was in the mood. On a few occasions, he noticed a painful expression flicker across her face, and it concerned him.

Kellan spoke to their family doctor about Moira's discomfort, and the doctor advised him that some women might have difficulty during intercourse if their pregnancy were not going smoothly, and it was apparent that Moira's was not. The doctor suggested possible remedies and advised him to be cautious, and to see if he and his wife could find ways to resolve the problem creatively between the two of them.

Kellan also spoke to his sister Eileen, who, as a doctor doing her internship in maternity, certainly had access to knowledge that he and Moira might find useful. Eileen was more than willing to help and said she would talk with Moira. Eileen reassured Kellan that there was nothing really to worry about, that Moira's discomfort was not uncommon, and there was a good chance that she would get through her pregnancy and birth without undue difficulty. Kellan was reassured upon learning that Eileen and Moira had talked, which eased his mind a bit more. Still, he remained very cautious with Moira, and as her pregnancy advanced toward its latter stages, he found himself willing and able to forgo relations for the sake of her comfort.

Moira was grateful for his concern, and promised him that once the baby was born, she would again be able to enjoy sex with him as before. "I miss it as much as you do," she said one night as they lay together. "I love you all the more for your worrying about me." In a moment she said, "Oh, did you feel that? The baby just kicked."

"Does that hurt?" he asked.

"No, no, it's just so strange—and wonderful—to have something alive inside me! Something that's part of you."

He held her close and kissed her on the forehead. "You're going to be a wonderful mother," he said.

Boston Lawyer

Kellan set about learning the legal profession from the inside with determination. The other young attorneys in the firm, two of whom had recently graduated from law school themselves, recognized that Kellan held a favorable position at Phillips, Shannon and Steinberg because of his father's former status as a partner. Kellan went out of his way not to take advantage of his situation, and although he called Benjamin Steinberg "Ben" in the office, he kept any contact with his mentor on a professional level, at least in the presence of other members of the firm. Ben, of course, was solicitous of Kellan's status as an aspiring associate, and he also took a continued interest in Moira, as well as the other members of Kellan's family. He had been Uncle Ben to all of them.

Two orders of business were on the table for Kellan. First was the Massachusetts bar exam, which Ben had told Kellan was something he certainly needed to accomplish, but there was no huge rush for him to do that, as he had a great deal to learn about the international legal business that his firm conducted. In that regard, Kellan brought the insight based on his studies in Dublin to the discussion, and he began to find that senior associates and partners who specialized in the international practice were not hesitant to solicit his opinion on matters involving other nations with whom they did business. Ben had suggested that Kellan accompany him on a trip to London to meet with members of the law firm with whom they had a formal relationship. Kellan, however, regretfully asked to be allowed to forgo the trip on account of Moira's pregnancy, as it seemed from time to time to be especially difficult. "That's fine," said Ben. "Julian's going over in January and you can go along then if you like."

Kellan began to read himself into the agreements that the firm had with their clients, and to study the contracts and legal arrangements under which their international clients operated. It was clear that as he expanded his professional knowledge he would have to pay heed to the ramifications of legal practice among the European partners, which varied from nation to nation. As memories of the Second World War faded, German firms with whom they had dealt had fairly well escaped the stigma of their nation's history. French firms, on the other hand, seemed to take their cue from national hero Charles de Gaulle, tending to deal with lawyers from other countries and non-French firms with more than a touch of arrogance.

British firms, as Kellan quickly recognized, tended to stay somewhat aloof from whatever legal squabbles arose from time to time, their posture reflecting the isolated status of their island nation. Kellan's opinions of the British in general were naturally colored by his four years of study in Ireland, although he was certainly aware that the British attorneys with whom he was likely to do business did not take a disparaging attitude toward the Irish, or anyone else. But the British could be annoyingly stiff and formal, and were often fussy about the details of legal agreements into which they were preparing to enter.

Those three nations were the ones with which Kellan would most likely have the most contact, but as Ben had made him aware, they would also be dealing from time to time with firms that had connections in Switzerland, Austria, Italy, or Spain. If the practice of their firm were to grow and expand, as the senior leadership had suggested they were interested in fostering, it was likely that they would seek to spread their areas of interest to Scandinavia and perhaps even Eastern Europe, though in the latter case obvious barriers existed. Kellan had much to learn, and it was clear that once the baby was born, and assuming that all went well with Moira and their child, he would be spending time out of the country, not necessarily a great deal at first, but as he saw his career track materializing before him, he knew that he would often travel across the Atlantic. He hoped that he would be successful enough that Moira and their young offspring might be able to travel with him from time to time, perhaps stopping in Ireland to visit her family. It was clear to him that she wanted to keep in close touch with her parents, brothers and sister. She wrote to them several times a week and received an abundance of mail in return. She also corresponded with Kathleen, expressing from time to time some concerns about whether Kathleen might be too closely involved with Liam's political activities. Kathleen's letters generally contained a note at the end bidding Moira to give her love to Kellan, which Moira delivered with no sense whatever of suspicion.

Summer turned to fall. The New England air grew crisp, and the trees began to turn color. Kellan and Moira attended two Boston College football games, and they might have gone to more if Moira had been more comfortable. For the remaining games that Kellan wanted to attend, Kellan would go with Tom and Eddie, both of whom had also attended Boston College, and Moira, Mary, and Eileen if she was not on duty, would spend the afternoon together, usually at Tom and Mary's home. Moira graduated from her driving program and was able to get around comfortably, even driving downtown to meet Kellan for lunch from time to time. He generally took a bus to work, but he talked about getting a second car, perhaps after the baby was born and Moira was recovered from her pregnancy.

Just after Thanksgiving Kellan told Moira that Julian wanted him to make the trip to London in January to get acquainted with the members of the English law firm of Ashford and Kingsley, with whom they shared business. Although Moira said that she was comfortable with him going, he still hesitated. "Are you sure you won't mind? Julian will understand, even though I can see why he wants me to go. A lot of our business goes through London, and I'm going to have to learn it sooner or later."

"Of course, I understand," Moira said. "I have plenty to keep me busy for sure. And besides, Eileen and I talk almost every day, and Mary is always available. I'm sure I'll be fine."

As the pace of Kellan's work life slowed down for the Christmas holidays, he was able to spend more time with Moira, which was fortunate. During her regular checkups, their doctor had shown mild concern for Moira and urged her not to overtax herself during the latter phases of her pregnancy. She naturally wanted to be fully engaged in preparations for the coming holidays, but she did her best, with Kellan's encouragement, to pace herself and not try to do too much. "We'll probably be spending a lot of the holidays with Eddie and Eileen," he said. "And Tom and Mary will expect us to spend some time with them as well. There's no need for you to think that we have to do a lot of entertaining. I just want you to be comfortable and healthy. That baby you're carrying is our top priority, and everybody in the family understands that."

"I just want to do my share," Moira said. "Your family has been so lovely to me, that I feel …"

"I'm sure that you feel you want to repay their kindness, but believe me, they'll be pleased just to have you around the rest of the family." He went over to her and put his arms around her and told her, as he had done repeatedly, that she would never have to worry about anything regarding his family.

The Maguire clan celebrated Kellan's first Christmas at home with enthusiasm. They spent Christmas Eve in Shrewsbury at the home of Tom and Mary Wells before going to midnight mass at St. Paul's in Worcester. Tom and Mary's home was not far from Nora Maguire's apartment. The family enjoyed Christmas dinner together at Eddie and Eileen's home in Westborough, which was also not far from the rest of the family. Edna Steinberg had taken Moira shopping and educated her on the practice of Christmas in America, which in fact was not very different from the way it was celebrated in Ireland. Kellan helped Moira in buying gifts from the two of them for other members of the family, assuring her that whatever they gave Eddie and Mary, Nora and the rest of the family, would be well received. Moira also bought presents to send to her family in Mallow. As it turned out, Christmas in the Maguire clan was a festive and happy time, with plentiful good food and drink.

Kellan and Moira decided to spend a quiet New Year's Eve together. The firm opened the office, as the large windows in the conference room provided a good view of the fireworks. Kellan and Moira enjoyed the show but left for home well before midnight. They had also attended a holiday party at the firm between Christmas and New Year's Eve. In all, Moira and Kellan enjoyed the spirit of the holidays, though it was clear to Kellan that from time to time Moira could not help thinking about her family celebrating without her. The trouble she was having with her pregnancy, while apparently not serious, also dampened her spirits over the holidays.

Moira's baby was due in late February. The Massachusetts bar exam was scheduled for early February, and Kellan hoped to complete it before Moira's delivery date. Looking over the preparation materials provided by the firm, he realized that his studies in Dublin had not been designed to address American law practice, but Ben and Julian assured him that he could master the material in time. If not, he could always retake the exam at a later date.

Julian, Kellan and Charlie Wright, another young associate in the international law practice, left for London on a Sunday evening, planning to check into the Waldorf Hotel in downtown London early Monday. After resting, they would make their way to the offices of Ashford and Kingsley, their partner firm on Fleet Street. Julian obviously knew the Ashford and Kingsley barristers quite well, and he introduced Kellan and Charlie to the members with whom he frequently corresponded. They settled into the conference room to begin two days of meetings. The London partners reviewed the contracts and ongoing negotiations with European firms that also had business in America, overseen jointly by Ashford and Kingsley and by Phillips, Shannon and Steinberg.

The British gentleman expressed an interest in the fact that Kellan had studied extensively in Ireland, and two or three of them seemed to be curious as to why Kellan had selected Trinity in Dublin rather than a British university—Oxford, Cambridge or the London School of Economics. Julian had warned Kellan that this might come up, and Kellan had decided simply to point out that his family was of Irish heritage. His not too distant ancestors had come to America from Ireland, and it seemed appropriate for him to study where his family had roots. Not only that, but the fellowship he was awarded upon graduation from Boston College had steered him toward Trinity. Julian whispered to Kellan during a lull in the conversation, "If these sons of bitches knew anything about Boston College, they would have understood why you wanted to go to Dublin. That Irish connection has always been important at BC."

The meetings concluded with a pleasant dinner at a London club, of which many of the Ashford and Kingsley partners were members. Several of them told Kellan they looked forward to his next visit to London, and one or two suggested they might be in Boston at some time during the coming year. Kellan was slowly beginning to understand that one of his jobs in the firm would be overseeing negotiations, with an eye toward keeping the relationships among their client firms friendly. He gathered quickly that it would not always be an easy job when interests crossed national boundaries. Kellan realized that he had a lot to learn, but he also understood that his study of European economic history had given him valuable insights into the challenges he would be facing as his role in the firm expanded.

On the flight back to America, Julian had the stewardess bring him a martini, and he took the opportunity to explain in further detail what the firm had in mind for Kellan. "I knew your father well," he began. "Edward was an excellent lawyer, but he was an even better mediator. He had that gift—I suppose you could call it that Irish gift—of talking people into getting along with each other. We are in the business of facilitating economic development between United States and the rest of the world by getting the companies we deal with to enter into long-term contractual agreements beneficial to all concerned. The legal points are important, and certainly challenging, given the differing jurisdictions in which we operate.

But Ben and I and the other partners have plans for you, and if you can see your way clear to accepting the challenge, we intend for you to walk in your father's footsteps."

"I'm not sure I can pick up where my father left off," said Kellan. "I appreciate your saying what kind of a man he was, and I understand that of course. But I never learned very much about how he practiced law."

"You're young," said Julian. "Though from what I've seen so far, I could say you are mature beyond your years. You have adjusted to your situation in the firm very smoothly. People are impressed. Everyone, from the secretaries to the young associates, has gained a considerable amount of respect for you in a short time. Being able to accomplish that is a skill nobody can be taught; you're born with it. Your father had it, and you've got it." Julian lifted his glass in salute to Kellan, who smiled and lifted his glass of cola in return.

As Kellan and Julian walked from the ramp into the waiting area, Kellan noticed a familiar face, Daniel Shea, who had driven Kellan and Moira from New York upon their arrival. Julian approached the driver and said, "Hello, Daniel, I didn't know anyone was meeting us."

"Actually I have a message for Mr. Maguire," said Daniel. He handed Kellan slip of paper.

Kellan unfolded it and read, 'Please call me at the office as soon as you land.' It was signed 'Ben.'

"As soon as Mr. Maguire makes his call, I'll be glad to drive you both back to the firm," said Daniel.

"Kellan, thanks for calling," said Ben. "I wanted to reach you right away—this is going to sound a little ominous, but it isn't. I wanted to talk to you before you heard anything else. Moira is in the hospital."

"Oh my God, what's going on?" said Kellan.

"Kellan, it's nothing serious. Edna spoke to the doctor and said they just want to keep an eye on her for a day or two. The pregnancy has been a little difficult, I'm sure you know that. Edna is there with her right now, and says she's doing fine. Daniel is going to drop Julian here at the office and then take you to the hospital."

"Thanks so much, Ben. I know it's been a little bit difficult for her ..."

"I'm sure she's going to be fine. Edna will wait until you get there, and she can tell me what's what when she gets home. You take care of yourself, son."

Moira looked a little pale, but she sat up and smiled as Kellan walked into the room. Edna was standing on the far side of the bed, and Kellan said, "Thanks so much for being here, Edna." He took Moira's hand in both of his and kissed her on the forehead. "How are you doing, Honey?"

"I'm feeling much better now. I'm sure everything's going to be all right—they said the baby is doing fine. The doctor said I could go home as soon as you got here, but he's told me I have to stay in bed until the baby's born."

"Well that doesn't sound too good," Kellan said. He tried to keep his tone on the light side.

"It's just precautionary," said Edna. "The doctor said it would be best if she stayed here tonight, since it's already late afternoon. She can go home first thing in the morning." Edna took Moira's other hand and squeezed it.

"You've been so kind to me," Moira said to Edna. Then she lifted Kellan's hand to her lips and kissed it. "Why don't you stay just a little while and tell me how your trip was. Then you need to go home and get unpacked," Moira said to Kellan.

"Sure." He walked around the bed and hugged Edna. "I can't thank you enough."

Despite the encouraging words, Kellan could not keep from worrying. He had another phone installed in the bedroom so he could reach Moira from the office without having her get out of bed. He tried to call her often enough to reassure her, but not so often as to disturb her rest or make her even more apprehensive than she already was. Despite his concerns, Moira seemed cheerful enough, but she was clearly uncomfortable.

Several days after she got home from her brief stay in the hospital, a letter arrived from Ireland. Kellan had come in from the office, saw the letter and took it straight up to their bedroom. She looked at the envelope and said, "It's from mother." She opened the letter and started to read. The expression on her face turned to one of surprise and she sat up and put her feet on the floor and looked at Kellan. "Mum is coming over here!" she said.

"To America?"

"Yes. She says there's a direct flight from Shannon to Boston, and that Brendan said he would take her to the airport."

"To Shannon?"

"Yes, it's not that far from Mallow." She continued reading the letter, looked at Kellan with the same surprised look and said, "What day is today?"

"Wednesday, the thirteenth."

She thought for a moment. "That means she'll be here next Monday. Good Lord, I have a lot to do!"

"What do you mean, you have a lot to do?" Kellan smiled at her. "You don't have to do anything; the house looks fine, we can put her in the extra bedroom, and she'll be very comfortable. We might have to get some extra sheets and maybe a blanket or two, but that's no big deal."

Moira finished reading the letter, glanced through it again, smiled at Kellan. "She says she's always wanted to come to America, and now she has a perfect excuse. She told me not to worry, she would take good care of me." She laughed softly. "Not that you aren't already doing that." She held her arms out to him and he sat down next to her and hugged her. "It will be wonderful to see her," she said. "Everything is wonderful here, and I'm so happy with you, but I do miss my family."

"I know. It will be good to see her."

Two days later Moira got another letter from her mother, and this one disturbed her a bit. "Mum said she has been in touch with Kathleen, and Kathleen seems to be worried about me. I haven't told her anything other than what I've told Mum and Dad, so I'm not sure why she says that. Oh well, Kathleen always did sort of worry about me."

Libby Connolly's Aer Lingus flight was right on time and landed at Logan Airport at five thirty in the afternoon. She got through customs quickly and smiled broadly as soon as she spotted Kellan. "Oh Lord, am I glad to be on the ground again! That's the first time I've ever been in an airplane."

"How did you like it?" Kellan said.

"Oh, it wasn't so bad, I guess. But I couldn't help worrying about the fact that we were over water so long. If anything had gone wrong, we'd have been sunk."

"They've been doing transatlantic flights for quite a while now," said Kellan. "It seems to be safe enough."

"Oh, I'm sure it is," she said. "I guess I could get used to it, though I said my rosary several times on the way over." She hugged Kellan again. "I can't wait to see Moira! How is she?"

"We'll be there in about half an hour, and you can see for yourself," he said, smiling. "She's really excited about seeing you."

Libby and Moira embraced each other with tears and smiles. Libby stepped back and held Moira at arm's length. "Look at you!" She was looking at Moira's bulging tummy. "You look as if you're ready to pop."

"Oh, I hope so," said Moira. "I'm tired of being pregnant; I just want to get it over with."

Libby hugged her daughter again and then stepped back once more. "You're going to be fine," she said, but Kellan sensed a trace of anxiety in Libby's voice. She had come because she thought she would be needed to see her daughter through her delivery, one that she sensed was not going to be easy.

With Libby staying in their home, Kellan was able to devote extra time to his preparation for the bar exam. He stayed later in the office than usual, knowing that Libby would be taking care of Moira and preparing meals for the three of them. He was as solicitous of Moira's feelings as always, but he was pleased to see that she and her mother were enjoying the chance to visit. Moira wanted to know everything that was going on back at the family home in Mallow, and Libby wanted to hear everything that Moira could tell her about her life in America so far. Kellan asked Libby if she would like to do some sightseeing, but she declined, saying that it could wait until after the baby was born. She obviously did not want to leave Moira alone. Libby's presence in his home was as comforting for Kellan as it was to Moira.

Kellan got through the first day of the bar exam without much difficulty. The second day required the completion of five essays on assigned topics, best described as case studies. As an experienced writer, he welcomed the challenge of answering the essay questions. He was also prepared to use a skill he had learned during his years of education. It was called examsmanship, the ability to answer difficult questions, even if the answers seemed elusive. He recalled an old joke about a student who had showed up for a final examination prepared to answer a question that the professor was known to have given every year for some time. Lo and behold, when he arrived at the exam, the professor had written a different question. The student went ahead and answered the question for which he had prepared and hoped for the best, pleading that he found the question asked less interesting than the one he chose to answer. Kellan knew he had to answer the questions that were presented, but he also knew that he could convey information about his knowledge of the general subject area as part of his answer, even if he was not sure of the details.

Kellan had completed four of his essays and was just getting started on the fifth when he heard someone enter the examination room. The apparent intruder was William Shannon, the senior partner of Kellan's firm. He watched, curious, as Mr. Shannon walked up to one of the proctors and began a whispered conversation with him. The discussion went back and forth for a few minutes, and then the proctor began looking around the room, and Mr. Shannon's gaze followed. Their eyes fell on Kellan, and he immediately felt concerned; Mr. Shannon's presence must have something to do with Moira. The proctor approached Kellan, whispered for him to pick up his examination papers and follow him. They went into an anteroom, where William Shannon was waiting.

Mr. Shannon reached out and grasped Kellan's hand. "I'm so sorry to disturb you, Kellan," he began. "I have asked Mr. Johnson" (nodding at the proctor) to excuse you from the rest of the examination."

"Sir, I don't understand," said Kellan, now clearly worried.

"Moira has been taken to the hospital," said Mr. Shannon. "Although they said the situation does not constitute an emergency, they felt that your presence at the hospital would be a good thing. I understand that Moira's mother has gone with her."

"How …?"

"They were taken by ambulance." Kellan's face had gone white, and he clutched his exam papers tightly in his fist. Mr. Shannon continued. "I spoke with an old friend of mine on the Massachusetts bar examination committee. They will evaluate the work you have done so far and waive whatever you have been unable to finish. Whatever the outcome, they have assured me that they will take the situation into account." He turned to Mr. Johnson. "Thank you for your kind assistance," he said. "I'd better get this young man to the hospital."

"Certainly, sir." Kellan handed Mr. Johnson his completed work and followed Mr. Shannon outside.

"I understand that you don't have your automobile with you," said Mr. Shannon when they were outside. "I'll be more than happy to drive you to the hospital." As they got into the car Mr. Shannon said, "Your proctor is Susan Johnson's husband. Were you aware of that?"

"No," said Kellan, "but I was wondering why he seemed to know me."

"Your reputation precedes you."

When they entered the waiting room outside the hospital operating area, Kellan was shocked to see his brother Edward and Ben Steinberg already there, along with Libby Connolly, who had obviously been crying. Eddie walked up to him. "They're doing everything they can," he said. "The doctor came out a few minutes ago and told us that the baby had been delivered and seems to be doing fine. Apparently Moira has had a lot of bleeding, and they're trying to stop it."

"Oh, God," said Kellan. He shook his head. Ben came over and put his hand on Kellan's shoulder. "We've all been praying for her," he said. "But you have a healthy daughter."

Kellan managed a half smile, sat down on a chair, folded his arms across his chest and stared at the floor, still shaking his head. Mr. Shannon came over and placed his hand on Kellan's shoulder. "I think you're in good company," he said. "We'll be hoping and praying for the best." Kellan stood up and shook his hand and thanked him. Mr. Shannon whispered a few words to Ben, and left the waiting room.

Kellan sat down next to Libby and took her hand. Libby looked at her son-in-law, patted his hand and tried to smile. "I'm so glad you're here," he said. After a moment or two he added, "And now you are a grandmother."

"Yes, for the second time." Kellan had forgotten that Brendan's wife Deirdre had delivered a baby daughter a few months earlier. She managed a smile. "Caitlin is a beautiful child. She and ... your baby will practically be twins." Kellan had not even thought about a name—they had discussed some possibilities, and had agreed only on the fact that she would have an Irish name.

Libby picked up on Kellan's train of thought. "Moira and I discussed names," she said. "She thought Fiona was a lovely name. She hoped you would like it, as she certainly would not choose a name unless you agreed with her." She reached out and took Kellan's hand again. "She loves you so much ..." She put her hands over her face and dissolved into tears again, then quickly collected herself, looked at him and said with as much courage as she could muster, "I'm sure she's going to be all right. Oh, Kellan, she has to be all right!" Kellan, fighting with his own emotions, could only nod.

About an hour later the doctor appeared again and Kellan, Libby and the others stood up to hear what he had to say. He was not encouraging; they were still doing their best to stop the bleeding and to deal with the crisis. Nothing much had changed, but they were still hoping for a "favorable outcome."

Ben came over and sat down next to Kellan. "I'm going to have to run along," he said. "You be sure that you let me know how everything is going. I've talked to Julian; you don't need to worry about coming in tomorrow morning. We'll see you through this thing."

"I know you will, Ben. Julian has really been great to work with." He thought for a moment. "It was really nice of Mr. Shannon to come and get me," he said.

Ben looked at Kellan as if considering what to say. "Yes, I had planned to go and get you, but it was really his idea."

"Oh?" Kellan wasn't sure what was coming, but Ben was obviously not finished.

"Two reasons, really. First, he is highly respected in this town and since it required a favor from the Bar Association, he thought it would be best if he got you out." He paused for a moment. "The other reason is something you might not be aware of—or maybe you are." He paused again and rubbed his jaw for a moment. "Kellan, what do you see when you look at me?"

"I'm not sure I understand."

"Well, you see a man named Benjamin Steinberg. Am I right?"

"Sure, but I can't seem to grasp what you're getting at. When I look at you I see a kind, wonderful man who has been a friend of my family for as long as I can remember. Now you're also a mentor, someone I can turn to while I'm learning the ropes. That's what I see."

Ben smiled. "It's what you don't see that can be important. You don't see a Jew."

"What does that have to do with anything?" Kellan was puzzled.

"As smart as you are, you can still be awfully naïve. This is an old, conservative city in many ways. Jews have had to struggle to get along here. Do you know how few Jews there were as partners in law firms when I started? They could've held a meeting in a phone booth." He chuckled. "Your father had none of that in him, and it's one of the reasons I loved him. You're cut of the same cloth. But there will be times as long as you and I are both in the same firm when I will be invisible in certain cases. Believe it or not, after everything the world has been through in the last twenty or thirty years, you can still find educated people in this city who would prefer not to have to deal with me because I'm a Jew."

86

He chuckled for a moment. "It's very interesting that you wound up in Brookline. You will discover that you have quite a few Jewish neighbors." Kellan smiled. "It's also part of the reason that Julian took you to London, even though I'm just as familiar with some of the issues you went to discuss as he is. Anti-Semitism hasn't ended, my friend, and there's plenty of it around in Europe, even in jolly old England."

"I understand," said Kellan. "I've run into that, of course. I just considered it to be an old-fashioned prejudice that really makes no sense anymore. But you're right; it's there. I just never thought of it as being something you would have to be concerned with. I can't imagine anyone …" He didn't know how to finish this sentence, but Ben put his hand on his shoulder and stood up.

"No reason you should—you don't think in those terms. Anyway, I'm glad I can help. Anything I can do, you be sure to call on me."

Kellan stood and looked at Ben for a moment, then hugged him. "I love you, Ben."

Ben kissed Kellan on the cheek, turned and left the visiting area.

Kellan and Libby spent the night in the waiting room. About three o'clock in the morning a nurse came out of the intensive care area and touched Kellan on the shoulder. He had been curled up on a couch sleeping fitfully. "Your wife is sleeping peacefully," she said. "I don't think we should wake her, but I thought you might like to come in and see her for a few moments. You could hold her hand."

As he followed the nurse through the door she whispered to him, "I probably shouldn't be doing this, but I thought you might like to see her."

Moira was pale, and there were tubes in both arms. Her breathing seemed shallow to him, but regular. He sensed a feeling of pain from what her face showed even in sleep. He sat down next to her bed and took her hand in both of his. She stirred lightly at his touch but did not wake up. He watched her face, trying to think positively. He had never doubted that he loved her, but now the thought of life without her was beyond his ability to imagine. He thought of the baby girl, whom he had not yet seen, who must be somewhere nearby. He couldn't begin to imagine having to raise her by himself. He was almost relieved when the nurse appeared quietly and he felt her hand on his shoulder. "Probably best to leave her to her rest," she said softly. Kellan glanced at the name tag on the nurse's blouse—Maureen Kelly.

He stayed a few more moments, then walked slowly back toward the waiting room. As he passed the nurses' station, which had been unoccupied on his way in, another nurse, older, stood and said in a harsh tone, "May I help you?"

"No thanks." He hoped that Nurse Kelly would not get in trouble for having sneaked him in.

When he got back to the waiting room Libby opened her eyes and sat up. "Did something happen?" She looked frightened.

"No, she's sleeping," he said. Libby's face was drawn and pale, ashen. She was exhausted, as was Kellan. He sat down next to her and closed his eyes.

Edward and Eileen arrived at 8:00 am. "How's she doing?" Edward asked.

"The same," said Kellan. He had heard nothing since his brief visit during the night. He looked at Eileen, surprised to see her.

"I'm off today," she said. "I just got off a thirty-six hour shift last night. I'll see if I can find out anything for you." She went through the doors into the emergency area. Eileen had worn a doctor's white jacket and had a stethoscope sticking out of the pocket—she had obviously planned her reconnaissance.

Edward put his hand on Kellan's shoulder. "Why don't you and Libby go home and get some rest. Eileen and I can stay for a while. We'll call you if anything happens."

Kellan glanced at Libby and noticed how distraught and tired she looked. "Would you like to go home with me for a while? Eddie and Eileen will keep watch."

"I guess I'd better. I'll need to be rested up when she and the baby come home."

"As soon as Eileen comes back, we'll go."

A few minutes later Eileen came out of the emergency area. "She's okay for now," Eileen said. "They had to stop the bleeding again early this morning." She took Kellan's hands in hers. "I did some asking around," she said. "Used my somewhat shaky medical credentials, but I did get to talk to the doctor who worked on her." She looked closely at Kellan, and her expression was pained. "I'm sorry, Kellan, but it doesn't look good. The doctor said if the bleeding stays stopped, she might be okay. He said it's maybe fifty-fifty."

"He didn't tell us that," he said. "I guess he didn't have to."

88

Kellan looked at Libby. "I think I'd better stay here," he said. "Why don't you go home and get some rest? This could be a while."

"Oh, no, Kellan, I'll be fine. I need to stay here with you."

Minutes later nurse Kelly came up to Kellan and whispered, "Mr. Maguire, there's an empty bed in a room down the hall. Perhaps your mother-in-law would like to rest in there for a while."

"You're an angel," said Libby as Nurse Kelly led her down the hall.

Kellan stretched himself across two chairs and dozed for a while. He woke up as Eileen came back from the cafeteria with coffee for him. "You look as if you need this," said Eileen as she handed him the cup. "I'll go see if anything's going on."

"Are they okay with you going in there?" asked Kellan.

Eileen smiled and took his hand. "I was in med school with one of the interns in the OR. He vouched for me." She disappeared through the heavy doors.

Tom and Mary arrived while Eileen was still inside. "How is she?" asked Mary.

"I don't know. Eileen has been in there a while, so maybe something's going on. Mary, would you mind getting Libby—she's in an empty room right down there." He nodded toward the hallway.

"Sure." Mary squeezed his hand. Moments later she was back with Libby, still pale with worry.

Ten minutes later Eileen came out of the OR; she looked worried. "They're working on her now," she said. "The bleeding started again." Eileen took both of Kellan's hands. "Kellan, I'm afraid it doesn't look good."

"Christ!" he said. Libby began to cry again. Minutes went by slowly, and Kellan and his family spoke hardly at all. It was almost an hour later that one of the emergency doctors came out of the OR. He had his surgical clothes on, and there was blood on them. Kellan knew instantly what the verdict was.

"I'm sorry," said the doctor. "We did everything we could."

They left the baby at the hospital. She was doing fine, but one of the maternity nurses, aware of all that had transpired, suggested that it would be all right to leave her for a few days. Kellan and Libby went in to see her again before they left the hospital. "I think Fiona is a lovely name," Libby had said. "What do you think, Kellan?"

His voice cracked as he said, "It was her last wish." Libby nodded.

Back at Kellan's home the family gathered and talked about next steps. Edward said he would talk to Father O'Malley about a funeral mass. He also called a funeral home to make arrangements for picking up Moira's remains. When they started talking about a burial site, Libby interrupted Kellan and his brother and sister and said, "I want to take her home."

No one said anything for a few moments. Then Eddie spoke. "There will be some expense in shipping her to Ireland," he said.

"I don't care about that ..." Libby began.

Kellan interrupted her. "Are you sure that's what you want?"

Libby came to him and took both his hands. "Kellan, she hasn't been here in America very long," she said. "As much as she loved you, she wasn't feeling quite at home here yet. She was not unhappy—just a bit homesick. I'm sure she would want to be buried back home."

"Then it's done," said Kellan. He looked at his brother. "I'll take care of it."

"But flying a casket ..." Eddie began.

"She doesn't have to go by air. There won't be any rush, will there?" Kellan looked at Libby.

"No, of course not, as long as she's laid to rest where she was born."

They picked up Fiona from the hospital the following morning. Kellan carried the tiny infant out to the car and held her all the way home. Mary had driven them, and she promised to help Kellan and Libby take care of the baby. Eileen's current rotation was in obstetrics and gynecology, and she would help whenever she could consistent with her training schedule. Her physician supervisor had generously consented to give her the time she needed to aid her family. They arranged for Fiona to be baptized at St. Mary's Church in Brookline, which Kellan and Moira had attended. Father O'Malley would perform the service as well as the funeral mass.

Ben Steinberg called and asked if he and Edna could drop by to pay their respects. They arrived about half an hour later and joined the somber gathering. Ben told Kellan that he had discussed the situation with the partners, and Kellan was to take whatever time he needed to make arrangements for dealing with Moira's death and the care of Fiona. Somehow the word got out into the neighborhood, and people began to stop by the Maguire home with offerings of food, casseroles and other ready-to-eat dishes. Charlie Wright and his wife Cynthia stopped by to pay their respects—he and Kellan had been working together closely since the trip to London. Kellan and Moira had dined with the Wrights several times, and Cynthia and Moira had gotten along well.

Eddie spoke at the memorial service, which was held at St. Mary's a few days later. In addition to Kellan's family, most of the partners of the firm and several associates with whom Kellan had worked were also in attendance, as were several neighborhood families.

"My brother spent four years in Ireland," Eddie began. "We all missed him, but when he came home with his beautiful young wife, we were more pleased than I can possibly say. I love my brother dearly ..." He paused to collect himself, then began again. "I love my brother dearly, and as I said, we missed him, but in the short time I knew Moira, I quickly began to love her as a sister. We all did." He looked at Tom and Mary and Eileen, and nodded as they smiled in agreement, even as their tears began once more. "We loved her Irish brogue, her Irish smile, and her wonderful personality. My brother is a pretty smart guy; after all, he has spent almost all his life in school." That brought a few chuckles from the audience. "But I'll tell you something: Moira was a match for him. She was a librarian, she loved books and literature, and in her understanding of the language she spoke, she put us all to shame. And on top of that, she also was fluent in Irish, a language that has sadly been forgotten, even in parts of Ireland."

He paused for a moment. "What a wonderful mother she would have made to our new darling Fiona. As sad as we are for losing her, we must also be just as sad over the fact that Kellan's daughter will never know her mother. But we have also been blessed to have Libby Connolly, Moira's mother, with us for the last few weeks." He smiled in Libby's direction. "And in just that brief time, we have seen firsthand where Moira got her charm and her beauty. Although Fiona will not know her own mother, she will know her grandmother Libby, and she will be the richer for that. Libby, we know how difficult these past few days have been for you, but we have been blessed to have you here with us, just as Moira was blessed to have you with her near the end."

As they gathered back at Kellan's home following the service, after all but the family and one or two neighbors had departed, Libby sat down on a couch next to Kellan. "I've been thinking," she said. "I know how much you loved Moira and I know how much you will love Fiona. And believe me when I say that I have thought about this as much as I could and have prayed over it. But I think I should take Fiona home with me."

"Libby, I …" He wasn't sure how to proceed. "I've been thinking about that. I was hoping that you might be able to stay here for a while."

"Of course I'll stay here with you, Kellan," she said. "But you know, Patrick needs me around the house. I was thinking that since Brendan and Deirdre have the baby, that perhaps they could take Fiona for a while. I took the liberty of calling Brendan on your phone—I hope you don't mind—and he said that they would be more than happy to take care of Fiona, at least for a while."

"Libby, I don't know what to say."

"You don't have to say anything, but just think about it. Kellan, you're a wonderful man, and Fiona will be lucky to have you as a father. But you're just getting started in your legal career. Moira told me that you would probably be traveling a great deal, and it will be very difficult for you to care for an infant by yourself. Also, I was thinking that as you will be traveling to Europe, you could stop with us and visit every so often. I promise you from the bottom of my heart, if Fiona comes to live with us, for no matter how long, you will always be a part of her life. Just think about it." Libby took his hand and squeezed it, and kissed him on the cheek.

Home Again

Dr. Janssen, who had attended Moira during the last stages of her childbirth, recommended that they not take Fiona to Ireland until she was at least six weeks old. Libby called Patrick and convinced her husband over his mild protests that it would be best for all concerned if she remained with Kellan and Fiona until it was time for them to bring the baby back to Mallow. She told him that Kellan would be returning to Ireland with his daughter when the time came. Kellan got on the phone with Patrick and thanked him for his patience, adding that he was grateful to have Libby with him to help him take care of his daughter. "I couldn't do it without her—I'm sure you understand that, Patrick."

"I do, I do," said Patrick. "What a shame this is." Kellan sensed that Patrick's voice was shaky and that he was feeling the loss of his daughter along with everyone else. Kellan thanked him profusely and said he looked forward to being in the Connolly house once more, even under such sad circumstances.

Eddie helped Kellan make arrangements to ship Moira's remains to Ireland. The sealed casket would be shipped in time to arrive in Ireland about the time that Kellan, Libby and Fiona would be there. Kellan returned to work and accepted the sympathy of his colleagues in the office. He found it difficult to concentrate on legal matters for the first few days back, but he gradually welcomed the distraction of work as it took his mind off the ordeal he had been through.

Mary and Libby took care of Fiona during the day while Kellan was at work. Several days a week Mary would drive to Kellan's home in the morning and take Fiona and Libby back to her house so that three-year-old Brian would be more comfortable. Eileen dropped in from time to time to look the baby girl over, reassuring everyone that Fiona was a normal, healthy baby. Although Eileen was not yet a year into her internship, she was already considering OB/GYN as her career specialty. She obviously loved being able to hold her niece. The women were amused by how much Brian seemed to be taken with his tiny new cousin. Dr. Janssen assured Kellan that there was no reason for concern regarding Fiona's coming

93

journey to the old country. Kellan snuck out of the office once or twice a week to visit his daughter, calling ahead to make sure the women would be at his home.

Kellan immersed himself more and more in work, but when he was at home he spent as much time as he could with Fiona, holding her, helping with feeding, and changing her whenever the women would allow it. It was soon clear to the ladies of the house that he adored his daughter. Libby tentatively explored the possibility that Kellan might change his mind about having her raised in Ireland, but he agreed that it would be the best thing for her. In his innermost thoughts he hoped that he was not being selfish in avoiding his fatherly duty; on the other hand, he knew that raising her himself, even with help, would be difficult. He was sure Fiona would be happier in the bosom of a warm family rather than being raised by nannies and day care. Nevertheless, with each passing day he became more painfully aware that he would miss her, just as he missed her mother.

Over the weeks before the time came for the trip, Kellan struggled with feelings about the loss of his young wife. He had loved Moira deeply, and the wound would take time to heal. When a well-meaning colleague suggested that Kellan might start thinking about remarrying, Kellan shut him off abruptly. "The guy's a clod," Charlie Wright said. "How he got through law school or more important, why we hired him, I'll never know."

"He means well," said Kellan.

"I suppose so," said Charlie. They were sitting in a conference room taking a coffee break. After a while Charlie said, "You mentioned that other woman you knew in Ireland, Moira's friend. I forget her name."

"Kathleen" said Kellan. "What about her?"

"You said you really liked her. I was just wondering … you know, you have that beautiful little girl, and I know it's going to be tough not seeing her."

"Are you suggesting …" Kellan began.

"I'm not suggesting anything, Kell. I just know you're hurting, and I wish there were some way to ease the pain. If that woman Kathleen is available, who knows?"

"She's not," said Kellan abruptly. "Anyway, that wouldn't work right now. I just have to get through this."

"I know," said Charlie. "You will, my friend. I'm going back to work." He stood and grasped Kellan's shoulder for a moment, then left. Kellan sat for a while staring out the window at the Boston skyline.

As the time approached for Kellan and Libby to undertake their journey to bring his deceased wife and baby daughter back across the Atlantic, he began to wish he had not agreed so readily to the move. He had to keep reminding himself that Libby's plan was the best possible thing for Fiona. Still, being able to love his daughter, to hold and kiss her, to rock her to sleep, to minister to her needs, was something he felt he would need for his own emotional recovery. He was shocked at how much pain he felt at the thought that he would not be able to see her every day. He promised himself, just as he would promise Libby and the rest of the Connolly family, that he would visit them as often as he could.

As it turned out, the six-week wait on Fiona's behalf eased the problem of shipping Moira to Ireland, as cross-Atlantic shipping was easier to arrange as winter turned into spring. A few days after Moira's casket had been delivered to the shipping company, Eddie drove Kellan, Libby and Fiona to Logan Airport, from where they would fly to Shannon. Brendan would meet them there. They had arranged for Moira to be shipped to the Port of Cork aboard a passenger vessel sailing from Boston directly to Ireland. Kellan would stay at the Connolly home until Moira arrived a few days later. Cork lay about twenty five miles south of Mallow, and a funeral vehicle would collect her and bring her home for the service. Brendan and Kellan would accompany the funeral driver.

Fiona slept for much of the flight from Boston to Shannon, but grew restless as they landed. "She knows she's home," said Libby with a smile.

Brendan Connolly had tears in his eyes as he hugged his mother and then Kellan. After offering words of comfort to Kellan, Brendan kissed the baby on the forehead and held her up at arm's length. "Ah, what a lovely lass," he said. "You're a lucky man, with such a lovely daughter, Kellan Maguire."

As they drove slowly back toward Mallow, Fiona was wide awake. "This is where your mum grew up," Libby said, holding the baby up so she could look out the window. "Isn't it pretty?"

Patrick, Deirdre, Kevin and Molly were thrilled with the baby and delighted to see Kellan again. Libby smiled at the enthusiastic greetings for the newer family members. "Well, I can see how much you missed me!"

she said. "I might've stayed in Boston for all you care." The sadness in the family was evident, but there was comfort for them in seeing Kellan and the baby. "We did miss you, Mum, really we did!" said Molly. "But you haven't been gone as long as Kellan has."

Two days later Brendan and Kellan drove with the funeral director to the shipping office in Cork. Brendan placed his hand on Moira's casket as they loaded it into the funeral car. "We didn't expect you home so soon, Lassie," he said, his eyes moist with tears. Kellan and Brendan talked quietly during the return drive to Mallow, but the mood in the vehicle was somber. Back in Mallow the funeral director dropped Kellan and Brendan at the Connolly abode and took the casket to the funeral home. The family had decided against the traditional parlor wake, given the length of time since Moira's death.

Brendan and Patrick had arranged for a funeral mass at St. Mary's church followed by burial in the church cemetery three days after Moira's remains arrived. As Kellan and the Connolly family stood outside St. Mary's waiting for the casket to be taken to the front of the church, Kellan looked up and saw Kathleen approaching. When Kellan saw her he drew in his breath, surprised at how glad he was to see her. She came up to the group, kissed Patrick, Libby and Brendan, then came over to Kellan and hugged him. "I'm so sorry," she said. "In her last letter she said that she was looking forward to me coming to America to visit. I was looking forward to it."

"There's no reason you can't still come," said Kellan. Kathleen smiled, but then turned away and greeted Deirdre and the younger Connollys.

Since the family had forgone the traditional wake, Patrick and Libby waited outside the church to greet guests. The pallbearers, friends of the Connolly family, lifted Moira's casket from the funeral coach, carried it into the church and placed it on the catafalque. Kellan and Libby followed the casket down the aisle; Patrick, Brendan, Deirdre and the children followed. Libby had invited Kathleen to sit with the family and she took a place next to Deirdre in the front pew. Father McGuire, who had married Moira and Kellan, conducted the service, recalling that happier event in the words of his homily. Brendan gave a brief eulogy in remembrance of his sister, struggling to get the words out. It was a warm tribute to Moira and included words of comfort for Kellan.

Following the burial at the family plot in the cemetery, the company repaired to the Connolly home. Patrick and Libby had engaged two girls from the church to assist guests with food and drink. Kellan knew few of them, but he accepted their condolences graciously, then stood off by himself and listened to the quiet conversations. After a while Kathleen made her way over to Kellan, stood next to him and slipped her arm through his. Neither of them spoke for a few minutes. Then Kathleen said, "My heart goes out to you, Kellan. I know how much you loved her."

Kathleen's words reassured Kellan. She had loved Moira as much as Kellan, though differently, but she had never tried to disguise her feelings for Kellan. She kept her regrets to herself nevertheless. "What a lovely person she was," she said. "She and I were nothing alike, except for being Irish, but we were as close as sisters." Her words were spoken without a trace of irony.

"It would've been nice to have you visit us in Boston," he said. "I'd like to think that still might be possible someday." Kathleen said nothing for a few moments. Then she said, "Liam has asked me to marry him."

The comment struck him sharply. He took a breath, forced a smile and said, "That's wonderful. I guess congratulations are in order."

She looked down at the floor and shook her head, then looked up at Kellan. "I'm not sure. There's so much tension in his life, so much danger. I understand why he does what he does—I believe in the same things—but I'm sure I would worry myself sick every time he went out the door. So much violence!"

"I can imagine how difficult your decision will be," he said. "All I can do is wish you happiness in whatever you decide. Moira would want you to be happy—and so do I."

She tightened her grip on his arm and smiled at him. "I know."

After a few moments he asked, "How long will you be staying here?"

"Just tonight. I'm staying at the hotel down on Main Street. I'll get the 10:30 train back to Dublin in the morning."

"Maybe I could join you for breakfast," he said.

She looked at him questioningly for a moment, then answered, "That would be lovely." She squeezed his arm again and drifted off to talk with some of the other guests.

Molly came up to Kellan, took his hand and rested her head against his chest. "I wish you could stay here with us, Kellan," she said plaintively, looking up at him.

"That would be nice," he said. "But I have a job back home, and I'd best get back to it."

"I know. But you still have to promise to come back and visit."

"I will. You couldn't keep me away with a team of horses." He smiled and kissed her on the forehead.

"Are you still related to me? I mean now that Moira is, you know…"

"I will always be your brother-in-law. In fact, you can just think of me as your brother." He put his arms around her and hugged her, kissed the top of her head. She put her arms around his waist and rested her head on his chest again. "You and Kevin and Brendan and your mum and dad will always be my family," he said.

When all of the guests had left, Libby made a pot of tea and brought cups to Patrick and Kellan, who were seated in the living room. Patrick said, "I think you're wise leaving Fiona here for a while." Kellan nodded. "We'll see how it goes. Deirdre is a wonderful mother. Fiona and Caitlin will be like sisters—they're only a few months apart." Deirdre came into the room with a cup of tea and sat down. "We were just talking about you, Darlin'," said Patrick.

"Oh, and I suppose you'll be wanting to know if my ears are burning?"

"I was just telling Kellan what a good mother you are," said Patrick.

Deirdre looked at Kellan. Then she looked down at her hands and seemed to be blushing. Looking at Kellan again she said, "There's something I've been meaning to ask you about," she said. "I've spoken with Libby, and I know that Fiona has had to be bottle fed since she was born. What I wanted to say was …" She hesitated for a moment. "I'm still nursing Caitlin. I think it would be a good thing if I nursed Fiona. I think it's a fine thing for a child to nurse at its mother's breast. And since Moira is …" She shook her head and wiped tears away from her eyes. "I just think it would be a good thing. But if you had any objection …"

"Why would I object?" said Kellan gently. "I think that would be wonderful for you to do."

Deirdre stood up and came over and sat down next to Kellan and took his hand. "I just want you to know, we will do everything possible to raise her as we think you and Moira would wish. I know this will be difficult for you, because I have already seen how much you love her, even in the few days you have been here. We want you to be part of her life, and she will never forget that you are her father."

Kellan understood what Deirdre was saying. Fiona would be staying in Ireland for an indefinite period of time. Unless Kellan were to remarry, it would be difficult to imagine Fiona coming back to live with him, at least until she was of school age. But he would write to her, and until she was old enough to read herself, he was sure that Brendan and Deirdre would read his letters to her and keep him alive in her thoughts. He would visit as often as he could, and he had already determined that his responsibilities with the firm's overseas clients would offer opportunities for him to travel to Ireland to see his daughter.

Instead of sleeping in the guest room in the back of the house where he had stayed during his first visit and at Christmas time, Kellan was sleeping in Moira's old bedroom. He felt her presence strongly, and as he lay awake that night following the funeral, he felt the loss of her intensely. He slept fitfully, then awoke, got out of bed and sat by the window, looking out over the moonlit pastureland behind the house. Even in the dim light, the fresh greenery of spring was visible. It was a time to think of new life, even though his thoughts were with Moira.

After a while he got up and tiptoed into Molly's room where Fiona was sleeping. He bent over the crib and saw that she was awake. She yawned, and he put his finger on her hand and she gripped it tightly. He picked her up and dandled her in his arms. He tiptoed out, holding her and went back to his room and sat down on the bed. He held her so that her head rested on his shoulder and rubbed her back. After a moment she burped loudly and he chuckled. He continued to hold her and she soon fell back asleep. He took her back to Molly's room and laid her back in the crib.

Then, back in Moira's room, for the first time since Moira's death he broke down and was wracked with sobs. He wrapped his arms around himself and rocked back and forth, trying to stifle his crying so as not to waken anyone. At last his grief ran its course. It was almost dawn when he finally fell asleep.

The next morning when he went downstairs Patrick looked at him and said, "Molly tells us you were sneaking around last night."

Kellan smiled. "I didn't know I wakened her."

"Ah, no matter, she didn't mind a bit. Said you came to visit your daughter."

"Yes. I'm going to miss her."

"I know you will," said Patrick. "But don't you think it's best?"

"Best for Fiona, for sure," said Kellan. He stood up. "I think I'll go for a walk."

"It will do you good, son," said Patrick.

At the hotel Kellan inquired at the front desk after Kathleen and was told that she was in the dining room. She was sitting by herself at a table next to a window, smoking a cigarette. She looked up as he approached and smiled. He sat down opposite her. There was a pot of tea on the table, and he gestured to the waitress for another cup. "I take it you haven't eaten yet," he said.

"I'm not really very hungry, but I suppose I should have something before I get on the train. How about you?"

He gestured for the waitress again and they ordered food. He poured himself a cup of tea, added milk in the Irish tradition, and took a sip and set his cup down. "So you and Liam are getting married," he said. He had not intended to bring it up—but he realized instantly that he was hoping—probably against hope—that she might dismiss the idea.

She smiled. "That's what he wants, but I'm not sure it's what I want."

"Do you love him?" He tried to keep his voice neutral.

"We've known each other a long time. He needed some money, so he got himself a job in Dublin. We've been living together in the same apartment where Moira and I lived." She laughed, but it was a bitter laugh. "We're living in sin," she said. "My dear departed mother would be shocked to death if she weren't dead already." There was an unmistakable bitterness in her tone, which didn't really surprise him. Kathleen had a hard edge that Moira had always been aware of.

"Well you know I wish you well, whatever you decide to do. I think of you often. Maybe ..."

She interrupted him. "Let's don't get into that," she said. "There's nothing to be gained from it."

"Kathleen," he began tentatively. "What happened between you and me was more than just a, how do they call it?—brief encounter. It meant something, even if I didn't want it to."

"Kellan, there's no point. Moira was my friend, and I should never have let that happen. But I have feelings too, and I was attracted to you the first time I saw you. If we hadn't drunk all that Jameson, who knows?"

"You deliberately got me drunk," he said, smiling.

She smiled back. "Maybe. But I don't recall having to twist your arm."

"You're probably right," he said. "Anyway, it was more than just the whiskey."

"Oh, Christ, we'll always have that hanging over us, won't we?"

He shook his head. "Right now feelings are very raw. When I saw you at the funeral, I have to admit I was really glad to see you. I'd been hoping you would be here. I'll always consider you a friend, at least. More than a friend."

She pondered that for a few moments. "I might never see you again." Her voice was heavy with the sadness she probably did not mean to convey. He could see that she was fighting tears. He wanted to tell her that she should not marry Liam, but he knew he had no right.

"I'll be coming over to see Fiona as often as I can. I have no way of knowing how long she'll be here, but I expect it may be a long time. I like to think that if I were here, that I could see you somehow. Of course, if you're married to Liam, that might be awkward."

"I won't make any promises," she said. "That would be foolish. But Patrick and Libby will know when you're coming, and I plan to keep in touch with them in any case. They saw me through some bad times when Moira and I were living together. I've had a much more complicated life than you know."

"I gathered as much from what Moira told me, though she never went into much detail. In any case, none of that would matter to me. I was just hoping …" He paused.

"Hoping what?"

"You know, that someday you and I might find a way to be together."

"Kellan, we went over all this before. If you and I had met earlier, things would be very different. Who knows, maybe we would have gotten married. But right now, you need to understand one thing. You are the father of a baby girl, and if you and I were to marry, that would make me her mother or stepmother or whatever. It doesn't matter. The point is, right now I'm in no condition to take on the job of raising a child. I'm not cut out for it, and I don't think I could face it. Believe me, my love, it has nothing to do with you. It's all about me."

"We could always get help. It wouldn't necessarily have to be a burden."

She took a deep breath. "Yes, and I must admit I've thought about it, but I just can't see my way clear to coming to America and taking over as the mother of your child and your wife. Maybe if the baby had not survived—oh, God I hate saying that—maybe things would be different. But they aren't. They never are. Kellan, I love you. You know that, but let's just give it some time."

"Well, that's one thing I seem to have plenty of now." He didn't try to hide the bitterness in his voice.

"Look, I don't know what I'm going to do about Liam. I love him, but not the way I love you, but he has had a difficult life, just as I have and he needs somebody. He's very dependent on me for emotional support, and I somehow feel I owe him something."

"Why? What do you owe him?"

"I believe in what he's doing, and therefore I believe in him. These people who are still struggling for the integrity and freedom of Ireland deserve the support of their countrymen, and too often they don't get it."

"So what you're telling me is that you will stay with him for what? For political reasons?"

"Kellan, that's not fair and you know it. I do agree one hundred percent with his principles, except for the violence. I've known him a long time, as I said. And I do feel that he needs me, and you can't turn your back on another human being.

"As we talk, I'm realizing that I need you too. I understand why that can't happen right now, but I beg you to just keep the door open."

"I will." She reached across the table and squeezed his hand. "There will always be a place for you in my heart, I promise. Who knows what the future will bring?"

He walked her to the railroad station and stayed with her until the train pulled in. Before she got on, she set her bag down and put her arms around him. "Promise me you'll always be my friend," she said. She stepped back, smiled, and then kissed him on the lips. It was a long kiss, and he started to put his arms around her, but she broke away, picked up her bag and hurried onto the train. She turned, smiled and blew him a kiss as it was pulling away. He stayed there watching until the train was out of sight then turned and walked slowly back to the Connolly home.

"You're looking a bit glum, Laddie," said Patrick. "I gather you saw Kathleen off?"

"Yes, I did," said Kellan. "But I'm a bit tired. I didn't sleep very well."

"I thought I heard you stirring a bit," Patrick said. "Kathleen's a lovely girl. Moira adored her." He looked over the top of his eyeglasses at Kellan.

"Yes."

"Ah, well, I expect she'll keep in touch. She seems to relax here, and we always enjoy having her."

"She may be getting married to Liam," Kellan said.

Patrick looked sharply at Kellan and frowned. "She'll find nothing but trouble there," he said, and then turned back to his *Irish Times*.

Next morning Brendan pulled his car around to drive Kellan back to Shannon. Deidre was holding Fiona as Brendan came back in, and Kellan asked if he could speak with the two of them alone. "You said you would always be a brother to me," Kellan said to Brendan. "And you are my brother, so please don't take this the wrong way." He handed Brendan an envelope containing a check.

Brendan opened the envelope, looked at the check and showed it to Deidre. "So what's this?" said Brendan. He looked confused.

"Oh, Kellan, that's not necessary," said Deidre.

"It surely is not," said Brendan.

Kellan smiled. "I was afraid you might take it the wrong way. Look, you two are taking on a huge burden, and I know you can afford it. I just need ... I don't know, I just want you to know that I more than deeply appreciate what you are doing. Just put that aside for emergency, or for Fiona's education. Please accept it with my gratitude." He looked at Deidre. "And with my love."

Deidre handed the baby to Brendan and threw her arms around Kellan. She was crying. "I watched you with her," she said. "The way you look at her and hold her, it breaks my heart."

Kellan put his arms around Deidre. He felt tears flood his eyes and roll down his cheeks. Brendan put a hand on his shoulder. "Not to worry, brother. Jesus, Mary and Joseph, we love you, Kellan."

The family came out of the house to see him off. Patrick and Libby hugged him. Deidre was holding Fiona, her cheeks still damp. Molly threw her arms around him and said, "I'll help take care of Fiona, Kellan. I'll make sure she doesn't forget you."

"Thank you, Sweetheart."

103

Kevin had gotten too big for hugs so he shook hands with Kellan. Kellan ruffled his hair and told him to be a good boy. "We'd best be off," said Brendan.

Kellan put his bag in the back of the car, and waved as they drove off. Libby and Molly were both wiping away tears. The drive to Shannon was relaxed and pleasant. Kellan appreciated the fact that Brendan seemed to sense Kellan's mood as he kept the conversation light. Kellan was content with the thought that he could not have left Fiona in better hands than with Brendan, Deirdre, and the rest of the Connolly clan. Brendan spoke of how he and Patrick were planning to extend their domains by another fifty acres or so later that spring. They were planning to try some new crops and perhaps start producing some finished farm products at home—butter, cheese and perhaps some baked goods. The small town and the surrounding region were growing, and Ireland was beginning to come out of its economic doldrums. Times were better, and the future looked promising.

Brendan and Kellan exchanged warm handshakes and hugs as they said their farewells. In Kellan's mind, Brendan was as fine a man as he could hope to know. Ireland had spent generations in the British imposed dark ages, exacerbated by famine and economic hardship. But the men and women of the Republic of Ireland were dedicated to improving their own lot as well as the condition of the country at large. Brendan and the rest of the Connolly family typified the hopes of the modern Irish state. As Kellan boarded the plane, he turned at the top of the stairway and waved to Brendan one last time. In a few moments the door closed behind him and he would leave Ireland completely behind for the first time in over five years. As the airliner winged its way across the Atlantic, Kellan dozed off from time to time, and when he awoke he was touched with a deep sadness counterbalanced by the conviction that he had made a wise decision with regard to his daughter. Still, he knew he was going to miss her. Kellan Maguire would be leaving a lot of himself in Ireland.

Attorney at Law

Eddie picked up Kellan at Logan airport and they drove to Tom and Mary's house where Kellan would have dinner. "Why don't you stay with us tonight?" Eddie said. "Eileen's got a night shift, and we can watch some b-ball and have a couple of beers."

"That' sounds good," Kellan said. "You're sure Eileen won't mind?"

"For Christ's sake, why would she mind? She said just before she left for work that she thought you would find it comforting not to have to spend your first night back in the States in an empty house."

"I appreciate it," Kellan said. "You're right, it's going to be kind of strange."

"You should move, brother. Find yourself a place near the firm." Kellan nodded.

The dinner at Tom and Mary's was quiet and comfortable. "How did it all go?" asked Mary.

"Very nice," said Kellan. "I wish you had gotten to know them that summer when you were in Dublin. Of course you got to know Libby."

"She's a sweetheart," said Mary. "What a wonderful grandmother for Fiona. And you say they live right next door to Brendan and Deirdre?"

"Yup. It's actually one big family farm with two houses." Kellan described the funeral and talked more about the Connolly family. He told them of the warmth and love with which Deirdre had accepted Fiona, virtually as one of her own. It comforted Kellan to share with his own family the warm feelings that he had carried with him from Ireland. "She couldn't be in better hands," said Kellan. He caught a look on Mary's face and reached out and touched her hand. "Heck, Sis, you could have done it, I know. But they lost their daughter, and it just seemed …"

Mary squeezed his hand. "I know, Kellan. It's okay—we all think you did the right thing. Getting to know Libby as I did, I couldn't imagine her not taking Fiona home. But I would have loved having her."

The next morning Eddie drove Kellan to his house and waited while he showered and changed into a business suit. He drove Kellan to the firm offices and dropped him off. As Kellan walked into the receiving area of

105

Phillips, Shannon and Steinberg, Susan Johnson got up and came over and hugged him. "We're glad to have you back, Kellan. We can hardly imagine all you've been through, and we'll do anything we can to help."

Kellan went into his office, looked around briefly, then visited the offices of Messrs. Shannon and Phillips to let them know he was back and prepared to buckle down. They both expressed their sympathy for his loss and were gratified to hear of the arrangements he had made for Fiona.

Kellan went to Ben's office next. Ben stood up and hugged him, then stepped back and held Kellan at arm's length. "How are you holding up, son?"

"I'm good, Ben. The service was nice, Fiona is in wonderful hands— I'm going to be okay."

"I'm sure you will," said Ben. "Edna knows you're back and wants you to come for dinner tonight. She's worried about you."

"She doesn't need to."

"Yes, but you know Edna." Kellan smiled and said he would be pleased to come to dinner. The two friends chatted for a while as Kellan filled Ben in on the details of his trip.

His last stop was in Julian's office. The head of the international law department was glad to have him back, he said. After offering his condolences, followed by some pleasant small talk, he brought Kellan up to date on the latest issues before the section. "Charlie can fill you in on the details," Julian said. "There's nothing critical at the moment, but I think it will do you good to get up to speed fairly soon. I know this is a difficult time for you, but I've always found that work can be a useful palliative, even as we grieve."

"Yes, sir, that's my plan."

"Good. Anything I can do to help, I'm always here."

Charlie Wright collected a bundle of folders, and he and Kellan went into a small conference room where they could spread them out and go through them at leisure. Alice Schreiber, who had been Julian's secretary for over ten years, and Anne Clark, a paralegal who worked in the international law division, joined the two attorneys as they went over files, discussed contracts and divided up tasks. Charlie thought it best if he took the lead on the issues with the shorter deadlines, giving Kellan time to catch up with what he had missed during his absence. Kellan agreed; he had worked on some of the issues during the time between Moira's death and when he left for Ireland, but he had understandably been distracted.

Back at home Kellan went through Moira's things one more time, and packed up some of the personal items that he thought should be sent back to the Connolly family. He would dispose of the rest with Mary's help, but was in no hurry to do so. He and Moira had purchased the house with the expectation that one or more children would become part of the family while they lived there. Now, as Kellan walked around in his eerily quiet home, he soon concluded that an apartment nearer the office would serve him better, as Eddie had suggested. He made a note to himself to contact the realtor who had found the house for them and ask her to put it back on the market. Meanwhile he would have Susan Johnson help him find a nice apartment, preferably within walking distance of Phillips, Shannon.

Before long it was spring again, and Kellan moved into his new apartment even while his former home remained unsold. The realtor had informed Kellan that he could expect a good price for the attractive house, and that sales would pick up as spring approached summer. "People don't want to move until the end of the school year," she said. That was fine with Kellan; he was earning a comfortable salary and could afford to support two residences for a short time. Two weeks later she called Kellan and announced that she had a buyer. He thanked her for the good news. He bought an attractive bookshelf for his apartment and spent some pleasant hours in a neighborhood book shop, purchasing a few volumes.

Eddie had managed to get three tickets for the last game of the basketball playoffs, which saw the Boston Celtics winning another championship. Since Bill Russell had joined the historic franchise, they had come to dominate professional basketball, to the delight of Boston fans. A few weeks later it was baseball season again. Kellan spent a lot of his leisure time at Fenway Park with Tom and Eddie, as well as with Charlie Wright and some of the other young associates at the firm. Charlie's wife Cynthia enjoyed having Kellan for dinner. They had no children yet but enjoyed entertaining.

As the year wore on, some of his friends began to make suggestions about Kellan dating again, but he put them off. "Maybe I'll meet somebody sort of by accident, and we'll see what happens," he said. "But I don't want to be fixed up with any blind dates. I just don't feel like it yet." One night after a long work day, Kellan invited Anne Clark to join him for dinner. He enjoyed her company but was in no hurry to follow up. They also went out to lunch together from time to time, but in answer to probing questions from colleagues, he would smile and answer, "We're just friends." Anne was a superb assistant, and she seemed to welcome his friendship. But she was no more interested in romance than he was; she was getting her law degree from an evening program at Suffolk Law School.

As he fell comfortably into a work routine, Kellan found himself spending long hours at the firm. He urged Charlie not to stay as late as he did, telling him that he needed to be with his family, especially as they would be traveling quite a bit. He started dismissing the secretaries and assistants at normal quitting time in the late afternoon unless they were working with other associates. "Call me if you need me," said Anne Clark. "I can get back here in fifteen minutes."

Kellan smiled—Anne was a hard charger and always seemed to anticipate Kellan's needs. "I'll be fine," he said, "but thanks."

Kellan was content spending evenings in the office with the radio on his desk playing classical music quietly on WGBH. The delicatessen and a Chinese restaurant within a few blocks of the firm office provided him all the sustenance he needed, and it was not unusual for him to be in the office until midnight. He didn't feel as alone there as he did in his apartment, and when he got home, he generally went straight to bed. He usually slept well.

In May Kellan received a letter from the Commonwealth of Massachusetts Supreme Judicial Court Board of Bar Examiners informing him that he had passed the bar exam. He took the letter to William Shannon's office and asked the secretary if the senior partner was available. The secretary ushered him in, and William Shannon stood, came around his desk and greeted Kellan with a handshake. "I see you got your letter from the bar committee," he said.

"Yes Sir."

"Congratulations, Kellan. We had no doubt that you would pass."

"Actually I wasn't so sure myself, considering everything that happened, that I didn't even finish the exam."

"The board of examiners were aware of your circumstances," Mr. Shannon said.

Kellan was unsure whether to proceed, but he decided to clear his own mind. "I hope I made it on my own," he said tentatively.

"Oh indeed you did," said Mr. Shannon. "You did very well. The portion that you did complete convinced the committee that you had a firm grasp of the law. I assure you that I exerted no influence whatsoever. I merely made an inquiry, informally, because I was concerned. I never had any doubts about your qualifications or your ability to pass the exam," he said. "But I knew that your wife's condition had placed you under considerable stress." He reached out and patted Kellan on the shoulder. "No, no, you did it on your own. Congratulations again."

Mr. Shannon paused for a moment. "I know how devastating it must have been for you to lose your bride. Julian and Benjamin have told me that you are managing quite well. I think your decision to allow your daughter to be raised by your wife's family was a wise one. When the time comes that you want to bring her back, please know that we will do everything to help you."

"I have been tremendously grateful for the firm's support, especially yours, Sir."

Kellan turned and started to leave, and Mr. Shannon patted him on the back. "We'll have to get together for lunch soon. I want to see what you're up to."

Kellan stopped by Julian's office and passed the good news on to him. After accepting Julian's congratulations, he went on to inform Julian of the contracts on which he and Charlie were working. Later that afternoon he brought Julian some letters and other documents he was preparing for clients and asked Julian to look them over. He was in the habit of seeking Julian's advice from time to time. Julian occasionally made minor suggestions but generally reassured Kellan that he was doing quite well. He thanked Kellan and said he would get back to him soon.

Later Julian told Kellan that he was planning a trip in June and would take Charlie with him. Kellan could not conceal his disappointment, but Julian said, "We'll only be flying to Amsterdam and then to Hamburg and then home. It will be a brief trip, and there wouldn't be time for you to visit Ireland." Julian smiled. "I know you want to see your daughter, and I've got another trip planned for August that will take us to Paris and London. I am sure we can let you come home on your own via Dublin. Meanwhile, you are doing terrific work, and this trip will involve things that Charlie was working on before you got back."

"I understand," said Kellan.

"I must say, Kellan, that in all my years as an attorney, I've never seen anyone pick up the ball as fast as you have. The other partners and I have discussed your progress, and we see you moving up very fast. Charlie is a hell of a good lawyer, but he'll have to go at top speed to keep up with you."

"I really enjoy working with Charlie," Kellan said. "I've learned a lot from him. He's a good man."

"That he is," said Julian. "You two are becoming a fine team, I'm happy to say."

The trip to Paris and London in August went well. Kellan briefed several of their European clients about contract proposals for acquisitions or for new agreements that would benefit both the European companies and their American partners. Once they had ended their business in London, Kellan was able to make a brief visit to Mallow to see Fiona and the Connolly clan.

"I wish I could stay for a few days," he told the family, "but I'm apparently needed back in Boston to go over what we've done on this visit. They've promised me that next time I'll be able to stay longer."

"So you are busy at learning the practice of law, are you," said Patrick. "Saints preserve us, what a waste of talent—sure you'd make a fine farmer!"

Kellan laughed. "I don't know about that. I've seen how hard you and Brendan work."

Kellan saw instantly that Fiona had taken to Deirdre, which was no surprise. He laughed as he watched Fiona and Caitlin playing together—they were fussing at each other over a toy stuffed lamb. Fiona was six months old, Caitlin almost nine.

"They're a pair, those two," said Brendan. "They keep Deirdre hopping."

"I don't mind a bit," said Deirdre. "I'm so glad Caitlin has a playmate to grow up with. Maybe Brendan and I can wait a while before having another."

"Ah, don't be foolish, now," said Patrick. "You know Libby is expecting you to have at least half a dozen!" He was smiling broadly. "Especially since …" He stopped abruptly. "Well, anyway, whenever you two are ready." At that moment Kellan found himself wondering whether Fiona would be his only child.

By mid-October Kellan had settled comfortably into a routine in the international law department. Early in November Julian dispatched him to New York to meet with members of a large import-export firm, clients of Phillips, Shannon. The meetings went well, and Kellan was glad to become acquainted with several of the young executives of the large, prestigious firm, including the company's in-house counsel, Rob Foster. Rob had an extra ticket to a Broadway show and asked Kellan to join him and two other friends.

Rob suggested that Kellan meet him at the theater. When Kellan got there Rob had two young ladies with him. He introduced Kellan to his sister, Sally, and his sister's friend Kathy. "Kathy's date couldn't make it," Rob said to Kellan, "so you're filling in." After the show, which Kellan enjoyed—it was the first real entertainment he had had in some time, except for sports events—they went to the famous Café Carlyle for drinks and a late dinner, where Rob had made a reservation. During the course of friendly conversation, Kellan began to realize that Rob, who was well acquainted with several of the young associates at Phillips, Shannon, had done a little research. His sister Sally and Kathy steered the conversation towards Kellan's social life, and Kathy ventured to ask politely, "I understand you lost your wife not too long ago? I'm very sorry."

Kellan glanced at Rob, who seemed embarrassed at the turn the talk had taken. Kellan decided very quickly not to take offense. "That's right," he said. "She died in childbirth."

"Oh, how sad," said Kathy. "Was the baby ...?" She seemed to realize she might have gone too far.

"My daughter is doing just fine," he said. "Right now she's being raised by my wife's brother and his wife. They have a child about the same age and it seems to be working quite well."

"Oh, that's wonderful. Are they close by?" said Kathy, warming to the subject.

"Actually, they're in Ireland," he said. The heck with it, he thought, let's get it all out. "I did my graduate work in Ireland and met my wife there. We were married there before I came back to the States, and I got to know my wife's family quite well. Fiona's in good hands."

"Fiona?"

"My daughter."

"What an interesting name," said Kathy. "Is it ...?"

Kellan glanced at Rob, who seemed ready to intervene, but Kathy was on a roll. "It's Irish," said Kellan.

Undaunted, Kathy seemed to sense that Kellan had not been offended by this turn in the conversation and plunged onward. "I'm sure you're looking forward to getting her back some time. I assume you would have no hesitation to starting another family."

111

Rob deflected the flow of conversation by signaling for the waiter.

This is a setup, Kellan thought. Kellan's young friends back at the firm who had been suggesting none too hesitantly that he might want to start dating at some point were behind this. He had politely told them that he would think about dating when he was good and ready; they would be the first to know when that time came. So, he concluded, Rob had called a couple of his friends in Boston and inquired about Kellan, and somebody had said it might be nice if Rob could fix Kellan up with an attractive single young woman. Kathy was indeed attractive, pleasant, and she seemed to be good company. He fought down feelings of resentment that he had been handled, as he put it to himself. He concluded that whatever was done was done in good faith.

He accompanied Kathy home in a taxi, and she invited him to come in for a nightcap or coffee. He politely declined, saying that he had more meetings to attend the next morning and then was catching a train back to Boston.

"Next time you're in town, why don't you look me up," she said. "Rob can give you my number."

He thanked her, got back in the cab and asked the driver to take him to his hotel. He wasn't sure whether to be angry or just amused. He decided on the latter. Later on, however, as he lay in bed in his hotel room listening to the faint hum of New York City traffic, he reflected on the evening, letting himself contemplate the possibility of opening up to a romantic relationship. As he thought about the possibilities, his mind drifted back to his last brief meeting with Kathleen. She was in his thoughts more frequently than he would have expected.

As the winter holidays approached, Kellan spent a Saturday in downtown Boston shopping for gifts for Fiona, Kevin, Molly, and Patrick and Libby Connolly, and of course Brendan and Deirdre. He wrapped and mailed them in time to arrive in Ireland by Christmas day. He thought about flying over for a brief visit during the holidays, but Julian had told him that another trip was coming up shortly after the first of the year, so he decided to postpone his next visit until then.

Kellan attended midnight mass with his family and spent Christmas day at Tom and Mary's house. Brian had turned four and tore through his packages with gusto. Eileen was working a shift at the hospital, but Eddie arrived in the early afternoon along with their mother. Later, when Eileen had finished her shift at the hospital and joined the rest of the family, they sat down together for their Christmas dinner, prepared by the women with help from Eddie, who announced grumpily that with Eileen working so much, he'd starve to death if he didn't know how to cook.

Eddie led the family in grace. Following the traditional Catholic blessing, Eddie added, "Lord, we ask that you look after our friends and family far away, and that you continue to comfort our brother."

Nora looked across the table at her son and murmured "Amen." She wiped a tear from her cheek, but then smiled. Eileen and Mary, on either side of Kellan, both squeezed his hand.

Kellan decided to spend most of the holiday time in the office. It was a quiet period, and he could dress casually and work at a relaxed pace. Having worked on Christmas day, Eileen Maguire had New Year's Eve off, and she and Eddie threw a party to celebrate. Along with Nora, Tom and Mary, other friends were there, some of whom Kellan remembered from the years before he had gone abroad.

Several young doctor interns, fellows of Eileen at the hospital in Worcester where she was working, were also at the gathering. Kellan observed with amusement as the young doctors celebrated with raucous enthusiasm. In his conversations with Eileen, he had learned just how grueling the life of an intern could be, and he understood that they needed to let off a little steam. Thirty-six hour shifts were *de rigueur*, and the physicians at the excellent hospital demanded much of the young doctors.

Eddie and Eileen had married just before Kellan left for Ireland. He had grown very fond of Eileen since his return, and his affection for his sister-in-law grew every time he was with her. She seemed to be interested in his legal career, and he was completely absorbed in hearing about the medical profession from her viewpoint. She seemed firm in her intention to develop a career in the pediatric or OB/GYN field, and was beginning to plan her residency toward that end.

Kellan was sorry to have missed Mary and Tom's wedding, but he had been in the middle of a semester at Trinity. Mary seemed content being a stay-at-home mother. Her husband Tom's position in an architectural firm in Boston was going very well, and she felt no pressure to find a job. She had majored in English at Tufts and shared with Kellan her plans to write a novel in her spare time. "Brian will be in school next year," she told Kellan. "And I ought to be able to find time to work on it."

"I thought you were planning a big family, Sis," he said. "There are three of us—I thought you'd at least try to match that."

She punched him on the arm. "Bite your tongue! Brian is a handful—didn't you see him on Christmas day? I need a break." She huffed, but then grinned and kissed her brother on the check. "I know you like being an uncle," she said. "I'm not saying never. I'm just saying not right now."

"Got it," he said. He smiled at her and squeezed her hand. He looked around the room. "Moira would have enjoyed this," he said.

A week into the new year Kellan received warm letters from the Connolly family. Libby and Deirdre each wrote to tell him how well Fiona was doing and to thank him for the gifts. Kevin and Molly included a note to "Uncle Kellan" asking him to be sure and come back for a visit soon. They sent him a book of Irish poetry bound in green velvet, which he placed on his bookshelf next to the similar volume he had received from Moira's friend Darcy. He smiled as he recalled Moira's farewell party at The Pig's Ear. He returned their letters, saying that a trip had been planned for February and that he would be sure to visit them in Mallow.

As it turned out, the trip included business with an exporting firm in Hamburg and a shipping company in Amsterdam, the same companies Charlie had visited a few months earlier. Kellan had become familiar with almost all the international clients, and Julian wanted him to meet their officers. The Amsterdam company, Gros Expediteur, was planning to expand its business contacts in the United States and would be generating a lot of legal work for Phillips, Shannon. The meetings went well.

Kellan had hoped to make a visit to Freiburg to call on Professor Schweiger, his old sparring partner from Trinity, but he decided to spend the extra time in Ireland. By good fortune, their business in Europe concluded a few days before Fiona's first birthday, and Kellan was pleased to be able to spend extra time with the family to celebrate the occasion with her and the rest of the Connollys.

Fiona took to him almost immediately. Kellan picked her up and she gurgled and smiled. Patrick laughed and said, "By golly, Kellan, she knows who she's talking to!"

"Look at her," said Libby. "She adores you."

"She's my girl," said Kellan, and he kissed her on both cheeks.

Everyone in the Connolly family laughed and agreed that Fiona knew Kellan was her father. He was pleased to note that there were no jealous feelings about his daughter's affection for him. The Connollys had embraced Kellan from the moment they had first met him. As he held his daughter in his lap in the Connolly living room, he reflected once again that his choice of turning her over to Brendan and Deirdre, her grandparents and her niece and nephew had been a wise decision.

Holding Fiona reminded him of how much he had loved her mother and how much he missed her and his daughter. Being back with Moira's family intensified his sadness while at the same time comforting him with their obvious affection. As they celebrated her birthday, he sat next to her high chair and helped feed her, smiling when she tried to share a bite of food with him. She waved a spoon at him and said "Da!"

"Well saints alive, she knows her father!" said Libby as everyone laughed.

As they sat in the living room talking on the day before Kellan was to leave, Patrick asked Kellan if he had been in touch with Kathleen. "No," said Kellan, "I was going to ask you if you knew of her whereabouts. I was wondering whether she was in Belfast or back in Dublin."

"She's still in Dublin," said Patrick. "She calls us from time to time just to say hello. She and Moira were very close, as you know, and she was very much saddened by Moira's death. Every time we talked to her she was thinking about visiting you two in the states. But now ..."

"I was quite fond of her," Kellan said. "She's very different from Moira, but she still a very interesting person."

"Oh she's interesting all right," said Patrick. "A real beauty, she is. But a bit wild, I guess."

"So Moira said, but I found her to be quite thoughtful all the same," said Kellan, "She's very smart."

"I've no doubt of that, Laddie. But I also gather she was quite fond of you," Patrick said. "She's still living in that apartment that she and my Moira had. I think she let it out for a while, but she's back there. It seems she can't make up her mind whether she wants to live in Belfast or Dublin. I'm sure that if it weren't for that Liam fellow, she'd be settled in Dublin and maybe have a boyfriend who didn't have his head up his behind." Patrick paused for a moment. "We have her number here. Maybe you could stop by on your way to the airport and see her—why don't you give her a call?"

Kathleen was pleased to hear from Kellan. She sounded very excited as they exchanged pleasantries; then she asked, "So you are leaving tomorrow? What time does your plane leave?"

"A little after eleven. I'll be driving up early in the morning. I thought maybe I could stop and see you."

"Why don't you leave early and I'll meet you at the airport," she said. "It would take you too far out of your way to come all the way into the city and then back to the airport. I'll just get myself out there on the bus and we can have a cup of tea. What's your flight number?"

Kellan gave her all the information about his Aer Lingus flight and they planned to meet near the departure gate an hour or so before the flight boarded.

Kellan turned in his rental car and proceeded to the check-in desk for his flight to Boston. As he was standing in line waiting for his bag to be checked, he felt a hand on his shoulder. He turned and saw Kathleen smiling at him. "Hi, stranger," she said.

He collected his boarding pass, turned to her and said, "Let's go find a place where we can sit and talk."

When they were seated at a table with their tea, he said, "So, what have you been up to?"

Kathleen smiled, reached across the table and took his hand and squeezed it for a moment. "I'm just trying to keep my head above water," she said. "Sometimes it's difficult to know which way to turn, but I'm getting along fine." She had been looking at him with a pleased expression, but her face turned sad. "You know, I know how much you must miss Moira, but I tell you true, I think I probably miss her almost as much, though differently, of course. She was my anchor, she kept me level; whenever I didn't know which way to turn, she had an answer."

"But you always seemed very sure of yourself, as though you understood where you were in your life and where you wanted to go. I don't quite understand what you're saying about Moira; you don't strike me as someone who needs a lot of help."

"Oh that's just because you don't know me as well as you think you do," she said. "A lot of my life has really been a mess. I've never talked about it very much because I don't like to. But I had to get out of a wretched family life and go up and live with my aunt in Belfast. She was wonderful to me, and I didn't mind living with her. But I never felt as though I was really home, that the North was the place where I was meant to live. Belfast is the seat of a great deal of discontent, but the city has its charms, and I got my education there at Queen's University."

116

Kellan was aware that marches through Catholic sections of Belfast each summer celebrated the victory of William of Orange over the Catholic supporters of the deposed King James the Second in 1689. "Do those marches come through your aunt's area?"

"No, my aunt had married a Protestant, an Ulsterman, and that's where they lived. She wasn't fussy about her religion. She'd go off to mass on Sunday, and her husband could do as he pleased. They didn't let it bother them, and the whole time I was in Belfast I found that a very common trait among those people. They went out of their way not to pay any attention to who was Protestant and who was Catholic, and if they knew they made a point of ignoring it. It was the only way they could live and work side-by-side without constant tension. Of course there are those on both sides who are always pushing things, and that's where most of the attention gets directed. But it didn't really affect me that much."

"How about you and Liam? Wasn't that an issue?"

"I'd really rather not talk about Liam today," she said. "He's part of my life that I just have to deal with, and I do care for him. Maybe I even love him. But he's hard to be around sometimes, he gets so worked up; he's angry a great deal of the time and that's not pleasant to be around. I think some of my anger feeds off of him, and I don't like that feeling either."

"Well then let's talk about how your writing and editing work is going." He smiled and reached for her hand again.

She seemed to relax. She took a deep breath and looked down at the table and shook her head for a moment. "You know, I wish my life were confined to my work." She looked at him with inquiring glance. "I suspect your life is like that now that Moira's gone. Unless you have somebody else in your life, I'm guessing that you focus yourself on your work and try not to think too much about other things."

"You're right," he said. "I have a couple of women friends, and from time to time we'll have dinner or go to a movie. But I don't really feel myself opening up to anything like that in my life, at least not until the pain goes away. I didn't expect to feel this much pain, but I do miss Moira." He squeezed her hand again. "I do love seeing you, please understand that, and I'm not looking at you as someone to replace Moira. But I am looking at you as someone I'd like to spend a lot more time with, where we could both shut the door on the past and move forward."

"That would be lovely," she said. She looked up at him and smiled, and her eyes flashed with pleasure. "I'm just not ready to turn everything over and leave my country. Please understand, if you were here or I were over there and we were together, who knows what might happen?" She smiled again. "It could be a lot of fun!" He smiled and nodded.

She went on. "The day when you and I were together and you kissed me, that was the day that I took the measure of you. Oh, I wanted you so badly, but we knew we should stop." She reached for his hand. "Kellan if you had pushed just a little bit, I'd have done anything you wanted. But you didn't. You sat down at the table—I can still see the look on your face—and I knew you wanted me, too, but you loved Moira, and you were true to her.

"If we had gotten in bed together, no one never would have known except the two of us. But you couldn't do it. After that I knew I really loved you, and I knew you loved Moira, and I knew that if you and I were ever together, you would be absolutely true to me. I've held onto that. And for some strange reason, I've got to be true to Liam. It's not the same thing; I don't love him the way you loved Moira, but I feel a sense of loyalty to him. I don't know where it comes from—maybe it's all those years I spent up in Belfast where I could see the turmoil that never ended. He's in the middle of that, and I just don't feel like I can desert him."

"I understand," said Kellan. "I know your feelings about Ireland—the troubles and all that—and I would never expect you to turn your back on someone you believe in. Maybe someday…"

She smiled and gripped his hand. "Let's leave it at that, shall we? Maybe someday. For right now that will have to be enough for us. Can you live with that?"

"I can, and I will. I'm still dealing with Moira's death, and I worry about Fiona, although I know she's in wonderful hands. I miss her too, terribly, and I never realized how much I would. But the good thing about that is that she will always bring me back here, and when I'm here, maybe you and I can have a cup of tea and hold hands."

She was still smiling, but she blinked back tears.

"We'll just have to keep in touch," he said. "Just promise me that you will always give me an address where I can reach you. I'll write, not as often as I should, maybe, but I promise I'll try. You have my address at the firm, and it will always be good. I'm not sure where I'll be living—I'm in an apartment right now and it's kind of cramped, so I'll be moving. But

118

just send anything you want to get to me to the office, and I'll be sure to get it."

She wiped her eyes with a handkerchief. "I'm a mess," she said, "but I'll be fine." She brushed back her long auburn hair, shook her head and smiled.

"You look wonderful," said Kellan, and she smiled.

"So, how's your legal practice going?"

"To be honest, I think I'm getting fairly good at it. They let me appear in court from time to time, no big trials or anything like that, but I've argued a few motions and gotten a feel for the way things go in court. Fortunately, one of my friends is a regular opponent, and we sort of lean on each other. He graduated from Harvard and is a superb attorney, and when I go up against him, I know I've met my match. But we're friends, and when we're done in court, he's perfectly happy to tell me what I did wrong." He laughed. "Seriously, he's a good friend, and I am learning the business. That's why I'm over here in Europe, visiting an important client. And I'll be back this way regularly."

She smiled. "That's a good thing. She reached out and took both of his hands. "Kellan, I do love you. Maybe it's not the kind of love that you had with Moira, but it's true. I care very much about you—I always will."

"Right now, that's good enough for me. I guess I loved you before … well, you know before everything else happened. I remember those long talks we had; the hours seemed to fly by. It was always such fun talking with you, to watch your face, to see you walking around the room all full of fire. You have a way about you that's absolutely striking."

An announcement sounded for the boarding of his flight, and he squeezed both her hands. "Well, I guess that's it. Walk me to the gate and give me a proper hug."

"I'll do more than that," she said. When we got to the gate she put both her arms around him and kissed deeply, warmly. He held her for several moments enjoying the feeling of her body close to his. He didn't want to let go, but he kissed her again, turned and walked toward the gate. As he went through, he turned back, waved and smiled at her, and she blew him a kiss.

Sad as he was to leave her standing there, he had a wonderful feeling about their friendship. He vowed never to let go of it.

Back in Boston he settled into a comfortable routine with the firm. He worked closely with Julian, Charlie, and the other associates and partners in the international law department. He enjoyed lunches and visits with Ben and Edna; they seemed to assume the role of surrogate parents for Kellan, and he relished their warm friendship. He attended sports events with Brendan and some of his old college friends, and he dined frequently with Tom and Mary. He made a point of dropping by Eddie's home when Eileen was off duty. Charlie and Cynthia Wright had him over for dinner regularly.

Later that spring Mary told him that she was pregnant again. "I told you so, Sis!" said Kellan.

"Well, Brian wants a little sister. I think he was taken with Fiona. We'll see what happens."

"Are you sorry?"

"Well, Tom's happy and Brian's excited, so what's there to be sorry about?" She smiled and reached out for Kellan's hand. "We need another girl in the family," she said. She was quite ready to put up with Kellan's teasing about how quickly she seemed to have changed her mind.

"I hope it's a girl," said Kellan.

"It better be!" said Mary with a laugh. "And what about you, brother? Don't you want to have a family?"

"I already have one," he said gently. "I'm not quite ready to start another. We'll see."

Encouraged by his friends, Kellan gradually became more open to meeting young women. Every so often one or two single women would materialize at a party to which he had been invited, sometimes obviously for his consideration. The fact that he had become a widower at such a young age seemed to have an effect on the women he knew. It was a sort of nurturing instinct, he concluded. They seemed quite ready to offer comfort and affection to an obviously lonely man. At least it was obvious to the women. He asked Mary about it.

"Just enjoy it," she said. "Who knows? You might get lucky!"

Kellan didn't feel particularly lonely. He enjoyed the law work, he found it easy to relax with his brother and sister, his brother-in-law and other friends, and casual friendships with women seemed adequate. He enjoyed female companionship, but on occasion when a relationship with a woman became intimate, he could not open himself to the possibility of a permanent arrangement.

As his knowledge of American law matured, Kellan found himself in court from time to time, and the firm recognized his budding skills as a promising trial attorney. He faced his friend Jordan Montgomery from time to time, and the friendship that had carried them through Boston College made them friendly but fierce adversaries. Jordan worked for the other firm in Boston best known for its international law practice, which tended to involve them in the same kinds of cases.

Without betraying the needs of their clients, Kellan and Jordan found it useful to work together in seeking settlements of issues in dispute. But when they faced each other in court, all bets were off. It would have been unethical for them to bet on outcomes, but when they opposed each other in court, it could quickly turn into a verbal sparring match that could easily turn sharp. When colleagues at their firms became aware that the two would be facing each other, they might be seen sitting in the back rows of the courtroom as spectators. It was possible, though kept secret, that a certain amount of betting might take place among the young associates at the two firms.

Later that spring Kellan and Jordan spent two days before a judge arguing a motion. When the hearing ended in favor of Jordan's client, he and Kellan walked out onto the front steps of the Federal District Courthouse in Boston. Kellan stuck out his hand. "Congratulations, you son of a bitch. You owe me a drink."

"Let's go to Foley's. I'll drive."

They sat at a table looking out on Berkeley Street in South Boston. "You love this place, don't you?" said Jordan.

"It's okay. Not too bad for an American pub, but not really like the ones in Dublin."

"Yeah, I know, you really enjoyed yourself over there." Jordan took a sip of his beer. "Tell me, do you ever think about getting married again?"

"Lots of people ask me that. The answer is, I just don't feel like it."

"How long has it been since Moira died?"

"Well over a year now. Hard to believe—it doesn't seem that long."

"I guess it takes a while. You'll eventually get over it, my friend. I guess you met lots of gorgeous women in Ireland."

Kellan smiled. "Yeah, there were a few. But Moira was something special. She was nice, you know, one of the most decent people I ever knew. I never once heard her say a mean word about anyone. And she never got angry, even when she was miserable right before Fiona was born. I've really never known anyone else like her."

"A beautiful Irish lassie, she was," said Jordan. "And a good Catholic too!"

"That she was. She was good for me; I was kind of falling away when I met her, but she got me going to mass again. It's funny, I've hardly been to mass at all since she died."

"It must've been difficult, the whole thing." They took a sip of the Guinness and were quiet for a while. "What was the name of that other woman you knew over there? I think she was Moira's roommate."

"Kathleen Morrissey," Kellan said. "Yeah, I remember her all right."

Jordan looked at him. "You're smiling," he said. "Did you and she have something going?"

"We might have, but I was engaged to Moira, and they were best friends."

"But you still think of her, too, right?"

"Sometimes."

"You should go back over and visit her again."

"I saw her the last time I was in Ireland for Fiona's birthday. She's very close to Moira's family. We're still sort of in touch."

"Write her a letter. Invite her over for a visit. Who knows what might happen?"

"She wouldn't come," Kellan said.

"Why not? Wouldn't she want to see you?"

"That's not it," Kellan said. He thought for a moment. "She's too Irish. She's kind of pissed off at America because we don't do enough to help the Irish and their cause. Not that we could do any good in that mess. But I understand how she feels."

"Well, I'm glad you do."

"And she's got some guy she's sort of attached to. He's got something to do with the IRA."

"Jesus, that's doesn't sound too good. Is she in that too?"

"No, she doesn't like the violence, but she sure hates the British."

Jordan shook his head. "Man, that's a mess." After a while he said, "Have you ever given any thought to going into politics?"

"Me? Not a chance. I like what I'm doing and have never even thought about it. But you have, right?"

"I've been thinking about it. My grandfather was a senator from Massachusetts, I guess you knew that."

"Yeah, he was a Republican, right?"

"My whole family is. If I ever ran for office, I would have to run as a Republican. My Dad has mentioned the possibility a few times—he was proud of his father, sort of the old *noblesse oblige* idea. I think he would be happy for me to carry on the family name in public office. You wouldn't run as a Republican, though, would you?"

"Jesus, Jordan, your ancestors were fighting in the American Revolution while mine were still growing potatoes in County Clare. Naw, my family's all Democrats through and through. I don't think I could get anywhere with that."

"Well, then run as a Democrat. Hell, I'd even vote for you!" Kellan laughed and shook his head. "And the Kennedy brothers seem to be doing all right. Is it true that old Joe is planning on using his money to create an Irish Catholic dynasty in the United States?"

Kellan laughed again. "Well, some folks are already talking about Bobby succeeding Jack."

"Yeah, well, Jack's got to get reelected first. He's just getting started."

They finished their Guinness, and Jordan drove Kellan back to the courthouse where he had left his car. "Thanks for the lift," Kellan said. "See you in court!"

"Right. By the way, Shelley wants you to come for dinner Sunday. Can you make it?"

"Sure, I'd love to. I've hardly seen her since you guys got married."

"She'll be glad to see you."

Kellan watched as Jordan's speedy little sports car zipped away. He smiled, shook his head and walked to his own car, a sedate sedan. He drove slowly back to his office, thinking about their conversation. He concluded that he would not be surprised if Jordan did decide to run for office. As for his own future, perhaps in politics, he would stash that idea away for a rainy day.

Kellan started keeping a journal of his legal experiences, and made notes to himself on subjects about which he might one day feel like writing. As a young attorney, he leaned more toward practical applications of the law, but occasionally he encountered situations where the depth of knowledge he had gained during his intense study in Ireland made him aware of an indistinct line between theory and practice. Perhaps one day he would put pen to paper and address those things, but for the time being he was content to practice law to the best of his ability.

Part 2

Off to Parliament He Shall Go

Twenty Years Later

*All legislative power herein granted shall be vested in a
Congress of the United States, which shall consist of
a Senate and House of Representatives.
—U.S. Constitution, Article I, Section 1*

Running Man

Kellan stood in the door of the office of Martin Downey and knocked. Downey looked up, nodded and motioned Kellan to a chair in front of his desk. He continued working at the document on his desk, making notations as he went. Kellan didn't mind waiting, didn't feel insulted. Martin Downey was not only the managing partner of the New York office of Phillips, Shannon, Steinberg and Rush; he was one of Kellan's best friends.

"So, Mr. Maguire," Marty began in a mock Irish brogue, "what brings ye to the foot of the throne today?"

Kellan laughed. Marty had that kind of wit and charm that could get laughter out of a jury in a courtroom even in the midst of a difficult trial. In one famous instance, he had even made the crankiest, most irritable federal judge in the United States Courthouse of the Southern District of New York laugh. Marty was liked and admired by his legal adversaries, who knew that he could turn that wit into a rapier-like weapon. A devoted family man with a lovely wife and three children, he was demanding of the attorneys who worked under him, but also understanding. Kellan was one of his most trusted and faithful colleagues, one on whom he often called for services that might have been difficult for a married attorney with a young family.

"You never quit, do you?" said Kellan. "Court jester and king of the hill at the same time!"

"Ah, well, it never costs me a dime to play the fool," said Martin in the same brogue. In a conventional voice he continued, "Seriously, what can I do for you?"

"Most of my active cases are well under control," he began. "All my guys are up to speed, and there are no critical issues pending, so I thought this would be a good time."

"A good time for what?"

"I'm going to run for Congress."

"Yeah, yeah, you've been saying that for years—months anyway. What else is on your mind?"

"I'm serious. I'm really going to do it. I've done some research, touched base with a few important people, and I'm ready to start the ball rolling. I've got a couple of good people on board, and I think it's doable."

Marty leaned back in his chair and looked at his friend with an expression that bordered on amusement. "Okay, I hear you. You've been meddling around in politics for a couple of years—you worked on the governor's campaign. So what does that mean for us and the firm?"

"I'd like to turn all my cases over to the guys who can handle them. We have a good group, and there won't be any dropped balls. I plan to stay in touch and help out whenever needed. But I don't want to take on any new clients."

"Go on."

"I'd like to take a leave of absence while I'm running my campaign. I'd like to hope that I could return to full time with the firm in case I'm not successful."

"So you want a safe landing place in case you fall on your ass?" Marty was smiling.

"Something like that." Kellan chuckled. "I've scoped out the political landscape pretty carefully. I think I have a good chance. Donovan is running for the Senate, and his seat is going to be open. It's my district, and no heavy hitters have stepped up to make a run for it yet. I'm thinking that if I get in early, I may have a good chance to preempt a lot of support."

"You're serious, aren't you?" Marty had stopped smiling. He stood up and came around and sat on the front of his desk right in front of Kellan. Kellan nodded. "So where are you? You must have some sort of an organization put together, right?"

"Of course. What do you think, that I'm going to run the campaign on my own?"

"Knowing you, what the hell?" Marty was smiling again.

"I've spoken with Lynn Patterson. She's got a lot of political savvy, and she seems interested. I'm having dinner with her this evening."

"Lynn Patterson, Jesus! Where's old George in all this?" George Patterson was a high-powered Wall Street financier. He was one of the wealthiest and most powerful men in New York. His wife Lynn was an experienced political operative. She had helped the current governor of New York get elected, where Kellan had first met her. She had also worked on the unsuccessful campaign of a candidate for the United States Senate. The conventional wisdom had it that if her candidate had followed her advice, he would have been elected. In other words, no one blamed her for the defeat.

"George is where he always is, downtown making money. Lynn has promised me that he won't interfere—he has always given her a free hand in what she does in politics."

"Where are you having dinner with her?"

"The Algonquin."

"Wow! I gather that's her idea." Kellan nodded. "So what makes you think she'll get on board with your campaign?"

"I think she likes me." Kellan smiled. "Actually, we've had a couple of conversations, and she thinks I might be able to win. With Donovan out of the race, it's wide open, and the Republicans are still squabbling over who their nominee is going to be. She thinks I can beat whoever gets it."

"She told you that?"

"Nah, I just made that up. Actually she told me I didn't have a snowball's chance in hell."

"All right, all right, I believe you. So when are you thinking of leaving us?"

"Lynn and I are going to talk it over tonight. We'll figure out a timetable, start thinking about opening a campaign headquarters, hiring a couple of assistants and canvassing for volunteers. It will probably take us a couple of weeks to figure things out. I should probably get it into gear by the first of March."

"That's not a whole lot of time to get things turned over, is it?"

"Like I said, I've been working on it for a while now. I didn't want to go to Lynn with a lot of loose ends, and I didn't want to bring it up with you until it looked like it might really happen."

Marty stood up. "All right, my friend. I know you've had a bug up your ass about politics for at least a year. When you worked on Governor Ross's campaign, I figured you were just learning the ropes." He held out his hand. "I wish you well, pal. Anything I can do to help, just let me know."

"I haven't said anything to Boston yet. You might help me with that."

"Ben Steinberg's retired, so is Julian. You don't have any more real close contacts up there, do you?"

"I still talk to Charlie Wright quite often." Charlie had become a partner in the firm and was running the international law section. "But it's been ten years since I left Boston. Of course, it was their idea to send me down here to help you set up this place. I don't really feel as if I owe them anything. I'll take a run up there sometime in the next couple of weeks and talk it over with the senior partners. I doubt they'll have any problem with it; a lot of our business rubs up against politics, and I'm sure they wouldn't mind having someone in Congress they could go to."

"Okay. Let me know how that goes with Lynn. Don't get too close to her, my friend. She'll fry your ass. She's a real piece of work."

"You know it. I'll be careful."

Lynn Patterson met him at the lobby of the Algonquin Hotel on 44th Street. She was tall, slender with light brown hair and was wearing an attractive suit. She had on a gold necklace with matching earrings, a large diamond ring and wedding band, but no other jewelry. They shook hands, and she said, "We're in the Round Table room."

The maître d' greeted Lynn with a smile. "Good evening, Mrs. Patterson. Nice to see you again. Right this way please."

A waiter approached as soon as they were seated. She smiled at Kellan. "Cocktail?"

"Sparkling water would be fine," he said.

"I'll have my usual and we'll have a Perrier to go with that," she said to the waiter; then she looked at Kellan. "Don't you drink?"

"Not very much. You know, the Irish curse." He went into a mock brogue. "'God invented whiskey to keep the Irish from takin' over the world.' My dad drank too much, and when I was studying in Dublin I met some young guys who had taken the pledge. They call them the Pioneers. I didn't join, but I drink very little."

Lynn smiled and nodded. "You've got that accent down pretty good."

"Well, I was there four years."

"Anyway, it sounds like a good idea for a politician."

The waiter reappeared with their drinks. Her 'usual' looked like a Manhattan cocktail. "You must come here often," he said.

"Oh, you know, George likes this place. It has a lot of history, and it's still relatively civilized. You can't say that for every place in New York these days."

Kellan realized that wherever he might be in the company with Lynn Patterson, she would know her way around. She obviously enjoyed being in the driver's seat, and although not as powerful as her famous husband, she knew how to throw her weight around; she didn't have to use his name to get what she wanted. Kellan knew that with her helping with his campaign, his chances of being elected would be excellent. The question was, given some of the campaigns she had been involved with in the past, would she be willing to work with him?

"So, Kellan Maguire, tell me a little bit about yourself. Why do you want to stick your toe into this muddy political water? I hear you're a pretty good attorney and have done very well for yourself. It seems to me that the United States Congress might not necessarily be a step up for you."

Kellan chose his words carefully. "Well for starters, I could give you some patriotic boilerplate about wanting to serve my country, and it wouldn't all be nonsense. I spend a lot of time overseas, and I am your basic red-blooded loyal American. As you know, however, my area of interest in the firm has been in international business. I know quite a bit about trade and commerce, and I'm not sure that our financial interests as a nation are always being served well. To be honest, I think I might have something to offer."

"So you're giving me the old JFK pitch: 'Ask what you can do for your country.' Okay, I'll buy that. After all, you started your life up in Kennedy country."

"That's right. But I've been a resident of New York for ten years and I think I have a pretty good handle on the politics of my district."

"You live in Scarsdale, so you're in the 19th district. Have you lived there ever since you moved to New York?"

"Pretty much. I had a place here in Manhattan for six months and then I moved up there. It will be ten years by the time of the election."

"So they can't get you for being a carpetbagger like Bobby."

"Let's hope not."

The waiter reappeared and asked if they were ready to order. Lynn said, "Do you mind if I order for both of us? I know what's good here." He hadn't even glanced at the menu, and it was obvious that she wanted to keep the conversation moving, so he readily agreed. Besides, he didn't really care what he would be having for dinner. She ordered salads, lamb chops, asparagus and a baked potato for both of them.

"What I'm really after at this point," she said after the waiter had left, "is whether you are in this for the right reasons. I've been asking around about you, and I'm guessing that you probably are. You studied law in Ireland, right?"

"Yes, law and economics. I had a fellowship but I stayed on for an extra year." He was not quite surprised that she knew that, but it wasn't exactly common knowledge.

"That surely won't hurt you in this state," she said. "Let's talk about what you think you can bring to the people of your district." She took a sip of her Manhattan. "For example, what do you bring from your practice of the law?"

Kellan was prepared for the question—he had been thinking about the core issues he would use in his campaign for quite some time. "What I've been dealing with at Phillips, Shannon is international business. Look, every time a German car company decides to build a car using components made in the United States, a bunch of contracts have to be worked out. The two companies have to agree for starters, and then there are contracts with shipping companies on both sides, import-export issues, tax issues and so on. Every foreign producer—Italian shoe companies, French wine growers, Swiss watch makers—all have to deal with contracts with American distributors, tariffs, and all that. There's a lot of legal work involved, and that's what we do. That's what I've been doing for twenty years, and believe me, there have been times when I wanted to go down to Washington and kick some butt. Congress tries to help American business and keep our balance of payments under control, but it's not easy. Yeah, there are lots of lawyers in Congress, but not many of them have worked in international trade."

"Wow," Lynn said. "I guess I pushed your hot button."

Kellan laughed. "Sorry about that. But you did touch a nerve. Hell, it's why I'm running."

Lynn didn't say anything for a few moments. She took a bite of food and looked at the table and around the room—not at Kellan. He could see that she was mulling over what he had said. Then she looked at him and said, "Good." She nodded. "Very good." She smiled and seemed to relax.

Throughout the rest of the meal she asked more questions, encouraging him to talk about himself, his experiences, his ideas, his favorite political figures, and other topics, not all of which struck him as being pertinent to what he was planning on doing. Lynn was obviously building a portrait of him in her own mind, and the thrust and variety of her questions made it clear that he would not be able to steer the conversation himself. She knew where she wanted to go, and as her demeanor came across as being friendly to what he had to say, he was happy to let her steer.

By the time they had finished with their dinner and were waiting for dessert and coffee, he decided to do a little probing of his own. "You obviously have had a great deal of political experience," he said. "I've done little asking around myself. To be frank, I have to wonder why you would find it interesting to work with a political beginner trying to become a first-term congressman."

She smiled. "And what's wrong with that?" He noted that she was very attractive when she smiled, and even when she didn't. She was a few years younger than her husband, which made her perhaps a few years older than he was.

"Nothing in particular," he said. "I might've thought you'd have bigger fish to fry."

She laughed and shook her head. "It's not the size of the fish that interests me," she said. "It's what the fish has to offer. And so far I'd say you would be a pretty interesting catch. I think you'd make a damn good congressman."

When the waiter brought them the check, Kellan reached for his wallet, but Lynn waved him off and grabbed the bill. "Don't even think about it," she said. "George has more money than God. This one's on me."

He thanked her and they left their table and walked out into the lobby area. "Sit with me for just a few more minutes," she said, heading for a quiet corner. When they were seated, she leaned toward him and said in a quiet voice, almost a whisper, "There's one thing I need to ask you about. It's personal, but if you're getting into public life you may as well face the fact that your private life will become public quite rapidly."

"I have nothing to hide," he said.

"As far as I can tell, you've never been married. Am I right?"

"You *have* been doing some digging," he said. "I gather some of it has been in the Boston area. You wouldn't have found anything there."

"Okay, so were you? Do you have an ex-wife floating around somewhere who might jump up and cause problems later on?"

He leaned back in his chair and gave her a hard look. "I was married. I got married not long before I left Ireland. I brought her back to the States with me, but she died in childbirth almost on our first anniversary."

"I'm sorry, I didn't know."

"Not many people do. I've never tried to hide it, but I don't like to talk about it. It's a part of my life I've just decided to keep private. Especially now that I'm thinking of running for office, there are parts of it that I would just as soon keep to myself. There's nothing there that could hurt me, but there are some things—some people—that I don't want to have involved."

"What sort of people, if I may ask?"

"You may, but it stays between you and me. If it should ever get out, which I doubt, I'll deal with that when the time comes. But I don't want it coming out on my side."

"Okay, I can deal with that. But I'm taking your word for it that there's nothing that could damage you politically anywhere in your background. The fact that you never married again may raise questions, but we'll deal with them when and where necessary." She formed her hands into a pyramid and looked at him with an interesting expression. "Do I dare ask whether there have been any other women in your life since your wife died?"

"Sure, you can ask. I've had some women friends, some of them pretty close. I've thought about remarrying a few times, but there have been reasons why I didn't want to do that."

"Do you have something against marriage?"

"Not at all. Let's just say that once or twice I might have wanted to get married, or at least thought about it, but the other party was not available."

"Married," she said. "Is there anything there that might prove embarrassing?"

"Nothing. Anybody who might have anything to say would probably be embarrassed more than I would. Let's just say that I'd like to keep as far away from that topic as possible."

Lynn Patterson thought for a few moments, then she said, "That's probably manageable. Of course the fact that you seem never to have been married might have people thinking that you're gay."

He laughed. "That's the least of my worries," he said. "I think if they checked with a couple of the women in the firm they might be disabused of any notions like that."

"Office sex? I guess that's not too bad as long as it doesn't qualify as sexual harassment. Have you been screwing around with the hired help?"

"I never slept with anybody I outranked," he said. "But I won't give you any clues about who to ask about that. I don't kiss and tell."

"Don't worry, my guys will find out all we need to know."

"Your guys?"

"Well, I have hired help too. I have a couple of pretty good investigators. It's an absolute necessity in this business, because you can bet your ass that the other side will have them. If there's anything to be found out, I want to find it first."

"So your guys are good at that."

"Actually, it's one guy and one gal. They're both very good. They've both been with me a long time."

Kellan was aware that the subject of Fiona had not come up, but it might not have occurred to Lynn that a child had survived the difficult birth. He might have to deal with it later, but he knew would be hard to uncover; nevertheless, he decided it was best to get it out on the table. If Lynn's agents were good enough to track that down, he would be impressed. But she might be disappointed that he had hidden something from her; it was better not to leave that possibility open.

"There's one more thing that you probably ought to know about," he said. "I have a daughter in Ireland. She survived the birth, and since I was a young attorney just getting started, my wife's mother, who was here during the birth, thought it would be best to take the baby back to Ireland. I knew the family well—I spent a great deal of time with them while I was over there.

"Anyway, my wife's older brother was married, and his wife delivered a daughter a few months before mine was born. This is a long story so I'll make it short. They took her in and agreed to raise her until I got married again, or wanted her back. I saw her often, and she was very, very happy with that family. She had a sister almost the same age, another little brother, and a very loving family. For legal reasons we decided it would be best for them to adopt her, since it didn't seem as if I was getting married again. It was an extremely difficult decision, but I think was the right one."

"So where is she?" asked Lynn.

"She's studying in Dublin. Her name is Fiona—Connolly since she was adopted—and I don't want her privacy compromised at all."

"Wow," said Lynn. "I'm very glad you told me, and I promise you, this will never get out from my end. Even though I can see why it probably wouldn't do you any harm, I understand why you want to protect her."

"Someday she might want to come over for a visit, and I would look forward to that. But for now she's where she is, and I like it that way."

"Done," said Lynn.

He smiled, glad that he had gotten it out. "Anyway, I'm wondering, will I ever get to meet your guys?"

"You'll never even know they're there." She smiled and stood up. "I tell you what. You said the last time we met that if you got into this you'd want to set up your campaign headquarters in White Plains. If you like, I can look into that."

133

"So we have a deal?"

"Yes sir, mister future congressman from the state of New York, we have a deal." She held out her hand and shook his firmly.

As Lynn was leaving, he noticed a tall black man dressed in a black suit nod and open the door for her. Not a hotel employee, he was obviously her driver. He held the front door of the silver Lincoln Continental open for her. As she got in, she turned and waved to Kellan. Not bad, he thought. Not bad at all. He decided right there that he would enjoy the campaign. He walked the few blocks to Grand Central to catch his train to Scarsdale.

During the ride to Scarsdale he reviewed the conversation and noted to himself that the subject of expenses had not come up. As a senior partner at Phillips, Shannon he had done very well, and he lived modestly. He assumed that he would have to do some fund raising, and also that Lynn had a pretty good idea of his net worth. He would be willing to spend his own money on the campaign and was well fixed in that regard. Besides, he was satisfied that Lynn and her people would manage that aspect of the process well.

The next morning Kellan gathered the associates, paralegals and secretaries in his department in the firm's large conference room. His secretary, Fran Kuzniak, had ordered coffee and pastries from a shop down the block from the firm's entrance. Lyle Stevens, the other partner in the group, stood next to Kellan as the ladies and gentlemen filed in and sat down, most of them helping themselves to the refreshments before they took places. He chatted and joked with some of the attorneys, then nodded to Lyle to take a seat.

Kellan remained standing. "I'm guessing most of you have probably heard of my plans, so I won't beat around the bush. I have decided to run for Congress from the 19th district." The gathered colleagues smiled at Kellan and broke into a round of light applause. A couple of them hollered, "Good show!" or "Go get 'em, tiger!"

Kellan laughed and held up his hands. "All right, all right, I appreciate the support." He smiled at his friends—he was a demanding boss, but everyone who worked for him seemed to like him a great deal. He continued. "Most of you know where that is, but just in case, it covers most of Westchester County and some of Rockland on the other side of the river. I've lived in the district for ten years and will be making my campaign headquarters in White Plains. Lyle is going to take over the section for me, and I'm betting none of you will miss a beat. I'll be wrapping up my full-time duties here in a couple of weeks, but I'll stay in touch. If you have any issues or questions, I'll always be available."

He smiled and looked around. "Of course, if I'm not successful, I'll be back here in the fall with my spurs on and a whip in my hand to thrash you back into shape since you will have been goofing off since I left." They all laughed. "If I win"—he was interrupted by a couple of 'yeah, yeahs'—"then you'll have to make an appointment with my administrative assistant if you want to talk to me." More laughter.

"Seriously, I do have an agenda, and it is related to the work I've done here at Phillips, Shannon for the past twenty years. I'm going to run on a heavily economic platform, which shouldn't surprise any of you. We've had to wrestle with some of these issues on a daily basis, and you and I all know that our government could do a better job of greasing the skids for us and our clients. Anyway, I just wanted you all to hear that directly from me. So stick around for a few minutes and enjoy the coffee and goodies, and in about half an hour I'll send for the Cossacks to drive you back to your desks."

They applauded again, and most of them stood and came and shook hands with Kellan and wished him luck. For a moment or two, he suddenly had regrets about what he was about to embark on because he was very fond of the people he worked with. Although he would stay in touch, he knew he would miss them.

Kellan went back to his office and continued clearing up last-minute issues prior to his leaving. In a few moments Fran came in with the coffee and leftover pastries from the meeting. "You'll probably have some visitors," she said. "We're all going to miss you." She turned away quickly and he saw her wipe a tear from her face. He walked over to her and put his hand on her shoulder. She turned and put her arms around him and said, "You've been very good to me."

Fran had been hired in the Boston office about a year before Kellan had left and had been assigned to his department. She had soon become his personal secretary, and when he was told that the firm was transferring him to New York, he asked her if she would like to come with him, and she quickly accepted. "Hey," he said. "If I make it to Washington, I'll be hiring people. You can let me know if you might be interested—I would sure love to have you down there."

"Thanks, Kellan. Don't forget me."

"How could I?"

135

As he sat at his desk a voice said, "I hear the real reason you are leaving is that you're tired of my whipping your butt on the basketball court." Alexandra Crowell had played varsity basketball at the University of Maryland. Alex and Kellan often played basketball together, either one-on-one or on pickup teams with others in the office who used basketball to stay in shape. Kellan had been the ninth man on the Boston College varsity as an undergraduate and still enjoyed the game. Although a decent basketball player, he was hardly a match for the athletic young woman standing in his doorway leaning up against the jam. Alex was a senior associate who had joined the firm shortly after the New York office was opened. Tall and slender with close cropped blonde hair, she stood in the doorway in an all gray outfit—slacks, soft blouse and a grey cardigan sweater—looking fit and beautiful. "Come here," he said and held out his arms.

Alex embraced him and rested her head on his chest. She held him for a few moments and then said, "You know, if I were straight, I could really go for you."

"If I grab you on the ass, would that help?" He kissed her on the cheek.

"Shut up," she said, and laughed. Then she turned serious again and said, "Man, it's gonna be dull around here without you. You're still the best player in the office."

"When you're not in the game, maybe," he said. Then he added, "I'm going to miss you too, Sweetie."

"Sweetie?" she said indignantly. "Where the hell did that come from?"

"Come on, you know I love you," he said. She hugged him again and said, "Me too."

He left the office early that afternoon, took the train to Scarsdale, changed clothes and packed a few things in an overnight bag, got into his car and headed for Massachusetts. He wanted to meet with the family and fill them in on his plans, even though they already knew that he had been contemplating running for office for some time. He planned to spend the night with Eddie and Eileen, who now lived in Worcester. As he drove along the Merritt Parkway and Wilbur Cross Highway, he couldn't help wondering whether his experiment was going to work. At last he took a deep breath and rested his mind, confident that having cut his ties with the firm, informing the family would be easier.

The Family First

When Kellan arrived at Eddie and Eileen's home, he was pleased to see that Eileen was not on duty and that they could enjoy the evening together. Eddie had made a fire in the fireplace and they relaxed in the living room as Kellan told them he had finally made up his mind for good. "So, big brother, you decided to get your hands dirty in that mess in Washington," Eddie said. He had never had much use for politicians, though he had not challenged Kellan's decision to run for office.

Eileen was now a senior physician in the OB/GYN section of St. Vincent Hospital and was an active member of a Massachusetts women's health group. Edward had moved his real estate business to Worcester. As a busy physician with increasing responsibilities, Eileen kept irregular work hours, and Eddie kept his schedule flexible so that they could spend plenty of time together. Although they did not have any children, Eileen's practice had her in constant contact with mothers and their children, and she had never been ready to take on the demands of motherhood herself.

"I think it's a fine thing you're doing," said Eileen. "Good Lord, we surely need good people down there. We definitely need to take a hard look at our national healthcare system."

"And a little kick in the butt for the economy wouldn't hurt guys like me," said Eddie.

"Well, I'm going to focus on economic policy in my campaign, and if I get elected I'm going to try to get on the committees that deal with that stuff. I've had some talks with Jordan Montgomery, and he's given me some ideas."

"Our Senator and old family friend, huh? Well, he sure knows you well enough."

Kellan laughed. "Yeah, that's the good news and the bad."

"I remember when we were in high school, he lived near us. But he's a Republican and you're a Democrat; what's up with that?"

"He's a Republican, but he's one of the good guys. We see eye to eye on a lot of stuff, and he's part of the reason I decided to run."

"Why would a Republican want you to run for a Democratic seat?" Eddie said.

Kellan smiled. "There's an old tradition in New York politics going all the way back to Theodore Roosevelt. He and his cousin Franklin always felt that principle was more important than party."

"FDR?" said Eddie. "You're kidding me."

"During his New Deal years he was pretty partisan. But don't forget that during World War Two, his Secretary of War and Secretary of the Navy were both Republicans. He was able to work with the other side when it really mattered. Look, the country is becoming more polarized politically, and people who are willing to find the middle ground are important. Jordan is still a liberal Republican, even though they're a dying breed, and I intend to run as a centrist. I've never been a knee-jerk liberal."

"You think you can get elected like that?" Eddie said in a skeptical tone.

"Look, Eddie, a lot of people said Jordan could never get elected in Massachusetts as a Republican, but he's done fairly well."

"You might say so." Eddie's tone was sarcastic. "I have to admit, I voted for him, but only because he was your friend."

"I'll make sure he never finds out. Anyway, my district is right on the edge of some pretty firm Republican turf," Kellan said. "I've checked out the political landscape, and the parties are pretty closely divided in my district. I should be able to get some crossover votes from Republicans. Hell, I'll lose some Democrats because I'm not liberal enough, but I think it will all wash out in my favor."

"You sound pretty confident," said Eddie.

"Well, I'm not getting into this with the intention of losing. Look, I might win, I might not, but I wouldn't leave the firm if I didn't think I had a decent chance. Anyway, I've talked it over with my campaign manager already, and she seems to think I can do it. She wouldn't have agreed to help me otherwise."

"Who is she?" said Eileen. "I forgot who you said you were talking to."

"Lynn Patterson. I've been lucky to get her," said Kellan.

"George Patterson's wife?" said Eddie, and Kellan nodded. "Jesus Christ, brother, how did you pull that one off?"

Kellan smiled. "I bribed her with flowers, candy, and booze" he said. Eddie laughed. "Actually, what happened was that we met a few times and she chose me. I had asked around a bit, and we were introduced."

"Not bad, brother. You're playing in the big leagues now."

"We'll see about that," said Kellan.

Before they sat down to dinner Tom and Mary arrived. Tom's career at the architecture firm was going well, and he had designed several important projects in New England. Tom and Mary had three children, two boys and a girl, and the two families—the Wells and Maguires—spent a lot of time together. Mary's three children, especially the two boys, loved their Uncle Eddie, and as they had grown older, he took the boys to sporting events and other activities, with his niece often in tow. Brian had graduated from Holy Cross and was serving in the Marine Corps. Their daughter Angela was a freshman at Holy Cross and was planning to go into nursing. Her Aunt Eileen was urging her to consider medical school, but Angela was still undecided. Their youngest son, Edward, Ned to the family, was still in high school.

As Eddie and Eileen had forgone having children, their relationship with the Wells youngsters had been especially close. The families celebrated holidays and birthdays together, and the two families often vacationed together at Cape Cod or some other attractive spot. Kellan had joined them whenever he could.

"So you're off to Dublin tomorrow morning, are you?" said Mary. "I expect Fiona is quite a young lady by now."

"That she is," said Kellan. "I'm hoping she'll be able to come over for a visit soon; it has been quite a while since you all saw her, and I really want her to keep in touch with our whole family."

"Well, be sure to give her all our love," said Mary. "Tell her how much we miss her."

The next morning Eddie saw Kellan off at Logan Airport. Upon arriving in Dublin, Kellan passed quickly through the customs gate and into the waiting area. Fiona spotted him immediately, rushed over and threw her arms around him. "Hi, Kelly," she said. She had told him a few years back that she wanted to call him Kelly instead of Dad, because she called Brendan Dad, and when Kellan visited she didn't want any confusion. Brendan liked being called Dad, and Kellan didn't mind being called Kelly; when he was a boy, his mother had called him Kelly, and so had some of the kids in school and at BC.

He held her at arm's length, then kissed her on the cheek again, and said, "Let me take a look at you." He backed up a few steps and looked her over. She was tall like her mother and quite mature now. She had her mother's fair skin and light brown hair. She also had her mother's build— broad shoulders and hips, but she still looked slender—she had a gorgeous figure. She was wearing black slacks with a pale green pullover sweater and a loose-fitting dark green jacket. Even with flat shoes, she appeared to Kellan to be almost six feet tall. He held out his arms. "Come here and give me another hug."

He collected his luggage, and they walked out to the terminal where they boarded a bus for Merrion Square. He was staying at the Davenport Hotel, a few blocks from Trinity College. Fiona and her father chatted amiably on the bus ride into the city. He checked in at the Davenport and took his luggage up to his room while Fiona waited in the lobby. Her apartment was on Foley Street, across the River Liffey from Trinity College. Neither Fiona nor her roommate, whom Kellan had not yet met, owned an automobile, but everything they planned to do was within walking distance. Anyplace else they might want to go was easily accessible via the convenient Dublin Bus service.

The weather was brisk, temperature in the mid-40s, overcast, but with no sign of rain. They decided to walk to her apartment, which was only about a mile from the Davenport. On their way they strolled through the Trinity grounds, and he suggested that they drop in to the beautiful library where he had spent the best part of four years of his life. Fiona had her arm in his as they walked through the magnificent structure. He stopped at one of the reference desks, looked at her and said, "This is where I met your mother."

Fiona smiled and rested her head on his shoulder for moment. "I know, Kelly, we've been here before."

"Yeah, I know, but I wasn't sure you'd remember."

She backed away and looked at him with a mock scolding expression. "Of course I remember!" she said. "I could never forget how you and Mum met."

They stood there for a few minutes without saying anything as he gazed around at the familiar structure with its high, arched ceiling, memories flooding back through his mind. Then he said, "Okay, let's go look at this fancy place that you're living in. And I want to meet Celeste." Celeste Jourdain, Fiona's roommate, was also a student at the University. She hailed from France, and she and Fiona had met in a seminar about a year earlier and had decided to share the apartment.

They walked across the River Liffey Bridge onto Memorial Road and up to Talbot Street. From there they strolled through Joyce's Walk to Foley Street. Fiona's living area was much more modern than Moira's had been; then again, although the city of Dublin had lost none of its character and charm, bits and pieces had become modernized in the twenty plus years since Kellan had completed his studies. Signs of the Celtic Tiger—the economic boom in Ireland—were everywhere.

The apartment was small but nicely appointed, with comfortable looking furniture and modest decorations; he noticed a photo of himself on a table. The magnificent old Customs House was visible from one of the windows, and although the neighborhood was part of a business area, it seemed reasonably quiet. Celeste was apparently not at home, so Fiona offered Kellan a bottle of sparkling water and they sat down in the living area. Although Kellan had slept on the flight somewhat, he was pleased to be able to lean back and rest while he and his daughter chatted.

"So, father," Fiona said. "Tell me about this new venture! You're going to run for the Congress, is that correct?"

"I'm running for a seat in the House of Representatives from the state of New York. It's the equivalent of your Dáil Éireann, your lower house, and it has important legislative functions. Our Senate, or upper house, has more power than your Seanad Éireann, and it is elected directly by the voters in each state. And of course our head of government is our president, who is not a member of either the House or the Senate, unlike your Taoiseach. The Speaker of our House of Representatives merely controls the doings within that house and has no power over any other branch."

"So I guess I'm going to have to learn more about American government," she said.

Kellan was charmed by her natural Irish brogue; her voice was much like Moira's and of course had the same accent. "I wouldn't worry about it," he said. "Heck, I haven't even been elected yet. In fact, I haven't officially started to run. But I've taken leave of the law firm, so I'm pretty well committed." He took a sip of his sparkling water, then said, "Tell me about your studies. I need to catch up."

"So far we've been pretty much concentrating on the history of political ideas," she said. "We started with Greece and worked our way through Rome to the Holy Roman Empire, and all that stuff. We have also studied about the other parliamentary systems in Europe, including the one in Iceland. Did you know that the Icelandic Althing is the oldest Parliament in the world? It goes back to about 900."

"I vaguely remember something like that," he said with a smile.

"I really like history, but I'm not sure I want to do anything with that." She launched into a discussion of her other courses, which he found fascinating and not the least bit boring. She might have been talking about the history of needlework for all he cared, as her enthusiasm and obvious delight in the process of learning held his interest and reinforced the pride he had developed for his daughter. She obviously valued his attention, and his affection for her as his daughter and only child. The love he felt for Fiona was returned in full, and that knowledge warmed him immensely. It reminded him of how much he still thought about and missed her mother.

"Have you decided what you want to do with your life once you've finished your studies?" he asked.

"I don't know," she said. "My mom—my real mom—was a librarian, but I don't think I want to do that. I'd rather be doing something more active; I just want to be able to help people."

"Your mother was wonderful at that. It's how we first got acquainted, and certainly part of the reason why I fell in love with her. But you don't have to do what she did."

"I suppose you would like me to be a lawyer," she said.

"Not necessarily."

She smiled as if relieved. "I've been thinking about going into medicine or nursing. I guess I still have time to think about it."

"Your Aunt Eileen would be thrilled with that. They all want you to come over for a visit soon; they really miss seeing you. And Eileen could tell you everything you want to know about the medical profession."

"I miss them too," she said. A wistful look crossed her face. "I wonder what it would have been like to grow up in America."

"Probably not all that different from here," he said. "You would've grown up in a warm and loving family just as you have done here. I certainly would have enjoyed having you close by." She stood up, walked across the room and hugged him. "Me too," she said.

He had been there over an hour when the door opened and Celeste bounded in. As he stood up, she came over to him, took both his hands and kissed him on each cheek in the French style. "Monsieur Maguire, I am so pleased to finally meet you!"

Celeste was considerably shorter than Fiona, petite, he would have said, and she had short very curly brown hair and bright brown eyes. She was wearing a medium length skirt with black tights underneath and soft shoes. She also wore a long-sleeved flowered blouse and over that she was wearing a jacket that looked like dark blue corduroy. She looked very European, Kellan thought. She came across as bright and bubbly, and Kellan liked her immediately.

Celeste went to the kitchen, opened the refrigerator and poured herself a glass of wine. She offered one to Kellan, who refused. For the next two hours the three-way conversation went from politics to fashion to music, with various side excursions into other topics. The two young women were full of opinions and ideas—typical students, he thought, and very bright ones at that. As the afternoon wore on he said, "I would love to take you two young ladies to dinner if there's a nice pub nearby."

Fiona and Celeste went back and forth with a few suggestions and finally came up with a decision. They would go to the famous Temple Bar near the O'Connell Street Bridge. "I've been there once or twice before," said Kellan with a smile. "I'll bet it hasn't changed a bit."

After a pleasant meal with much animated conversation, especially from Celeste, who had a delightful French accent and loved to talk, Kellan walked the two women back as far as the bridge and then strolled back to his hotel, where he spent a restful night. In the morning he breakfasted in the hotel dining room while reading the *Irish Times*. Fiona had classes until noon, when she joined him at the hotel. They spent the afternoon visiting some of the spots Kellan remembered, finishing up at the beautiful old Archbishop Marsh's Library near St. Patrick's Cathedral. On their way back they stopped at The Pig's Ear, a pub on Nassau Street across from Trinity, where they enjoyed a pint of Guinness before walking on to Fiona's apartment. He remembered having dined at the old pub with Moira, and he told Fiona about the farewell party Moira's library friends had held for here there.

That evening Fiona and Celeste decided to prepare dinner at their apartment. It turned out that Celeste was quite a cook, and the two women put together a very pleasant meal. Celeste was especially interested in Kellan's new political career and questioned him endlessly about every topic she could think of, including a few for which he had no ready answer. Her view of politics was more than a little bit skewed by her familiarity with the French variety, but it was an interesting and stimulating conversation nonetheless.

Before turning in for the night Kellan arranged for a rental car to be delivered to the hotel early next morning. He picked up Fiona at her apartment and they set off for Mallow. Fiona had arranged for someone to take notes for her in the classes she was to have attended that day. It was Thursday, and his flight back to Boston was leaving Friday morning, so they would have to come back that evening rather than staying at the Connolly home. But the trip down and back would give him additional time to visit with his daughter. He needed to discuss with her the implications of his coming public life.

When they had been on the road for a while, he said, "I think you need to understand that my running for office back in the States might have some effect on you."

"How could that be?" Fiona said. "I don't see how it could possibly affect me."

"I'm not sure the press here in Ireland is anything like the press in America," he said. "But I can tell you, when you run for public office in the United States, so far as the press is concerned, anything is fair game." He glanced over at Fiona. "That includes you."

"Why would anybody be interested in me?"

"Because you're part of my family—you're my daughter. Not many people back home know that I was married to your mother. Since we were married here in Mallow, there are no records of it back in the States. For a long time I didn't think much about it one way or the other. Then when Brendan and Deirdre adopted you, you didn't have my last name anymore."

He glanced over at Fiona again and she looked troubled. "I didn't realize that that bothered you," she said.

"No, no, it never bothered me," he said. "It made all kinds of sense for you, and since they were always open to my seeing you anytime I wanted, I was never anything but grateful to them for raising you."

"Mum and Dad always told me how much you helped them, and you are paying my tuition and sending me an allowance. I didn't know there was a problem with that."

"There isn't," he said. "There was never a problem with my relationship with Brendan and Deirdre. I think you're misunderstanding what I'm trying to say." He looked over and smiled at her. "If I ever had any regrets, it was because every time I saw you when you were growing up, I was reminded of how much I loved your mother, and how much I wished I could have seen you grow up every day instead of just a few times every year. I was lucky to have a job that allowed me to come and visit so often. And those times you came over to the States to visit me, even though the visits only lasted for a few weeks, they were wonderful. I especially loved that trip when we went to Niagara Falls."

"That was fun," she said and seemed to relax. After a while she said, "Are you really worried about me because you're running for Congress?"

"I know there are going to be a lot of questions about my private life. Reporters will want to know why I was never married, or if I was, why there's no record of it. I have seen some good people hurt by careless publicity, and I don't want you or Brendan and Deidra to ever have to deal with that."

"But I'm proud of what you're doing. I will be bragging to my friends that my real father is a member of Congress in the United States. Do I have to keep that a secret?"

He laughed. "No, not at all, you can tell your friends all you want. You can even tell your friends that your real father is Kellan Maguire. When I become famous they'll say 'Wow!'" He laughed and paused for a moment. "Maybe I'm being silly about all this. If you think so, just tell me. We can talk it over with the family when we get to Mallow."

"I guess I understand. Whatever you want is okay with me." She slid over and rested her head on his shoulder, and he glanced down and kissed the top of her head.

They didn't say anything else for a while as the scenery rolled by. Then she asked, "Are you going to get in touch with Aunt Kathleen on this trip?" Kathleen had told Fiona once when she was younger that her mother had been like a sister to her, and Fiona had started calling her Aunt Kathleen.

"No, I won't have time," he said. "I really need to get back tomorrow."

"Every time I see her, she asks me to give you her love. She must've really liked you."

"I was very fond of her," he said. The awkwardness that he always felt when he recalled the relationship between him and Kathleen all those years earlier never failed to come back to him at times like this. He could not tell Fiona that one of the real reasons why he wanted to keep things private was to protect Kathleen; there was probably no way that anything in their past could ever hurt Kathleen, but she was still part of his Irish life—his other Irish connection.

"So how about you? Any boyfriends?"

"No one special," she said. "There's one boy from Belfast that I really like. We go out for a pint every so often."

"Belfast, huh? That's interesting."

"He's Catholic, Kelly. Nothing to worry about."

"Who said I was worried?" He smiled at her, and she punched him on the arm.

145

They arrived in Mallow just in time for lunch. The Connolly family were delighted to see Kellan and disappointed that he would not be able to spend at least one night with them. Patrick, now in his sixties, was still his old robust self. Libby was beginning to look a bit frail, as she had had a prolonged bout of pneumonia a year earlier. She was still thrilled to see Kellan, however, and like Patrick, she wanted to hear all about his political plans. Molly and Kevin had both grown up and moved away. Molly was married, had a child and lived in Waterford, where her husband Tim worked at the famous crystal factory. Kevin was still single and had a good job down in Cork. Kellan caught up with doings in their lives while he talked with Patrick and Libby.

It was a pleasant afternoon talking about old times as well as new, and Libby planned an early dinner so that Kellan and Fiona could get back to Dublin at a reasonable hour. "Oh, Kellan, I wish you had more time to spend with us," Libby said.

"Mother, the boy's a busy man," said Patrick, smiling at Kellan. "I'm sure he'll get back whenever he can." He looked at Kellan. "So, running for office, are you?" Kellan nodded. "Well that's a fine thing, it is," said Patrick. "And I gather you're running as a Democrat, the same as Kennedy. That's good."

"Maybe we can come over for your inauguration," said Libby.

Kellan laughed. "I'm not running for president," he said. "A congressman being sworn in is not a very big deal. There are usually a couple of dozen newly elected freshmen, and it's over pretty quickly."

"Well, we'll be sure to make the trip when you do get elected president," said Patrick with a smile.

Kellan just shook his head, though he smiled at Libby and Patrick. "You'd make a wonderful president," said Libby. "Lord knows, I would certainly vote for you. You have always been so wonderful to us."

Brendan and Deirdre arrived well before dinner and joined in the conversation with Kellan and Fiona. She was glad to see her parents, though she got home quite often. Deirdre scolded her for not being in class. Fiona laughed it off. "It's just for one day, Mum. Besides, someone's taking notes for me. Anyway I'd much rather spend the time with Kellan than be sitting in a classroom, I won't miss anything important."

"Well, with what you're tuition and fees are costing, it better damn well be important," grumbled Patrick. Even Deidra laughed.

The Connolly family had done very well. Brendan and Deirdre were building a new house with extra space so that they and Patrick and Libby

146

could live together comfortably. Fiona's sister Caitlin had a job in Galway and was doing very well, though she had decided to forgo a university education. She had taken some courses in business and accounting and had a responsible position with a good firm in the old city. She had sent her love to Kellan via her parents, and Kellan was pleased that she was doing well.

During the trip back to Dublin, Fiona told Kellan that she really wanted to visit America again during a future vacation. She asked him if that might be possible once he got elected to Congress. (The entire Connolly clan, Fiona included, took it as a foregone conclusion that Kellan would be elected.)

"Sure, that's more than possible. If I'm serving in Congress, I'll be living in Washington much of the time. There's an awful lot to see down there, and I would love to be able to show you around." He thought for a moment. "Concerning what we were talking about on the way down, would you be upset if I introduce you as my niece instead of as my daughter?"

Fiona didn't answer right away. Then she said, "Kelly, I understand that you're trying to protect me. And I appreciate that, truly I do. But I'm a big girl now, and I can't imagine how anything that involves you could ever be upsetting to me." She thought for a few moments. "But I know that you love me, and I love you, and anything that you want to do will be okay with me. But I don't want to be your niece. I am your daughter. I like calling you Kelly, but only for my dad—my other dad's sake. But in America I want to be your daughter. And I want to be able to call you Dad."

"Okay, princess. Your wish is my command. We'll do it your way and the press be damned." She leaned over and kissed him on the cheek and rested her head on his shoulder. He took one hand off the steering wheel and hugged her for a few moments. Then he reached down and squeezed her hand and she squeezed his. He smiled at her and again felt the sadness that he had seen so little of her life. Maybe in the future there would come a time when they could spend more than a few weeks together. He would treasure that. He was her dad, and that was that.

They didn't talk for a while, and then Fiona said, "Kelly, I have another question."

"Okay."

"How come you let Mum and Dad adopt me?"

He thought for a few moments. "It was a hard decision. Mostly it was for legal purposes—for your welfare. If you had an accident, or got very sick and needed surgery, or something like that, having you legally adopted here in Ireland would avoid complications. If anything happened that needed permission of a parent and they couldn't reach me … you know, that sort of thing. We all thought it was for the best."

"I guess I understand," she said. Then she added, "Yes, that makes sense."

It grew dark as they drove along, and Fiona leaned back in her seat and drifted off to sleep. When they got to her apartment it was late, and he needed to get an early start from the hotel for his plane back to Boston. He hugged her, kissed her good night and goodbye and told her again how much he loved her. She wiped a tear from her face and kissed him again on the cheek. "I love you too, Kelly," she said.

On the flight back to Boston Kellan reflected on what he and Fiona and the rest of the Connolly clan had talked about. It had occurred to him that he had made too big a deal of his desire for privacy, even though he had decided to run for public office. It was just that so many times he had seen public figures dragged through the mud, often unfairly, and he just didn't want his Irish family to have to go through any of that. But Fiona's wishes had changed his mind. She wanted to claim him as her father, and she knew that 'Mum and Dad' would understand that. Back in Ireland he would be Kelly, but in the states he was going to be Dad.

The Primary Cause

As Kellan's plane was rolling up to the terminal at Logan airport, a first-class flight attendant handed him a note. "A message just arrived for you, Mr. Maguire." He unfolded the piece of paper and read, 'Call me as soon as you're in the terminal. Important. Lynn.' The note included a number with a New York City area code. As soon as he found a phone, he inserted a credit card and dialed the number.

"I just landed," he said when Lynn answered. "What's up?"

"I've got some good news and some bad news. Which do you want first?"

"I'm kind of tired from the flight. Give me the good news first."

"Okay. The good news is that the Republicans are going with Preston Fuller. He's a dork. Not only that, he's a pompous ass. I have no idea how he wound up with the nomination, but it looks like a done deal. The good news about that is that if you get the Democratic nomination, the general election will be a cinch. That's where the bad news comes in."

"Okay, Coach, I can take it. Shoot!"

"You've heard of Anthony Parisi, I assume."

"Sure. He used to be the mayor of White Plains; is that the guy you're talking about?"

"The same. Now he's in the New York legislature but I hear he's decided to go for the Democratic nomination for the seat in the 19th; so he'll be your opponent. The other guy dropped out when he heard about Parisi, so it's probably for real."

"Okay, what does that mean?"

"It means you've got to get your ass back here as soon as you can. Tony Parisi has some baggage from when he got into a pissing contest with the White Plains Police Department, but there are a lot of chits he can cash in from the party faithful. So far it's only a rumor, but it's pretty solid. If you get your name out there first, that would be a huge advantage for us. I'm setting up a press conference for you in White Plains on Monday morning. Any reason you can't make that?"

"Nope. I'm staying here in Boston tonight, but I can get there tomorrow."

"That will be good. I'll get a few people together on Sunday and we can figure out what you're going to say. We need to try to make a splash so it will get some attention. If people get to know you in a hurry, you can drain away support that might otherwise go to Parisi. Time is of the essence, my friend."

"I'll call you as soon as I get there. I'll be staying at Eddie's tonight—I think I gave you that number."

"Got it."

Kellan arrived at his townhouse in Scarsdale at dinnertime Saturday evening. He checked his mail and his phone messages—there were two from Lynn, but both had arrived before he spoke to her from the airport—poured himself a glass of sparkling water and dialed Lynn's number.

"So, what's the plan?" he asked when she answered.

"Tomorrow morning about 10 o'clock. Your place or mine?"

"You've never been here, so if it's all the same to you, I prefer to do it here. I can meet you at the Scarsdale station, or you could come on your own."

"My driver can bring me, and I'll be bringing a couple of people with me, if that's okay with you."

"Sure. I'll pick up some soft drinks and snacks and maybe a couple of bottles of wine. Do you have a preferred drink?"

"I'm like you," she said. "I don't drink very much, except when I'm not working."

"Well, I'll have some wine and beer; there's probably some hard stuff around here somewhere. We'll see you tomorrow than about ten." Before he hung up he gave her the address, which she said she already had. She added that her driver knew the way.

Now that Kellan knew he was going to have to make some sort of an announcement on Monday, he spent Saturday evening jotting down some points that he might like to make. Lynn would certainly have some ideas about how his speech ought to go, but he was reasonably comfortable speaking to groups and knew what he wanted to say. He didn't like to use a prepared text, although he suspected that he was going to have to learn how to do that. He figured that as long as he knew where he stood on the issues, he wouldn't need a script to be able to answer most questions. He was new to the game, however, and he would certainly welcome Lynn's advice.

Lynn's silver Lincoln arrived a few minutes before ten. He signaled for the driver to pull into his driveway. Lynn got out of the front seat, and a young man and a young woman got out of the back. Kellan shook hands with Lynn and invited the driver to come in with them and relax.

Kellan ushered the four people in, suggested that the driver could relax in the living room with a television set. He, Lynn and her two assistants would work at the dining room table.

"Kellan, this is John Morse. He'll be making some suggestions about your announcement and will be discussing some tactics as we go forward." John was an intense looking young man, dressed casually and wearing horn-rimmed glasses. He appeared to be about thirty. Kellan shook his hand and turned to the other assistant.

Lynn introduced the young woman, who appeared to be in her thirties. She was dressed casually in jeans, sneakers, and an NYU sweatshirt. "Jean Slater will be handling the media during the campaign," Lynn said. "She has some contacts in your district."

"Welcome, Jean," Kellan said. "You look like you're ready for work."

"Nice to meet you, Mr. Maguire. I've heard a lot about you from Lynn." He smiled, and she nodded and returned the friendly look.

Kellan had placed some legal pads and a tumbler full of pens and pencils on the table. He had also put out a couple of plates of snacks and a few coffee mugs. "I've got some fresh coffee, soft drinks, red or white wine or anything else you'd like," he said. "Let me fix you up and we can get acquainted."

Lynn and John opted for coffee, and Jean asked for a diet soda. Kellan went to the kitchen, brought in an insulated coffee server, cream and sugar and a couple of bottles of water. He went back and brought Jean a bottle of soda and a glass of ice. He went into the living room where Pete, Lynn's driver, had seated himself in front of the television and offered him a drink. Pete said he would like sparkling water.

Kellan came back to the dining room and seated himself at the table where the others had already settled in. "Okay," he said, "where do we begin?"

"Jean, why don't you start with the lay of the land," said Lynn.

Jean turned to Kellan, glanced at a small notebook and began. "We scoped out the territory pretty well and think we know where we ought to make your initial appearances. We'll try to get you an interview with the White Plains Reporter, and a spot on the local radio station. Television is harder to do, but we'll see how it goes. After that John can give you some ideas about the issues that should play well in your district. For your announcement tomorrow, we think the Westchester County Center would be a good location."

"Inside? Can we do that?"

"No, no," said Jean. "We'll do it outside at the entrance unless there's bad weather."

Kellan nodded. He had his own ideas about the issues he wanted to address, but it was clear that these two young people, like Lynn, were pros, and he welcomed their advice, though he had no intention of following it blindly. He had heard during his preliminary forays into the world of politics that dissension on a staff could be a fatal disease in a political campaign. He intended to do his best to see that the atmosphere within this group, and with any others who would be on the staff, would be friendly and cooperative as well as efficient.

Jean continued. "Mr. Maguire, or Kellan, if you prefer," she paused and looked at Kellan, and he smiled and nodded. "Okay, Kellan, first we'll go over the general plan for your announcement tomorrow—it's not very complicated—and then I'll give you the general layout of the rest of the campaign, and we can tweak it as we go along.

"We're going to set up two main campaign offices, one in White Plains and one in Yonkers. John will mostly operate out of the one in Yonkers, and my home base will be in White Plains. We have already located some office space on Hamilton Avenue that's available at reasonable cost, and we'll get some temporary office furniture and phone lines installed as soon as we can. Printing can be pretty expensive, and we'll check into renting a printing press or contracting with a commercial service.

"I've got some contacts at Pace University in Pleasantville, Briarcliff College and Sarah Lawrence in Yonkers. I'll see if I can find anyone who knows anything about the College of New Rochelle and Iona. College kids are good at this stuff because a lot of them are still idealists." Kellan glanced at Lynn at that remark; she raised her eyebrows and smiled. Jean continued. "Sarah Lawrence has an individual study program and I'm trying to set up something where a couple of students could work for us and get credit for it. That might also work at Pace. I'll check that out with a couple of volunteers we have from there."

"How do you go about doing all that?" asked Kellan. "I'm just curious." Lynn smiled at him, as if to say, 'Of course you are, dearie!'

"John and I have worked on campaigns before. You meet people, you make friends, you keep a couple of Rolodexes full of names and phone numbers. Later on we'll talk about people you know who might be willing to pitch in. Lynn said you had mentioned that one of your attorneys might be willing to help, and that would be great. Other than that, think about neighbors, neighbors' kids if they're old enough. All this will get done in due course. Right now I think our most important job is to get your initial announcement out there so that we can preempt Tony Parisi."

Lynn said, "Right now that's our first priority."

"I agree," said Kellan. "When I got home last night, I sat down and made a few notes on points that I think should be included. I'm assuming you guys will tell me what to steer clear of, and how to shape my remarks. But I've got a pretty good handle on what I want to use for my core issues." He looked at Lynn. "You and I have already talked about this."

"Right," Lynn said. "We need to establish some firm talking points for you, and you pretty much need to commit them to memory. Not verbatim, of course, but one fatal error that can occur is when you say one thing to a newspaper reporter and something else on the radio or TV. The other guys will be doing their best to catch you contradicting yourself."

"I'm pretty sure I know what I think," Kellan said.

"Of course you do, but a set of stock answers that you can pull out pretty much anytime, anywhere is a useful thing to have in your pocket," Lynn said. "Look, you're smart, but even smart guys make mistakes. You're a rookie, and the three of us and some others we'll bring in as we go forward have been down this road before, more than once. We're here to help you and make it as comfortable for you as we can, but we want to win."

"So do I," said Kellan. "Believe me, I know I need all the help I can get."

The conversation continued, with John and Jean doing most of the talking, Kellan asking questions and taking notes, and Lynn hanging back, apparently trying to gauge her candidate and figure out his strong points and potential danger areas. When she contributed, as she did from time to time, John and Jean immediately stopped and paid close attention. About one o'clock in the afternoon, Kellan suggested that they take a short break. "There's a nice little deli down by the railroad station where we can get a bite to eat if you like," he said.

"Do they have takeout?" asked Jean.

Lynn smiled. "You guys are gluttons for punishment. I like Kellan's idea." They roused Pete, who had dozed off on the couch in the living room, piled into Lynn's big Lincoln and headed for the Muscat.

Jean and John seemed a little antsy as they were finishing up their lunch, but Lynn was apparently in no hurry. Kellan hoped that the reason she showed no sense of urgency was that she had a good feeling about the campaign. In any case, after Kellan took care of the check, Lynn got up, and the five of them drove back to Kellan's house. They settled down to work again, focusing on Kellan's talking and speaking points. At about 4:30 Lynn said, "Okay, I think we're on track. We can probably wrap this up."

Kellan had determined that John was the quiet one, and Jean did the talking. She was serious but enthusiastic at the same time and seemed to have a wry sense of humor. She also struck him as very competent. As they were gathering up their notes, Jean said to Kellan, "Do you think it would be possible for me to stay here tonight? I know Lynn and John are going back to New York, but I want to get up to White Plains first thing in the morning and set up for your announcement. I've got a few calls to make tonight, and perhaps you could drive me up there? That way we can get a head start on everything." She looked at Lynn, then back at Kellan. "I know Lynn will want to be there for the announcement, but I want to check everything out in advance."

"Good idea," said Lynn. "Kellan?"

"Sure, that's fine with me. I have plenty of room."

Jean had a small overnight bag in the trunk of Lynn's car, which she fetched before they left. She brought it into the house, dropped it down on the floor and flopped onto the couch in the living room. Kellan turned on the TV, then asked Jean, "Would you like a drink? I think I'll have one."

"I'm not much of a drinker. Do you have a beer?"

"That's what I'm having."

Jean had her legs curled up under her on the couch. Kellan had CNN news on with the volume low. Jean asked him, "Lynn said you're not married—were you ever?"

"Yes, I was briefly, but it's not for publication. My wife died about a year after we were married—from natural causes." He added the last part to ward off any further questions on that subject.

"I'm sorry," she said. "Do you have a girlfriend?"

Kellan smiled. "I have some women friends, but no one special right now."

Jean mulled that over for a few moments and then asked, "Do you think you'll ever get married again?"

"Maybe, maybe not. If I find the right woman, I could get married again." Kellan assumed she was being nosy for reasons related to the campaign, but he decided to push back a little. "Why is that important?"

Jean shifted her body around a little bit and looked mildly uncomfortable. "It's not." She paused for a moment. "If there was a messy divorce or something like that, you know … but I was just curious." She took off on a new tangent. "What kind of law do you practice?"

"Well, as you know, I'm not practicing anything right now. But my specialty is international law and business. I'm not real happy with the way our government has been handling trade policy, and that's why I decided to run."

"That's what Lynn told us. She thinks it's a good issue, but you'll have to have some positive ideas about that—you can't get elected on being pissed off. Not that a lot of guys haven't tried."

Kellan laughed. "I've got some ideas," he said.

Jean asked a few more or less innocuous questions, and then they began chatting casually about nothing in particular. Kellan turned the volume on the TV news up a bit and pretended to be interested, but he was more focused what would be happening the next morning. After a while he clicked over to the ESPN channel to check on basketball scores. The Celtics had won and the Knicks had lost—beyond that he didn't care much. A few minutes later he said, "I have some stuff to eat here, but I'd just as soon go out to dinner. What do you say?"

"Fine with me," she said.

While he was still living in Boston, Kellan hadn't paid much attention to his diet. He had a few favorite restaurants and ate out a lot. He prepared simple meals at home from time to time, but nothing fancy. Following the move to New York, however, he had noticed himself getting a little puffy around the waist, and he started paying more attention to his diet. He learned how to prepare some simple dishes, and began to eat more salads, fish, vegetables and other healthy fare. He also made sure that he exercised regularly and now, in his early forties, he was in pretty good shape.

He and Jean dined at a nice nearby restaurant. When they returned to his house, she asked if she might use the phone to make a few calls in preparation for the next day's announcement. As the evening wore on, she finished what she was doing and came back into the living room where Kellan was reading a recent biography of Franklin Roosevelt.

Before sitting down on the couch, Jean stretched and then pulled off her NYU sweatshirt. She had some sort of tank top underneath, and he noted that she had an attractive figure. She had medium length brown hair, brown eyes, and although she had no makeup and generally wore a serious expression, when she smiled and relaxed she was quite pretty. She sat down on the couch, leaned back and asked, "What do you like to do in the evening?"

"If I'm not going out somewhere, I read a lot and watch the late news. When I was at the firm, I liked to go in early and have a short workout before starting the day. So I didn't often stay up late."

She stood up and stretched again, and he noticed that she was not wearing a bra. She smiled at him, sat back down, and he wondered idly if she was probing to see whether he might be open to something more intimate than mere conversation. When he turned back to his book, she stood again and said, "I guess I'll go up and get some sleep. It's going to be a pretty busy day tomorrow, and we should get an early start up to White Plains. I'd like to get there early and make sure everything's okay. I'll probably need to use your phone again before we leave. What time are you getting up?"

"Anytime you like," he said. "What time would you like me to wake you?"

"We ought to be up there by about 9:30 just to be sure everything's set." He agreed that they would be up in plenty of time to get to White Plains. His press conference was scheduled for 10:30. The weather report for the morning was favorable, and they decided that he would make his announcement in front of the Westchester County Center as planned. There would be plenty of parking nearby, even though they were not expecting a large crowd.

Jean made several calls in the morning as they were having coffee. As Kellan overheard Jean talking, he became more impressed with Jean's professionalism—she obviously knew her way around the political landscape. She had done some preparatory work before their meeting the day before, and now she was wrapping up loose ends. From what he could gather from her side of the conversations, she had laid the ground well. They got into his car and headed up the Bronx River Parkway to White Plains.

Lynn and John arrived at the County Center shortly before 10:00. Another car had pulled up behind hers, and two more people, apparently more of Lynn's assistants, got out. She gathered everyone together at the front steps of the hall and asked Jean, "Okay, what do we have?"

Jean flipped open her notebook, glanced at it and said, "There are nine newspapers in the area, all more or less local. At least six of them are going to have a reporter here, probably one or two more. The White Plains TV station said they would show up. Here they are now," she said, as a television truck with the station logo on the side pulled up near the front of the County Center. A TV reporter got out of the truck, and Jean waved to him. He waved back.

She continued her report. "There will be some people from the local Democratic committee here, and they're trying to round up some interested people." She looked over toward the parking lot where a couple of cars had pulled in. "I'm hoping somebody from the New York papers will show up. There is a good chance that the News or the Post will have somebody here; not sure about the Times. The Eagle's also a possibility. We'll see what we get. I think the word is out that Tony Parisi is going to go for it, and since nobody knows Kellan yet,"—she glanced at him and smiled—"they probably assume he'll have it locked up."

"No chance," said Lynn firmly. "Good job, Jean." They were standing on one end of the steps, and as they spoke another truck pulled up, and two young men got out and started setting up microphones near the center of the entrance to the large building. Lynn looked at Kellan. "You all set?"

"As ready as I can be," Kellan said. "I'm a little bit nervous, no question about that."

"Good," said Lynn. "If you weren't, I'd be real worried. Once they get the mics set up, we can check out how you'll sound." She looked around at John and the two new aides. "Okay, people, you know the drill. Mix around with the crowd, keep your ears open, and lead the applause. These people know why they're here, so if you can pick up any clues about what they're thinking, please do."

They had decided that Lynn would introduce Kellan. At a few minutes after 10:30, she stepped to the microphones. "Good morning ladies and gentlemen, thank you for coming. I would like to introduce to you your next Congressman from the 19th district of New York." She smiled and waited for a small round of applause, led by John, Jean and the other aides. A few other spectators joined in.

"Kellan Maguire is an experienced attorney who has specialized in economic and business issues and has dealt at length in the international trade arena. He is no stranger to politics, and has been involved in the campaigns of some of our fellow Democrats, including your governor. He hails originally from Boston, but has lived in New York for over ten years as a resident of this district. It's my pleasure to present Kellan Maguire."

Kellan nodded and shook hands with Lynn and stepped to the microphones. He held a single three-by-five card in his hand and glanced at it before he started to speak.

"Thank you very much for coming. I am here to announce my candidacy for the nomination of the Democratic Party for the congressional election in the 19th District of New York this coming November." Again, there was a smattering of applause.

"I have spent the last twenty years of my life conducting business on behalf of American corporations whose primary business is international trade. I am quite familiar with the ways in which our federal government assists these firms with legislation designed to enhance our trade opportunities. I think that Washington can do a better job of supporting American business, and here's why I think it's important to you.

"In my law practice I have become aware of how many people in this country depend on our overseas business for their livelihood. Thousands of American workers are engaged in businesses that sell products overseas, or that import products from overseas and provide them to American consumers. Millions of Americans benefit from the trade that results from the actions of those dedicated American workers. And millions more enjoy the fruits of their labor.

"You all know what a favorable balance of trade is. We get a favorable balance of trade when the total value of our exports exceeds what we spend on imports. We have had a favorable balance of trade for much of our history as a nation, but we could be doing much better. This depends on our international trade policy, as well as our support for American businesses. The United States government can add to the efficient operation of American corporations. We need to review tax policies and other incentives in order to make our businesses as strong as possible.

"As your congressman, that is what I intend to work for. As an attorney, I have worked in that field for the past twenty years. I intend to take what I know to Washington with me to make America a stronger nation.

"Thank you again for coming, and I'll be glad to answer a few questions."

Lynn stepped up next to Kellan to field the questions, as they had arranged. Jean had sidled up next to Lynn and was prepared to whisper in her ear if she sensed a hostile question coming.

A couple of hands went up, and the questioning began. Most of the questions were more or less friendly and generally on topic—routine questions with no barbs attached. Then a woman asked, "Sir, how does your family feel about you running for Congress?"

Kellan was prepared. "Everyone in my family supports what I am doing, without exception. I have discussed my plans with them at length and have no doubt that they will be behind me all the way."

The same questioner raised her hand again, and Lynn whispered "careful" in Kellan's ear.

"What does your wife say about it," she asked.

"I'm not married," he said.

"Why not?" said the woman.

Lynn nudged him. "Be nice," she whispered.

"What do you mean?" He tried to keep his voice in a friendly tone.

"Well, were you ever married?"

"Yes, briefly, a long time ago. My wife died of natural causes."

"What did she die of?"

Another nudge from Lynn. "I'm not sure that's relevant to my campaign. Are there any other questions?"

There was some muttering in the crowd following aggressive questioning about Kellan's private life. The same woman called out "Sir …?" but he ignored her and pointed to someone else. The few remaining questions were generally of a political nature. After a few more minutes Lynn stepped back to the microphone and said, "Thank you very much for coming, ladies and gentlemen. Kellan Maguire welcomes your support in his run for Congress."

Following one more brief burst of applause, the crowd dissipated. Jean went and spoke to a couple of the media people and then returned to the group. "Okay, good show," said Lynn. "What you say we go get some lunch and talk it over. Kellan?"

"There's a real nice little Italian restaurant about a mile from here on Tarrytown Road on the left side. Just follow me."

Five minutes later when they were all seated at La Manda's, one of Kellan's favorite restaurants, Lynn introduced the two new aides, Peggy Schiavoni and Joel Levi. "What do you guys do?" asked Kellan. They seemed to be a pair.

"We're both seniors at Pace University," said Peggy. "We're majoring in political science, and we're working on your campaign as part of our senior project. Lynn was nice enough to sign off on it."

"They'll be a big help with the college crowd," said Lynn.

"I'm hoping to go to law school when I graduate," said Joel. "Maybe you could give me some advice on that," he said, looking at Kellan.

Kellan assured Joel that he would be happy to do that. "Nice to have you guys on board," he said.

After they had ordered, Lynn opened the conversation. "Okay, I think it went pretty well this morning. We'll get some decent press coverage out of it, and Jean says they'll try to get it on the news on the White Plains TV station this evening. With a little bit of luck, we'll make a couple of the New York papers also. Any comments?"

After a few informative bits had been tossed around, Kellan asked, "Where did those questions about the marriage come from?" He looked at Jean, but Jean immediately looked at Lynn.

"Those were sort of planted," Lynn said.

"What do you mean?"

Lynn cleared her throat. "Look, we let it slip to some people we know in the other campaign that you are going to run and gave them some very basic background info. Believe me, Kellan, anything we let out yesterday will be common knowledge tomorrow. There's a kind of political underground that operates in every campaign. Stuff goes back and forth, usually with general consent on both sides. Nobody likes surprises, and we will surely get some information from the Parisi campaign as we go along."

"How come I didn't know about it in advance?" said Kellan a bit testily. He was obviously unhappy with what he was hearing.

"That was on purpose," said Lynn. Kellan glanced at the others, who seemed mildly uncomfortable. Lynn continued. "Look, you're going to get hit with stuff out of left field from now until the election. The other guys will poke and jab and try to find a chink in your armor. To be honest, I just wanted to see how you would handle it, and you did very well."

"In the future, I'd like to know about that kind of stuff before it happens."

"Hey, welcome to the club," said Lynn. "We all would like to know everything before it happens. But this isn't volleyball, my friend. It doesn't necessarily have to get ugly, but I'll guarantee you that between now and the election, somebody's going to throw a question at you that will set you back. And I promise you, it will be at a time when a bunch of reporters are shoving microphones in your face."

She looked at Kellan and smiled. "Right about now I bet you're wondering if this running for office was such a good idea, right?" The others laughed, and Kellan allowed himself a smile.

"I've got a lot to learn, no question about that."

Lynn patted him on the arm. "You're going to do fine. You're a good-looking guy, and you've got your head on straight. You have nothing to hide, and you have some damn fine credentials. Just be ready to step up to the plate, and be prepared for some curveballs. We'll get you through this, and then we'll have a big party on election night."

Two days later Anthony Parisi announced that he was seeking the Democratic nomination for the 19th Congressional District. Kellan's campaign headquarters on Hamilton Avenue was a small office opening on the street a block from the main shopping area of White Plains. Jean had had it furnished with chairs, tables, and telephones, and the campaign staff were watching a large television set during Parisi's announcement. In his introductory speech, Parisi made a somewhat disparaging remark about "people who think they know more than those of us who had been in the arena for a while." Later on, he made a similar sort of slur about lawyers. There was some grumbling among the staff—their loyalty was now firmly in place.

"He's a tough, old style New York politician," said Lynn. "He knows his stuff, but he's not very likable. If you get a chance to go against him one on one, you'll make him look like a street thug."

"We're working on that," said John, who until then had apparently not offered very much in terms of strategy. Lynn simply explained that John was the silent deadly type and would come up with good ideas in due course. As Kellan would discover, John was rather shy and presented his ideas to Jean, who then presented them to the rest of the staff.

"Actually, that's going to be a tough sell, John," said Lynn. "Tony is smart enough to know that he won't match up well against Kellan face to face. His guys will come up with some bullshit excuse about timing or weather or some damn thing. If he doesn't agree to debate, we use that against him. If he does agree, Kellan will kick his butt. It's a win-win situation for us."

Over the next few days Kellan got a firm feel for how the campaign was proceeding. Lynn gave him a list of names of people to call, suggesting that they might want to make a contribution to the campaign. She provided him a sort of rough outline of the kind of pitch he might make, and said that she would offer background on the people named before he made the calls. Kellan recognized a few of the names on the list, and he offered a few suggestions of his own, most of which Lynn readily accepted. Lynn suggested that he listen in on a few calls she made to wealthy potential donors.

Jean and John started planning for a few rallies at key locations around the district. They would use Peggy and Joel and some of the other volunteers to help drum up publicity for the appearances. They also started working on flyers for a mail-out campaign, and worked out a design for some posters. Jean had prepared some mailing lists and contracted with a printer a couple of blocks away so that they could start stuffing envelopes. Kellan offered to do some door-to-door campaigning if that would be useful. Lynn said that they would go over the district demographics and try to locate some areas where that would be productive. Northern Westchester—Chappaqua, Mount Kisco and Katonah—for example, was generally regarded as a Republican stronghold, and there wouldn't be much point in his going into a place like that.

The campaign took on rhythm of its own. Kellan would generally arrive at his campaign headquarters early in the morning, make a few phone calls, sign letters, and help with the other necessary busywork. The growing corps of volunteers came and went, and Kellan enjoyed chatting with them. Sometimes when not much was going on, the key players would gather at Kellan's home for strategy sessions.

The primary election would be held in the latter part of June, and by the end of May, it looked very promising for Kellan. He and Tony Parisi had met face to face twice, once at Sarah Lawrence College, and the second time at a White Plains radio station. Kellan performed well in both, and Tony Parisi's belligerent personality did not serve him well. At the conclusion of each session, Kellan received congratulations not only from Lynn and other members of the campaign staff, but also from some observers, who promised him their support.

At one meeting early in June, Lynn offered her opinion that if not home free, Kellan surely had reason to be optimistic. "Tony's really pissed," she said. "As he sees it, he's getting his ass kicked by an amateur. Some of the party regulars have abandoned him, and that makes him even angrier. Kellan, all you have to do from here on in is keep your cool and let him rant and rave. Unless he makes some outrageous claim, there's no need to respond. I'm not saying coast, I'm just saying keep doing what we've been doing and we should be fine. From everything I'm hearing from the Republican side, if you get the nomination, you have an excellent chance to wind up in Washington."

On the last Tuesday in June, Kellan and the staff, along with as many supporters as could crowd into the small campaign office, toasted the Democratic candidate for the 19th District of New York. He was on his way. He had taken 59% of the vote against an old political pro and former mayor of the city in which they were located. Four New York newspapers, including the Times and the Wall Street Journal, had given Kellan's victory front page coverage. Alex Crowley and Marty Downey called to congratulate him on his first successful foray into politics. It was an impressive start.

Campaign

The front page of the New York Daily News was posted on the bulletin board of the Maguire for Congress campaign headquarters: The headline read, MAGUIRE DEFEATS PARISI—WILL FACE FULLER IN NOVEMBER! The Times and several other papers carried front page stories as well.

Early that morning Jordan Montgomery called Kellan at home. "Hey, Kell, congratulations! I didn't have any doubts about the outcome, but you did real well. Really cleaned his clock."

"Thanks, Jordan. The tips you gave me along the way sure came in handy. I had a lot to learn."

"Don't mention it, pal. Anything for a friend. And you were lucky to land Lynn for your campaign—she really knows her stuff. Anyway, I'm glad you won."

"Even as a Democrat?"

"Come on, Kell, you know me better than that—you're one of the good guys. Anyway, I did call to congratulate you, but I also see that you're going up against Preston Fuller. I have no doubt that you can beat him, but I can guarantee you that he's gonna make your life miserable for the next few months."

"Yeah, I've already picked up some vibes. What can you tell me about him?"

"This is between you and me, buddy."

"Got it. If anything gets out, you can deny you know me."

Jordan laughed. "Actually, I can tell you quite a bit, some of it you probably already know. I did a little digging around, and here's what I found out. He's originally from upstate New York, somewhere around Kinderhook, where Martin van Buren was from, not far from the Massachusetts state line. When he started dabbling in politics, he moved over to Massachusetts and served one term in our House of Representatives from the district where my family home in Pittsfield is."

"Where your parents live now."

"Right. Shelley and I are going to move back out there too. Mom and Dad rattle around in that house—shoot, you've been there enough—they could turn it into a hotel tomorrow.

"Anyway, Fuller was sort of a gadfly, kind of an embarrassment to the rest of us in the party. Christ you should have heard my father go on about him!"

"He would never vote for a Democrat," said Kellan.

"Yeah, but he didn't vote for Fuller. He voted for a Libertarian or an independent. Anyway, Fuller didn't get reelected, so he moved back to New York, and a couple of years later he got elected to the New York State Assembly from Dutchess County. That's hard-core Republican turf, as you know. He's a right-winger, and I think he served a couple of terms. He was a decent campaigner, but he introduced some far-out legislation, and the voters kicked him out. Despite that, he got too big for his britches and decided to run for the State Senate. That district hadn't had a Democratic senator since the 19th century, but his ultra-conservative stuff did him in, and he got his butt kicked.

"So he was out for a while, and then he moved again, this time down to your area, to have another go at it—a real carpetbagger. He toned down his rhetoric and managed to get elected to the New York Assembly again. In New York State you only have to live in the district you're running in for a year in order to be eligible. I'm sure you knew that. Anyway, when I heard he was going to run for Congress from your district, to tell you the truth, I wondered what he'd been smoking." Kellan laughed.

"Listen, Kellan, I have no doubt that you can beat this guy, and I hope you do. But watch your back; he'll dig up any kind of crap he can find and throw it at you. He's a fierce campaigner, and he's pretty good at it. Shit, if all you had to do was run for office, he'd be governor of New York by now. It's when he has to work with others that he gets his ass in a jam. He'll try to rile you up, put you off your game. Just keep your cool, and you'll do fine."

"You think he's liable to get into my private life? You know, Fiona, and all that?"

"I doubt it, but I wouldn't put it past him. Like I said, just watch your back and be ready for anything."

"Thanks, Jordan. I'll pass this info on to my staff—without your name on it, of course."

"Good luck, buddy. Keep in touch."

A few days later Martin Downey invited Kellan to take a few hours off from campaigning and have lunch with his friends at Phillips, Shannon in New York. Kellan told his friends and colleagues—he still considered himself a member of the firm on a leave of absence—that the practice of politics was very different from the practice of law.

"Yeah, I know that a lot of politicians are lawyers," he said. "But Congress isn't a courtroom—there are no strict rules of evidence. And on the campaign, man, you can get away with almost anything at least once. I'm trying to play it straight, and so far I've been able not to tell too many lies. But when the other guys accuse you of stuff that you don't believe in, sometimes you have to stretch things a little bit."

"Why, Kellan, you know lawyers never lie!" said Martin. There were chuckles all around.

A few of the more conservative attorneys poked at him in a more or less friendly manner, but most of them were curious about how he was enjoying his foray into politics. "What's your staff like," asked Lyle Stevens.

Kellan turned to Alex Crowell. "Alex can tell you more about that. She's been helping out part time."

"Yeah, so we noticed," said Marty. "She's making noises about maybe jumping in full time if you go to Washington."

"I never said that," said Alex, but she was smiling.

"If you steal her, I'll kick your ass," said Marty.

"Why would you do that?" asked Kellan. "Hell, you might even win a b-ball game or two." Marty smiled and raised his middle finger toward Kellan as the others laughed.

Kellan's friends reacted to his candidacy with amused skepticism. They said that although he had never been accused of playing fast and loose with a law, his standards seemed to be slipping mightily. Kellan countered that Marty Downey, among others, had been known to pull a few fast ones in the courtroom. All in all, the partners and associates at Phillips, Shannon expressed their support, both verbally and with contributions to Kellan's campaign. As he left, Alex hugged him and said, "See you soon."

Kellan's White Plains campaign headquarters had moved to a larger office just off Main Street. Lynn Patterson remained as campaign manager, of course, with John Morse and Jean Slater still two of the top aides, but a new member had joined the staff, Ray Braxton. Ray was an experienced political operative who had been working on a primary in upstate New

York, but his candidate had lost. Lynn had called Ray the day after the primary and asked him to join Kellan's campaign. "He's a good man," Lynn told Kellan. "His candidate was a jerk; Ray did all he could, but it was not enough."

"Glad to have you aboard," said Kellan as he shook Ray's hand.

Kellan had gained confidence from the primary campaign, and Lynn was optimistic about his chances against Preston Fuller. Fuller's base of support was in the northern part of the district, on the edge of what was traditional Republican turf. Kellan had just finished reading a biography of Franklin Roosevelt, and recalled a story that FDR used to tell on himself. A commuter from northern Westchester County took the train into New York City every morning. Each day he purchased the daily newspaper from a paperboy and paid him a nickel. He would scan the front page and then return the paper to the boy and get on the train. After some time, the boy became curious and said to the man, "Sir, I appreciate getting the paper back, but I'm curious as to why you only look at the front page."

The commuter replied, "Son, I'm looking for an obituary."

"But sir," said the boy, "the obituaries are in the back, and you only look at page one."

The commuter replied, "Son, the SOB I'm looking for will be on page one!"

Kellan's district, however, stretched from above central Westchester down to the Bronx. All he had to do was break even from White Plains north, and the traditionally Democratic lower part of the district would carry him into Congress. Nevertheless, Lynn urged the campaign staff to move ahead with vigor, reminding everyone that in politics you could take nothing for granted. "Remember Tom Dewey," she said. "He thought he had it won until Harry kicked his butt."

Some of the staff members laughed and started singing, "Hang down your head, Tom Dewey, hang down your head and cry. Hang down your head Tom Dewey, poor boy, you're bound to die."

Kellan enjoyed the light-hearted, optimistic atmosphere in his campaign headquarters. Lynn kept things bustling, Jean, John and Ray were always in good spirits, and the younger, college aged volunteers were full of enthusiasm. Alex Crowell started taking the train up to White Plains on weekends to help out. When some of the younger volunteers were informed that Alex had been a second-team All American basketball player at Maryland, they quickly took to her. She proved to be a very good organizer and cheerleader for mundane tasks like envelope stuffing and manning the phone banks. She also made suggestions to Kellan from time to time on political points. She was warming to the whole idea of a political life—perhaps Marty had been right.

The political atmosphere in the off-year election did not become highly charged until after Labor Day. Lynn took some time off right after the June primary to travel to Europe with her husband George, and for much of July the campaign office operated in a relaxed manner. Jean Salter managed the staff more than adequately in Lynn's absence, and as the time approached to move things back into high gear, the office once again became crowded.

Kellan was scheduled to face Preston Fuller in debates three times in September and October, once at Pace Law School in White Plains, once at Bronx Community College, and once at Iona College in New Rochelle. There had been some wrangling over the locations, but the Fuller campaign had acknowledged that their candidate needed to gain support in the southern portion of the district near New York City in order to have a chance in the election. That meant that Kellan would be debating on fairly friendly turf, but Lynn, John and Jean pressed him once again to take nothing for granted.

Kellan's positions vis-à-vis his Republican opponent were strong. First of all, by any measure, he was pro-business. And the campaign issues he talked about were also aimed at the welfare of American workers, whose jobs depended upon the businesses that Kellan talked about. Kellan's Catholic faith, although he did not pursue it vigorously (in private he might even have conceded that he was a lapsed Catholic), that fact alone put him on the conservative side of some hot-button social issues. He refused to take strong positions for or against abortion, for example, saying that his personal beliefs would not override the right of women of all faiths to make their own medical decisions.

Kellan's other stands were consistent with traditional middle-of-the-road to conservative Democrats. As much as Fuller might try to portray him as a wild-eyed liberal, the campaign staff helped him work on responses that would keep that particular charge from gaining any traction.

The first debate between Kellan and Preston Fuller took place at Pace Law School in White Plains. There was a good crowd in the auditorium and plenty of media coverage. The moderator was the editor-in-chief of the White Plains Reporter Dispatch. Fuller came out swinging. In his opening statement Fuller laid out what was obviously designed to be a moderate program; his ultraconservative positions would not fly in this area of the state. His tactic was apparently to portray himself as a centrist while characterizing Kellan as a left-wing liberal.

"I'll tell you what my opponent stands for," he said while answering one question. "Mr. Maguire wants to see to it that everyone in the nation will get a free pass to college. He thinks government is the answer to every problem. He's a typical tax-and-spend Democrat who will pat you on the back and tell you how much he's helping you while he's picking your pocket. He'll tell you he's a moderate, but don't be fooled. He comes from the same school that gave you Boston's Mayor James Curley. And need I remind you that Curley's corrupt practices landed him in jail?"

The moderator couldn't help shaking his head, but he said to Kellan, "Sir, would you care to respond?"

"Indeed I would," said Kellan. "Mr. Fuller is absolutely correct." He paused for a few moments to let the audience wonder where he was going. "I was indeed born and raised in Boston. As for the rest of it, Mr. Fuller has obviously ignored my positions on a number of issues, which were well defined during the recent primary. We will get into more of that as the evening progresses, I hope, but I would again remind my opponent that I was attacked from the left by my opponent in the Democratic Party primary. If I am such a left-wing radical, how did that happen?"

Kellan's answer was followed by mild but sustained applause and a few shouts of approval. Many of the voters in the district were not familiar with Fuller's background, but it was apparent that they would soon see what he stood for. Kellan's tactic for the rest of the first debate was to reiterate his positions on economic issues, to reassure the audience that he had no radical social agenda, and to refute the occasional wild charges thrown out by his opponent.

The next morning's headline in the White Plains Reporter Dispatch read: "FULLER CHARGES, MAGUIRE SIDESTEPS." The article went on to compare the first debate to a bullfight, with Preston Fuller being the bull and Kellan Maguire skillfully wielding a cape to ward off the attacks. Kellan and the staff sat around in the campaign headquarters, reading bits and pieces from the coverage to each other, laughing and congratulating Kellan on his first debate performance in the new campaign. Lynn clapped her hands, called for attention and said, "Do we have a winner here or what!" Then she added her familiar strain, "Let's don't get cocky. This guy may be down but he's not out. He'll be back with a vengeance. We still have work to do." Following what was generally judged to be a significant victory for Kellan in the first debate, a few new volunteers showed up at the office and were welcomed into the fold.

Realizing that his first performance had not gone very well, Preston Fuller moderated his approach during the second debate at Bronx Community College. His staff had obviously done a little digging, and he had decided to attack Kellan's law background. He accused Kellan of helping foreign companies who wanted to do business in the United States at the expense of homegrown businesses. Someone had dug up a general accounting of Kellan's travels, and Fuller used that to point out how much time Kellan had spent overseas during his practice. He attempted to make it sound as if Kellan was insincere in his promises to do everything he could to aid the American economy. "Is Mr. Maguire really working for General Motors, or is he working for Volkswagen?" he demanded at one point.

Although the exchanges were not as sharp as during the first debate, Fuller soon found out that he was on Kellan's home turf. Kellan's staff had poked around in Fuller's record at the New York State assembly, and while it was obvious that he held typical conservative positions on business matters, his record was spotty. Kellan chose not to dwell on Fuller's shortcomings in terms of his economic background, instead emphasizing his own experience and reiterating his desire to improve the lot of American businesses and workers through better trade policies.

The results of the second debate were not as one-sided as in the first, but Kellan had obviously not lost any ground, and had probably gained a few points.

Meanwhile Kellan's campaign staff produced attractive flyers and position papers and spent many hours stuffing envelopes and licking stamps. Kellan made three or four public appearances every week, and on Lynn's recommendation, he attended a Boy Scout gathering, hoping to ward off any suggestions that he was insensitive to the needs of families and their children. As the campaign moved from September into October, he gave several short speeches at area colleges and universities. Although the college audiences generally included a few hecklers, some of whom tried to be funny and some of whom were just plain nasty, the students seemed to warm to his message, and his appearances were well received. By the time of the last debate, Kellan had a comfortable lead.

Iona College in New Rochelle had been carefully selected for the final debate. Iona was a small Catholic college that had been founded in 1940 by the Christian Brothers. It had a strong Irish flavor—indeed, one of its past presidents had been a native of Dublin. Iona's Hagan School of Business—

a highly regarded program that offered an MBA degree—was sponsoring the debate.

As Kellan, Lynn, Jean, and John sat around a table on the day of the debate, Jean said, "I've been talking to one of our contacts in the Fuller campaign."

"One of our spies," said Lynn with a smile. "Okay, Jean, what do you have?"

"She told me that when Fuller found out about the Iona debate, he was really pissed. He chewed his staff out for accepting the site. I guess he figured out that somebody named Maguire would probably do pretty well there. He'll probably come out swinging."

"You see," said Lynn to Kellan, "your Irish connection is turning out to be a bonus here."

"Every little bit helps," said Kellan. "I think we're in for an interesting evening."

The business school auditorium was full to the point of standing room only for the final showdown between the two candidates for Congress. Kellan was greeted warmly during introductions, Preston Fuller barely politely. The questioning, conducted by three graduate business students at Iona, began innocently enough, but it soon became apparent that Preston Fuller was looking for a chance to lash out. About a third of the way through the debate, Fuller found an opening when Kellan emphasized his experience overseas in furtherance of American business interests.

"Mr. Maguire has indeed spent a great deal of time overseas," said Fuller. "But I ask you, how much of that time was spent in Ireland, and what was he up to besides getting educated?" A few mild boos arose from the audience but were quickly drowned out by applause from the Maguire supporters. "I would ask Mr. Maguire to explain how his political views have been influenced by his Irish connections. Who were his closest friends in Ireland? I am fully aware that his term as a student in Dublin was a long time ago, but I have also learned that he has kept up those connections regularly. I would like to hear from Mr. Maguire how many of those friends of his were members of Sinn Féin. How many of them were members of the IRA? How much money has he contributed to that cause, a cause, by the way, that attempted to introduce a socialist government into Northern Ireland?"

With that the audience erupted in boos as well as a few loud cheers. The ruckus went on for a few minutes, and the three questioners stood and faced the audience and signaled with their arms out for everyone to be seated. As it quieted down, Fuller stood on the stage with what was supposed to be a triumphant look. Kellan had his head down and was shaking it back and forth slowly. As he lifted his head, he had a smile on his face. He thought to himself, 'you dumb bastard.'

"Mr. Maguire?" said the lead questioner, who was president of the student graduate business association.

"Well, I don't know what to say to that." His comment was followed by a few derogatory shouts, followed in turn by a few more boos. "I will tell you this: I had a friend in Ireland who had a friend in the IRA. I never met him, I only knew his first name, and I have no idea what his activities in the IRA were. If I ever met a member of Sinn Féin, I was not aware of it. It is true that I have sent money to Ireland. I have close family relatives in Ireland, and I help them out from time to time. I would be stunned if any of them had spent an Irish penny on weapons or any other political activities. Mr. Fuller's charges are outrageous, and I won't waste any more time responding to them." He looked at the questioners and added, "Please, let's move on." His statement was greeted with enthusiastic applause.

By the end of the evening, it was clear to everyone on Kellan's staff that the contest was over. Kellan was going to win by a landslide, as Fuller had spent much of the campaign shooting himself in the foot. Kellan, however, in the post-debate meeting back at the headquarters in White Plains, was not happy.

When everyone had gathered he asked to no one in particular, "Where the hell did he get that crap?" He looked at Lynn but she was shaking her head and had her arms folded across her chest. She was obviously unhappy as well as baffled. "I have no idea," she said. "I'm assuming—and forgive me for this Kellan, but I have to ask—I'm assuming that there's absolutely nothing to it. You and I have discussed this, but the rest of these folks"— she gestured around the room—"need to hear it."

"Everything I said in there was true. I had—still have, in fact—a friend who had a friend in the IRA. That's the sum total of my nefarious activities in Ireland. But god dammit, Fuller got wind of it somehow or other, even that tiny little connection. I sure as hell would like to know where that came from." It was the first time anyone on the staff had seen him really angry. He looked around the room.

"He just threw a handful of shit at the wall to see if any of it would stick," said Ray Braxton. A few chuckles followed Ray's remark.

No one said anything else for a few moments, and then Jean spoke up. "As I said before, Kellan, we have contacts in their camp, and it's quite possible that some of our people—I assume it's nobody who is here right now—might be spying for the other side. That stuff happens; we can't run background checks on everybody who volunteers. Hell, you were there for four years; you probably had dozens of friends, and who knows how many of them might have had IRA contacts? I'm guessing that he just threw it out there to see if he can get a rise out of you, like Ray just said. Although you kept your cool during the debate, maybe he managed to do that."

"Oh, for Christ's sake Jean, of course Kellan's pissed!" said Lynn. "So am I. But no damage has been done; Fuller buried himself, and we can celebrate that. The election is only two weeks away, and if I ever felt like we were home free at this point in the game, I can say that we are. But again, it's not over, and god dammit, if anyone in the press or any other outsider starts poking around and asking if there's anything to this IRA crap, you better keep your wits about you. It's not up for discussion, not now, not ever. Everybody got that?"

The room was quiet and most of the people nodded in agreement.

"Okay, then, the drinks are on me," said Kellan. "There's a keg and some snacks in the back room. Please help yourselves."

The tension in the room quickly evaporated, and the staffers applauded Kellan and allowed themselves a few shouts and cheers. They started to wander into the back office, emerging with plastic cups of beer. A couple of them brought plates of cookies and cans of nuts and placed them around the room. The mood quickly changed back to where it had started.

By Election Day Kellan's chances in the contest for the Congressional seat in the 19th District were such that several reporters and a couple of photographers followed him to the polls and took pictures of him emerging from the polling place. One of the reporters asked him if he was confident of winning. "I'm hoping for the best," he said. "But you never know until the results are in."

"But you're about 25 points ahead in the polls," the reporter persisted.

"Yeah, that and a buck or two will get you a cup of coffee at your local diner," he said with a smile. "We'll see what happens."

"Thank you Congressman," said the reporter in a sarcastic tone.

Back at campaign headquarters the mood of happy anticipation was hard to suppress. Lynn did not even bother to try. By late morning when many of the workers had already gathered, she had someone help her stand up on a table. She was wearing dark blue slacks, had on a white blouse with a pale blue scarf around her neck. Kellan thought she looked quite fetching.

Lynn clapped a few times, then held up her hands. "Okay, people, listen up. We've reserved the ballroom at the Crowne Plaza for this evening." Her announcement drew enthusiastic applause. "We're expecting a nice turnout, but it would be good if you would take a few moments to invite some friends, maybe your parents, roommates, boyfriends, girlfriends, significant others … "

"Anybody you find wandering the streets who's still sober," someone shouted.

"Seriously, it will be a big evening, there will be some TV there, and Kellan will of course be prepared to make appropriate remarks depending on the outcome." She smiled at Kellan and there was more raucous shouting and applause in the room. Her warnings about not being too cocky were not getting any traction this morning. The newspapers had pretty well declared the race over and were beginning to speculate about the impact that Kellan might have on the United States Congress.

Shortly before noon Jean answered a call in the office and shouted for Kellan. "Senator Montgomery for you," she said, holding out the phone.

"Jordan, thanks for calling."

"You're looking good, my friend," he said. "Even though it's too early for congratulations, I just wanted to extend my good wishes in case I can't reach you this evening. You'll probably be up on the roof of the hotel in your superman suit, so I wanted to catch you early."

"Yeah, right." Kellan laughed. "We're not home yet."

"Sure you are. People who know that I know you are already asking questions about you."

"Afraid I might come back to Massachusetts and run for your seat?"

"Not a chance, buddy. Don't even think about it!"

"Just kidding. Anyway, you've been a hell of a big help, Jordan," Kellan said. "I would sure like to sit down with you for lunch within the next few days. I've got to figure out who I want to hire for my staff and what I need to have in mind before I do."

"The first thing I would suggest is that you take yourself down to Washington and try to find out when the guy you're replacing won't be there. No sense bothering him. Just go in and introduce yourself to his staff, get to know them a little bit, and I'm guessing that they will be more than happy to show you the lay of the land and tell you where some of the bodies are buried."

"Good idea, I'll do that."

"Then drop in on the New York senators' offices; I know them both very well, and they'll be glad to see you. If they're not there, get to know their staffs. You're going to need their help with legislation. Before you leave, pay a courtesy call to the Clerk of the House—she's a good person to know."

"Are you going to be down there for the next few days?" Kellan asked.

"Sure. Just give me a call and we'll get together once you're in town. You already have my private number. I've told my staff to put you through to me any time."

"Great, I'll give you a call soon."

As it was an off year election, late afternoon news reports were calling the turnout in the 19th District moderate to heavy, unusual for an off-year election. Speculation seemed to attribute that fact to Kellan's growing popularity. He had run an efficient, positive campaign thanks to Lynn and the others, and it was clear that much would be expected of him when he finally got to Washington.

About five o'clock Kellan checked into the campaign suite at the Crowne Plaza to await the results. There were two large rooms in the suite and one smaller one for more private conversations. Lynn and the other staffers soon began to gather. They had ordered extra televisions to be brought in so that they could watch several channels simultaneously. The atmosphere was relaxed and warm, with a lot of friendly chatter and joking.

At about six o'clock, Alexandra Crowell appeared and was invited in. She sought Kellan out, took both his hands and said, "Hey, Kellan, you're looking pretty chipper!"

"You look pretty good yourself," he said. "Did they let you out of jail for the evening?"

She just laughed. "Marty might stop by later," she said, "and maybe a few of the others. They're all looking forward to the result."

"I'm really glad you're here," he said. "Let's go into the other room where it's quieter, and we can talk a little bit."

A waiter offered Alex a soft drink, which she accepted. She took a sip and sat down in a chair next to Kellan. "I've been thinking," she said. "What are the chances that I could come down and work for you?"

"That's if I win, of course."

175

"Yeah, like that asshole has any chance at all. No, I'm serious. What's it going to take?"

"What about the firm? What do you plan to do about that? Those jobs on the Hill don't pay very much."

"Look, I'm a cheap date," she said. "I've done quite well at the firm, and I'm comfortable. I can afford to take a pay cut for a while."

"You've never worked on the Hill, have you?" he asked.

"You forget that I majored in political science before I went to law school. I had an internship with a Congressman from Maryland between my junior and senior year. I learned quite a bit."

"Hmmm," he said, "I wasn't aware of that. Maybe you told me and I just don't recall."

"No big deal," she said, "but I'm serious. I believe in what you're doing, I know what you've accomplished at the firm, and I know where you're heading."

Kellan glanced at the clock. "Nothing's going to start around here for a while. I'm not going to have dinner, but why don't we sneak out and get a bite."

They found a table in the corner of the lounge and ordered sandwiches and coffee. "Look," Kellan said, "don't take this the wrong way, okay?" Alex nodded. "There's nothing I would like better than to have you working with me down there. But I need to ask you, what's your agenda, if any?"

"What do you mean?" she asked. "I thought you knew me."

"I do, and I've always liked and respected you. You're a damn fine attorney and you have a real good job. You've got a real shot at being a partner someday. I'm just wondering why you want to chuck all that to go work for a politician."

"First, I assume Marty would take me back if things didn't work out."

"In a New York minute."

"Well, thanks for that. But look, if you're afraid I might be going after some gay agenda or some radical feminist stuff, that's not going to happen. Kellan, I'm assuming you want to be there for a while. Maybe you want to run for the Senate someday, who knows? I don't have anything in mind other than to help with whatever it is you want to accomplish. I know what your agenda is, and I share that." She paused for a moment. "That said, I think it's pretty clear that it would be good to have someone on your staff who can pick up the little nuances about women's issues, whether gay or straight, and help you make sure you don't offend people."

176

"I try pretty hard not to do that," he said.

"I know that. But I can tell you that an awful lot of damn good people from time to time will let something slip that people can find insensitive or maybe even hurtful. They don't mean it; their hearts are in the right place. All I'm saying is, I'd be a somewhat different voice from whatever else you're likely to hear, and that might be useful at times."

He smiled. The waiter brought their sandwiches and they paused for a moment. Then he said, "Nothing you said surprises me, and I wasn't expecting that anything you said would be a problem. In fact, even if you had an agenda of some sort, that wouldn't necessarily bother me. Believe me, I asked more out of curiosity than anything else. If you're sure you want to do this, the door is open. I'm going down to Washington to meet with Jordan Montgomery next week, and I'll see what the possibilities are. Good enough?"

"That's great, Kellan. I really appreciate it. I enjoy practicing law, but ever since I was an intern I've had a little bit of an itch to stick my toe in political waters. Hell, I'd have a hard time getting elected to anything, but I think I would really enjoy working behind the scenes."

"You've got a deal," he said. "I promise that I'll see what I can do."

"Thanks, Kellan."

When the first returns began to come in, it was clear that Kellan was going to win by a wide margin. As the evening progressed the numbers grew more and more impressive. By the time the race was called, the first television station to make the announcement predicted that Kellan would win with more than 60% of the vote, a huge landslide. When the result was settled, a commentator on national network covering the day's results spent several minutes talking about the impressive victory of the new New York congressman, pointing out that his race had led to one of the more interesting and significant victories of the day. The people gathered in the suite smiled and cheered at that, and several of them congratulated Kellan for being separated from the crowd of newly elected legislators.

"All we have to do now is wait for Fuller to concede," Lynn said. "He'll probably take his sweet time at that." She leaned over and grasped both of Kellan's hands. "You're on your way, my friend."

Shortly before midnight Kellan appeared in the ballroom to great applause and gave a brief speech of thanks and acceptance for the office to which he had been elected. He thanked the campaign workers, many of them by name. Lynn, Jean, Ray, and John were up on the stage with

Kellan. As he finished his remarks, he went over to the edge of the platform where Alex was standing, reached out his hand and invited her to come up onto the stage, where he put his arm around her.

The handshaking, backslapping celebration continued until well past midnight. By 1:30 in the morning a small group had gathered at Kellan's home in Scarsdale to wind down and talk over the next steps. An hour later Lynn and a few others headed back to New York, leaving just Alex.

"I guess I'd better get going, too," she said. She stood up, stretched and yawned.

"Why don't you stay here?" Kellan asked her.

She gave him a kind of funny look. "Are you propositioning me?" she asked. He just laughed. "Are you sure I won't be a bother?"

"Yup. There's plenty of room up there."

"Cool," she said. "I may even call in sick tomorrow."

"That will be a first."

As Kellan lay awake reflecting on what he had accomplished, one of the most pleasing things was the fact that Alex would be coming to work with him.

Kellan and Jordan Montgomery were seated in the Senate dining room. It was not Kellan's first visit to the imposing historic dining area, but he was still impressed with the ambience. Jordan had introduced Kellan to members of his own staff before they left for their private meeting.

After they had ordered, they continued the conversation they had started earlier. "You mentioned staff," said Jordan. "I'm sure you know that you have fourteen slots for personal staff. Obviously the most important is your Chief of Staff, and you said Lynn Patterson isn't interested."

"Lynn's a dyed-in-the-wool New Yorker and really doesn't care for Washington that much."

"Strange for someone with all her political experience," said Jordan.

"Ah, you know, she likes to keep an eye on George. Anyway, what are the chances that an outsider could handle the job?"

"Well, of course that depends on the person. If you have someone in mind who's not too young and has his or her head on straight, it's not unheard of. Are you already thinking of someone?"

"Yeah, she's a rising star at Phillips, Shannon, but she's already told me that she'd like to come down here to work for me. She's a damn good lawyer and she's smart as hell. Stood near the top of her law class at Duke."

"Okay, not impossible, but you definitely want an experienced person for your chief of staff or deputy chief. I've done a little poking around about the folks in the office you're taking over, and I think there are at least one or two keepers. Carmen Montefiore is one of the real old pros on the Hill—I assume you've met him?"

"Yeah, I did. I told him I'd like to come back after lunch and meet with some of the staff. Hal's not in the office today, so it's a pretty good time."

Hal Wofford was the outgoing Congressman from the 19th District of New York. He had recently been named to replace the Under Secretary of Interior and had decided not to run again, which had left the seat open for Kellan.

"Hal's a good man, and you would do well to hold on to some of his folks. Carmen Montefiore is his chief of staff. He'd be a hell of an asset, but he may not want to stay."

"When I talked to him, I got the impression that he was open to the idea."

"Great. You couldn't find a better person to run your office."

"There are some other pretty good people on my campaign staff, and I'd like to bring a couple of them down here."

"Sure, why not? If you keep Carmen, you can bring in a few of your own folks. They must have done a hell of a job for you, considering the way you stomped Preston's butt. You had one of the highest winning percentages of any contested election ever. Sometimes an incumbent will get eighty five percent against a Libertarian or some other third party type, but you had a real fight on your hands, theoretically at least. Anyway, my friend, you can hit the ground running here. Your reputation precedes you, and I'm sure you will be very well received. I've spoken with a couple of folks over on your side about your committee assignments, and I think you'll be pleased with what they have in mind."

"That's great, Jordan. I appreciate it."

"Not at all. Let's go back to the office and we can go over a few of those staff names. What are your plans between now and when you get sworn in?"

"Well, I got a call from Fiona," Kellan said, smiling. "I told her that swearing-in for a congressman wasn't that big a deal, but she wants to come. I'm going to spend Christmas with the family up in Boston, but I think I'll go over there for New Year's and bring her back."

"I remember her well from when she came over here when she was, what, about ten?"

"Yeah, I remember that too. We stopped by to see you when we were on our way to Niagara Falls. She remembers you—she asked me if you would be in Washington during the swearing-in session. I told her we'd bring her here for lunch—she's already thrilled about that."

"I bet she's a stunner by now."

"She'll knock your socks off."

"I can't wait to see her."

Back in New York, Kellan's campaign headquarters had been shut down, but Kellan planned to convert it into his district office. He thanked Lynn profusely for her terrific support, and they promised to keep in close touch in the coming months. "Are you sure I can't convince you to come to Washington?" he asked her, and she laughingly said, "Maybe if George drops dead."

As soon as he returned from his visit to Washington, Kellan contacted John, Jean, and Ray and invited them to dinner at his place to discuss possible moves to Washington. It was a pleasant evening as they rehashed the campaign experiences, the good, the bad, and the funny. There were quite a few of the last, as most of the campaigning during both the primary and the regular election had been very upbeat.

When the discussion turned to Kellan's Washington staff, he started by asking if any of them were interested in working for him in Washington. "I met with Hal Wofford's chief of staff, Carmen Montefiore when I was down there. He's agreed to stay on as chief of staff. Other than that there are places available."

Ray responded first. "Kellan, it was an honor to work for you. I'd like to come to Washington, but I've got a pretty good job lined up, so I think I'll stay in this area. If you ever have a spot in your district office, keep me in mind."

"I'm in," said Jean. "I know Carmen, and I'd love to work with him. If you've got a spot for me down there, that would be great."

"You know the pay isn't that terrific, and there's not much I can do about that," said Kellan.

"Hey, I'm not high maintenance. As long as I can find a decent place to live, I can manage."

"I'm told that a lot of the staffers down there share apartments or houses. Parts of Washington are reasonably priced, and I'm sure you could find something. If you're serious, we'll talk it over later and I'll see what we can do."

"I'm serious," Jean said. "It's my dream."

"Good, you're hired!" said Kellan, and everyone clapped as Jean smiled broadly.

Kellan continued. "John, you did a hell of a job. What's your pleasure?"

"I'm good here, Kellan. Like Ray said, it was great to work for you. But I've lived in Westchester all my life, and I like it here. You can also keep me in mind for your district office, but I can get on the train and be in Yankee Stadium in less than an hour, and there's no baseball in Washington, right?"

"Well, you've got the Orioles in Baltimore."

"I hate the Orioles," said John, and everyone laughed.

"Well, then, I guess you're out of luck," said Kellan. "But let's keep in touch."

Kellan returned to Washington a few days later and leased an apartment not far from the Capitol. He contacted a realtor and put his house in Scarsdale up for sale. She told him that the publicity from his winning campaign for Congress would be a strong selling point, and she was confident that she could get him a good price. "I'm in no hurry," he said, "but I'll appreciate anything you can do."

Nora Maguire had passed away the previous year, but the emotions in the family from the loss of their last parent had subsided. Kellan spent Christmas with Eddie and Eileen, Tom and Mary and their children, and he visited with old friends and colleagues from the Boston office. Having been recently elected to the House of Representatives, he was something of a celebrity, and both his friends and relatives were full of congratulations and good wishes. It was a pleasant time, but he was distracted by thoughts of what lay ahead. He made a couple of quick trips to Washington on the Boston-DC shuttle to prepare for assuming office. He was in a hurry to get everything set up so that he could fly to Ireland and bring Fiona back with him.

Fiona was at home with her family in Mallow, so Kellan had decided to fly to Shannon Airport, which was closer than Dublin. He looked forward to seeing the Connolly family again; he rented a car and drove straight to Mallow. The congratulatory atmosphere in Boston had been pleasant, and he knew there would be more of the same once he rejoined the Connolly clan. He looked forward to renewing his Irish connections.

As he pulled up to the Connolly house, Kevin and Molly came bounding out. Molly threw her arms around him. "You're famous! You're going to be president someday!" she said. Kevin shook his hand. Then Fiona came out, embraced him in a hug. "I'm so excited!" she said. "Are you really going to take me back with you?"

"I've already got the tickets. First class, direct from Shannon to Washington." She hugged him again. Kellan looked over her shoulder at Patrick and Libby standing in the doorway. Libby was clapping her hands and had tears running down her face.

The Irish, Kellan thought, so emotional! He took Fiona's hand and walked toward the house.

Patrick shook Kellan's hand and clapped him on the shoulder. "Well done, Laddie!" he said. "We knew you had it in you!"

Libby took both of Kellan's hands and kissed him on both cheeks. Her eyes were still wet with tears and she just shook her head and smiled at him. "We are so proud of you!" was all she could muster.

Brendan engulfed Kellan with a huge bear hug, then stepped back and slapped him on the shoulder a couple of times. "Begorra, you've done it, brother!" he said. Deirdre was standing next to him and she hugged Kellan as well, adding, "Lord, we're happy to see you. What a thrill it was to read of your victory in the Irish papers!"

Patrick produced a bottle of Bushmills and poured a small glass for everyone. "A toast to our parliamentarian!" Then he added, "There's some Kinsale Irish Lager in the kitchen if anyone cares to wash down the Bushmills. Brendan went to the kitchen and brought back two bottles of Kinsale and offered one to Kellan. They seated themselves around the living room and Patrick said, "So, my lad, tell us how you pulled it off." He had poured himself another tot of Bushmills.

Kellan smiled. "I was very fortunate to have an opponent who tried to paint me as a member of the IRA." Everyone laughed. "Actually, he wasn't a very good campaigner, as it turned out. I had a lot of good advice from friends and some very fine people working on my behalf. I won't say it was easy, but it was well worth the effort. I'm looking forward to going to Washington."

"And our darling Fiona is going with you!" said Libby. Fiona just smiled.

"You're excited, aren't you Fiona?" said Deidre. Then she turned toward Kellan. "She'll be representing all of us, and be sure we'd all love to go. But we'll wait until you get elected president, and then we'll all troop over and clutter up the place with our Irish jabber."

"I'd love to have you all there," he said, "but getting sworn into Congress is not as big a deal as you might think. There are about eighty of us who got elected for the first time, so it will be a pretty big mob scene. It all takes place within the Capitol building, and will be over in a matter of minutes, except for the informal part, picture taking and that sort of thing." He paused and held up his drink in salute. "I would like to toast all of you for giving me a wonderful second family. I owe a lot to every one of you, and there is nobody I would rather share this with. Sláinte!"

They raised their glasses, and Libby took the crucifix she was wearing around her neck, kissed it and blessed herself with the sign of the cross. "My prayers worked," she said to Kellan triumphantly. He smiled, nodded and lifted his glass again to his mother-in-law.

Fiona came over and sat down next to him on the couch. She put her arm through his and rested her head on his shoulder. Deirdre looked at the two of them for a few moments, turned her head away and wiped a tear from her cheek. Then she turned back and smiled at them. "I'm happy for you, Darlin'," she said to Fiona. "I just wish I could go with you."

"I know, Mum. But Kelly said we could all go over maybe next summer. I'll bring back pictures, and I promise to tell you everything that happens."

"You can tell us all," said Patrick in a gruff voice. "We'll be putting you through your paces, Lassie!"

The happy conversation went on until dinner time, and Kellan caught up on the latest doings of the Connolly clan. They seemed prosperous and happy, and Kellan knew they lived fruitful, comfortable lives. But it occurred to him that they hadn't seen much of the world. As far as he knew they had taken a few brief vacations on the southwestern Irish coast, and once or twice along the Antrim Coast from Belfast to Londonderry. He also recalled that they had taken a trip to Scotland some years earlier. But they had never been to continental Europe or to the United States. He told himself he would try to rectify that. He knew that they all wouldn't be able to come at the same time, for someone had to keep an eye on the farm animals. But he could arrange for Brendan and Deirdre to come, and later Patrick and Libby.

Libby, of course, had been to the States during the latter stages of Moira's pregnancy, but except for a brief excursion to some of Boston's historic sites, she had seen little. And for her, the trip had had a tragic ending. He could scarcely recall ever hearing her talk about it, though she often voiced her recollections of her beloved daughter.

As always, the visit seemed to end too soon, but this time, instead of leaving everything behind, his daughter was going with him. As they said their goodbyes in front of the Connolly home, the rest of the family was sad, and Deirdre and Libby again tearful. But Fiona could not contain her excitement, even as she hugged her parents and grandparents. When they were finally on the road heading for Shannon, she said several times, "Oh, Kelly, I can't tell you how excited I am!"

Kellan smiled as he felt her excitement and absorbed her affection in a way that made him indescribably happy.

Congressman Maguire

Kellan Maguire's "low-key" swearing-in proved to be a pretty big deal after all. Among all the incoming freshman representatives, Kellan got a disproportionate share of the attention. His impressive victory over Preston Fuller, his reputation as an experienced attorney with a strong background in economic and trade issues, and his attractive looks made him a favorite with the press. The fact that he was an unmarried man in his mid-forties added to the attraction, at least among the female journalists.

In addition, Kellan had a pretty good crowd of visitors for the occasion. Tom and Mary had brought their children to witness the historic family event; Eddie and Eileen were there, as well as Alexandra Crowell and Martin Downey. Charlie and Cynthia Wright had flown down from Boston. Jean Slater had met with Carmen and was all set to commence work the next day as Kellan's Deputy Chief of Staff, so she was technically a guest. Marty pretended to be irritated with Kellan for stealing one of his prized attorneys, but he was sincerely pleased for Alex, who would joining Kellan's staff. "She'll do a great job for you, Kell," he said.

Of all Kellan's guests, Fiona got the most attention. She had her mother's beautiful skin, blue eyes, dark blonde hair and stunning figure. Kellan had gotten Alex to take her shopping the day before, and Alex had helped her select a gorgeous dress for the occasion at Woodward and Lothrop. He introduced her as his daughter, Fiona Connolly. A number of his colleagues seem surprised to know that he had a daughter, and given her different last name, they apparently assumed she was married. To his closer friends he simply introduced her as Fiona; most of them knew the history and were happy to see her. Charlie and Cynthia Wright told her how much they had loved her mother, and the friends from the New York office were excited to have finally met her. By the end of the day's ceremonies she had attracted more than her share of attention, but she seemed to enjoy it. She could not conceal her pride in her father's achievement, nor did she try.

Every corner of the United States Capitol was filled with men and women newly elected to Congress, along with mothers, fathers, wives, children, friends and former campaign workers, incoming staff members for the newly elected Congressmen and Senators, not to mention photographers and reporters looking for a story. Some of the journalists had noticed a young woman hanging close to Kellan and had discovered that she was indeed his daughter. "Congressman Maguire," one of them asked, "you have a very attractive daughter. We understand you are not married—would you care to comment?"

"Fiona's mother died in childbirth," he said. "I never remarried." He turned his attention to another reporter to avoid a follow-up. He had nothing more to say on the subject just then. He knew, however, that the subject was now out there, and that he would get more questions in the future. It was the sort of thing he wanted to shield Fiona from, but she seemed to take it all in stride. She had been standing next to him during the questioning and had responded to one polite query, "I'm just happy to be here with my father." There was some chattering about her Irish accent, and that would become part of the story as well. Her movie star good looks would add to the mystique. It was only a matter of time.

Kellan gave polite answers to a few more queries from the press, but he excused himself and ushered his guests back to his office area where many of his new staffers were waiting.

Kellan's Chief of Staff, Carmen Montefiore, had grown up in the village of Port Chester in Westchester County, son of Italian immigrant parents. A star football player at Port Chester High School, Carmen had won a scholarship to Fordham University. After college Carmen had helped his ailing father run his construction business. He served briefly in a management position with the Westchester County Department of Public Works and was later elected Westchester County Clerk. From there he was elected Mayor of White Plains. When former mayor Hal Wofford had been elected to Congress, he invited Carmen Montefiore to come to Washington as his chief of staff.

Carmen still had a football player's build and presented a rough exterior, until people got to know the gentle man underneath. Still, there was a running joke around the Longworth House Office Building that if you wanted a hit put out on someone, Carmen was the man for the job. Kellan had warmed to him instantly, and Carmen seemed to return the feeling. He knew his way around on the Hill, and he was familiar with the needs of Kellan's constituents back in New York. Kellan soon learned that the women in the office were quite fond of Carmen and lovingly called him 'the Godfather.' But when Carmen wanted something done, the office staff jumped to perform the task.

Carmen was the first to welcome Kellan's guests as they returned from the swearing-in. Tom and Mary's children had gone off with another group of children led by a guide who would take them around the Capitol. Kellan left his family in the office briefly while he went to join various groups for picture-taking sessions, including one of the entire freshman class of Congress on the Capitol steps. Carmen gave Kellan a few routine papers to sign, and Kellan's family and friends eventually made their way back to Kellan's apartment.

Alex Crowell and Jean Slater had joined the family gathering. In addition to Jean as Kellan's Deputy Chief, he had selected Alex to serve as Communications Director on his personal staff. She and Jean chatted with family members about how the office of Congressman Maguire was going to function. Alex was already well familiar with Kellan's general agenda, and Jean, a very quick study, had already hit it off well with Carmen, whom she remembered from his service in White Plains; she was rapidly learning the ropes of her new position. Aisha Washington, who had served as Hal Wofford's Legislative Director, had agreed to stay on for a year in that position.

As she had been during the ceremonies on the House floor, Fiona was the center of attention with Kellan's family. She already knew her Aunt Eileen and Aunt Mary from previous visits—Kellan had taken members of his family to Ireland several times—and the two women were anxious to find out what their very attractive niece was up to.

"So, Fiona, are you going to follow in your Dad's footsteps and go into politics and law?" asked Mary.

"I haven't decided yet," said Fiona. "Kelly and I have talked about it, and I've been concentrating on history and political science at Trinity, but I still have a way to go. I'm also thinking about nursing."

"Interesting," said Eileen. Then she added to the small group surrounding their Irish niece, "Don't you love her brogue? It takes me back to when we visited your family in Mallow," she said to Fiona.

"I wish they could have been here," said Fiona. She was still starry eyed from visiting the events at the Capitol and during her short time in Washington.

"Maybe you'll come back here to live someday," said Eddie. "I'm sure your dad can find something interesting for you to do."

"Sure, we've talked about that," Fiona said with a smile. "We'll see— I love Ireland and would hate to leave my family, or my country, but so many Irish people have come to live here … I can see why, I guess."

"Well you sure don't have to decide anything right away," said Tom. "You've got your studies to finish first."

"Would you listen to your aunts and uncles," said Mary. "Trying to run your life for you already!"

Fiona laughed. "Ah, I surely don't mind, you've all been so wonderful to me," she said. "I'm enjoying myself, truly I am!"

Later that evening Jordan Montgomery and his wife Shelley arrived and joined the gathering. Jordan immediately spotted Fiona, walked over to her and said, "My God! Look at you!" He held out his arms and she hugged him. Shelley Montgomery was delighted to see Fiona again, as she also remembered her from the visit years earlier. Shelley's family on her mother's side was of Irish descent, and she and Fiona soon got into a lively conversation.

Jordan had congratulated Kellan earlier on the floor of Congress, but they shook hands again and shared some thoughts on the new class, the new Congress, and the new year. It definitely had promise.

Jean sidled up to Jordan and poked a little fun at him. "Gee, Senator, I didn't know Kellan allowed Republicans in his house!"

Jordan picked up on the theme and responded in a mock gruff tone, "Well, if that's the way it is, I'll just drag Shelley away from Fiona and we'll be outta here!"

Jean smiled, reached out to shake his hand and said, "Senator, I know how much Kellan has depended on you for advice, and all of us truly appreciated it. I know you'll be working together on legislation."

"That we will, Jean. Kellan knows you have to be able to get along with people on the other side, or you'll have a short career, or at least a very ineffective one, in Washington. He tells me you're going to be his DCS, so we'll probably be seeing a lot of each other."

"Yes. I know Carmen from back in New York, and I'm looking forward to it."

"I'm sure you'll do a fine job, and please call me Jordan."

When the last of the guests had departed, Kellan waved his hand around the modest apartment. "This is your home away from home, any time you want to come, Sweetheart," he said to Fiona.

She hugged him yet again, and said, "I'm so glad to be with you." He kissed the top of her head.

Early in the morning on the day after he was sworn in, Kellan called his staff together in a small meeting room, leaving Jean in the office to field visitors, as she already knew what he wanted to say. He thanked Carmen Montefiore for being willing to continue as Chief of Staff. "I'm sure that all of us, especially me, will benefit from Carmen's wisdom and experience. He'll be helping Jean learn the ropes."

"Can we get him to arrange a hit on a certain politician back in New York?" said one of the young staffers who had been with Kellan during the campaign.

Carmen smiled, but Kellan quickly answered, "Okay, enough, or I'll report you to the Italian-American Anti-Defamation League." Everyone laughed. "Seriously, we don't need to be throwing that around." He glanced at Alex, and she nodded and applauded silently. It was the sort of thing that her antenna picked up very quickly. Kellan continued, as he nodded at his new Communications Director. "You have all met Alex Crowell by now, and I know she will welcome the assistance of all of you who have spent some time on the Hill. Alex is a superb attorney, and she's going to be an important member of the team." He smiled at Alex. "She gets to handle the press."

He turned to the elegantly dressed African American woman seated next to Alex. "I would especially like to thank Aisha Washington for agreeing to stay on as Legislative Director. She and Alex have already decided to be co-captains of our staff b-ball team." Alex and Aisha high-fived each other, to applause and cheers from the group. "Two All-Americans," said Kellan. "Wow!"

"Okay, now for the serious stuff. I'm fully aware that I'm one of the new kids on the block, and I know that freshman can get beat up by trying to get too big for their britches too fast. But I didn't run for office to come down here and do a lot of sightseeing. I do have an agenda, and those of you who worked with me in New York know what it is. For those of you who aren't quite sure, Jean has put together some outlines of my campaign speeches, and you might want to glance over them. I'm still working to find out what my committee assignments will be, and I will pick all your brains concerning other members on those committees."

He paused for a few moments and was pleased that everyone seemed well tuned in. "Finally, let's not forget that I'm here—we're here—to serve the people of the 19th District of New York. My door will be open to them as much as possible, including to the fruitcakes I've heard about who think the CIA is reading their brains and wants Congress to put a stop to it." A good deal of laughter followed Kellan's remark; he had already heard that personal staffs in Congress spent a lot of time dealing with people who thought their Congressman had a direct line to God and could fix anything. "I get that, and we'll have to separate the wheat from the chaff. But that's our job." He had been seated at a table at the front of the room, and now he stood up.

"I know we still have a couple of holes to fill on the staff, and I'll get to that as soon as possible with Carmen. But the last thing I want to say is that as much as I want to serve the people of New York, I want to serve my country at the same time. As you all know, I spent a good deal of my life overseas, and that has given me a view of things that shaped my thinking. As you learn more about me, I will surely be learning more about all of you. I welcome that, and I thank you for your past service. I look forward to the job that all of us will do together during my time here."

As the meeting broke up and the staffers made their way back to Kellan's office spaces, Alex sidled over to him. "That was real good, Kellan." He nodded and thanked her. "By the way, I've actually found a couple of people that I knew when I was an intern, believe it or not. And I've just been chatting with people I've met here and there. When they find out I'm new, and that I'm working for a freshman congressman, they're very quick to point out that a whole lot of newbies come in here ready to change the world and start ordering people around. Still, everyone I've met so far knows who you are. The only new guy who's better known than you is that ex-football player from Nebraska. I know you're not going to try to make a splash too soon; also, the guys on the staff already like you. That's a big plus. I'm really going to enjoy this, even though I know it's going to be a lot of work."

"You and Aisha seem to have hit it off."

"Oh, yeah, she was really a great player at Pitt. I didn't know her, but I've seen her play. She's tough. We're going to get along fine. In fact, she invited me to stay with her until I find a place of my own."

"Wonderful."

As Jordan had pointed out and Alex and Jean had already discovered, Kellan's reputation as an expert in international trade matters had preceded him to Congress, boosted by his impressive showing in the election. The Democratic Steering Committee had decided to place Kellan on two important committees, unusual for a freshman. He was to serve on the Energy and Commerce and the Financial Services committees, where he would focus his efforts on trade matters. He was also appointed to two subcommittees that dealt with economic issues; he was pleased with his assignments. Jordan, who had had a hand in seeing that Kellan got prestigious positions, advised him that the real work in Congress was done in committees. They had large staffs, and staff members had a considerable amount of expertise. Many of them were generally better versed in the details of committee business than the members who served on them.

Kellan would soon discover for himself what he had always suspected, that it was the career staffers who ran the show in Washington, not only in Congress, but in the executive departments as well. He also discovered very quickly that many senior staffers took a dim view of too much meddling by the new members, even to the point of revealing a supercilious attitude toward them that occasionally bordered on outright contempt. He had already encountered an annoying little freshman congressman from Arkansas who acted as though he had been crowned king of the Hill. Kellan quickly vowed to treat the committee staffers deferentially, and even the most jaded of them seemed to warm to him.

As much as Kellan appreciated the advice and counsel of Jordan, Carmen and the other veteran people he was getting to know, he knew there was much he had to learn for himself. So during his first few weeks as a member of the House, Kellan sought out key staffers of the committees on which he would serve, introduced himself and asked questions about committee business, as well as seeking background materials which he could study to get himself up to speed. He was again made aware that his reputation was already rather well known, considering his freshman status, and it was apparent that some of the senior members of the committees which he would join had alerted the staffers to keep an eye out for the young congressman from New York.

Kellan made a point of meeting each morning with Carmen, telling rest of the staff they were not to be disturbed. He was surprised at how much Carmen revealed in the way of the hidden operations within the House of Representatives. A great deal of congressional business was conducted dining rooms, exercise spaces, hallways, corridors and coat rooms, as well as in various locations off of Capitol Hill. Despite his obvious good nature, Kellan realized that Carmen certainly knew how to play hardball, and that he knew how to get things done in the often fractious political environment of Washington. Carmen also warned Kellan of how hard he was going to have to work, and of the long hours that he was going to have to put in, not only on the Hill, but at various embassies, receptions, dinner parties and social gatherings where the powerbrokers of Washington gathered in the evenings.

"It's kind of a good thing that you're not married," said Carmen. "But let me give you a piece of advice there. You may not need it, and I trust you won't be offended by what I'm about to say." Carmen paused and smiled. "I'm told you're a good Catholic," he said. "Just for the record, so am I, but you're more likely to find me here on Sunday morning than at mass. But believe me, the fact that you're a good Catholic isn't going to keep the skirts away. There are battalions of women in this town ready to drop their panties for anybody with a little clout. You're a good-looking guy, and you're single, and I'm assuming you're not gay, since you have a daughter." Kellan just smiled.

"I don't have to tell you this, my friend, but there's a bucket full of guys around this town who have gotten their asses in a jam because they couldn't keep their dicks in their pants, including a few who managed to keep it out of the press." He paused to let Kellan think that over. Then he said, "You were married once, though, right?"

"For about a year," Kellan said. "And you've already met Fiona."

"What a lovely girl she is," said Carmen. "She could be a movie star. The subject hasn't come up before, and I was actually unaware that you had a daughter until I met her. Is she your only child?"

"The only one," he said. "She was our first, and as it turned out, only child. And as you could tell from her accent, she was raised in Ireland. It was meant to be a temporary arrangement, but as I never remarried, she grew up there. She was eventually adopted by my brother-in-law and his wife. They have a daughter about the same age, so it did make sense. I've tried to be a big part of her life. There were good reasons for my leaving her in Ireland, but I've often regretted that decision. I often traveled to Europe for the firm, so I got to see a lot of her. And she has visited the States before. I didn't plan to bring her over for the swearing-in, but she insisted on it, and I'm thrilled that she was here."

"How come you chose not to marry again?"

Kellan paused for a moment. "There are reasons for that, I guess. I never made a decision not to marry again—no death-bed promises to my wife or anything like that. I've had some close women friends, but never really came close to marrying any of them. There is another woman who has been part of my life, and she's still in Ireland. Maybe she'll be a bigger part of my life someday, but she's married to someone else. That's the part I'd like to keep under wraps, and not just because she's another man's wife. There's more to it than that."

Carmen mulled that over for a few moments, nodding his head. "Thank you for telling me." He pointed at his temple. "It all stays right here. By the way, where is Fiona at the moment?"

"She's spending a few days with my family up in Massachusetts," said Kellan. "All of them are very happy for the opportunity to get to know each other a little better. Fiona has talked a little bit about coming to the United States to live, but that's still a ways off. She has to finish her studies at Trinity in Dublin first. After that, we'll see."

"Is she coming back down here?"

"Yup. She'll be down on the weekend. Alex and I are going to show her around a bit more. I've got some tickets for the National Symphony Saturday night. Her great-great-grandfather is buried in Arlington, and she wants to visit his grave. He fought for the union in the Civil War."

Carmen nodded. Then he said, "Jean and I are going to get along fine. I remember her from when she was just getting her feet wet back in White Plains. But tell me a little bit more about Alex," he said. "She's sharp as a tack, but she's got a little edge to her, hasn't she?"

"Well, for starters, you've probably figured out that she's gay."

Carmen rubbed his jaw thought about that for a moment. "Now that you mention it, I'm not surprised. Not that she said anything to make me wonder. I noticed she wasn't wearing a wedding ring, and for a looker like her, that always makes you wonder."

"She and I worked very closely back at the law firm," Kellan said. "She really understands international trade and commerce, and the legal issues involved in dealing with foreign businesses. The reason I hired her is for her help in that area. She has assured me that she doesn't have any other agenda, and she never raised any eyebrows in the office about the fact that she was gay." Kellan smiled. "I'll say one other thing about her that you will probably discover pretty soon. She was an All-American basketball player at Maryland, and she's already checked out the basketball court here. She and Aisha are already planning to rule Capitol basketball. I played against her often back at the firm, and I can promise you that she's going to embarrass some guys who think they're pretty good."

Carmen laughed. "My daughter plays basketball," he said. "I'll have to get them together. And Aisha has already reached out to her, as you said, and that's good. She'll teach Alex the ropes."

"Alex would be thrilled to meet your daughter," said Kellan. "Of course she doesn't have any children, but I can assure you that she really loves kids. I bet your daughter will really take to her."

"Okay, we'll see. Well, Mr. Congressman, you're off to a good start. I now have good reason to tell my friends why I decided to stay on—I'm looking forward to working with you. I did have a couple of other interesting offers, but I like it here on the Hill." He reached out, and he and Kellan shook hands on what promised to be a productive partnership. As he was leaving the office, Carmen said, "You'll have to come to dinner soon—the missus wants to meet you."

"Any time. I'd love it."

Fiona arrived in Washington on Friday afternoon. Kellan met her at Union Station and they walked the few blocks back to his office. As Fiona was chatting with Carmen—she found him fascinating, she said—Kellan took Alex aside. "Listen, I've got some stuff to finish up here. Any chance you could take Fiona to get a bite to eat, and I could catch up with you later?"

"You're going to turn me loose with your only child?" Alex said with a grin.

"I've always trusted you, Sweetheart."

"Sure," said Alex. "I'll take her to that pub over by Union Station, the Dubliner. Where shall we meet?"

"Fiona has a key to my apartment. I'll come by the Dubliner when I'm done here, and if you're gone, I'll meet you back there."

"Sounds like a winner." Alex reached out for Kellan's hand. "I have to tell you, Kell, you are a lucky man. She is one neat kid." She quickly picked up the sadness that crossed his face and squeezed his hand.

On Saturday morning Kellan, Alex and Fiona visited the grave of Patrick Maguire. "He was badly wounded at Fredericksburg," said Kellan. "They brought him back here to Washington, where he died. That's how he wound up here in Arlington. Back then a serious wound was a virtual death warrant."

"How come his name isn't spelled like yours?" asked Fiona.

"That happened a lot back in those days. It could be that the guy who enlisted him just got it wrong. Or maybe it happened after that."

Fiona said, "A lot of Irish fought in the American Civil War, didn't they?"

Kellan smiled. "When Robert E. Lee surrendered to General Grant at Appomattox, one of Lee's officers told one of the Union officers that the reason that the North had won was that they had more Irish. The Irish Brigade was one of the most famous outfits in the Civil War, and they got really hammered at Fredericksburg. If you look over the rolls of those who died there, you'll see a lot of Irish names. One of their regiments, the famous Fighting 69th, is still part of the New York National Guard."

Fiona knelt down and touched the gravestone. Kellan noticed her lips moving and assumed she was saying a silent prayer for a distant relative whom she hadn't even known existed until a few minutes earlier. She stood up and smiled at Kellan. "Thanks for bringing me, Kelly. Mum and Dad will be very interested that I was here. You all get behind the stone and I'll take a picture. Granddad will be interested to see another Patrick in the family."

"There's a whole lot of Irish history in this country," said Alex. "I know that, and I'm not even Irish!" Fiona laughed and gave Alex a quick hug. They sure are getting along, thought Kellan with pleasure.

On Saturday evening Kellan and Fiona attended a National Symphony concert at the Kennedy Center. Fiona was captivated by the large bronze sculpture of President Kennedy in the main lobby area. After they had dined in the Roof Terrace restaurant, they took their seats in the box area and heard Mstislav Rostropovich conduct a program that included Beethoven's Sixth Symphony, the Pastoral. Fiona loved music, and her first concert at the Kennedy Center was another experience that she would take home with her to share with the family. "They are all going to be so jealous!" she said. "They may all get on the next plane and come over here and pester you," she said.

"We'll see what we can do about that," he said. "Maybe this summer when Congress isn't in session."

"I would love that," she said. "Could I bring Celeste?"

"Sure, but I thought you two weren't getting along." On the plane ride over from Dublin, Fiona had been telling Kellan of a spat that she had had with Celeste over something to do with food. It had not made a whole lot of sense to Kellan, and he assumed that it was a recent event and that Fiona was simply getting it off her chest.

"Oh, you know, she starts something about once a week, but she always gets over it. Typical French attitude."

"You could get along with anybody, Sweetheart."

Kellan drove Fiona to Dulles Airport Monday afternoon for her flight back to Dublin on Aer Lingus. He took advantage of the special parking for members of Congress and accompanied his daughter to the gate. "Oh, Kelly, I've had such a wonderful time." She put her arms around him and rested her head on his chest for a moment.

"I wish you could stay longer," he said. "In fact..."

She looked up at him. "What?"

"I just wish you were here all the time," he said. "I've wished that practically every moment since you were born. The hardest thing I've ever done was to give you up. It was probably also the best thing I've ever done, for you if not for me." He put both his arms around her and squeezed his eyes shut against the tears that were forming.

She stepped back a bit, kissed him on both cheeks, then hugged him again and turned and walked down the ramp. A few steps past the doorway she turned, waved, and blew him a kiss. Kellan watched her go, then did something he didn't do very often. He went into an airport lounge, ordered a double scotch neat, and sat at a corner table thinking about what a full life he had lived in recent months. He was in no hurry to get back to the Hill, so he sat in the lounge for a while idly watching television, looking out the window at planes coming and going, and thinking about where he was going to go from here.

Round Two

Kellan Maguire was reelected to a second term without much of a fight. He was not challenged within his own party, and Kellan had buried Preston Fuller deep enough that he was no longer a factor. Two Republican candidates had beaten each other up sufficiently in their primary that Kellan did not have much to worry about. They were not anxious to debate Kellan, remembering as they did how he had handled Fuller; as the incumbent, he clearly had the upper hand. He limited his campaign to a few speeches, and the rest was handled under the guidance of Ray Braxton, his former campaign worker now on his staff. Ray was manager of Kellan's district office in White Plains and had kept his finger on the pulse of Kellan's district. He had proven to be a valuable asset.

At the time of his second election victory, again by a substantial margin, reporters questioned him about his future plans. For example, did he plan to run for the Senate?

"That wouldn't make much sense, now would it?" answered Kellan. The senior senator from New York, Joseph Parma, was in his third term and was about to become Senate majority leader. The other New York Senator, Republican Victor Kershaw, was in his first term, and he and Kellan had hit it off very well. Kellan had no interest whatsoever in challenging either senator.

The reporter persisted. "Then what about governor of New York?"

"I ran for Congress originally because I felt we needed some changes in international trade policy. With the cooperation of Senator Montgomery, Senator Kershaw and a few others, I feel we have been making progress in that area. I have no intention of leaving Congress for the foreseeable future. Of course I'll have to get reelected in two more years, but we'll deal with that when the time comes."

"Good luck, Congressman!" The reporter hurried off to meet his deadline.

Following the election Kellan took a few days off to visit his family in Boston, where he discovered that all was well. As usual, his brother Eddie lectured him on everything that was wrong with government in general and the United States House of Representatives in particular. And as usual,

Eileen told Eddie to zip it. Tom's architectural firm had won a contract to help design yet another new business center in downtown Boston, and Tom was very excited about the prospects. He had made major contributions to the design and would be at the center of the project.

Now that all her children were occupied with school and other teenage pursuits, Mary had become more and more involved with volunteer activities. She was even thinking about volunteering to help with a political campaign for the next governor of Massachusetts. Kellan encouraged her to get involved. "I might even want to run for office someday," she said with a smile.

"Hell, Sis, I'll be your biggest supporter!"

Mary's children had gotten over the thrill of having their uncle in Congress. Angela, home for the weekend from Holy Cross, gave him a quick, "Hi, Uncle Kell!" in passing and went about her business. Ned spent a little more time talking to Kellan, but neither did he linger.

"Good kids," said Kellan, and Mary nodded.

Kellan stopped by the Phillips, Shannon office to say hello to some of his old colleagues. He spent a pleasant evening with Charlie and Cynthia and their family, then made his way back to Washington to finish up some first-term business. As the activity on the Hill ceased for the holiday break, Kellan boarded an Aer Lingus flight to Dublin. He planned to spend a few days in Ireland during the Christmas holiday visiting the Connolly family in Mallow. Fiona had finished her studies and was working at an office of the Bank of Ireland in Dublin. Before she started in at the bank, she had spent a month in the States visiting with her father and his family. Alex had joined her in Massachusetts, and they went hiking in the Adirondacks for a few days, which both had enjoyed. They had become fast friends despite the age difference.

Fiona met her father at Dublin Airport and smiled and hugged him as he came out of the customs area. As a United States Congressman with a diplomatic passport, he had breezed right through. "You're looking lovely," he said to his daughter. She did, and he also noticed that her looks had matured. She was no longer a student, but a working woman, and it showed. Fiona had already rented a car for their trip to Mallow. Kellan followed her to the parking area, and they headed off. As they drove, Kellan was grateful for the opportunity to visit with his daughter. "So," he said, "are you happy at the Bank of Ireland?"

"Oh, it's okay for the time being, but it's not what I want to do permanently. I'm trying to make up my mind about something."

"What's that?"

"Kelly, do you think I would make a good lawyer?"

He glanced at her and smiled. She was looking straight ahead through the windshield and didn't seem to be in a hurry to hear his answer. "Of course you would. Are you seriously thinking about going to law school? I thought you were interested in nursing."

"I am, but you're such a good lawyer, I thought I should at least consider it. Anyway, I'm trying to decide whether to study law here, as you did, or maybe go to law school in the States. Which do you think would be better?"

"Well, that depends on where you intend to practice. From my experience I think studying here and practicing in the United States was challenging but not impossible. I think the other way around might be more difficult; if you studied in the States and then came to practice back here, it might take a little bit longer to adjust. Have you talked to anybody about it?"

"I talked to your friend Sean," she said. "Of course, he's not a lawyer, but he seems like a pretty good person to ask for advice. You always liked him, didn't you?"

"I still do. I was hoping to see him this trip, but it didn't work out. We still keep in touch."

She didn't say anything for a while and seemed to be nervous; she was rubbing her hands together as she continued to stare at the landscape going by. After a while she said, "Maybe I could come over and stay with you for a while. Would that be all right?"

"Of course. You can come and stay with me anytime you'd like. You can stay with me in Washington, or Eddie and Eileen would be tickled the have you stay there for a while. Boston's a pretty good place to be if you want to go to law school. Of course there are some good ones in Washington too—Georgetown, George Washington, Catholic. There's a test in the states called the Law School Admission Test, which you would probably have to sign up for somewhere. That shouldn't be too difficult to arrange."

"They call it the LSAT, right?" Fiona said, and Kellan nodded. "I hear that they're starting to give that at University College in Dublin. I could take it there, I'm sure."

"You're right, now that I think of it. They are starting to give the LSAT everywhere all around the world. I assume your score would be good either here or in the United States."

"Did you have to take it?"

"I'm pretty sure I took an exam called the GRE—the graduate record exam. About the time I would have taken the LSAT I had already been awarded a fellowship to Trinity, so I don't think I took it. That was quite a while ago."

"I just can't make up my mind what I want to do."

"There's no hurry, but you should think about it carefully. Law school can be pretty demanding, and so can nursing, medical school if you decided on that. But I'm sure you would do fine at whatever you choose. You've got your mother's brains."

She smiled at that. "What happens if you start to go to law school and then change your mind?"

Kellan laughed. "That happens quite a bit. Either guys decide they don't really want to be lawyers, or they think it's too hard, and some of them just can't hack it. It wouldn't be too big a deal if you decided to drop out and then picked it up later. Once you start, though, you're probably better off going straight through."

"I also need to talk to Aunt Eileen about nursing or medicine."

"That would be smart."

"I'll think about it all some more. Kelly, I'd really like to go to the States, but I know I'd miss my family."

"It's a lot easier to go back and forth these days—more flights, cheaper fares."

"Did you ever go by boat?"

He laughed. "Your mother and I crossed on the *Queen Elizabeth*. It was sort of our honeymoon. In fact, you were with us."

"I was? How old was I?"

"You weren't born yet. Your mother got pregnant with you before we left Ireland."

"Wow, I guess I never knew that." She thought that over for a while.

"How about boyfriends?" he said. "You've never said very much about your love life." He looked at her to see how she was taking the question. From the look on her face, it didn't seem to bother her.

"I've had a couple of boyfriends," she said casually. "They were very nice, but it never really felt like they were anybody I would want to marry. When I first started in at the University there was a teacher I was crazy about, but he was married. Teachers were off-limits anyway." She turned to him and smiled. "I guess I'm just not the very romantic type, not like Celeste was." Celeste had returned to France and had begged Fiona to come and visit her some time. "It seemed like she had a different boyfriend every week. I think she was sort of, you know, maybe too friendly with them or something. There were times when she would go out with a boy and not come home until the next day."

"Did that bother you?"

"I just didn't want her to get in trouble. She was always getting in trouble, you know, getting her work in late, losing stuff. If it was raining soup, she'd go out with a fork."

Kellan laughed. "I haven't heard that one for a while!" After a few moments he said, "Well, if you decide to go to law school, I'll do everything I can to help you along. I know a few people in the business."

"Lord sakes, Kelly, you could probably get me into Harvard."

"That's a thought," he said, and she laughed. "And Eileen could certainly help with the medical side, if you decide on that."

Kellan had a favorite chair in the Connolly living room. Libby would always bring him a cup of tea and some biscuits as soon as he sat down. They had always been gracious hosts to Kellan, but now that Libby was entertaining a United States Congressman, she went out of her way to make sure he was well taken care of. She loved to fuss over him, and Kellan found it embarrassing, though he had to admit to himself that he really didn't mind.

Patrick Connolly enjoyed very much telling Kellan things that he ought to do to fix everything that was wrong with America. He seemed to think that all Kellan had to do a snap his fingers, and problems would be solved. "You're a smart lad," he would say. "But some of those people are blockheads in your Congress. I mean, we've got our share of fools here in the Dáil Éireann ..." He just shook his head.

"I know what you mean, Patrick. I'm doing my best, but it takes time to change the direction of our government—it's been in business for two hundred years."

"I've met some of Kellan's friends," said Fiona. "They seemed pretty smart to me."

"Ah, sure, Kellan wouldn't be wasting his time with fools. I know that, Lassie."

"Now don't be bothering him, your Lordship," said Libby to Patrick. "He didn't come over here dying to get your opinion on the American political system."

"I know, Mother, I just want him to do what's right."

"Of course he'll do what's right!" said Libby. "He's a good boy."

Kellan smiled at the banter, as he always had.

Brendan and Deirdre joined them shortly after Kellan's arrival, and they exchanged warm hugs and greetings. Deirdre was particularly interested in questioning Kellan about his position in the United States House of Representatives. "You're in session all year round," she said. "That must get tiring."

"It does," said Kellan, "We do get some time off, but when the House is in session, the days can be very long. The people in my district are pretty demanding, and that keeps us all hopping."

"Kelly has a wonderful staff," Fiona said. "They have always been very gracious to me when I visited. His friend Alex has shown me a lot about the Capitol and how everything works over there. She's great. I really like to visit Kelly's office."

"Fiona tells me she's thinking about law school," said Kellan. "I can't say I've got a problem with that."

"I've heard that law school is pretty expensive," said Brendan.

"In the states, yes," said Kellan. "But it's manageable."

"You mean you can manage it, but does a congressman make as much as a partner in a law firm?" Brendan's tone was light, but Kellan picked up a thread of something, envy perhaps.

"Will you listen to yourself, Brendan Connolly!" said Deidra. "Fiona can find her way; she always has, and if Kellan can help her out, well that's a fair thing."

Brendan smiled. "I didn't mean anything by that," he said, though not defensively. "We all know how much Kellan has done for his lovely daughter." He looked at Kellan. "And don't think we don't appreciate it."

"I know you do. And I know you have been wonderful parents for Fiona. I've been fortunate enough to be able to help out along the way, but what I've done is nothing compared to your job of raising her."

Deidra said, "Ah, Kellan, Fiona was a treasure to raise. She and Caitlin were inseparable. The two of them had a wonderful childhood together, and they're still very close, aren't you Fiona?"

"Of course, Mum. We talk on the phone at least once a week. And we get together every so often. Did you know she has a boyfriend?"

"Aye, we've heard that for some time. There's been a parade of them through here."

"Oh hush up, Brendan. Caitlin and Fiona always had lots of friends, and sure they came parading through here, and weren't we lucky that they did! Jesus, Mary and Joseph, you'd complain if the Pope came to visit!"

202

The conversation went on pleasantly, but from time to time Kellan would pick up a little hint that something was not quite right. Eventually it dawned on him that whenever Fiona mentioned the possibility of going to America, possibly for an extended period or even permanently, the tension seemed to rise in the room. Brendan was still friendly with Kellan, but Kellan sensed that perhaps Brendan had the idea that Kellan was about to take their daughter away.

The fact that Fiona was also Kellan's daughter was apparently not part of the equation for Brendan. Whatever was going on, he would be sure to allow Fiona to make her own choices, and he would support them to the best of his ability. He didn't want to hurt Brendan or Deirdre, not to mention Libby and Patrick, but he wanted Fiona to be free to make her own choices. There was a crossroads ahead, he thought, and passage through that area was bound to be full of bumps and bruises. As much as he wanted to spare the feelings of Fiona's Irish family, he wanted very much to be a bigger part of her life.

As he thought more about it later on, he reflected on how often the scenario had been played out in Irish history: sons, daughters, loved ones, friends and relatives, all going to America. There were four million people in Ireland, and over 35 million Americans claimed some degree of Irish ancestry. It was a fact of life of Irish history, but often a painful one. And now it seemed as though Fiona might add to that pain. Naturally she had no intention of hurting anyone, but it was her life to live. The problem was that Kellan realized that his glamorous position as a member of the United States Congress had an appeal to it with which Patrick and Libby, Brendan and Deirdre could not compete. There was so much to draw her there, much less to keep her here. But it was out of his hands.

Back in Washington Kellan made a few changes on his staff. Jean was still Deputy Chief of Staff, and Alex took over the office of Senior Legislative Assistant following Aisha's departure; Aisha had been named Special Assistant to the Chair of the Congressional Black Caucus. Alex had developed good working relationships with the staffs of the committees on which Kellan served, and her legal background served her well as she worked on proposed bills that Kellan and his cosponsors were developing. She also worked with Jordan Montgomery's legislative assistants on cosponsoring legislation. Fran Kuzniak, Kellan's former secretary at Phillips, Shannon, had come to Washington to be his office manager.

Alex also turned out to be a very effective writer, and had published several articles in newspapers and magazines dealing with the proposed modifications to the system of international trade pursued by the United States government. A few weeks into Kellan's second term, she approached him with an idea for a book. "You need to drum up support for what you and Jordan are doing for American trade policy. We could call it something simple like 'trading for the future'," she said. "You would be the author, and I'd help with the writing. We could get Jordan to write the introduction."

"Are you saying I'm not keeping you busy enough?"

"Of course not. I'm working my ass off. But a lot of the work I do could easily be folded into a book. Marlene could give me a hand—she's a good writer." Marlene Worth was one of Alex's legislative assistants.

"What will be the focus of it?" said Kellan. "I mean, what will be gained by writing a book?"

"Look, you and I both know that getting the legislation we're working on through both houses is going to be a challenge. If we get the people stirred up, they could put pressure on their representatives to support it. If the thing gets published by a big New York publisher, as it surely will, you could go on a book tour and spread the gospel. It won't hurt you any in future elections either."

"You might have something there," said Kellan. He paced the office thinking about Alex's idea. Alex waited for a further response. In a few minutes he said, "Okay, why don't you have Marlene draft up an outline with proposed chapters or something like that. We would want to spend some time talking about the economies of our biggest trading partners—we could always go back to Phillips, Shannon for some advice there. Then we would want to look at tariffs, tax incentives for trading agreements, and so on. We might even go back and visit Adam Smith about how countries can best maximize their businesses for international trade."

"You mean, if the Italians make the best shoes in the world, why waste our time competing with them?"

"Not exactly, but something like that. We probably want to spend some time talking about big-ticket items like automobiles, considering ways that we can better compete with the Germans and Japanese by encouraging our automobile manufacturers to become more competitive."

"You know how that will go over on the other side," Alex said. "Kind of like a fart in church."

"Jordan can help with that. He's got some friends on his side of the aisle who understand economics."

"I'll get together with Marlene we'll start putting some stuff down on paper. We don't need to have a deadline on this. I'd say about six months before your next election would be a good time to bring it out."

"What would I do without you, except maybe get more sleep?"

She smiled and gave him the finger as she left the office.

Kellan read in a New York newspaper that George and Lynn Patterson had decided to go their separate ways. It was the sort of news that Kellan generally didn't pay much attention to, but since Lynn was a friend, he found himself reading columnists in the New York Daily News and other papers about the story behind the story. Not surprisingly, Kellan quickly learned that George had found someone else—the trophy wife, they were calling such women these days. The woman in question, who soon appeared in photographs in newspapers and magazines, was perhaps ten years younger than Lynn, very attractive, but in Kellan's judgment, not nearly as enticing looking as Lynn herself. He decided to phone her.

"Yeah," she said in response to Kellan's first query, "the old bastard got an itch somewhere and decided that a teeny-bopper might scratch it for him—get his juices flowing again."

"I thought she was much older than that."

"Listen, Kell, when you're my age, they all look like teeny-boppers."

He knew he was rubbing some raw nerves, but he went on. "Hell, Lynn, you're about the same age as me. I don't feel that old." He laughed, and he heard her chuckling on the other end of the line.

"Yeah, well men generally don't have to deal with this crap. She paused, then went on. "You know, I'm tired of talking about George. I'm tired of thinking about him. I'm tired of him, period."

"I can understand that. I didn't mean to pry."

"Sure you did, you son of a bitch. Oh hell, I didn't mean that."

"Sure you did. Okay, no more talk about teeny-boppers."

"Which reminds me," she said, "speaking of teeny-boppers and romance and all that stuff, how's your love life?"

"Oh, you know, I've got a few women that I see from time to time. Nothing serious, though, and definitely no teeny-boppers. Carmen slaps me around every so often to keep me in line, but I don't find myself being lonely very often. I work pretty hard, and I don't feel too much of an urge to go chasing after women every time I want to relax. Not that I haven't had any offers."

"I'll bet you've had more than your share. But you always were a boy scout," she said. "Anyway, I'm glad you called. I'm going to be in Washington next week and I wondered if we might get together. It seems that now that I'm a free woman, they want me to serve on the Democratic National Committee. That might be fun."

"You'd be perfect for the job," he said. "Are you going to take it?"

"We'll see. Actually I feel like going off and sitting on a beach somewhere for about a year, but I've agreed to meet with them."

"When will you be here?"

"I'm coming down next Wednesday and will be in town all day Thursday and Friday meeting with DNC people. I thought I might stay the weekend if you're free," she said.

"Sure, I'd love to see you." He gave her his private office number and told her to get in touch when she got to town.

A few days later Kellan got a call on his private office phone from Brendan back in Ireland. "Kellan, how are you, my friend?"

"Doing fine, Brendan. What's going on over there?"

"Well, lad, I've got some news that might be good or it might be bad. Kathleen came to see us; it seems Liam has been killed."

"Damn, that's a shame. How did it happen?" Kellan felt blood rush to his head. He sat down quickly and took a deep breath.

"Well, as you know, Liam has been pretty active with the IRA. As a matter of fact, things haven't been going very well between him and Kathleen. I guess he's been involved in some nasty stuff, and the last time she was here, she said she hardly ever saw him anymore. She came back to Dublin because she said she was tired of sitting around in an apartment in Belfast waiting for bad news. As it turns out, whatever happened to him probably occurred up in Derry. There's been a lot of scuffling up there in the last few weeks. Details have been hard to come by, but there's no doubt that he's been killed."

"I've seen some news about all that in the *Irish Times*, which I read every couple of days. How's Kathleen taking it?"

"I've spoken to her a couple of times, and it seems as though she had already resigned herself to the inevitable. She said it was just a matter of time before something like this happened."

"If you talk to her, please give her my condolences. I think about her from time to time, always fondly."

"Kellan, I say this as a friend and brother; I'm going to be frank with you. Ever since Moira died, it has become apparent to us that you and Kathleen were very close friends. Mind you, we never thought there was anything going on that was improper, since she was married, after all. But she loved Moira, and I have no doubt that she loved you as well. I could hear it in her voice every time she mentioned your name, and she always asked for you when she was here."

"I was always very fond of her," Kellan said. "Maybe it was even more than that."

"I don't blame you—by God, I love her too. Anyway, as you know, she never had much of a family. Her father died when she was young, and her mother had all kinds of problems—the juice of the barley, if you know what I mean. Kathleen came down here frequently with Moira, as I'm sure you know. We came to consider her part of the family. And as a matter of fact, we've invited her to come down any time since we got the news about Liam. We're expecting she might show up any day. I'll let you know."

"Be sure to give her my best, Brendan. No, to hell with that, give her my love."

"I will, Brother. And you take care of yourself now. I'll keep in touch."

Kellan was stunned by the news. As he went about his business that day, he could not keep from turning over in his mind the meaning for him of Brendan's news. That night he stayed up late, sitting on his balcony overlooking the Potomac River, sipping on a glass of scotch. He was sorry for Kathleen, and sorry for Liam, even though he had never known him. He could not prevent himself from feeling excited, no matter how much he tried. He told himself that he could not in good conscience be happy about another man's violent death, especially a man who had been close to a woman he truly cared about. But it didn't work. He suddenly saw a door open that had been closed for some time, and he could not suppress the feeling he had that Liam's death might have deep implications for his own future. He found himself thinking over his coming responsibilities in Congress, wondering about a time when he might be able to get away for a few days.

'Patience,' he said to himself. 'Whatever happens will happen in due course. You can't afford to force this thing. You don't even know how she still feels about you.' He mulled that last thought over for a while, but he didn't really believe it. He slept very little that night.

Lynn was waiting for Kellan in the Occidental restaurant of the Willard Hotel. She was already seated at a table in the corner when the maître d' directed him to her place. She stood, took both his hands and kissed him on the cheek. "Long time, no see, stranger." She held her arms out for a hug.

"So," he began once they were seated. "You have had a lot going on in your life."

"Yes, George and I have finally split. It has been in the works for some time—I knew he was getting tired of me, and to tell you the truth, I was a little tired of him quite a while ago. I knew he fooled around, you know, rich men and power and all that—you can't keep the young ones away."

"I hear that a lot around here," he said. "Especially from Carmen."

"He's a dear," said Lynn. "I've known him since he was mayor of White Plains. You were smart as hell to grab him for your Chief of Staff. He probably knows more about Washington than the next ten guys put together."

"I'm lucky to have him." The waiter interrupted them to take orders for drinks and dinner. Lynn ordered a martini, and Kellan opted for sparkling water. "So what have you been up to?"

"Well, I don't really have to do anything for a while. Needless to say I got a nice settlement from George. He knew he was being a bastard, and he was willing to pay to get my forgiveness. I left him enough for lunch money and football tickets." She laughed. "I'm sure he's got stuff stashed away somewhere." She drummed her fingers on the table for a few moments. "And what are you doing? I heard you're not running for the Senate—no surprise—and you're not interested in governor. Ambassador to Ireland, maybe?"

Kellan smiled. "Not much chance of that," he said. "The White House isn't too happy with me these days."

"Oh?"

"They know I'm working with the other side on finance and trade issues, and I don't think they like where that's going. They think I'm too pro-business, don't pay enough attention to the little guy, et cetera, et cetera. But helping business will help the little guy—it's business people who give them their jobs. It's also one way to attack our budget deficits. After all, they pay a lot of taxes. Conversely, higher tariffs may bring in more revenue, but in the long run I think they're counterproductive.

Anyway, I haven't made any friends over there except maybe in the Treasury Department."

"Sounds like you might be in the wrong party," Lynn said.

Kellan laughed. "That's the same thing they've been saying about Jordan Montgomery. Maybe we should just exchange parties and to hell with it. There have always been people who are willing to work with members of the opposition, but it's getting harder and harder to do that. The best men were always the ones who weren't afraid to step across the aisle when it mattered—it's a shame that that's not true anymore. The hard-core people on the ends of both parties consider that political treason. So far it hasn't hurt me in my home district."

"I think it has helped you. New Yorkers aren't stupid, after all. You and Jordan aren't afraid to do what's necessary."

"Yeah, and we're called mavericks, which is fine with me. But the press loves to stir stuff up—conflict is their bread and butter."

"You got that right." She paused for a moment, then said, "Anyway, let's not talk any more politics," she said. "I'm trying to break the habit."

"That's fine with me. I get tired of it too."

"Bite your tongue!" They both laughed.

As they were finishing their meal over coffee, Lynn said, "I've enjoyed talking with you, Kellan. Please come up and have a drink with me before you go."

Back in Lynn's comfortable suite, Kellan took off his suit jacket and relaxed in an overstuffed chair. Lynn took off her jacket, kicked off her shoes and sat in a chair facing Kellan. She had offered him a brandy, which he accepted, and poured herself one. Kellan brought her up to speed on the people from their first campaign who were still with him—Jean, Ray, and Alex, whom she didn't know very well. Lynn nodded politely, but she didn't seem particularly interested. "I hear your friend Alex is doing quite well," she said.

"She figured out the political world on the Hill really fast. She's been a great help to me."

Lynn mulled that over for a few moments. Then she sat up, leaned toward Kellan and smiled. "There's something I've been wondering about for quite a while. How come you never made a pass at me?"

Kellan put down his drink, leaned forward and put his elbows on his knees and folded his hands in front of him. Looking directly at Lynn, he said, "Well for starters, you were married then."

"Christ, Kellan, you knew George fooled around. It wouldn't have bothered me."

"I guess I was kind of naïve. More important, though, was the fact that you were running my campaign, and I had no idea how you might react to something like that. I never gave it any serious thought." He looked at her. "What would you have done if I had ...?"

"I'd probably have said no at first, but you were too much for me to resist." Lynn leaned toward him. "I guess that's not really what I meant to ask," she said. "What I want to know is, would you have been interested in me in different circumstances? I mean, did you ever see me that way?"

"I've never been with you in different circumstances, until now. If you're asking if I found you attractive, the answer is, of course I did." He paused for a moment. "I remember the day we won the election; you were standing on a table talking to the staff. I remember you had on blue slacks and a white blouse. You were happy—we were home free, and I was thinking, maybe we should go get a room and really celebrate."

Lynn blushed and smiled. "If you had suggested that, I'd have gone with you and had your pants off before you closed the door."

"Anyway, we're in different circumstances now," she said. She sat back in the chair and fiddled with the buttons on her blouse.

After a few moments Kellan looked at her and said simply, "Yes."

She stood up and reached for his hand. "Come with me."

He knew instantly where this was going, and as she led him into the bedroom part of the suite, he wondered for a moment whether it might be a mistake to follow her lead. Something in the back of his mind made him hesitant, but common sense told him there was no real danger ahead. Lynn would be discreet; there would not be any aftermath that the press could get their teeth into.

Besides that, she had changed. Perhaps her divorce from George, which had to have been humiliating on one level, had made her less sure of herself, more humble. She was softer now; even her dress and make up had a less commanding tone. Her hair was longer, and she no longer wore a look of authority on her face. Even her eyes, which he had seen bore intently into those around her, seemed to have softened. In all, she seemed much more feminine, more alluring than he had ever seen her before.

"Take off your tie," she said. It was a request, not a command. She unbuttoned her blouse, loosened her skirt, let it fall to the floor and stepped out of it. She started unbuttoning the buttons on his shirt. As he shrugged out of his shirt and let it fall, she tugged his undershirt out of his trousers and put her hands underneath it on his bare skin. As she reached around his back and pulled him close, she lifted up her head and kissed him on the lips. It was a long, slow, burning kiss that got an immediate response from him. She pressed her body against him as he put his arms around her and unfastened her bra.

She moved back, unbuckled his belt, and loosened his trousers. He stepped out of them and tossed them onto a chair. When the ritual of undressing was complete, she took his hand led him to the side of the bed and lay down; he lay down beside her, drew her to him and began exploring her body with his fingers and with his lips. "Oh God," she said as he touched her intimately. "I've been thinking about this forever. Come to me, Lover."

He moved on top of and she guided him inside her body. She was warm and ready, and she moaned with pleasure as he moved. "Take as long as you can," she whispered. "This is heaven." He moved slowly, but his desire grew and he moved faster until he climaxed. She gasped and whispered, "Stay inside me. I want you to stay inside me." She shuddered and pulled him tight against her. "Oh, Lord," she said. He pushed himself up and looked down at her. She was smiling.

"What's the matter?" she said later. They were still in bed but relaxed. "You've drifted off somewhere."

He looked at her and smiled. "I'm still here." He leaned over and kissed her.

She propped her head up on her hand with her elbow on a pillow and stroked his chest with her other hand. "How come you never married again?"

He rolled over on his side so that he was facing her. "Is it important?"

"It might be, depending on where you intend to go from here with your career."

"I'm pretty content where I am."

"Come on," she said, "you've made a real name for yourself in the House. Surely you're not going to be content with that forever?"

"Maybe not," he said. "But as far as I am concerned, the Senate is blocked for me unless either Kershaw or Joe Parma disappears, which I don't see happening anytime soon."

"That leaves you only two options," she said. "You can wait for somebody to pick you for vice president, or you can go for broke." He smiled but didn't answer. "Seriously, I know you're not a saint, but there hasn't been a murmur about you and women for as long as I've known you. It's hard to believe you been celibate ever since your wife died."

He rolled back and put his head on the pillow. "Back at the firm in Boston there was a woman who was a partner when I was still an associate. She was young for a partner but older than I was. Some of the guys in the office were kind of mean to her; they didn't think she was very attractive, and they would joke about how she couldn't have slept her way into a partnership. The problem was, they didn't know her."

"But you did?"

"She had a fantastic mind. We worked together on some cases where she was defending clients who got tangled up legally over some trade issues. We spent a lot of time together, and I was fascinated by the way she thought. To me her physical appearance meant nothing; she wasn't what you would call a looker, but people who thought she was unattractive couldn't see what lay underneath. In fact, she was by no means unattractive, but the better I got to know her, the better she looked. Even though she was senior to me, that didn't really matter."

"How long did it last?"

"Quite a while. Several years, in fact. After I went to New York, I would still go up and see her from time to time."

"You never thought of marriage with her?"

"It might have worked; I think the firm would have accepted it, but we never discussed it seriously. She took her career as a lawyer very seriously, and she might have thought it would jeopardize her position if her relationship with me became known. I guess I sensed that and respected her situation. It was one of the things I really liked about her—that we could be together without any complications. I guess I was in love with her, but not enough to put her in a compromising situation."

"Very thoughtful of you, but that's not the whole story, is it?"

He turned his head toward her and smiled. "No wonder you're so good at what you do. You see right through people, don't you?"

"Goes with the job. Or it used to."

"What about you?" he said. Do you think you'll ever marry again?"

She smiled and kissed him. "Is that a proposal?" He smiled but didn't answer. She lay back on the pillow. "Not any time soon," she said.

They were silent for a few moments. Then she said, "Anyway, tell me what else was going on in your furry little brain."

He thought for a while, then let his true feelings rise to the surface. "I loved my wife, Moira. I'm sorry you never met her."

"You hardly ever spoke of her."

"When I met you, she had been gone a long time; as you know, she died giving birth to my daughter. While we were still in Ireland, I spent a lot of time with her and her apartment mate in Dublin. Her friend was a classic Irish beauty, red hair, green eyes, though she had some rough edges. After Moira died, I realized that I had been really attracted to her friend also."

"So why didn't you do anything about it?"

"She had a boyfriend, or at least a guy she was very close to. I never met him, but from the way she talked about him, I knew he was one of those passionate Irish revolutionary types. He was in the IRA and spent most of his time in Northern Ireland. Moira's friend—her name is Kathleen—believed in many of the same things he was involved in, though she never became directly involved herself. Eventually they got married, but it was almost, I don't know, maybe a political marriage."

"But she was in love with you?"

"She was. We were together enough that I knew she had strong feelings for me, because I had them and she knew it. And she never tried to put me off."

"Are you still in touch with her?"

"Sort of. She was very close to Moira's family, and I think they sensed that Kathleen and I were attracted to each other—after Moira had been gone for a while. We kept in touch through them."

"So you never followed up on your feelings because she was married. That's very noble of you."

"I'm not sure noble is the right word." He rolled over on his side and looked at her again. "It's kind of funny that we're talking about this right now. I just found out a couple of days ago that her husband was killed by the British, apparently in Londonderry."

"Jesus Christ."

"I'm not sure what to do now."

"But you still love her?" He nodded. The expression that crossed her face told him more than he wanted to know. "I knew you were somewhere else, even when we were making love a few minutes ago."

"Lynn, I wasn't thinking of her then. Believe me, I was with you all the way."

"I always knew you better than you know yourself," she said. "But that's okay. I love you, but I'm not in love with you. I know you know what I mean."

He leaned back and rested his head on the pillow. "Yeah, I know what you mean."

Lynn rolled over and pressed her body against him and stroked his chest. "You're a good man," she said.

The next morning Lynn ordered breakfast to be sent up to the room for the two of them. There was some tension in the air between them, but Kellan realized that enough had been said already, and there was no point in probing any deeper. Lynn seemed relaxed and content. As she sipped her coffee, she held the cup in both hands in front of her lips with her elbows on the table. She peered over the top of her cup with a quirky smile. "Did you see that guy from the Washington Star camped in lobby as we were getting on the elevator last night?"

"No."

"I wonder if he'll be down there when you leave."

"It never ends, does it?"

"Not as long as Washington is Washington. That stuff really bothers you doesn't it?"

"I don't have anything to hide— why should I worry about it?"

Lynn chuckled. "Nothing except a whole goddam family and a girlfriend in Ireland that nobody knows about."

"I'll deal with that when I have to."

"Well, my friend, if you have plans for anything bigger than the United States House of Representatives, that might come sooner than you think." Kellan took a sip of coffee and looked at her but didn't answer. "You're thinking about running for president, aren't you?"

He smiled, put his coffee cup down and stirred it idly with a spoon. "I won't deny it has crossed my mind."

"When you get ready, you have my number."

"I'll keep it in a safe place."

A few minutes later, as he was leaving, Lynn put her arms around him, hugged him, and kissed him again on the lips. "I really loved last night," she said. "Even if ... "

He cut her off. "Lynn, I didn't mean... "

She put her hand on his lips. "Shush. Just get out of here before you get caught by the sex police."

He kissed her again and reached for the door. He didn't bother to look and see if a reporter was camped in the lobby.

Author, Author

The review, written by Jeffrey Sachs, a professor of economics at New York University and a published author, was on the front page of the Sunday Book Review of the New York Times. It began:

Congressman Kellan Maguire has written a book that will disturb his political allies, thrill his opponents and be largely ignored by much of the population. It should not be ignored. In fact, it should be required reading for everyone from the White House to our college population. It is the most sensible argument about how to improve our economic and trade policy to be made since the time of Adam Smith. Young people especially should be exposed to Congressman Maguire's ideas, for their futures depend on a successful implementation of the kinds of ideas detailed in this compelling work. Written with his legislative assistant Alexandra Crowley, Maguire's book includes a forward by Senator Jordan Montgomery.

Two weeks later Kellan and Alex's book appeared on the non-fiction best seller list of the Washington Post, where it remained for several weeks. Though it did not make many other best seller lists, it was discussed on radio and television political talk shows. The reviews that appeared in the Atlantic, Time, Newsweek, the New York Review of Books and several less prestigious forums were generally positive. The National Review complained that the book had not been written by a Republican and suggested that party leaders might want to consider urging Congressman Maguire to jump ship and join the Grand Old Party. The Nation opinioned that it was all about the rich getting richer while the poor remained in the economic doldrums. One television host remarked on the air to Kellan, "Well, Congressman, you're getting beaten up from both the right and left, so you must be doing something right"—an idea attributed to Harry Truman, among others. Kellan and Alex appeared together on the new C-SPAN network to discuss the book.

Sales were respectable enough that the publisher ordered a second printing, despite a generous first run. Kellan made a limited number of public appearances and autographed hundreds of copies in the weeks following publication. Pundits began to speculate about a possible run for the White House by the New York Congressman, even though he was only in his third term.

Not long after the book was published Kellan got a note from a friend in London he had met during his years of traveling there for Phillips, Shannon. Jeffrey Parsons had left the world of business to take a position at the London School of Economics. He was quite interested in Kellan's ideas about international trade. He thought he might like to find a venue to comment on the implications of Kellan's ideas for the British economy. Kellan responded immediately that his agent was in negotiations with a British publisher to come out with a European edition. Kellan's agent suggested that Mr. Parsons might want to write a forward for the British edition, or perhaps even contribute a chapter.

Jeffrey Parsons responded quickly to Kellan, thanked him for the information, and welcomed the opportunity to contribute. He suggested that Kellan might find time to come to London to discuss the possibilities. Kellan called Jeffrey, then his agent, and they quickly agreed on a time for a meeting in London. Next he sent for Alex.

She flopped down on the couch in his office and said, "What's up?"

"How would you like to go to London? You know we're doing a British edition, and I've set up a meeting in to discuss it with the publisher. You certainly ought to go along—it's as much your book as mine."

"I'd love to go. I've only been to London once, that time when I went on a trip with you, but it was all business. I have always wanted to go again, maybe do some sightseeing. Of course this will be business too, but not quite as intense as it was back then."

"Great. I'll get Fran to set it up, and we'll arrange a little time for sightseeing. I might want to do a little personal business while I'm there as well."

"Something Irish, I presume?" she said, raising her eyebrows and smiling.

"Something like that," he said. "I'm not sure that'll work out, but we'll see."

As soon as Fran Kuzniak, who handled travel arrangements for Kellan, made reservations, he wrote to Kathleen. He also called his agent and asked him about the publishing house where Kathleen was working. His agent told him that the house was one of Ireland's better-known publishers, and that they regularly brought out works on political subjects. Kellan suggested the possibility of an Irish edition, but his agent said it would be better to concentrate on the British version for the time being.

Kathleen was living in Blackrock just south of Dublin, where she was working as an editor at a publishing house. He expressed his condolences over Liam's death and asked if she could meet him in London for a few days. He mentioned the book idea despite what his agent had said, but mostly he wanted to see her "just for old times' sake."

About two weeks later he got a letter from Kathleen.

'Dear Kellan,' it began. 'Thank you for your kind words on Liam's death. As sad as it was, it was quite predictable. His political activity had become quite intense, and he was wanted by the RUC—the Royal Ulster Constabulary, in case you've forgotten. When they found out he was in Derry, they went after him and some others, and he was killed in a gunfight. That's all I can tell you. We will probably never know whether he was betrayed by one of his own, or whether the RUC found out by other means. In the end, it doesn't really matter.

'Actually I had seen very little of him in the months before he died. I probably never should have married him in the first place, but I felt that he was a lonely man doing a nasty job, and I thought I might make his life a little happier. I guess I loved him, at least for a while. But he became so preoccupied with what he was doing that I became little but an afterthought in his life.

'I would love to see you again, but I need to think it over and clear it with my boss. Your suggestion about an Irish edition might work. I will keep in touch, however, and perhaps I can manage it. I have the dates, so don't worry about arrangements. I can make my own.' She signed it 'Much love, Kathleen.' She added a PS: 'Hardly a day goes by that I don't think of you.'

He decided to push his luck. He purchased a round trip ticket from Dublin to London for dates that would overlap his. He didn't want to seem condescending, but he didn't want her to forgo the trip because she might not be able to afford it; he had no idea whatsoever of her financial situation. In the letter that included the ticket he told her where he would be staying and said that he had reserved a room for her. He sent the ticket off to Kathleen's address in Blackrock.

Kellan invited Alex to accompany him to lunch away from the Hill. He told her he had a personal matter he wanted to discuss with her and didn't want to do it in the Rayburn Building. He hailed a taxi and gave the driver the name of a small, quiet restaurant on Wisconsin Avenue in Georgetown. When they were seated, he said to Alex, "I need to talk to you about our trip to London."

217

She looked at him with a curious smile. "What did you have in mind? Personal business?"

"You know about Kathleen." It was not a question.

"Sure. I mean, you don't talk about her very much, but I gather that she means a great deal to you. Maybe you could fill me in if she's somehow involved in our trip to London. I guess that means you're going to take a couple of days and go visit her." She seemed pleased by the idea.

"Nope," he said. "I've invited her to join us in London. I sent her an airline ticket, but I'm not sure she'll use it. In any case I wanted to let you know and to see if you have any thoughts on the matter."

"Gee, Kellan, I thought this was going to be a getaway for just you and me." She smiled; she enjoyed teasing him about their relationship, which some people on the Hill had seen as something other than what it really was. Alex didn't advertise the fact that she was gay, nor did she hide it. But clearly there were people on the Hill who would believe anything, whether or not they knew she was gay.

Kellan laughed. "Oh, I was thinking maybe you and I could take off for Bermuda. The diving's pretty good there, I hear."

"Any time, Cowboy."

"Seriously, she is important to me—you know that. Her husband was killed a while back—that's a long story that I won't go into. But she and I go way back; she was my wife's best friend."

"I sort of gathered that." She looked at Kellan for a few moments. "From the look on your face, and the fact that you dragged me off to Georgetown, I'm guessing this is a serious business. Are you in love with her, or should I say still in love with her?"

"I haven't seen too much of her lately; in fact, I saw her only rarely while she was married. I'm not sure what kind of a marriage it was. I wouldn't say it was a marriage of convenience, but I think it had something to do with her loyalty to the man she married. As I said, that's a long story."

"You still didn't say whether you are in love with her."

"I know. She and I were very close a long time ago, maybe closer than we should have been, given that she was Moira's best friend. You can make whatever you want of that, but I know that I loved her, and I still do. I'm just saying that it's been a long time, and feelings are hard to judge."

"You know, a whole lot of people wonder why you aren't married. People ask me about it every so often, almost always women. Single women, mostly, no surprise. Look, you are obviously the most eligible bachelor on the Hill, with the possible exception of that senator from Wyoming. And there are plenty of women on the prowl on the Hill, and many of them don't give a damn whether the guy is married or not. When they start poking a little bit too deep about you, I tell them to bug off. Some of them think you and I have something going, and so far as I'm concerned, they can go ahead and think that. You know I love you, Kellan, as a friend, and I think you're pretty fond of me. So what do we care what people think?"

"Of course I love you, Alex. I've told you that dozens of times. You know how much I respect you and value your friendship, not to mention your professional skills. Yes, technically you work for me, but so what? You have always been a personal friend more than an employee. And I want you to understand that this is something very important that I need to talk about with someone I trust.

"I've confided in very few people about this, and for now I'd like to leave Carmen out of it. He wouldn't cause any problems or anything like that, but he doesn't need to be concerned about my private life and whatever may happen with Kathleen."

"What do you want to happen with Kathleen?"

"It's kind of delicate, I think. But if she would be willing to marry me, that's what I'd want."

"Well, go for it, dammit! Why shouldn't you?" She paused for a moment. "I've known you a long time now, and you've always been pleasant to be around, kind and thoughtful to everyone you deal with. But I've never been sure that you're really happy. So you should ask her to marry you."

"There really isn't any reason why I shouldn't, except that if I'm really honest with myself, I'm not sure what I'd feel like if she refused."

"Yeah, I understand that," said Alex. "If that's all there is to it, then take a chance." She smiled and said, "You might as well be miserable as the way you are. But I'm guessing there may be something else."

"This might matter, and it might not, but her husband was in the IRA for years and was killed in Londonderry by the British. I'm absolutely sure she never belonged to the IRA nor took part in that stuff. She abhorred violence just as much as she hated what the British had done in Ireland for generations. I don't know where she stands now on all that, and that's partly why I asked her to come to London."

"Jesus Christ, Kellan, I hadn't really put all this together before. That could be a real can of worms for you. Look, I know you're thinking big about your future. You've never come out and said it, but you know people are talking about you as a possibility down the road for the White House. You could have squashed that talk if you wanted to, but you just kind of ignore it. That's cool, that's smart. You haven't slammed any doors, but you sure haven't opened them. But if you do decide to go that way, a possible IRA connection could jump up and bite you in the ass."

"I know. But I know Kathleen, and I know it doesn't have to be an either-or situation. There is nothing in her background that could compromise my position. I'm certain of that, even though I haven't been in close touch with her recently. Hell, if she had been into that stuff, she'd have been up in Derry with him. In fact, she was back in Dublin when he died, even though they lived in Belfast."

"Yeah, but just think what the press could do with that. They'd have a freaking field day. How do you think Kathleen would handle that?"

"I can answer that. She'd tell them to fuck off."

Alex laughed. "Man, that would be really fun to watch. I'd love to see her going on CNN and blowing up the set."

Kellan laughed and shook his head. "Look, I want you to meet her in London. I want you to kind of poke around a little bit, you know, maybe tease her little bit. Get to know her."

"So I'm to be the examination committee: 'Your mission, should you accept it, is to determine whether Kathleen is suitable material to be the first lady.' Is that about it?"

He laughed again. "Yeah, that's about right."

"I hope you choke on your shrimp salad," she said, laughing. Then, in a more serious voice she said, "The fact is, I'm dying to meet her. If she's kept you preoccupied for what? Over twenty years? She must be one hell of a woman."

"She is."

Kellan was waiting when Kathleen came through the passenger gate at Heathrow Airport. She didn't see him at first, paused and set down her bag. He noticed her hair first—it was still long and looked a bit darker, but still reddish. As she turned and saw him, she smiled as he walked toward her. She was still beautiful, but her face showed signs of strain—she looked tired. He held out his arms and she embraced him. "God, I hate flying," she said. Then she laughed. "Just what you wanted to hear, right?"

She stayed in his embrace for several moments. "I'm glad you're here," was all he could manage to say.

"So am I." She stepped back a bit, then hugged him again. "God, I've missed seeing you."

"Have you been in London before?" he said in the taxi on the way to the hotel.

"Once," she said. "A long time ago. I was also in Liverpool a couple of times and have been to Scotland. But I haven't traveled much."

"I'm glad you came."

She reached out and squeezed his hand. "Yes."

There was so much to say, but it would take time. All he dared wish for was that there would be no missteps, no rushing, and no forcing issues. He wanted to leave London with the gap that had existed between them since Moira's death closed. Although years apart, the loss of loved ones had touched them both. As if reading his mind, she said softly, "I still miss Moira. And I'm sure you do too."

They said very little during the rest of the ride, but for Kellan it was a comfortable silence. She was sitting next to him; that was all that mattered. They had a little over three days before them—it seemed like a lot, but he knew it would pass too quickly, especially since he would be in meetings part of the time.

He accompanied her to her room and placed her bag on a stand at the foot of the bed. She took off her coat and put her arms around him. "This feels so good." He held her tight and kissed her hair. She backed away and smiled.

"Maybe you'd like to rest a bit."

"Just let me freshen up from the trip. Shall we meet in the lobby? Say, fifteen minutes?"

"Take your time," he said. He smiled at her. "But don't be too long."

Kathleen smiled back, and for the first time since she had walked out of the gate, she started to look relaxed.

She got out of the elevator wearing black slacks and a dark green cardigan sweater with a white blouse underneath. She had touched up her makeup and brushed her hair and she looked fresher and even more relaxed than fifteen minutes earlier. He stood up, walked to meet her and said, "Why don't we have a drink and just chat for a while?"

"Perfect," she said.

Kellan ordered scotch and soda, and Kathleen ordered Jameson on the rocks with water on the side. "Here's to us," he said, reaching his glass toward her.

She tipped his glass with hers and said, "Sláinte." Then she smiled and added, "Or should I say, kiss me, I'm Irish."

He laughed. "I never learned much Irish; I didn't hear it very often in Dublin, and it's pretty difficult."

"They're beginning to resurrect it by teaching Irish in school. It's spoken much more in the western counties."

"Very few Americans know that many of the Irish who came over in the 1800s couldn't speak English."

"I know. And under the British it was a crime to speak Irish in Ireland." She took a deep breath and exhaled. "Let's don't get into history; I've seen enough of that lately."

"I know. I'm really sorry for everything you had to go through. I just wish I could've seen more of you."

"It's just as well you didn't. I wasn't very happy, and I was angry at a lot of things. I was even angry at you from time to time." He cocked his head a bit and looked puzzled. "I was mad at you for marrying Moira, though I had no right. I was jealous of her and her happiness. I was jealous of her going off to America and leaving this Irish mess behind. All I had to treasure was that one time that we promised we would forget. But I could never do that."

"Neither could I. I was never angry with you, but I know what you mean. I was angry with myself, angry that I didn't meet you before I met Moira. Of course, since you were hardly ever in the library, that never would've happened. Please understand, I loved Moira, and I was never sorry I married her."

She reached across the table and took his hand. "Kellan, whatever you and I have before us, looking back won't make it any easier. We both loved Moira, and she's gone, God rest her soul." She squeezed his hand. "This may sound strange, but I think if it turns out right between you and me, Moira's hand will be in it. And wherever she may be, I'm sure she'll be happy for us."

Kellan squeezed his eyes shut against the tears that he felt forming. All he could think of was, there is a future for us after all. "I'm sure she will be," he said. "And I don't think we will ever need to feel ashamed or embarrassed by thinking of her, or speaking of her. We have said our Hail Marys and Our Fathers."

"Yes," she said. "I'm not very religious, but I have prayed for Moira's peace. And a bunch of other stuff that you will probably never know about."

"I don't go to confession or communion very often, but I think that what's in our hearts is more important than what we do."

Neither of them said anything for a few moments. It was a good silence, a settling silence. To Kellan the room seemed warmer, friendlier, and he looked at Kathleen and thought she had never been more beautiful. After a while he said, "Shall we get some dinner?"

"Something light," she said. "Let's not go anywhere fancy."

"We could get room service," he said. A few moments later they were in the elevator.

Kathleen kicked off her shoes and sat down on a large bed in Kellan's room. Kellan took off his jacket and sat down next to her. Then he thought better of it and stood up. "Would you like me to order something?"

She stood up and said, "I'm not really very hungry right now." She put her arms around him and leaned her head on his chest. "Are you scared?" she said.

He chuckled. "That's one emotion I'm feeling, but it's not the only one."

"I know," she said. She stepped back, looked at him and smiled. "Let's just lie down for a while, I just want to hold you and be near you; it's been such a long time, and I wanted to be with you so much."

He kicked off his shoes and they lay down side-by-side on the bed facing each other. He reached out and stroked her hair and ran his fingers over her cheeks and her lips. She caught his finger gently in her teeth, then kissed his hand. She sat up and pulled off her sweater and tossed it onto a chair. And she reached out and touched his face just as he had touched hers. He took her hand and kissed her palm, and moved her hand away and leaned over and kissed her on the lips, very softly, very gently. She inched closer to him until he could feel her body touching his. He kissed her eyes and then moved his lips slowly across her cheeks and back to her mouth. She parted her lips, put her arm around his back and pulled herself tight against him.

They let the fire build slowly, not wanting to let it burn too brightly before they were ready. They kissed hungrily for a long time and then he started to unbutton her blouse. At the same time she began unbuttoning his shirt. They both sat up, and she took off her blouse and she took off his shirt and undershirt. He reached around her back and unfastened her bra and tossed it away. They kissed again with more intensity, exploring each other with their tongues. He ran his hands up and down her back and moved to caress her breast. In a few moments she said softly, "Let's finish getting undressed."

He stood and took off his trousers and sat on the bed. He took her hand and pulled her in front of him. He unfastened her skirt and she stepped out of it. He put his hands inside her panties and slid them down over her thighs. He pulled her close and kissed her breasts, her stomach, and lower. Then he leaned back onto the bed and pulled her down beside him.

They held each other tightly, nothing between them now, and Kellan moved his hands down Kathleen's back to her buttocks and pulled her body tight up against him. She moved against him, inflaming him further and then she slowly rolled onto her back and pulled him up on top of her. He entered her slowly, teasingly, and she rose to meet him and they were locked together. As he moved within her she dug her fingers into his back kissed him hungrily, bit the tip of his ear, kissed him again and whispered, "Yes, my love—come with me, my love."

"I'll always be with you," he said, and they exploded. He stayed above her, resting on his elbows.

"Put all your weight on me," she said. "I want to feel all of you."

"I'm too heavy for you."

"You'll never be too heavy for me." He relaxed his arms and let his full weight press into her. She sighed with pleasure and held him tight.

He started moving inside her again, his excitement growing as before, and this time their passion grew more slowly but lasted longer, blessedly longer, until they both arrived back in that sacred place they had longed for. "I've always loved you," she said. "Even when I wasn't allowed to, I loved you."

"I have always loved you," he said. "Right or wrong."

"It doesn't matter now."

They lay beside each other for a long time, not saying much, stroking each other's bodies, smiling, laughing softly, and kissing over and over as they talked.

They had not turned any lights on, and it grew dark in the room. Kellan turned on a bedside lamp and said, "Are you hungry yet?"

"What do you think?" she said with a sly smile.

"I mean for food."

"Well, I guess you and I will have to do something to keep up our energy, right?"

He got a menu from the writing table and sat back down with her. "What do you think?"

"I think we had better put some clothes on before we order," she said. "We don't want to give the gent who brings the food too much of a thrill. Might be cheaper than a tip, though," she said with a laugh.

After they had eaten he said, "Why don't we get all the stuff out of your room, and you just stay in here?"

"Should I check out?"

"No, let's not do that. Just in case anybody gets nosy."

"Oh that's right, Mister Congressman. I'm sure Fleet Street has people parked out in the hall right now."

"I wouldn't be surprised," he said. "But there is someone here I want you to meet. She knows about us, but she wants to meet you, too."

"She?" She raised her voice a little bit in a mock accusing tone.

"She's an old friend, and my Chief Legislative Assistant. We're very good friends, but you have nothing to be jealous of, I promise you. I have a feeling you'll really like her."

"I'll try to keep an open mind," she said with just a touch of sarcasm. He just smiled. He was looking forward to seeing Kathleen and Alex together—two women he loved.

Girl Friends

Kellan met Alex in the lobby; Kathleen had said she would join them shortly. "So now I get to meet the mystery lady, huh?" said Alex.

"Here she is now."

Kathleen stepped out of the elevator, started walking toward them and smiled. Alex said, "Wow!"

Kellan had rarely seen Alex flustered, but when Kathleen walked up to her, put out her hand and said, "You must be Alex. I've heard a lot about you, all of it good." Alex actually blushed. She didn't do that often.

"I'm glad to meet you too, at long last."

"Let's go get some breakfast," said Kellan. He wasn't quite sure what was going to happen once they sat down, but whatever had happened during the first moments when Kathleen and Alex met suggested that it was going to be more than interesting. He was not disappointed.

Kathleen opened the conversation once they had ordered coffee and something to eat. "So, tell me what you do for Kellan," she said, without a trace of anything resembling jealousy.

"Well, as you probably know, I'm his Legislative Assistant. That means I oversee the drafting of legislation we put forth. I'm also in charge of reviewing legislation that comes to us from other members, and I spend a lot of time with the staff members of the committees Kellan serves on."

"You were also a lawyer in his firm, if I'm not mistaken."

"Right. We've known each other about ten years, and we've worked together for most of that time. When Kellan got elected to Congress I twisted his arm to hire me."

"Smartest thing I ever did," said Kellan.

"And what about this book project? I've heard a lot about it." She turned to Kellan. "Did you know that Sean Levinson reviewed it in the *Irish Times*? The faculty at Trinity have been talking it up, and I've noticed it in the window of a couple of bookstores in Dublin."

"Yes, I sent him a copy, several copies, actually. I asked him to give them to some of the people at Trinity who might remember me."

"You know he's also written a book," said Kathleen. "In fact, the publisher I work for, Mercier Press, brought it out before I went to work there. I actually got to meet him and asked if he knew you. Turns out he was your advisor. Now he's head of the Economics Department. Small world, huh?"

"Getting smaller by the minute," said Alex, and they all laughed.

"Have you read it?" asked Alex of Kathleen.

"I specialize in literature," said Kathleen pleasantly. "Economics is the moon to me. But I enjoyed seeing your photos on the cover flap. You're prettier than your picture," she said to Alex.

"Well thank you," said Alex. "You're not so bad looking yourself."

Kellan started laughing. "What's going on here?" he said.

Alex leaned over and whacked him on the arm. "Don't worry, boss, I'm not going to hit on her."

Now Kathleen laughed. "Hmmm," she said, "that might be interesting."

"Jesus Christ, what have I done?" said Kellan.

Kathleen reached over and squeezed his hand. "Don't worry, lover boy. I just said interesting."

Kellan was well aware that Alex was no stranger to the world of literature, and she and Kathleen soon got into comparing notes on books and authors. Eventually the conversation turned to politics, and it quickly became apparent that Alex and Kathleen would have no conflicts in that area.

"Kellan has got me interested in Irish history," Alex said. "He even got me reading James Joyce." She turned serious. "He's told me some of your story," she said. "I'm very sorry about the loss of your husband. This religious fighting makes no sense to me."

"It's only religious on the surface," said Kathleen. "And thank you for your sympathy. As Kellan may have told you, my husband Liam had friends and relatives killed by the British. When I was in Belfast, and I spent quite a bit of time there while Liam and I were married, a large part of the population really didn't give a damn whether you were Catholic or Protestant. But they cared like hell whether you were a Unionist or a Nationalist, or worse yet, a Republican."

"I'm not sure I understand what all those terms mean."

"The Unionists are those who want to see Northern Ireland remain part of the British Empire. Sometimes they're called Loyalists. Nationalists are those who want to see Northern Ireland fully independent; Republicans are those who want to see all of Ireland united as a free republic. The whole thing is more political and cultural than religious. I was in a pub in

Belfast one day and a journalist who didn't know his ass from Sunday asked some of the people how they could tell the difference between Catholics and Protestants. One guy looked at him and said of the Catholics, 'Their eyes are closer together.'"

"Jesus. And this has been going on for a long time."

"Every summer the Unionists march through Belfast celebrating the Battle of the Boyne. That was when William of Orange—he was the William of William and Mary to you Yanks—defeated the Catholic supporters of King James II. The whole thing had more to do with King James and the English Crown than it did with Ireland, but nobody remembers that anymore."

"So that's why they call them Orangemen," said Alex. "I was wondering where that came from."

"I congratulate you on your knowledge," said Kathleen. "Most Americans probably don't know an Orangeman from a catfish."

"If it weren't for Kellan, I wouldn't know anything about Irish history. I've never met anyone who knows more about Ireland than he does."

"Well, after all, I did study in Dublin for four years," said Kellan. "I picked up a lot of history along the way."

"Moira always told me that you lived in the library for four years," said Kathleen.

Kellan turned to Alex. "That's where I met her," he said. "She was head of the reference section."

The lively getting-acquainted talk continued until Kellan said, "Alex and I have a meeting to go to. Why don't we meet back here about noon?" He looked at Kathleen. "I'm sure you'll find something to keep you busy, he said with a smile.

"I might just take a nap" she said. "I didn't get much sleep last night." She smiled at Kellan.

"I'm going to pretend I didn't hear that," said Alex, grinning. She held out her hand to Kathleen. "It was wonderful to meet you," she said.

Instead of taking her hand, Kathleen hugged her. "I'm sure I'll see a lot more of you, and I look forward to it. Kellan has told me a lot about you." She started for the elevator, turned back and waved to them, and got into the car.

Kellan and Alex left the hotel and walked toward the meeting place. "That went well," he said. "I was pretty sure you two would get along, but you never know."

Alex hooked her arm in his. "I'm so glad I got to meet her. Believe me, I can understand why you love her. I can imagine how difficult it must've been for you to keep your feelings under wraps for so long. I admire you for that."

"It took a lot of practice," he said.

By the end of the day Kellan and his agent had reached an accommodation with the British publishers. They would bring out a British edition with a long forward written by Jeffrey Parsons. He would receive a share of the royalties earned by the British edition. Thinking of Kathleen's publishing house, Kellan inquired about the possibility of a separate Irish edition. Unsurprisingly, the British rejected that proposal and quickly turned the conversation elsewhere. Kellan's agent simply shrugged his shoulders; they had agreed in advance that an Irish edition probably was not going to happen. Alex was not too happy about it either, but she recognized the realities involved.

Later she said to Kellan, "I'm beginning to understand this British-Irish thing a whole lot better. When we were taking a break I went down to the newsstand and asked for a copy of the *Irish Times*—just thought I'd check it out. Some guy standing next to me looked at me and said, 'Oh it's you lot again.' I guess he didn't pick up my American accent."

"Kathleen told me that from time to time Irish people are still called white niggers to their face."

"It makes you want to join the IRA," Alex said. "Jesus Christ, where does it all end?"

That evening Kellan, Kathleen and Alex dined at a fine British restaurant. Kellan noticed that Alex paid close attention when Kathleen was ordering, apparently trying to detect any subtle response from the waiter on hearing Kathleen's Irish brogue. He concluded that two American accents and a brogue didn't require a response; the staff at this elegant dining venue were probably too well-trained.

"How do you feel about being here in England?" asked Alex.

"I wasn't sure how I would feel," said Kathleen. "I've been out walking around a little bit, and when I speak, I know there's going to be a reaction. I didn't expect to be assaulted or attacked, but it's clear that there's a lot of tension here. Things are not very good right now between the British and the IRA up north. I have no idea how many have been killed, but it must be in the many hundreds."

"It's hard to understand," said Alex. "I know that during the Saint Patrick's Day parades in New York, there was always some tension, always a feeling that there was some kind of an agenda underneath it all. I know many Irish Americans sympathize with the Irish cause, but it's complicated."

"I'm not sorry I'm here," said Kathleen. "But I must admit, I do feel a bit like a fish out of water. I have friends who worked in London, and they've told me that they simply need to remind themselves, turn the other cheek, so to speak, when somebody makes a comment."

"That's hard to do," said Alex.

"Yes. And it's one thing that my friend Liam never could do, he never could turn the other cheek. And that's why he's dead, killed by the Royal Ulster Constabulary. The bastards."

Any misgivings Kellan might have had about how Kathleen and Alex might get along had long since disappeared. They were already making plans about what they would do when Kathleen came to Washington, as Alex assumed she would be doing in the not-too-distant future. The conversation was light and accompanied by an abundance of laughter once they stopped talking about "the Troubles." Each woman had a finely honed sense of humor, and Kellan simply sat back and enjoyed the banter for much of the evening.

Back at the hotel, Kellan and Kathleen said good night to Alex at the door of her room and retired to their own space. They stretched out on the bed still clothed and talked about things that might be possible in the future. "Alex sure is looking forward to your coming to Washington," he said. "I wish you could come back with us right now."

"I know," she said and kissed him. "The problem is that with what I brought on this trip, I'd run out of clothes in about two days."

"Who said you need clothes?"

She swatted him on the arm. "Don't think I wouldn't like to. But I promise, as soon as I can schedule a vacation, I'll come and see you."

"Didn't you have to take vacation to come over here?"

"My boss knows about your book. I convinced him that this was a business trip. I'll simply tell him that as hard as I tried, your British publisher wouldn't hear of it."

"Well, that's true. I could have brought you into the meetings, but I knew there would be no point. And most of it was just us fussing over rights and stuff like that. You'd have been bored to tears."

"I'm sure you're right, I didn't even want to think about work. And I have to go back tomorrow. God, I wish I didn't."

He pulled her close and kissed her. "It won't be too long." After a few moments Kellan said, "Fiona wrote me that she sees you from time to time. I'm happy about that."

"Yes, whenever I'm in Dublin I make a point of stopping by her bank. If she's free, sometimes we visit a pub for a pint or a bite. She calls me Aunt Kathleen."

"Well, you were like a sister to Moira. We'll have to tell her about us—I think she'll be pleased. She's very fond of you."

"She already knows, I'm sure," said Kathleen. "When I talk about you, I can see it in her face. I love her to death. It was fun watching her and Caitlin grow up. I know she misses you."

"I know, and I miss her. That's the one thing I've always had regrets about, even though I know it was the best thing for her to leave her with Brendan and Deirdre." Then he added, "Speaking of telling Fiona about us, there is something else I need to ask you."

"I know. I know what you're going to ask, and the answer is, I want to be married to you someday. There's still some unsettled business with Liam's death, and I need to sort out my personal affairs with work."

"That shouldn't take too long, should it?"

Kathleen sat up and looked at him. "Kellan, I'm not Moira." He started to speak, but she put her fingers on his lips. "Please hear me out, it's not what you think. All I mean is I'm not a twenty-five-year-old who can pull up roots and go off to America with scarcely a second thought. Leaving Ireland is going to be very different for me than it was for her. Please understand that I want to be married to you, and I hope we can spend the rest of our lives together."

"That's all I want," he said.

"Don't take this the wrong way, but it's always the woman who has to pack up and move. Suppose I told you that I would only marry you if you would come to Ireland to live. I mean, forget about the fact that you're in Congress. I know you have a political career, and I'm excited to get involved in it. But if you just had a regular job, say that you were still in your law firm. Even if you could get a position with a good Irish firm, how would you feel about pulling up roots and coming over here?"

He sat up and leaned back against the headboard. "Well, I have a lot of family, and that matters. I also have friends, people like Alex, and a senator named Jordan Montgomery, whom you'll get to meet when you come over. I've got some friends in my firm that I still like to see now and then. I understand that, and I know you have connections here. It's just …"

231

"I know what you're going to say, I don't have any family except the Connollys. That's true, but I do have friends and connections. My connection with Ireland goes way down deep into my soul; it's part of the reason why I married Liam. It's partly because I still feel that there's a lot of unfinished business here in Ireland, and although I've done little to contribute to it, I still believe in the struggle. Part of me feels that if I left, I'd be turning my back on Irish suffering. Oh shit, I know I haven't really suffered, except for Liam. And I pretty much accepted that even before we got married. I'm surprised Liam lasted as long as he did without getting shot. But my Irishness is deeper than that; I can't really explain it."

She turned to him and kissed him long and hard on the mouth. "Listen, my love, I want us to spend as much time together as we can. And as soon as I can get my head around it, I will come and live with you. And I promise I'll marry you, but I think we should get married in the States."

"Why?"

"I'm not sure I know. I guess it's that if I end my life here in Ireland, I don't want to start my new life here. I want to start it over there with you. Does that make any sense?"

"Sure. I haven't thought about this very much before now, but it occurs to me that marrying Moira here in Ireland probably had a lot to do with the fact that Fiona grew up in Ireland, even though she was born in the States. We had to get married in Ireland; there was no way her family would've been comfortable with her going off with me to America unless we were already married. And I really didn't want to leave without her."

"She really adored you. She would have gone anyway."

"I know, but I couldn't ask her to do that." He started to say something more, but it was ground they had already covered, ground he didn't want to cover again. "I'm going to come back and see you whenever I can. I have reason enough to make official trips to Europe, but I'm not going to abuse that. I'll fly over on my own nickel if I need to, but I don't want to go another long time without seeing you. I feel like the luckiest man ever, and I don't want to stop feeling like this."

She was silent for a while, and then she said, "This is kind of scary."

"Yes."

"I haven't had a terrible life compared to millions of people. But it hasn't been a walk in the park either. I've never been in a place like this before, I mean, a place that feels like this. I feel like I'm floating on a boat at sea, and as good as this feels, I'm still afraid of sinking."

232

"I'm not going to let you sink." He pulled her close and kissed her deeply, feeling his passion begin to rise once more. Her eyes told him that she wanted him again, and their kisses grew warmer. They undressed each other and made love again, and their lovemaking left them breathless as before. They fell asleep with her tucked tight against his body, his arms around her.

The next afternoon he went with her to Heathrow to catch her flight back to Dublin on Aer Lingus. As they stood near the gate she held onto his arms with her head on his chest. He had one hand on her back and was stroking her hair. They didn't say much. As the final boarding call came, she kissed him and said, "You will always be with me."

He couldn't find words to say goodbye with, so he just kissed her and hugged her one more time. He followed her with his eyes down the runway until she disappeared through the door of the plane. He found a seat next to a window and watched the aircraft back away from the terminal and head out to the takeoff runway. Even when the airliner had disappeared from sight, he lingered where he was.

As he was sitting there, a nice-looking young woman walked up to him.

"Congressman?" she said.

He just stared at her. "Aren't you Congressman Kellan Maguire?"

He relaxed and smiled. "Last time I checked, I was."

"Was that woman you're saying goodbye to a member of your family?"

"Who are you with?" he asked.

"I'm with the London Bureau of the New York Times. We're doing an article about the British edition of your book, and I thought it was a huge coincidence that I should run into you. Of course I knew you were here."

"Ah, I see."

"Do you mind my asking who that woman was?"

"No, I don't really mind. Let's just say she's a member of my extended family."

"It looked to me as if you two are very close. Would you mind giving me her name?"

"Her first name is Kathleen. That's all I'll give you."

"I noticed that her plane is going to Dublin. So she's Irish?"

Screw this, he thought to himself. "Actually, she's Icelandic. She's changing planes in Dublin for a flight to Reykjavik."

The reporter's expression changed from friendly to aggressive in an instant. She made a point of taking a notepad and pen out of her pocket. "I didn't know you had family in Iceland."

"Well, you learn something new every day," he said. He turned away and started looking out the window again.

"Thank you, Congressman," she said. He waited for her to walk away, then stood up and headed for the exit to the terminal.

When Kellan got back to the hotel he stopped at the desk to check for messages. The clerk handed him an envelope from the Embassy containing two tickets for him for a new production of *A Midsummer Night's Dream*. He hoped Alex would enjoy it. When he showed her the tickets, she teased him about his choice. "I always knew you were a romantic," she said. They enjoyed the performance, which featured a young, very talented cast. As they walked back to the hotel, Alex hooked her arm in Kellan's. "That was fun," she said.

"Yes. I can't remember the last time I saw a Shakespeare play. It was when I was with the firm in New York I guess."

"I remember that. Several of us went, I think. I don't remember what the play was; I was never a huge Shakespeare fan."

They shared a nightcap in the hotel lounge and headed for their rooms. They had an early departure. He kissed her on the cheek as they said good night. "I really enjoyed meeting Kathleen," she said again as she opened her door and went into her room.

The next day on the flight back to the States, they had plenty of time to reflect on their visit. There wasn't much to say about the book deal; it seemed to be in good order. Alex told him that she had been invited to appear on a PBS program concerning the book, and she had agreed. "Sounds like a great idea," he said. "It will probably drum up a few more sales."

"Have you thought any more about the royalties?" she asked. He had talked about donating his share to some worthy cause.

"No, I'm just going to let them sit and gather interest for a while."

"I still think you're being unfair to yourself," Alex said. He had insisted that she receive seventy-five percent of whatever the book earned for them. But it was selling fast enough that they had long since passed what the advance from their publisher had brought.

"You did most of the work," he said.

"So what? If your name hadn't been on it, it would have sold about fifteen copies."

"I'm sure you'll find a good use for it," he said.

A while later the conversation turned once more to Kathleen. Alex had said several times how much she liked her. "So, do you know when you'll be seeing her again? I know you're going to have her come to Washington."

"We're working on it. She has some stuff to tie up from her husband's death. And she has to decide what to do about work. I was thinking about trying to help her find an editing job in the States. Most of the good houses are in New York, of course, but we're not very far down that road yet."

"Any chance there's a wedding in the picture?"

He smiled at her. "So you're a romantic too," he said. "We talked about it. It's going to happen sooner or later. I hope it's sooner. We'll see."

"I really connected with her," she said.

"I noticed. Is it fair of me to say that you seemed to be attracted to her?"

She didn't answer for a while, and he wondered whether he had crossed a line. But she looked up at him, smiled and said, "If you mean romantically, I'd have to say no. Let me ask you something; when we were sitting in a lounge last night there was a good-looking woman at the next table—that blonde—and I noticed you noticing her. Could you say you were attracted to her?"

"Yeah, I remember her. That was some dress she had on. But was I attracted to her? I guess if I were loose and unattached and she'd been alone, I might've tried to strike up a conversation. But without even exchanging a word, I can't really say I was attracted to her. I just thought she was attractive."

"Interesting."

"But you spent quite a bit of time with Kathleen. That's sort of different, isn't it?"

She thought for a few moments. "I guess so. Look, she and I really connected on some level. And no question, she's a damn good-looking woman. If someone asked me what a classic Irish beauty looks like, I would think of someone just like her. But did I have romantic feelings towards her? I mean sexual feelings? I didn't pick up any vibes from her. I know she liked me, but there was nothing sensual about it. I don't how it is with straight people, but before you get those kinds of feelings, something has to click, doesn't it?"

"But if you come across another woman who is gay, do you pick up some vibes? I mean, can you tell just by looking at or being around a person?"

"Sometimes. Sometimes you miss a message, or sometimes you get a false message. That can be embarrassing."

"I gather that's happened to you?"

"Yeah, when I was at Maryland. There was a girl on the basketball team that I thought was really hot. I can say I was attracted to her, and I made a sort of casual advance in that direction. She shot me right down. I later found out that she was going with a guy on the football team. She carried herself like a real jock, so I guess I assumed something that wasn't there."

"I'm on real shaky ground here, but I want to understand this. Have you ever had a regular partner?"

"Not now, I live alone. It seems to suit me just fine."

"But did you ever have a regular girlfriend?"

"I had a roommate at Maryland who was gay, and we were together for a couple of years. Then she dropped off the basketball team and went in some other direction. We parted friends, and I guess I have to say I didn't miss her very much. Then when I was in law school at Duke, I had a relationship with another student in my class. That lasted until we both graduated and went our separate ways."

"Did you ever think about following her to wherever she was going so that you could continue the relationship?"

"I probably thought about it. But I was pretty set on going to New York, and when Phillips, Shannon made me an offer, I jumped at it." She looked at him and smiled. "You were on the interview committee. Do you remember that?"

"How could I forget? One more question and then I'll leave you alone. When did you figure out that you were gay?"

"When did I first know?" He nodded. "I have a brother and a sister. When I was still pretty young, I remembered that I was more interested in playing with my brother's toys than with my sister's dolls. I guess you could describe me as a tomboy when I was growing up. I was pretty athletic, and once my brother, who was a year older than I was, got in a fight with a bully at school. This must've been about eighth grade. Anyway, when I saw my brother had a bloody nose, I went after the bully. I guess I was so angry over what he'd done to my brother Billy that I scared the crap out of him. I got in a few good punches and he backed off.

That was probably about the time that I began to feel more like a boy than a girl." She looked at him with a quirky expression. "When did you first figure out that you were straight?"

"I don't know. Probably about the time I got my first erection. It's kind of strange for boys; you have all this plumbing and it begins to act kind of weird. Takes a while to figure out what's going on." He laughed. "Young guys are always sort of comparing notes on what's going on. You know, 'does yours do that too?'"

Alex just shook her head and chuckled.

"I guess I do have one concern about you," he said. "I sometimes have the feeling that you might be lonely, that you'd like to have someone in your life you could go home to every night."

"No lonelier than you. It's funny, now that I've met Kathleen, I understand why. But you always seemed like a lonely person to me." She took his hand for a moment and squeezed it. "I'm really happy for you, Kellan. Kathleen and I are going to be real good friends. I've got a feeling I'll be a lot less lonely when she's around a lot. And I know you will be!"

He squeezed her hand in return. "I'm sure glad I was on that interview committee, and that we hired you. You will always be one of my favorite people."

"I'm glad," she said. She pushed her seat back, stuck a pillow behind her head and closed her eyes.

Their flight arrived back at Dulles Airport in midafternoon. Kellan suggested that Alex go straight home and rest, but she wanted to go with him back to the office. Carmen Montefiore was sitting at Kellan's desk when they walked in. Carmen smiled at them and asked, "So how was London?"

"London was great," said Kellan. "And what's going on around here?"

"Same old, same old," said Carmen. "Things have been kind of quiet. You picked a good time to be gone."

"How does my schedule look for tomorrow?" Kellan said. Carmen handed Kellan a sheet of paper and he scanned it. "Okay, there doesn't seem to be anything urgent on here. You must have some stuff for me to sign."

Carmen stood up from Kellan's desk. "I'll have the girls bring them in right away. Good to have you back, Kellan. You too, Alex. I gather the trip was worthwhile for you?"

"Right you are, Carmen. I learned an awful lot." She looked at Kellan, and they both smiled.

"Something going on over there that I need to know about?"

"Nothing right now," said Kellan. "The book meetings went very well. I'll fill you in on the rest of the details."

A few days later Kellan got a note from Fiona. She wrote that Kathleen had come by to see her after she returned from London and had told her that she and her father were planning to be married, though no date had been set. 'I'm really happy for you, Kelly,' Fiona wrote. 'I have always loved Aunt Kathleen, and I know you will be very happy. She said you would be living over in America. That makes me want to come over there even more. We can talk about it the next time I see you, which I hope will be fairly soon. Much love, Fiona.'

As he sat in his office with his hands behind his head looking out the window, Alex came in. "Kellan, we may have a problem." Without turning around he answered, "Tell me something I don't know." He turned around and smiled. "Okay, let's have it."

"There are two reporters out here who claim to be from The Tunnel."

"What the hell's The Tunnel?"

"It's that sort of underground newspaper that started up about the time they started building the Metro. You know, they're going to dig tunnels under the Potomac. Anyway, they want to know if you want to make a statement. "

"About what?" Alex now had his full attention. He had his hands flat on the desk and his feet on the floor.

"It seems to have something to do with your family in Iceland. What the hell is that about?"

He laughed. "Sweet Jesus, how the hell did they find out about that?" Alex sat down in a chair opposite his desk. She looked bemused, and asked, "How come I haven't heard about your family in Iceland?"

Kellan filled her in on his encounter with the reporter at Heathrow Airport. "I was just being a smart ass," he said.

"Well, somehow or other it seems to have made it over here. Who were you talking to, for Christ's sake?"

"She said she was from the London Bureau of the New York Times, but I didn't ask for her credentials or anything. I don't recall that she was wearing any kind of press pass, but it was an open area. All she saw was me saying but goodbye to Kathleen, and yes, it probably looked quite intimate, which it was." He leaned back again, put his hands behind his head and shook his head slowly.

"Well, what you want to do about it?" she asked. "If I send these two away, they'll just go digging around somewhere else. If you don't say anything, they'll think there's something there."

"They won't find a goddamn thing. The worst that anyone can find out is that there's a woman in Ireland that I'm in love with. And I can sure as hell live with that, because they're gonna see a lot more of her."

"Okay, so what do we do?"

"Bring them in here and we'll do a standup. If they try to sit down, say I'm late for a meeting."

The two reporters seemed to be in their mid-20s, and were appropriately dressed for a Saturday afternoon picnic. Kellan was standing in front of his desk. "What can I do for you?" he said in a friendly tone.

"We got a report from a friend in England that you have relatives in Iceland, and we just wanted to follow-up a little bit. It sounds very interesting to have a family there. We might do a story on it." The woman was speaking, and her face showed what was obviously a forced smile.

What a crock of shit, Kellan thought to himself. He decided to clear the air. "Okay guys, here's your story, and you can say you got it straight from me. I was saying goodbye to a dear friend at Heathrow Airport. She had recently suffered the loss of her husband, and I was wishing her well. The last thing she needed was some reporter chasing after her, so I told whoever that person was who was posing as a New York Times reporter that she was going to Iceland. I lied. Got it?"

The man spoke. "Um, could you tell us the woman's name so we can wrap this up?"

Kellan was tempted to say he could wrap it in cheesecloth and stuff it where the sun don't shine. Instead he smiled and said, "No, I won't tell you her name. She has been through a lot and I would ask you to respect her privacy."

Alex said, "Congressman, you're going to be late for your meeting." She pointed toward the door and the two 'reporters' shuffled out. The woman turned and started to say something else, but Alex put her hand on the woman's back and gently eased her on her way. When they were gone, she came back in and sat down.

"I hope that kills it," he said.

"Kellan, if it doesn't, fuck 'em. Look, I'm thrilled for you and Kathleen. She's coming over, and eventually you guys are gonna get married, right?" He nodded. "I think you've killed it for now, but don't think it's not going to rise like the Phoenix when our noble press corps gets a look at that redheaded bombshell from Ireland." She grinned, and Kellan laughed and shook his head.

"We'll see about that, won't we?"

"You bet your ass!" She turned and started out, then said over her shoulder, "That meeting you were late for has been canceled, by the way." As was her custom, she hoisted her middle finger as she went out the door. Kellan shook his head and thought to himself, 'man, I love that woman.'

Ten minutes later Alex and Jean came in, both looking upset.

"What's up? Are they back?"

"Who?" asked Jean.

"Those reporters," said Alex. "No they're long gone. It's something else. Have you been watching the news?"

"No, why? What's going on?"

Alex walked over, turned on his television and selected CNN. A reporter was speaking.

"... and that's all we have for now. As I said, first reports are that it was the IRA, but nothing definite yet." Behind the reporter was an image of the smoldering ruin of a building.

"Jesus Christ, where is that?"

"London. It's an office building about three blocks from where we were staying," said Alex.

He went over and stared at the television screen and shook his head. "Well, at least Kathleen was out of there before it happened."

"Thank God for that."

Carmen came into the office. "The Speaker just called," he said to Kellan. "He wanted to make sure you were back safely."

Kellan nodded. "Thanks, Carmen. All safe for now." He looked at Alex. She was still watching the screen. Then she wiped a tear from her face. 'Damn,' he thought, 'she never cries.'

Part 3

Run for the Rose Garden

"He serves his party best who serves the country best."
—Rutherford B. Hayes

Out West

Fiona and Kathleen were smiling as they came out of the international arrivals section at Dulles Airport. Kellan and Alex were waiting for them, and the four of them shared hugs, kisses and warm greetings with smiles and laughter. Kellan was delighted to note that Fiona and Kathleen had formed such a close bond. He was not surprised; Kathleen was, after all, Fiona's "Aunt Kathleen," but their relationship had taken on a new dimension now that Kathleen was, in a sense, going to become Fiona's stepmother. Kellan had thought about the implications of that, and he and Alex had talked about it on their way to the airport. But now that the two women had arrived, defining relationships seemed superfluous.

"Where are we going?" Fiona wanted to know. She hooked her arm in Kellan's as they headed for the parking lot, pulling their suitcases-on-wheels. Kathleen was holding his other arm, and Kellan looked back and forth and noted, "I guess I'm the thorn between two roses." He turned toward Fiona. "We'll go to my apartment on the Hill, and I'll show you what I have in mind for your visit."

"You said we were going on a trip?" Fiona asked.

"If you want to," said Kellan. "We've been working on it, but it's easy to cancel."

"Where would we be going?" Kathleen said.

"West," he said. "San Francisco for starters. Then we'll see."

"That sounds like fun," she said, but Kellan didn't pick up much enthusiasm in her voice. He assumed she was tired from the flight from Dublin.

Kellan had moved to a larger apartment following his reelection to a third term. He had placed the investments he had made while still at Phillips, Shannon in a blind trust, but had arranged it so that he could withdraw funds as needed without violating the trust's provisions, thus maintaining his integrity as a lawmaker. He had decided to invest his share of the royalties from his book in certificates of deposit and mutual funds. In all, with his congressional salary and other assets, he didn't consider himself wealthy, given some of the company in which he had traveled, but he was certainly well off. He did not maintain a full-time residence in his district in New York, choosing instead to engage in short-term leases as needed. In his new apartment across the Potomac in Arlington, he now had plenty of room for Fiona, Kathleen, and even Alex, if she wanted to stay over.

The drive back into Washington was pleasant. Kellan had engaged a limousine with driver, and he sat in back with the three women. He didn't say much, but just enjoyed the banter, as at least two separate conversations seemed to be going on all the time—Fiona and Alex, Kathleen and Kellan, Kellan and Fiona, Kathleen and Alex and various combinations of the above. When they reached the apartment, Kellan carried Kathleen's suitcase into the room where she would be staying. The room adjoined his bedroom, and nobody expected that she was going to sleep by herself. He put down her bag and they embraced each other. He kept his arms around her and she held him close. "It's so lovely to finally be here with you," she said.

"I could hardly wait," he said. She kissed him warmly.

Alex had helped Fiona with her bags, and Kellan smiled as he heard the two of them chattering out in the living room. Alex was still officially his Chief Legislative Assistant, but she had become much more than that. She functioned as a combination of social secretary, personal advisor and trainer, but most of all a loyal and trusted friend. Kellan consider her part of his family, an adopted sibling. She knew her way around his apartment as if she lived in it, which, in fact she occasionally did. She lived nearby, had a key to his place, and felt free to drop in unannounced. She seemed to bask in the warmth of the affection that Kellan showed her. If jealousy existed among the rest of the staff, he was not too concerned. The fact that everyone in the office knew that she was gay served as a protective shield in a sense, as there was little thought of romantic attachment in their relationship.

Kellan's other friend in the office besides Carmen was Jean Slater, who had been with him since the beginning of his first run for Congress. As Deputy Chief of Staff, she managed the other aides efficiently with a mixture of good discipline and common sense. Jean had matured into a highly effective aide with a good handle on political issues, legislative matters, and the routine, mundane business that dominated the office of any congressman. She was also very adept at handling the press, whose demands had increased as Kellan's reputation on the Hill had become stronger. She had formed a solid working relationship with Carmen, and as they were both from the same area in New York State, they had much in common. Both of Kellan's two senior staff members were more than capable of managing the entire operation of his office, and when Kellan traveled, often with Alex along as an on-the-road assistant, Kellan never worried for a moment that his office was not in the best of hands. Alex and Fran Kuzniak, his office manager, remembered each other from their Phillips, Shannon days.

Kellan got drinks for everyone, and after they had stood out on the balcony for a few moments admiring his view of the Potomac, nearby Washington landmarks and the Virginia shore, they settled in the living room. Kellan took out a map of the United States and unfolded it on the coffee table. "Jean has pretty much mapped out our trip," he said. "Okay. We're flying to San Francisco, and from there we'll drive up along the coast through redwood country and on to Seattle. There's a lot to see along that route. From Seattle, Jean has reservations for us to fly to Denver. From there we have two options: drive north through Wyoming to the Badlands of the Dakotas, Mount Rushmore and some of the other places along that path; the other option is to drive south from Denver along the eastern edge of the Rockies and into New Mexico. There's a lot to see there, also. When we get to Denver, I'll let Jean know where we are flying home from, and she'll do the rest."

"That looks exciting, Kelly," said Fiona.

Kellan smiled. "I thought you were going to call me Dad once you were here."

Fiona was sitting next to him and she swatted him on the arm. "I can't help it," she said. "It's force of habit." She leaned over and kissed him on the cheek. "The travel plans look great, but it seems like a lot of ground to cover."

"It is," he said. "But for someone who was raised in the East like me, traveling out West is like going to another country. The history of the Great Plains, the Rockies, and everything west of there is very different from the history of old Massachusetts and Virginia. Then you've got the whole South, the Cajun area in Louisiana, and the whole history of Texas, which was a separate republic for ten years before they joined the United States."

Kathleen stared at the map for a while and then pointed at it. "That's West Virginia, right?"

"Yes."

"And you once told me that Ireland is about the size of West Virginia." Kellan nodded. "Jesus, that's just a tiny little piece of this country." She shook her head. "Is it really that different out West?"

244

"In many ways. For example, the highest point in my home state of Massachusetts is about the same as the lowest point in the whole state of Wyoming. And the highest point in Wyoming is about two miles higher than the highest point in Massachusetts. Another contrast is that the population of Massachusetts is about eleven times that of Wyoming, but the area of Wyoming is twelve times as large as Massachusetts. Four states in the northern Great Plains, Wyoming, Montana, and the Dakotas, are ten times as large as Ireland, with half the population. There's lots of open space out there."

"There's so much to see," said Fiona. "We're only going to see a small part of it. I have so much to learn about this country." She shook her head.

"Now's your chance," said Alex. "I'm glad I'll be going with you." Alex had "volunteered" for the trip, saying she could help take care of business while they were on the road. Kellan didn't ask what business that might be. He knew he would be glad to have her along.

"Have you traveled much in the States?" said Kathleen to Alex.

"I've been out West a few times," Alex said. "When I was playing basketball at Maryland, we occasionally traveled out West. And I had some friends in San Francisco that I used to visit. And I've been to the Grand Canyon."

"Kellan, you seem to know a lot about the West," said Kathleen.

"When I was a kid, my parents took us to the Grand Canyon. I have cousins who live in Wyoming, and I visited them from time to time. But I haven't been to see them since before I came to Congress."

"Can we see them on this trip?" said Fiona.

"Maybe," said Kellan. "We'll see if we have time."

Dinner turned out to be a group project. Kellan prepared a roast and put it in the oven. Alex made a salad, and Kathleen and Fiona worked on potatoes and vegetables. Before dinner they enjoyed cheese and crackers with their wine. It was a festive occasion, and, as Fiona noted, the first time the four of them had all ever been together at the same time for more than a few moments. Fiona talked a lot; she and Alex bantered back and forth, trading wisecracks and mock insults. Fiona had a well-developed sense of humor, and, like Kathleen, she had a great facility with language. Kathleen sat at the end of the couch with her legs drawn up next to her; she spoke little, but smiled a lot. When she caught Kellan's eye, he could see her smoldering passion building. Tempted as he was to drag her into the bedroom, he thought about what the evening would bring and reminded himself to be patient. Kathleen would smile, as if knowing exactly what he was thinking. The glances they shared were filled with meaning, deeply but silently expressed.

After dinner they relaxed again in the living room, music playing softly on the stereo. As Kellan watched the three women talking, smiling, laughing, he was conscious of the fact that he had rarely found himself in such a happy setting. He was pleased when Kathleen stretched her arms and yawned. "It has been a long day," she said. She stood up, kissed Fiona on the cheek and embraced Alex. "Does anybody mind if I turn in?"

All three of them turned towards Kellan, and he found himself blushing. "It sounds like a good idea," he said. "We'll be getting an early start in the morning."

Alex stood up as if getting ready to leave, but Fiona said, "Oh, Alex, don't leave yet. We have so much catching up to do!"

"You know where the extra bed is," said Kellan to Alex. "Stay as long as you like, all night if you want."

"Yeah, Kellan, I expect you're dead tired and will be asleep in five minutes, right?" Alex grinned at him.

"Something like that," he said.

Kathleen stopped at the door to the bedroom turned, looked at Alex, shook her head and laughed. "Jesus, Mary and Joseph, a fine bit of foolishness you are!" she said.

Much later Kellan and Kathleen lay side by side, his head on the pillow and her head resting on his chest. They had been talking softly, and Kathleen mentioned something about Liam. Her former husband's name had not come up very often, and Kellan felt there was some lingering doubt concerning how Kathleen's marriage had ended. "This is something you need to tell me about Liam?" he said. She didn't answer right away and he said, "Never mind—I guess there's nothing I need to know."

"Maybe later," she said. "But not tonight. Tonight I just want to be with you." She ran her hands over his chest, down to his waist, and lower. He rolled on his side facing her, kissed her and let his hands range over her body. She bit his earlobe gently and pressed herself into him. She pushed him on his back, pulled herself up and straddled him. "My turn to drive," she whispered. She lowered herself onto him and began a slow rhythmic motion. Her hands resting on his shoulders, her arms out straight, and she was almost upright. He took her arms and started to pull her down towards him, but she smiled and said, "Not yet. I want to watch you from up here."

246

He gently massaged her breasts and watched her face, and she began to move just a bit faster, then slower, then faster again, teasing him. Her face was a picture of pure pleasure. And he let her set the pace until the time came when she embraced him and felt him rise to meet her. She remained on top of him for a long time as he stroked her back and her buttocks and kissed her over and over. There was nothing they needed to say. Their bodies had said it all. When he was aware that she had fallen asleep he gently eased her off onto her back and pulled the covers over her. He rested his head on his elbow and watched her until he too was ready for sleep.

The next morning as they drove to Kellan's office, Kathleen looked out the window at the buildings and monuments as they crossed Memorial Bridge and drove along the mall past the Smithsonian to Capitol Hill. Kellan watched her, not knowing whether she was impressed, or whether, indeed, she should be. He knew that she had always had mixed feelings about the United States, not necessarily about its place in the world of nations, but about the American relationship with Ireland.

Jean Slater stood and greeted them as they came into Kellan's office in the Longworth Building. She hugged Fiona. "Wonderful to see you again," she said.

"It's great to be back," said Fiona.

Jean turned to greet the other visitor. "You must be Kathleen," she said. "I've heard a great deal about you. It's wonderful to finally meet you. I'm Jean."

"Ah, the Deputy Chief of Staff. Kellan has told me how much he relies on you; he's lucky to have you."

Alex came out of her office and greeted everyone. Kellan had no idea when she had left the apartment; it had apparently been sometime early in the morning. "How's everybody?" She looked around smiling. "I assume everybody got plenty of sleep, except for Fiona."

Kellan looked at his daughter. "Alex and I talked till about three o'clock this morning," she said. "We would probably still be talking if I hadn't gotten so sleepy."

Kellan took Kathleen into his own office, where Carmen, as usual, was seated at Kellan's desk. He immediately stood up and came around the desk and held out his hand to Kathleen. "Welcome, my dear," he said. He stood back and looked her up and down. "Just as advertised," he said with a smile. He looked at Kellan and nodded. "So, you will be leaving shortly for your little inspection tour of our western provinces, am I right?"

"Something like that," said Kellan.

"Well, that's wonderful," he said. He asked Kathleen, "Have you ever been in the States before?"

"No, this is my first trip across the Atlantic," she said. "I'm already impressed."

"It's nice that you could come by the office, but the real sights are where you're going," Carmen said. "We have some pretty fancy buildings in DC, but the real scenery is west of the Mississippi." He turned to Kellan. "Jean and I are going to split the time while you're gone. One of us will be here every day, but both of us probably not at all. There's not much going on right now, so I don't expect any problems. The rest of the staff is lying low until after the Democratic Convention. It's gonna be slow around here for a while. You'll be back before you head for New York, right?"

"Right. If you need me to come back to sign anything, just let me know, and I can make a quick trip back here and catch up with them maybe in Seattle. I think everything is covered."

Carmen excused himself and Kathleen strolled around the room, looking at the pictures, the books on the shelf, and other memorabilia that were part of the furniture of every Congressman's office. "So this is where you run your little corner of the country, hmmm?" She looked at him with her quirky smile.

"We do our best."

She strolled over and sat down in his desk chair looking over the items on top. Her picture, a picture of Fiona and a picture of the two of them together were prominently displayed. She put both of her hands flat on the desk looked around and said, "I'm impressed."

Kellan took them through the tunnel to the Capitol building itself, where neither house was in session. There were plenty of tourists on hand, however, as schools were on summer break. Kellan took Kathleen and Fiona onto the floor of the House, describing briefly how their business was conducted. From there they walked to Statuary Hall, where the two women looked at the figures displayed as well as the magnificent artwork that covered much of the inside of the spacious room. He took them down to the old Senate chamber where Chief Justice John Marshall had run the Supreme Court. From there they went up to the Senate side and into the gallery.

Back in the Longworth Building Kellan took them into two of the committee rooms, one large and one small. "Most of the real work of Congress is done in committees," he told them. "Most of what happens in

248

my office deals with constituent issues. When the full House is in session, most of what happens there is a product of the work done in the committees. By the time a bill gets to the House floor for a vote, it has been pretty well worked over."

"Fascinating," said Kathleen. "And you serve on how many committees?"

"Two committees and two subcommittees," said Kellan. "They keep me busy."

As they sat in Kellan's office following the quick tour, Jean went over their itinerary. She handed each of them a copy, which showed the flights they would be taking, the hotels where they would be staying, and some of the highlights they might expect to see at each stop or along the way between stops. As they would be getting on and off planes several times, she advised them to pack light and wear comfortable shoes.

"This looks wonderful, Jean," said Fiona. "It was good of you to take care of all this for us."

"Part of my job," said Jean. She looked at Kellan. "Just another inspection tour, right, boss?"

"You got it," said Kellan. He glanced at Kathleen and Fiona. "Actually, this one's not on the taxpayer," he said. "Can't push my luck too far."

"The car will pick you up at your apartment at noon and take you out to Dulles," Jean said. "I hope you guys have a wonderful trip."

"I'll be at your apartment by noon," said Alex as she hurried off.

From their rooms on the top floor of the Fairmont Hotel in San Francisco, they could see out across San Francisco Bay and much of the city, as well as Berkeley and the other suburbs on the other side of the bay. "That island over there is Angel Island," he said to Kathleen, Fiona and Alex. He looked at Kathleen. "You've heard of Ellis Island, no doubt; most Americans have, especially those of us who grew up on the East Coast. But Angel Island was the West Coast equivalent, and thousands of Chinese, Japanese and other Asians and a number of Mexicans came into the country right over there. It was different from Ellis Island, and there's not much there anymore. But it's a piece of our history."

Kellan was glad that Alex had been able to come on the trip as company for Fiona. They were happy to share the comfortable room at the Fairmont, while Kellan and Kathleen shared the adjoining room. Kellan was aware that Fiona was still interested very much in law school and in fact had taken the LSAT. Alex had shared her experiences at the Duke Law School as well as her time at Phillips, Shannon with Fiona. Kellan overheard one of their conversations during breakfast on their first morning at the Fairmont and said to Alex, "If I didn't know better, I'd swear you were trying to recruit her for Duke."

"With her scores on the LSAT, and her record at Trinity, I'm sure she can go anywhere she wants." Alex paused. "But I'm not convinced that's what she really wants. She keeps talking about nursing."

"Kelly, sure I've been thinking about going to law school in the United States," she said, "but Alex is right. I haven't made up my mind yet, but whatever I do, I want to study here. I know Mum and Dad are going to be terribly disappointed, but there's so much to see here, and so much I haven't seen. I know I'll be able to get home and see them every so often." She paused for a moment. "I guess I should call them Brendan and Deirdre while I'm here, to avoid confusion."

"I don't think that's going to be a problem," said Kellan. "But have you told them your plans yet?"

"No," she said. "I thought, if it's okay with you, that I'd fly home and tell them in person. I think it might go over better."

"Maybe after the Democratic Convention," he said. "There will be some down time before the Republicans kick off their big show."

That night Kellan and Kathleen sat in their darkened room looking out the window at the lights of the city and the town surrounding the bay. "It's beautiful here," said Kathleen. "Even when we were flying over the Rockies, I could see what you meant about how different it was out here. I've never been to Germany or Switzerland, but I guess the Alps must look like that."

"The Cliffs of Moher are one of the most spectacular bits of scenery anywhere," he said. "My first summer when I was studying at Trinity, a couple of us rented a car and took a tour. We took the boat tour out along the cliffs, and I still remember how rough it was. We got soaking wet as the waves broke over the side of the boat. My friend actually got seasick."

"I spent a few days in Doolin once," Kathleen said. "I guess I was about ten or twelve, and I went with my mother and father. We took that boat tour also, as I remember, but I don't remember it being so rough. That was one of the last times we were together. My father died about a year later."

"I guess you know a lot more about me than I know about you," he said. "You've never really talked very much about yourself, or your family.

I gather from Brendan and Patrick, and what I remember Moira telling me—that was a long time ago, to be sure—is that you've had a lot to deal with in your life."

"Everybody does at one time or another," she said.

"I'd like to know more about you, if you ever feel like talking about it."

"About what?"

"Any of it. Your mother, your father, what it was like growing up, you and Liam if you feel like it. I don't think there is anything you could possibly tell me that would change the way I feel about you. I hope I'm not making you uncomfortable."

She reached over and squeezed his hand. "No, that's not it. I have to tell you one thing, and it may muck up our plans." She was still holding his hand, and he leaned toward her turned her hand over and kissed her palm, something she said she loved. She smiled at him. "I'm not sure where to start," she said.

"It doesn't really matter, does it?"

"I just want to get it right. I don't want there to be any secrets between us. You and I had that one big secret—that we loved each other—that we had to keep, but that was different."

"Yes it was."

"Okay, I'll start more or less at the beginning. My aunt, my father's sister, married a man from Belfast and she moved up there. After my father died, my mother's drinking got much worse. I guess you knew she had a drinking problem."

"Patrick sort of hinted that," he said.

"Well anyway, it was bad. She embarrassed me in front of my friends more than once, and I finally got good and pissed off and went up to stay with my Aunt Michaela in Belfast. While I was up there, I got a little wild myself. Aunt Mikki threatened to ship me back home, but she knew about my mother's problem, so she put up with me, and I finally calmed down a little bit. But then I met Liam and some of his friends in a pub, and he started paying a lot of attention to me, and I liked it. I guess because of my mother's drinking, I didn't have a very good opinion of myself, and when Liam started treating me like a princess, I just ate it up.

"He was older than I was, and when I met him he was just getting interested in the IRA. His uncle was very active, and when he got killed by the British, it turned Liam right around. He was bent on avenging his uncle's death, and he started running with an IRA crowd. He still made

251

time for me, and being young and stupid as I was, I thought what he was doing was exciting and heroic. Then one night we were drinking in a pub, and a bomb went off nearby. Liam went rushing out to see what happened, and I followed him. There were two mangled bodies lying in the street; one of them was a woman. She was badly torn up, and I immediately threw up. It was horrible.

"Liam used that incident to convince me that what was going on was war, and he was a soldier. I guess I bought that because I stuck with him, even though I realized that he was getting into more and more dangerous stuff. I thought I needed to back off for a little bit, so I went home, and found my mother just as I had left her. We lived in Cork at the time, but I left and went up to Dublin. I got my degree in Belfast and had always done pretty well in my studies.

"Anyway, I needed to support myself, so I got a job at a Dublin newspaper. I was a good writer, and I told the editor about my experiences in Belfast and said I wanted to cover the IRA and politics. I remember that the editor laughed at me and told me to come back when I was all grown up. Well, that pissed me off, so I went out and did some digging, and wrote a couple of stories that impressed him. Later I landed a job with the Dublin News and was on my way to becoming a writer and a journalist.

"I always loved literature, and I read all the time, probably as an escape. You could say I was a compulsive reader. I would often start a new book and go nonstop until I finished reading it, even if it took all night. But the more I read, the more my writing improved. I wanted to do longer pieces than the newspaper needed, so I started sending stuff to magazines. I hung around places where writers gathered, and I eventually met an editor at a publishing house. We got acquainted, and he offered me a job. I still did my research at the library at Trinity, and that's where I got to know Moira. She helped me a lot."

"Me too."

"Moira was nothing like me; she came from a good, tranquil home, strong family, and she had her head on straight. I was still half strung out, and somehow I figured out that it would be good for me to make friends with her. I think she sort of claimed me as a reclamation project. Anyway, we became friends, and we eventually moved into that apartment where we lived when you met her. She really became my family, like a sister, she was. And when I got to know her family, they adopted me too. Christ knows what I would have become if they hadn't taken to me."

"It was the same for me. The way they helped me after Moira's death was amazing. And then when they raised Fiona ..."

"I know. They are quite wonderful."

She paused for a few moments. "Anyway, I guess Liam convinced himself that he was in love with me, because he would come down to Dublin from time to time and we would connect. He was so intense and focused on what he was doing that I had a hard time imagining how he could even remember who I was. But I guess I thought he really needed somebody to keep him grounded, and I guess I felt sorry for him. But I had seen enough of the stuff up in Belfast that I began reading more and more about what the British had done to us, and I paid a lot more attention to what we might call the revolutionary press. I learned a lot about Sinn Féin and got pretty politicized myself.

"Liam kept asking me to marry him, but I knew that was a losing proposition. He was no more ready to settle down to married life than he was to swim across the Irish Sea to England. Even sex with him wasn't very good—his mind was always somewhere else. I kept putting him off, but he was persistent. So sometime after you and Moira left for the United States, I decided to go ahead with it. Mind you, by that time I already had feelings for you, as you are no doubt aware. When I heard that Moira had died, I was heartbroken for her and for you, but I was also confused. Anyway, Liam and I finally got married, or at least I thought we did."

Kellan had been loath to interrupt her and had been listening patiently. But here he had to ask, "What do you mean, you thought you did?"

"As I said, Liam was older than I was. In fact, he had been married before, although I didn't know it. Eventually I found out about it when one of his friends up in Belfast let it slip. I confronted him about it, and he told me that his first wife was dead. I believe that he actually thought she was, but later I found out that she had not died. She had fought along with the IRA and been badly wounded in some kind of fight. Liam and his boys thought she was dead, but she apparently recovered. She was still in British custody, however. When a friend of Liam's with an RUC connection inquired, they told him, 'Just tell your friend his wife is dead.' But she wasn't—those bastards! Anyway, as it turned out, he was apparently still married to his first wife when he married me. That did it. I left him and went back to Dublin; I told him not to follow me, I was done with him."

"What a mess," Kellan said. "Jesus, I had no idea you had gone through all that. I'm so sorry."

"Don't be. The problem is, I'm not sure exactly what my status is. I'm not sure Liam was really married to that woman, Bridget something or other. There are some benefits for widows in Ireland, but I'm not sure I qualify even as a widow. Now that Liam is dead—I know that he is; I was at the funeral, for Christ's sake—I want to get it all straight. But beyond that, who knows? I hired a solicitor just before I left, and he's checking into it for me, but I'll need one more trip to Ireland before you and I get married just to make sure everything is cleared up."

"I can't see why we need to wait," he said gently. "You are definitely not married; that's one thing you know, that we know for sure."

"I know that, but remember when we were talking a while back—I think was in London—I told you that leaving Ireland for me was not going to be a simple matter? I don't want to leave anything behind. I never thought I would come to America for good, but now I know I want to spend the rest of my life with you, and I know you're not going to give up your position in Congress and run for the Irish Parliament."

She got up from her chair and knelt down in front of Kellan and put her arms around his waist, her head against his midsection. She started to cry. Kellan stroked her hair, stood up and lifted her with him and took her over to the couch, where they sat down side by side. He had both arms around her and she had her head in her hands, still crying. "I just can't believe ..."

"It's okay, it's okay," he said.

"I just can't believe I could have been so fucked up for so long. I mean, I look at your life, and even your short life with Moira, and I just don't see how I could ever wind up in a life like that. It's more than I have any right to expect."

"What do you mean? Nothing you've told me suggests that anything you did was your fault. For God's sake, you never got a break anywhere. Everything you have made of yourself you did on your own. You're a wonderful writer, you're smart as hell, and you're everything I need to make my life complete. I know it's not going to be easy to get used to life over here, but I can be patient. I can help. I promise you, I'm going to do everything I can to see to it that you have a good life. And I don't just mean a good life with me, I mean a fulfilling life. Hell, I don't know what you're going to wind up doing here in America besides being married to me, but I know it's going to be something worthwhile, something noteworthy. God, woman, you have so much to offer the world!"

She stretched out on the couch and put her head in his lap. She didn't say anything for a long time, but her tears had stopped. He felt her body relax, and she looked up at him pulled his head down and kissed him on the lips and then put her head back down in his lap. They stayed like that for a time, then he lifted her off his lap stood up, took her by the hand and said, "Let's go to bed."

They didn't make love that night; she lay in his arms saying nothing and eventually fell asleep. He wondered what the strange, wonderful, beautiful woman was going to wind up being in his life. He was unsure of how he was going to help her find a full life alongside him. He might give up politics and go back to practicing law; being the wife of a politician was stressful. On the other hand, Kathleen knew enough about politics that she understood the demands on a politician's time and attention. He was planning to run for his fourth term in November, and no serious challenger had appeared on the horizon. There was a good chance that he would be able to run unopposed, or if not, that a victory would be if not certain, at least very likely. He had never thought about not running, but he had time to drop out if he really wanted to. He would have to wait and see.

The Beginning of Chaos

They were just finishing up breakfast in the Fairmont hotel dining room when a woman wearing a hotel staff nameplate approached the table. She leaned over and spoke very softly to Kellan. "Congressman Maguire, I'm sorry to disturb you, but you have a phone call in my office. Would you care to come with me and take it?"

He followed the woman to her office and picked up the phone. "Congressman, this is Betty from Congresswoman Alice Sutton's district office here in San Francisco. I just got a call from your office in Washington from Jean—I guess she's your DCS. She asked if you would call her; she says it's urgent. She tried to get your room, but there was no answer."

He thanked Betty and asked the woman who had brought him from the dining room if he might use their phone. "Of course, Congressman." He dialed Jean's number at the office.

"Hi, Kellan, thanks for calling. I'm really sorry to disturb you, but it's Carmen."

"That's okay, Jean, what's happening?"

"It's apparently a heart attack—seems as if it's pretty serious. They've taken him to Bethesda. I can hold the fort, but I thought you ought to know about it right away."

"Thanks so much for calling, Jean." He thought for a moment. "I'm going to leave the ladies here. Alex can take care of them for a while. I'll be on the first plane I can get back to Washington. I'll call you from the airport. Anything else you can tell me?" Jean filled him with a few more details, none of them promising, and he thanked her again, thanked the people in the office and headed for the dining room. The ladies had already left.

Fiona, Kathleen and Alex were standing by the elevators waiting for him; Alex had signed for the breakfast. As he approached them, Fiona said, "Dad, you look worried. What's the matter?"

"It's Carmen," he said. "I spoke with Jean; he's apparently had a heart attack and it seems that it's pretty serious. Jean said he was on the way to Bethesda Naval Hospital, and as far as anyone knows he's still alive."

"That's terrible," said Alex. "What are you going to do?"

"I think I'd better get back there. From what Jean told me, they weren't able to revive him before they put him in the ambulance. It doesn't sound good."

Moments later they were gathered in Kellan's suite. "Alex," he said, "I think it's best if I go back by myself. I can get a single seat on a plane pretty easily." He looked at Kathleen and Fiona. "Look, I'm really sorry, but I think it's best if you guys and Alex stay put here for another day. I'll be back in Washington this afternoon and I'll go straight to Bethesda. I'll call you here soon as I know anything, and we can plan from there. Depending on how serious it is, I can either get you back to Washington, or, if it's not as serious as it looks, I can come back here tomorrow."

He walked over and put his arms around both Kathleen and Fiona, hugged them and kissed each one.

Kathleen looked up at him. "Kellan, I'm so sorry. Please don't worry about us—we'll be fine, won't we?" She looked at Fiona.

"Of course we will, Dad." She managed a smile and looked at Alex. "Alex can probably handle the two of us, right Alex?" she said.

"I've handled worse than you two," Alex said with a smile. "We'll be fine Kellan. Just take what you need and we'll pack up the rest. If you can get to see Carmen, tell him he's in my prayers. We'll hang loose until we hear from you."

He looked at his watch. "If I can get out of here by noon, I'll be in DC by dinnertime. I'll be in touch."

The taxi delivered Kellan to the main entrance of Bethesda Naval Hospital. It was just after six pm. "I'm Congressman Maguire," he said to the woman at the information desk. "I'm here to see about Carmen Montefiore."

The woman directed him to the waiting area outside the emergency room, where Jean and Carlos Gutierrez, a new addition to Kellan's staff, were waiting. Jean walked up and hugged him. "He's been there all day," she said. "I've been here since about 3 o'clock. The doctors have told us it doesn't look good. Fran's in charge of the office—she'll be fine."

Kellan nodded. He noticed a nurse about to enter the emergency area and stopped her. "Excuse me, nurse, I'm Congressman Kellan Maguire. Could you ask somebody if they could give me an update on Carmen Montefiore?"

"Certainly, Congressman."

A few moments later a doctor came out. He extended his hand to Kellan. "I'm Doctor Nayak, Congressman. I'm afraid it doesn't look too good. We're keeping Mister Montefiore alive, but just barely. I'm sure you want the best information, and frankly, I doubt he'll last the night. I'm very sorry."

"Thank you, Doctor."

"Carmen's wife and son are down in the main waiting room," said Jean. "I thought they would be more comfortable down there, and I told them I'd let them know as soon as I heard anything. I'm not sure she knows how bad it is."

"I'll go down and speak to them," said Kellan. "Carlos, I want you to stay here in case anything develops—let me know if it does. Jean, can you come with me? We probably ought to talk a bit about options."

Carmen Montefiore died at 1:34 am. Jean had suggested that Stella Montefiore come up to the emergency area when the doctor had alerted them that the situation looked dire. When the doctor came out with the bad news, Kellan hugged Stella and did his best to comfort her. After the doctor had provided details of the efforts to save Carmen, Kellan and Jean took Stella back to the waiting area and did what they could to comfort the rest of Carmen's family. He assured them that his office would help with the funeral arrangements, and that he, Jean or another member of the staff would be in touch. Stella had been in the office from time to time and knew most of the people in Kellan's office. He gave Stella his private number and told her she could call anytime. He sent Jean and Carlos home, and as Jean was leaving, he said, "We've got to get Alex and the ladies back here. It's too late to call now, but we'll do it first thing in the morning California time. You get some rest." Kellan sat with the Montefiore family until they too were ready to leave the hospital.

Kellan and his staff arranged for Carmen's funeral to be held at the Basilica of the National Shrine of the Immaculate Conception on the campus of Catholic University in Northeast Washington. He had been in Washington for over three decades and had many friends. The family would hold another memorial service later back in New York prior to his burial in Gate of Heaven Cemetery near Valhalla, just north of White Plains, where such notables as Babe Ruth, Jimmy Walker, James Cagney and Dutch Schultz were interred. "Interesting company," said Jean as she investigated the history of the famous cemetery. "Carmen will fit right in."

Attendees at the funeral in Washington included a good number of Congressman and their staffs, several senators, including both from New

York, and the vice president representing the White House. Kellan was pleased that Carmen was receiving the respect he deserved for his years of service, not only to himself, but to all those who had preceded him. Undersecretary Hal Wofford, Carmen's previous boss on the Hill, shared some thoughts with Kellan following the service. "Keeping Carmen was the smartest thing you ever did, Kellan," said Hal. "I sure as hell could've used him where I am now."

Alex, Kathleen and Fiona had returned from San Francisco. Kellan assured them that they would resume their sightseeing journey later, but for the time being he would be preoccupied with reorganizing his office. He would retain Jean as Chief of Staff; he assured her that she was more than capable of holding the position. He decided to move Alex to Deputy Chief of Staff; she would continue to oversee legislative affairs until he could choose a new legislative director. Fran and Carlos would anchor the rest of the staff. The summer prior to the presidential election was generally a slower time on the Hill, and the loss of Carmen would not prove as critical as it otherwise might have been. Still, Kellan felt his loss deeply; he had become a friend as well as a key assistant.

Back in his apartment on the night following the funeral, Kellan, Kathleen and Fiona relaxed in the living room. "I hardly knew him," said Fiona. "But he was always wonderful to me. He was a sweet man."

Kellan smiled. "You could get some argument on that score on the Hill," he said. "But everybody respected him. He will be missed."

After Fiona had retired, Kathleen drew Kellan onto the couch and took his hand. "I've been thinking about what I told you about me and Liam out in San Francisco. Kellan, I know this is not a very good time, but I need to close that chapter of my life once and for all."

"Sure, I understand. What do you need to do?"

"I spoke with my solicitor on the phone. He has all the information I need to wrap things up, but he suggested that it would be best if we discussed it in person. Kellan, I really need to do this. I'm going to go back to Dublin and meet with him. I'll only be gone a few days." He didn't respond right away, and Kathleen took his hand again. "If this really upsets you, I can probably do everything from here. Or I can wait a while. We still have to decide when we're going to get married."

"You know I wanted to marry you the day you got here," he said. He smiled. "You've been testing my patience."

She kissed him. "I know, I know. Don't ever doubt for a moment how much I love you, but all this is not easy for me. My whole life is starting over, and I just don't seem to be able to let go of the past. We've been over this before, but here I am in my forties and thinking like a teenager. I just can't get my head around all this right away. Please be patient with me, Darling. I promise that one day soon I'll get good and roaring drunk, sleep it off, wake up with a headache and be ready to start my life over."

"What's all that nonsense about the luck of the Irish? I'm lucky as hell to have found you again, but it seems like someone's banging me on the head with a shillelagh. I know it's all going to end soon, but we've been waiting a long time."

"I know. It will be over soon, and we can get on with our lives. Just hold me." He put his arms around her and she rested her head on his shoulder. They didn't say anything for a while, until she stood up and took his hand and said, "Let's go to bed."

After talking with her solicitor, Kathleen decided that the best time for her to go back was during the Democratic convention. Kellan had wanted to take her along so she could watch the proceedings up close, but he agreed that he would be pretty busy and she would be left by herself a lot of the time. She intended to fly back to Dublin, take care of her business there, then go down and visit with the Connolly family for a few days before returning to the States. "They're really the only family I've had since I was about twenty," she said. "They as good as adopted me, and strange as it may seem, I got even closer to them after Moira died. They always told me that they had accepted her going to America because they knew they could see her now and then. But when she died, that was different. I want to let them know we will always be thinking of them."

Kellan saw Kathleen off at Dulles Airport a few hours before he himself was to depart for New York and the convention. The media had poked around a bit trying to discover who Kellan's lady friend was, but with the presidential campaign approaching, as well as other issues that had broken out in Washington, they were occupied elsewhere. "They've got other fish to fry," Kellan had said to Kathleen when she asked him about the American press. "I'm not the only Congressman who's a bachelor, and I'm sure as hell not the only one with a girlfriend, bachelor or not."

She laughed. "You better not have any other girlfriends or I'll cut your privates off."

"I just love your delicate way of putting things," he said.

The quadrennial Democratic convention in New York was a typically raucous affair. The delegates were certainly going to re-nominate the incumbent president, Walter Mayhew, even though many in the Democratic Party thought an alternative might be in order. The president's tenure in office had been rocky, with suggestions of improprieties on the part of certain members of his staff. Two of his cabinet secretaries had resigned under pressure, and his relationships with Congress had been disappointing. Still, he was an effective speaker, and his approval ratings had hovered close to the fifty percent mark.

President Mayhew was seen as weak enough that a few possible candidates had their names bandied about. One of them was Congressman Kellan Maguire of New York. When his name was first mentioned, several media personalities tracked him down and stuck a microphone in his face with a cameraman standing by. "Is it true that you are considering a run for the Democratic nomination?" one of the questioners began.

"Absolutely not," he said. "I'm not sure I have the experience to be president; after all, I've only been in Congress for three terms."

"So you're saying that when you get a little bit more experience you will be running for president?"

"Did I say that? What I said was that I absolutely do not have any plans to run for president, now or at any other time. I promise you, if I make that decision, you'll be the first to know."

"Thank you, Congressman."

When the reporter had gone off in search of other prey, Kellan turned to Alex. "Well that should do the trick until the next one shows up," he said. The next one showed up about ten minutes later, and the previous conversation was repeated more or less verbatim.

Another boomlet got going for a popular Democratic senator from Illinois, but that one also fizzled out, and the convention got down to the business of re-nominating President Mayhew and arguing over platform issues. Given that the convention was in New York, and both the Yankees and Mets were in heated pennant races, the convention failed to draw the attention that the party faithful might have hoped for. But at least most of the televised coverage outpolled the summer reruns on the major television networks. The convention adjourned with ringing hopes for a solid victory in November. The Republicans, of course, had other ideas.

In the weeks between the two conventions, Kellan was out of sorts. Alex complained to him that he was cranky and irritable. "How come you don't give me the finger anymore when you leave the office?" he said one afternoon.

"Shit, Kellan, you're bad enough as you are; I don't want to make you any worse."

"You're so thoughtful," he said. "What would I do without you?"

They had dinner together a few times and she tried to cheer him up. "When is she coming back?" Alex said as they were finishing up dinner at a restaurant one night. There was no need to identify the 'she' in question.

"I was hoping she'd come back before the Republican convention," he said. "We'll have a little down time while that's going on. She's still with the Connolly family in Mallow. I guess she'll come back when she gets good and ready."

"You sound pissed," Alex said.

"Yeah, I know. I just have this uneasy feeling that somehow this thing isn't going to work out with her."

"What do you mean, for Christ's sake? She's crazy about you, and you can't think for a moment that she won't be happier than hell to spend the rest of her life with you."

"I know that. It's just that after those years of sort of having her in the back of my mind, and then having her with me again, it just seems too good to be true. I've never really been a pessimist, but I just wish she would get back here so we can get married and things will settle down. Like with Carmen dying, for example; we were having such a good time and then, bam! The bottom falls out."

"The redwoods aren't going anywhere. You and she can always get back to that."

"I know, I know." He stirred his coffee for a moment. "I've been thinking about maybe flying over there to see what's going on, but I'm not sure that would be a good idea."

"Why not?" Alex said.

"Well, suppose for some reason she's not ready to come back. She might think I was trying to force her and get upset. She's told me a lot about her life recently, and a lot of it wasn't very pretty. Coming over here to marry me and live in the States permanently is a big deal for her. I just don't want to do anything to frighten her off."

"Do you really think it's that bad, that she's that nervous about everything?"

"Hell, I don't know. I just thought she'd be back by now. All that business about her former husband has been settled. As far as I know, there's nothing keeping her there. She's with Moira's family, of course, and that's a really comfortable place for her. I think the best thing for me to do is just take a deep breath and hold on."

"Probably." Alex thought for a moment. "How's Fiona doing?"

"She's doing great. She thinks she wants to go to law school here. With those LSAT scores and her record at Trinity I might be able to pull some strings and get her accepted somewhere, but first she has to decide what she wants to do. I'm not convinced she really wants to be a lawyer."

"Well don't push her. She may be talking about going to law school because she wants to follow in your footsteps. Have you pushed her in that direction?"

"Hell no. I've just tried to be helpful—I guess it might seem that way." He paused and thought about that. "Anyway, if she does want to go, NYU looks promising; as a congressman from New York, I could probably get her accepted even at this late date. The advantage of Catholic, of course, is that it's right here and she could live with me. Or, she could get into a night program. Both Georgetown and George Washington have part-time evening programs."

"That might be good. Part time would take longer, but it might be a bit more relaxed. She said she wants to work while she's going to school."

"Yeah, she told me the same thing, and I said she didn't have to work. But she is pretty adamant—told me I had supported her long enough."

Alex smiled. "That's just like her. God, Kellan, she adores you. I swear, there are thousands of kids who grow up not knowing their fathers as well as she knows you, and vice versa. My dad didn't know me."

"Did your being gay have anything to do with that?"

"I don't know … probably. He wasn't mean to me or anything. Just kind of aloof. And of course I had two brothers, so naturally he focused on them. That's probably why I became a jock."

"To get your dad's attention." She nodded, and Kellan just shook his head.

During the Republican convention Kellan flew up to Boston to visit Eddie, Eileen, Mary and Tom, and to spend a little time with Fiona away from the capital. They discussed her law school plans, and she agreed with Alex's notion that part-time in Washington might be better. "I just want to be doing something productive," she said, "and I met a couple of people I really like down there."

"Yeah, that guy on Senator Montgomery's staff sure took a shine to you, didn't he?" Fiona blushed, and Kellan thought, 'I knew there was something going on there.' "He seems like a pretty decent chap."

"I think your friend Jordan sort of arranged it that we would meet," she said.

"Did you mind that?"

"No, Jerry is really nice. He told me to let him know when I was coming back to Washington."

"So that's why you want to come and live with me?"

"Come on, Dad, I wouldn't want to go to school somewhere just because of a boy. Besides, I've been talking to Aunt Eileen about doing nursing—I'm still thinking about it. Anyway, Jerry is nice, but I'm not going back to Washington just to see him. "

He smiled. "A lot of women do that."

"Yeah, do you think I'd have gone to medical school if it hadn't been for your Uncle Eddie?" said Eileen.

"Oh, for Christ's sake," said Eddie. "I had to find a job up here because you were going to medical school. I was all set to go to New York to make a million dollars."

Fiona went over to Eddie and gave him a hug and kissed him on the cheek. "I always knew you were a good guy," she said.

Since all of Kellan's family knew Jordan and Shelley Montgomery, they got together at Tom and Mary's house to watch Jordan's acceptance speech. He was a good speaker, and the delegates roared with approval as he outlined his plan for gaining the White House. The Republicans smelled blood in the water, knowing that President Mayhew was vulnerable. They were anticipating a victory in November and whooped it up with enthusiasm.

"I'll vote for him even if he is a damn Republican," said Eddie.

"Well, then, if you're going to vote for him, I guess he's home free," said Eileen.

Mary chimed in. "Jesus, Eddie, not long ago you said you wouldn't vote for a Republican if the other guy running was a convicted felon."

"Oh, for Christ's sake, we all know Jordan. He's as straight as an arrow, and not one of those damned stuffed-shirt Republicans, the kind who get pissed off if you say Jesus Christ was a Democrat."

"Yes, you can tell Jordan that our whole fuckin' family is voting for him," said Eileen to Kellan.

"Eileen, watch your mouth, for Christ's sake!" said Mary, glancing at Fiona.

"Oh, and I suppose she's never heard that word before!" said Eileen.

"What about it Fiona? Do the Irish cuss a lot?" said Tom, who always enjoyed it when the Maguires got into a verbal brawl.

"I think we invented it," said Fiona. "You ought to hear Grandpa Patrick and Brendan when a piece of machinery breaks down. It's fookin' this and fookin' that. Grandma Libby opens the door and yells, 'Jesus, Mary and Joseph, you two will curse the leaves right off the trees! I can hear you in here with the windows closed!'" Everyone laughed.

"That's what we're famous for," said Eddie. "Cursing and drinking. You know what they say, wherever you find four Irishmen, you'll find a fifth."

"Actually a lot of young men don't drink these days," said Fiona. "There's a group in Ireland called the Pioneers. They are very religious, and the boys who are members take a pledge not to drink until they are eighteen. Most people in Ireland are aware of the drinking problems. Weekends in Dublin can be pretty rowdy."

"Is that why you're staying here in America?" asked Mary.

"No. Not really. I guess I'm like my mum. My birth mum. You all knew her." He smiled. "My family says that one of the reasons that Mum fell for Kelly was that he would take her to America."

"I'd like to think there was more to it than that," said Kellan.

"Your mother was a sweetheart. We adored her," said Eileen. "And she adored Kellan. That was the saddest thing that ever happened to this family as long as we have been alive. But we got you, Fiona. And Lord, how much we see your mother in you! You surely take after her."

"I wish I had known her," said Fiona softly. The room was quiet for a while, and Fiona's eyes filled. Kellan went over and sat next to her and put his arm around her shoulders. "I'm sorry," she said. "You all are so good to me!"

Kellan and Fiona flew back to Washington the next day. Fiona went off to visit Georgetown and George Washington in order to investigate the possibilities for part-time law school. She told Kellan that she didn't want him to have to pull strings to get her into a law school long after admissions had been completed. "Besides," she had said, "I want to get a job. You can pull some strings for me on that if you want to," she added with a laugh. "But I don't want to start anything until next year."

265

Alex had gone off hiking along the Appalachian Trail with some friends. Jean was holding down the fort in the office quite effectively in the aftermath of Carmen's death; she seemed quite comfortable with her new responsibilities. Kellan was also aware that she had become close with a member of one of the staffs on which Kellan served; Kellan had seen him hovering around Jean's desk. Kellan asked her if it was getting serious.

Jean blushed, something he didn't see her do very often. She smiled. "Could be," she said. "We've been seeing each other a lot."

"He's a good guy," said Kellan. "You two make a nice couple. Are you thinking, maybe, about marriage?"

"We've talked a little bit about getting married in December, you know, after the election. It will be pretty slow around here at that time. You'll have to give me away, Kellan; you know my dad died a couple of years ago."

"I'd be honored," he said. "I think that's wonderful, Jean." She was approaching the age when professional women in Washington either got married or resigned themselves to life as a single woman.

On the Monday morning after they had returned to Washington, Kellan got a call from Kathleen. "I can't stand it anymore," she said cheerily. "I miss you! I'll be there Wednesday afternoon."

"Wonderful! I was beginning to wonder if you were coming back at all."

"Don't be silly, Lover. There's no way you're getting rid of me. I just wanted to leave here in peace, and I've found it. I'm ready to become a Yank!"

"You'll never be a Yank, but you can be happy here. You can stay as Irish as you like and I'll always love you." He took down the information on her flight number and promised to be in Dulles airport with open arms when she arrived. The sense of relief he felt when he lowered the phone almost moved him to tears. He had known in his mind that she would be returning, but his heart needed reassurance, and now he had it.

He was back in his apartment when Fiona came in from her fact-finding journey into the law school world of Washington. "Guess what? I think I have a job. I was over at Georgetown law school, and I talked about wanting to work while going to school, and a secretary told me about a position in the law library. So I went and talked to them."

"Great. When do you start?"

"Dad, it's not definite yet. In fact I told them who my father was—they asked me where I lived and I said I lived with you; it sort of just came up."

Kellan laughed. "Hey, don't worry about it. So your old man's a politician—you might as well get something out of it for yourself."

"Dad, I wouldn't do that!"

"I know. Just teasing."

She walked over and put her arms around him. "Anyway, I'm thinking about getting my own apartment once you and Kathleen get married," she said. "But I'll have to get that job first. They're going to have me back for an interview."

"There's no rush to do that. There's plenty of room in the apartment for all three of us."

"I know, but I don't want to be horning in on your marriage."

"Hey, you're my daughter! I've missed you all these years, and now you want to move out on me?"

She hugged him again. "I just want to support myself," she said, then turned and headed for the kitchen. "I'll start fixing dinner." Kellan smiled and turned on the television to watch the evening news. Jordan had won the nomination but had not named his vice presidential running mate. Now the pundits were full of speculation about who it might be. Kellan heard his name mentioned, but tossed it off as nonsense. There were plenty of other suitable candidates. He would wait and see.

Into the Cauldron

By the time Kellan got back to his office spaces from his meeting with Jordan in the Senate dining room, he was no longer smiling. Jean stood up as he walked in, took one look at his face and said, "What did he want?"

He didn't answer. He just said to Jean in a stern voice, "Come on in here and close the door," and ducked into his office.

"Jesus Christ, Kellan, what's going on?"

"Is Alex back from wherever she was?" he said gruffly.

"Yeah, she called a little while ago. She'll be in tomorrow morning."

"Call her and tell her to come in right now if she can. Use this phone right here."

Jean stepped over to his desk, picked up the phone and punched in Alex's number. While it was ringing she said to Kellan, "What should I tell her?"

Kellan had spun his chair around and was staring out the window. "Just tell her to come in."

He kept looking out the window while Jean spoke to Alex. "Kellan wants to know if you could come in to the office … Right now … He didn't say why … He's sitting here staring out the window and there's something going on … I don't know. He just came back from a meeting with J … "

Kellan interrupted her. "No, no, don't say anything. Here, give me the damn phone." He put it to his ear said, "Alex, I'd really like to see you as soon as you can get here; it's important. … I'll tell you when you get here. … Okay, great!" He hung up the phone.

Jean was sitting down again, looking very nervous. "Kellan, will you please tell me what the hell is going on! What did Jordan want?"

"Okay, starting right now, everything we say stays right here in this room. Jordan wants me to run for VP on the ticket with him."

"Holy shit!" Jean looked surprised, but couldn't keep a smile from flitting across her face. "What are you going to do?"

"As soon as Alex gets here we're going to talk this thing through. Fiona is out somewhere—she'll be back by dinner time, and Kathleen is arriving tomorrow afternoon at Dulles. But the three of us need to think through whether this is a good idea."

Jean just stared at him with a puzzled expression on her face. Then she shook her head. "What do you mean, Kellan? He's your best friend on the Hill. How can you turn him down?" She paused. "Was he really making the offer, or just asking if you'd be interested?"

"It was a real offer. And he's in a hurry for an answer."

"God, he's got to give you a little time, doesn't he?"

"You know what the press is doing. They're bugging the shit out of Jordan and his team. They have a short list of possibilities, and everyone in this town is placing bets on who the lucky guy—or girl—is going to be."

"Your name has come up."

"Yeah, but just barely. The Democrats made some noise about that also."

"Well, it shows you're popular in both camps." He shook his head. "One thing's for sure—you can't give him an answer until you talk to Kathleen. You can't just dump it on her. Could you maybe call her?"

"Are you kidding? She might never get on that plane tomorrow. No, I have to do it face to face."

"Okay, so that means you have to hold Jordan off until at least tomorrow evening."

"Yeah, and he wants an answer by tomorrow morning."

Jean thought for a moment. "You could say no."

"Yeah, but he'd want to know why, and I'd have to bring up Kathleen, and it would eventually get back to her that she's the reason I'm not running for VP." He thought for a few moments. "No, I can't do that. I'm going to have to stall him off."

"Shoot, Kellan, just tell him Kathleen's coming back tomorrow and you need to discuss it with her."

"Jean, I've known Jordan since fifth grade. He's real nice and patient, but he's just been nominated to run for President of the United States. When he gets his mind made up on something, he doesn't fool around. Years ago he told his firm back in Boston that he was going to move back to Pittsfield where his family was from and run for Congress. I thought he was just thinking about it, but the next day he walked into the senior partner's office and handed in his resignation."

"Just like that?"

"Just like that. And that's probably the way he decided on me, and now he wants me to give him an answer by tomorrow morning, and he was being nice giving me that long."

There was a knock on the door and Alex peeked in. "Can I come in?" Kellan's door was usually open unless he was meeting with someone in private.

"Sure, sure," said Kellan. "Come on in, Alex, and thanks for coming."

Alex was wearing a sweat suit and running shoes. She looked as if she had just gotten out of the shower; her hair was still damp. "So, what's going on? Are we going to declare war on Russia?"

"Naw, it's not that simple," said Jean. "I wish it was."

"Tell her, Jean," said Kellan.

"Jordan Montgomery asked Kellan to run with him for Vice President," said Jean.

Alex sat down and stared at Kellan. "Jesus," she said. "Then we're going to have to start working on the campaign, right? Is that why you wanted me in here right now?"

"No, I'm trying to decide whether I should accept," said Kellan.

"What do you mean, whether you should accept? You're going to do it, right?" Alex looked at Jean as if summoning support for what she apparently felt must be a foregone conclusion.

Kellan stood up and started walking around. He looked at his watch, mumbled something to himself about what time Fiona might be back at the apartment, and sat down again. "Okay," he said. "Let's start with, what happens if I say no? What does that mean?"

"Too bad Carmen isn't still with us," said Jean. "We could sure use his input right now."

"Okay," said Alex. "If you say no, your relationship with Jordan is messed up. With him in the White House pushing the agenda that you guys have been working on, you could get a lot done. But if this really disappoints him, you might not have much of a voice over there."

"He's not like that," said Kellan. "I've known him too long."

"He's going to be president," said Alex. "There's no way Mayhew is going to beat him. And who is he going to have for advisers? They'll know you turned him down, and you'll be on their shit list. And over on this end of Pennsylvania Avenue, people will wonder what you have up your sleeve. Are you holding out for the Democratic nomination in four years, or eight years, assuming Montgomery gets reelected? You've got a lot of credibility up here on the Hill, and if you deny your friend, what's that going to do to your reputation?"

Jean said, "She's got a point, Kellan. The best thing you have going for you up here is that you're dependable. You're loyal to your friends and respectful of your opponents. That counts for a lot, in case you haven't noticed. And how are you going to feel four or five years down the road when you realize that you had a chance for something bigger and turned it down? This is a once-in-a-lifetime deal."

"I know. But so is Kathleen. Jean, you don't know her very well yet, and you don't know as much of the history as Alex does. Hell, you know a lot of people have wondered why I never remarried. Well, Kathleen is the reason. My feelings for her go back to the time before my wife died, when I was still in Ireland studying. Suppose I accept this, and she can't handle it?"

"She'll accept it," said Alex. "The way she feels about you, it would kill her if she thought she had denied you something like this."

"I'm not so sure about that. She's been sitting over there in Ireland for the last month or so, probably wondering whether she really wants to give up everything to come over here and marry this Yank. We've had some real long talks, and I can't say I'm sure what she might do."

Nobody said anything for a few moments. "Well, Fiona will be tickled to death," said Alex.

"She sure will," said Jean. "From everything I've seen of her, she'll be out there standing on street corners handing out flyers for you."

Kellan smiled and seemed to relax a bit for the first time since he had come back from his meeting with Jordan. "Yeah, she'd do that," he said. "Look, how about if we all go over to my place and wait for Fiona. We'll order some food and talk this thing over with her in on the conversation. When Jordan calls tonight, I'm going to tell him Kathleen's back tomorrow afternoon and I can't give him an answer until I talk to her."

"Is there anybody else you want to bring into this discussion?" said Jean. "There are going to be some huge repercussions one way or the other."

"Look, you two are my brains trust. You've been in this stuff with me longer than anybody else in this business. Let's just the three of us and Fiona work it out, and if I need to call anybody else, we've got time."

"Sounds like a winner," said Alex. "I'll go home and finish my shower and see you at your place."

"Good." Alex got up and bolted out the door. "Jean, let's you and I go over anything that's hanging fire and wrap it up. Tell the staffers to go home unless you think we might need them for something."

"Got it, boss."

Kellan sat back down in his chair, spun it around and adopted his thinking posture: his feet on a book shelf, hands behind his head, staring out the window. 'Man oh man,' he thought, 'I never saw this coming.'

Fiona came through the door of Kellan's apartment just as a pizza delivery man was leaving. "Hi, everybody! Are we having a party?"

"Something like that," said Alex. "Grab a slice of pizza and a beer and sit down, and we'll fill you in."

"Fill me in on what?" Fiona looked around and seemed to pick up on the fact that something big was going on. A few moments later she came back from the kitchen with her pizza and beer. She sat down on the couch, put her pizza on the coffee table and took a sip of beer. "Okay, I'm ready," she said.

Kellan decided to be the one to break the news. "Jordan Montgomery has asked me to run with him as his vice presidential candidate."

Fiona looked startled. "When? I mean, for this election coming? You're kidding, right?"

Kellan said, "Well I'm not going to say I wish I was kidding, because this is a pretty big deal. No, Sweetheart, he's completely serious and he wants an answer very soon."

Slowly Fiona seemed to grasp what was going on. As she did so, her excitement became obvious. She put down her beer and walked over to where Kellan was standing and took his hands in hers and looked at him. "My God, Dad, vice president of the United States! I can't believe it. Aren't you thrilled?"

"Sure I am. I was absolutely stunned when Jordan asked me, but it is an honor. I sort of protested, but he said he had thought about it and has made up his mind. I'm not sure it's a good idea?"

"Why not? When did all this happen?" Fiona asked.

"Just this afternoon. We're all here to discuss it, and you need to be in on the discussion. It's going to affect you, too."

"What do you mean, will we be living in the White House?"

Kellan laughed. "No, the vice president has his own quarters up on Massachusetts Avenue. It's on the grounds of the Naval Observatory and used to be the quarters for the Chief of Naval Operations. It's a pretty nice place—I've been there a couple of times."

"So, you and Kathleen would live there?"

"I'm afraid you'd also have to, Honey. You will have to put off the idea of your own apartment for a while."

"But why?"

Just then there was a knock on the door, and Kellan went to answer it. Two young men in dark suits were standing in the hallway outside his apartment. "Good evening, Congressman. We're very sorry to disturb you." The speaker held up credentials. "I'm Sam West, and this is Charlie Blackford, United States Secret Service."

Kellan smiled. "Well, I understand why you're here, but isn't this a little bit premature? I know that Jordan Montgomery has made an offer, but I didn't think it was settled yet."

"We're aware of that, Congressman. Actually there are two other names on the list; however, I can't disclose them."

"Come in, gentleman. I have some friends here, but they will certainly understand. But I was under the impression that Senator Montgomery's offer was fairly firm."

"We're not in a position to verify that, Congressman," said Tom. "But I can tell you that you are the first person we were supposed to visit, and to make sure that we got in touch with you before we talk to anybody else. I'm guessing that the other two names are a backup plan."

"Ah, I see. Okay, what can I do for you?"

"We won't disturb you, sir," said Charlie. "We just have a couple of questions. First, is this the only entrance to your apartment?"

"Yes, it is."

"Do you have any other residences where you might be living in the next few months?"

"Well, I was planning on vacationing somewhere, but this is my only residence."

"And how many people live with you here, Congressman?"

"My daughter, Fiona; she's here now. And my fiancé will be returning from Europe tomorrow. She'll be living here also; we're planning to be married soon." Fiona had come to the entryway to see what was going on, and Kellan beckoned her to come over. "These gentlemen are from the Secret Service, Fiona. It's just a routine visit. This is my daughter, Fiona," he said to the agents.

Sam gave a casual salute toward Fiona. "Evening, Ma'am. He turned back to Kellan. "Would you mind giving us your fiancée's name, sir?"

"Kathleen Morrissey."

"And does she have a current address other than this one?"

"No, she has been a resident of Ireland all her life and is in the process of moving her residence permanently to the United States. As I said, she'll be living here."

"Thank you very much, Congressman," said Sam. "If you don't mind, we'd just like to take a quick stroll around the apartment. It will only take a couple of minutes."

"Be my guest," said Kellan.

The two agents walked into the living room, nodded and said good evening to Alex and Jean, walked around and poked their heads into every room, thanked Kellan and excused themselves.

"Secret Service," said Kellan to Alex and Jean.

"Wow, they don't fool around, do they?" said Alex.

Fiona was standing there looking puzzled. Kellan looked at her. "That's why you won't be able to have your own apartment, Sweetheart. If I go through with this, you'll probably have Secret Service protection with you most of the time, at least after the election, assuming that Jordan wins. It'll be much simpler if you're living with me."

"Wow, I had no idea," Fiona said. "Why would they need to guard me?"

"There are lots of kooks out there," Kellan said. "It's the job of the Secret Service to protect immediate families of the President and Vice President. When there's an overt threat or an assassination attempt, it's all over the news. But I'm told by people who know that there are dozens of incidents every year that never make it into the press. A lot of those wing nuts just want their names in the paper, and the Secret Service wisely does not oblige them."

"Let's have some more pizza before it gets cold," said Alex. "We should go into the dining room."

They sat around the large table and continued their pick-up dinner. "I'm guessing that Jordan is assuming that you're going to accept the position," said Jean. "Otherwise, why would he have sent the Secret Service?"

"It's probably just a precautionary step," said Kellan. "They don't like surprises."

"So now all we have to worry about is Kathleen," said Alex.

"That's assuming that Kellan is comfortable with the political ramifications," said Jean. "Kellan, you'll have to agree that from a political standpoint, it's a no-brainer."

"That's right," said Alex. "You'll have everything to gain by doing it, and a lot to lose if you don't. I just don't see how you could possibly turn it down."

"Then all we have to do is convince Kathleen," said Kellan.

"Or not," said Alex. They all looked at her. "I mean, if for some reason she can't accept it, I think you'll just have to do it anyway. She could change her mind any time, but if you turn it down on account of her, there's no going back."

"Dad, she'll be thrilled, I'm sure," said Fiona. "Sure, she knows you're a politician, and she surely knows what that means. I mean, look what happened to Liam."

"Yeah, but starting a new life in a new country in a situation like that is not something that the average immigrant runs into when they first get off the boat. It's a huge step for her."

"She might actually like it," said Alex. "Hell, I've talked to her a lot, and she's full of ideas and opinions. As the wife of the vice president of the United States, she should have a pretty good platform to get her ideas out there."

"Yeah, that's the good news and the bad news," said Jean. "You all know her better than I do, but I gather she's no shrinking violet."

Fiona laughed. "I think you could say that, Jean. Nobody ever accused Kathleen of being shy."

"Okay, moving right along," said Alex. "Assuming that we're all in agreement that Kellan is going to accept Jordan's offer, all we have to do is figure out how to convince Kathleen to go along with it."

They talked for a while about the theoretical problem they had raised. The consensus began to grow that Kathleen would be able to accept the notion of possibly becoming the second lady of the United States. They agreed that they would have to put her on the fast track for citizenship, but that was not a problem. She knew enough about the United States that she could probably pass a citizenship exam without any additional study. Alex promised to look into it. Eventually they got around to discussing the implications of Liam's activities with the IRA. They were all convinced that Kathleen had never had any direct involvement with the IRA or Sinn Féin, but they would have to be sure of that.

"Sooner or later, the media are going to track that down," said Alex. "She's going to need somebody good to help her out with all the stuff. You're sure not going to have time if you're out there campaigning," she said to Kellan.

"How would you like the job?" said Kellan.

Alex smiled. "Might be fun," she said. "Wouldn't you just love to see her on 60 Minutes?"

"Bite your tongue," said Kellan. "Although it might be fun to see her go head to head with Zelda Brewer."

"No contest," said Alex, grinning.

The phone rang, and Kellan said, "That'll be Jordan."

"So tell me who you're huddling with," said Jordan after Kellan had answered the phone.

"Just the usual suspects," said Kellan. "Alex, Jean, and Fiona. And we had a surprise visit from the Secret Service a while ago; I guess you probably knew about that."

"Interesting," said Jordan. "They've been hovering ever since the convention was over. I guess they're just doing some background checking."

"I'm assuming they got my name out of the Yellow Pages," he said, and Jordan chuckled.

"They started asking about that right away, and I had to give them some names. To be honest, Kellan, I told them you were my first choice. I hope that didn't bother you."

"I didn't really expect to see them at this point," Kellan said. "But they were very nice. No problems."

"So," said Jordan. "Are you ready to give me your answer, or am I going to have to wait until breakfast?"

Kellan took a deep breath. "Jordan, I'm going to have to ask you to give me a little extra time."

"You've got to be shitting me, right?"

"Look, you haven't met Kathleen yet, but you know the whole story. Hell, you've known about her since we were back in Boston together. She has finally cut herself loose from Ireland and is on her way back here tomorrow. She's arriving in the afternoon at Dulles, and of course I'm going to meet her. Jordan, much as I would like to, I can't give you an answer until I've spoken with her.

"Alex and Jean have been with me since this afternoon, and we've gone over everything from my end of the deal. But look, Jordan, you have to understand this. Kathleen and I are planning to be married, practically as soon as she gets back. We would've been married before now except that she had some loose ends to tie up back in Ireland. Where she is concerned, I can't make any assumptions, and once you meet her you'll understand immediately what I mean. She's a very strong woman, and she's been through a lot of really rough stuff in her life. I think I told you about her husband being killed by the RUC. I think she's okay with all that stuff now, but this will be a huge thing for her to have to deal with."

"I understand, Kell, but I do need an answer. The media are hounding me."

"Look, Jordan, if it weren't for her, you'd already have my answer, and you don't have to guess what that would be. But I just need to be sure."

"Are you saying that she could veto the whole thing?"

"No, that's not what I'm saying. I just feel that I need to tell her about it before I give you a final answer. If you want a tentative yes, you've got it, my friend."

The line was silent for a few moments, then Jordan said. "Buddy, I know you've been carrying a torch for her for a long time. And believe me, I understand. Without Shelley, my life would be an empty shell. So I get it. But there's a hell of a lot of pressure on me to wrap this thing up. You'd think that with the nomination in my pocket, I'd be in the driver's seat, but let me tell you, there are a whole lot of guys who think that once you're President or a nominee for the job, somebody has to tell you what you're thinking. They know you're good enough to have won the nomination, but they don't think you're competent to run your own campaign, or Lord knows, your administration when the time comes."

"I understand, believe me I do. You have my tentative yes, and that's the best I can do. I promise that by six tomorrow I'll be able to confirm it."

"So you're saying that you will accept, even if she objects?"

"Let's just pray that it doesn't come to that. We're coming straight here from the airport, so you know where to reach me. Is there someplace I can reach you in case the flight is delayed, or something like that?"

Jordan gave him a number, then said, "Thanks, friend. We've got a hell of a future ahead of us."

"So, you told him tentative yes?" said Alex when Kellan had hung up.

"You were eavesdropping, I assume."

"Sure. Isn't that what you pay me for?"

"Sure," he said. "I just don't pay you to eavesdrop on me." He smiled at her.

"Wow, Vice President Kellan Maguire!" said Jean. "It sounds really good, Kellan."

"There's a lot of water has to go over the bridge before we're there," he said.

"It's over the dam, under the bridge," said Alex.

"Whatever."

"I still say there's no way Mayhew can win," said Alex. "Hell, he was even challenged for the nomination. Yeah, I'm with Jean, I like the sound of that. Mister Vice—that's cool. Jordan will keep you busy, for sure. You will not be like that guy who said that the office of vice president is like a bucket of warm spit. Who was that?"

"John Nance Garner, Franklin Roosevelt's first vice president. He was known as Cactus Jack, and what he actually said was 'a bucket a warm piss,' but they cleaned it up for him."

Fiona said, "You guys are kidding about all this, right? Patrick and Libby and Brendan and Deirdre are going to be absolutely thrilled, Dad. This time they will have to come to your inauguration, right?"

"I think we can arrange that," said Kellan. "But as I said, that's still a long way off."

"I can't wait to see Aunt Kathleen," she said. "I'm sure she's going to be just as excited as I am."

"You're probably right," said Kellan, and he smiled.

Marriage

"I hope you will be able to come to the airport with me to meet Kathleen," said Kellan over breakfast.

"I had a job interview set up for this afternoon. I could always postpone it," said Fiona.

"It's your call, Sweetheart, but this is pretty important."

"I know, Dad. I'll give them a call and change it to later." Fiona took a sip of her tea and put down the cup. "I still can hardly believe that Jordan wants you for Vice President."

"Pretty amazing, isn't it?"

Kathleen's plane was right on time, and she got through customs fairly rapidly. Fiona rushed up to her as she came out into the waiting area and hugged her. "Kelly has something to tell you," she said.

"Oh? And what's that?" She smiled at Kellan.

"We'll get to it," he said. "Let's get to the car first."

Once they were on the Dulles access road heading back toward Arlington Kellan reached out and took Kathleen's hand. "Okay," she said, "let's have it! What's the big secret?"

"Jordan Montgomery has made me quite an offer," Kellan said.

"I was thrilled when he got the nomination," Kathleen said. "I know you two are close friends; you must be excited for him."

"I am," said Kellan, "but he's put something out there that kind of takes it to the next level. He wants me to run with him on the ticket."

Fiona was leaning forward so that her elbows were resting on the back seat, her head between Kellan and Kathleen. Kathleen looked at Kellan for a moment, then at Fiona. "What do you mean?" Kathleen asked. "Do you mean for vice president?" Kellan nodded, looking straight ahead at the road.

"Don't you think that's exciting?" Fiona said.

Kathleen twisted around and looked at her for a moment. Then she looked back at Kellan. "My God!" Nobody said anything for a minute or so. Then Kathleen said, "When did you find out?"

"Yesterday afternoon," said Kellan. "I thought about calling you, but I wanted to tell you in person. I thought that if I told you over the phone, you might cancel your trip." He tried to keep his voice light, but he was half serious, maybe more than half.

After a long pause, Kathleen said, "No, I wouldn't have done that." She took his free hand in both of hers and squeezed it hard. "I'm committed," she said. "I'm not looking back. I wish you had … No, I take that back. I'm glad you didn't tell me. Maybe you are right; it might've scared me. But I'm here now, and you have to tell me what to do from here."

"I think we should get married right away. There's virtually no waiting time in Virginia; we can do it tomorrow at a courthouse in Arlington. We can have another ceremony at a church any time, but I think this should be something we do right away. If you agree, I'll tell Jordan, and if he has any second thoughts, well then it's his problem."

"Why would he have a problem?" she asked.

"I don't know—this is new ground for him, too. Damn, I wish you had met him. We've been friends since forever. I know he'll love you, but the first thing that happens when you get into that arena is that everybody gets real protective. There will be people checking you out, and it could get complicated."

"Kellan, I don't know … "

"Listen to me," he said. "You are the most important thing in my life, you and Fiona. There's nothing I know about you that could be a problem for anyone. But there's some stuff that could come up, and it probably will come up sooner or later, that will get people talking."

"Liam." she said.

"Most likely, but there's nothing there, and I know that. Hell, you had some pretty strong political ideas about Irish history and the British and all that, but that's history. That's Irish reality. My God, everybody in this country knows about the troubles in Ireland, and people understand that it's a real emotional issue for the Irish people. Your opinions are strong, but they're not crazy. And in all your writing, it's been years since you wrote about that."

They were approaching Interstate 66 and Kellan took that exit and headed in towards Arlington. "I just don't want anything to hurt you," Kathleen said. "I know enough about you and your politics to know that I believe in everything you've done. I mean, Lord, I don't know every vote you've taken over every piece of legislation that you supported. But I do know that you think straight, that you care about the people you represent, and that you only want what's good for your country. How could I disagree with any of that?"

280

"I'm more conservative than you are." Kathleen shrugged, and Kellan took her hand again. "Let's get married tomorrow. Do you think you can handle that?"

She rested her head on his shoulder. "Oh God, this is so overwhelming. But yes, I can handle it. I love you more than you will ever know, and as long as I know that you love me, I can handle anything."

"I've already talked to Eddie and Mary. If they can't get here tomorrow, we'll have another service later on that they can come to."

"I'll be there!" Fiona said enthusiastically. "I can represent the whole family, even yours, Kathleen. You are a member of our family in Ireland, and I know they'll be thrilled for you too."

"Maybe we can get them over here too," said Kellan. "But let's not think about that right now."

There was a message on Kellan's phone when they returned to his apartment in Arlington. Eddie had called and said that he and Eileen would be on an early morning flight to Washington and would take a cab to Kellan's apartment from National Airport. They would be able to stay through the weekend, as Eileen had taken a few days off. He said that Tom and Mary would try to make it down for the weekend.

Jean and Alex were still in Kellan's office, and he checked with Jean to make sure there was nothing pressing that he needed to come in for. "There's nothing going on here, boss," Jean said.

"Kathleen and I are going to get married tomorrow, right here in Arlington at the courthouse," he said. "We'd sure like it if you could be there."

"Are you giving me the day off?" Jean said.

"We're going to do it about 2 o'clock tomorrow afternoon. I'm assuming that will work for you."

"Sure, I'll be there. Would you like to talk to Alex?"

"Just tell her we're back and she can stop by anytime. We're not going anywhere this evening."

"Before you go, Jordan's office called and gave me a number where you can reach him anytime," said Jean. "He's back home in Massachusetts right now, but he'll be down here on Friday. He said he'd be in touch, but he'd like you to call him sometime this evening. He's planning a press conference for Friday and said he hopes you can be there."

"Thanks, Jean. I'll talk to him later. Stop by if you feel like it when you've wrapped it up here."

"Not much to wrap up these days," she said. "I'll see you later."

When Kathleen's luggage was stowed in the extra bedroom, they relaxed on the balcony overlooking the Potomac River. Kathleen appeared to Kellan to be happy, but understandably nervous. "I knew we were going to get married," she said to Fiona and Alex. "But this is still kind of sudden. I feel like I ought to at least have a new dress."

"Why don't Fiona and I take you shopping," said Alex. "Crystal City has some nice stores. It's only a few minutes from here."

"Why not?" Kathleen stood up, walked over and kissed Kellan. "It shouldn't take too long."

He took out his wallet and handed her a credit card. "Take this," he said. "Just don't let Fiona get her hands on it." He looked at his daughter and smiled.

While the women were gone, Kellan made a few more telephone calls. He called Charlie Wright up in Boston and gave him the news about himself and Kathleen. He was holding off on the announcement about the vice presidential candidacy until after the formal announcement, although Eddie had already been informed. He called Mary and told her told her that he was looking forward to seeing her and Tom whenever they could get to Washington. "Bring the kids if you're able," he said to her.

"I will, Kellan. And we're so happy for you!"

As Kellan suspected, the women were taking their time. Alex was not particularly fussy about clothes, though she always appeared well-dressed, but Fiona had taken to American shopping customs with enthusiasm. He had to keep reminding her that they didn't have unlimited closet space, which was apparently one reason why she was bound and determined to get her own apartment.

He made himself a Scotch and soda, sat down in the living room and flicked on the television to catch the evening news. He was not really surprised by the lead story, but he sat up and took notice as the announcer talked about the Republican nominee for president.

"Republican presidential nominee Jordan Montgomery has apparently completed his search for a vice presidential candidate. Although no formal announcement has yet been made, the speculation is that he has made a surprising choice in Democratic Congressman Kellan Maguire of New York. Congressman Maguire's office has refused to comment on the speculation, but it is believed that the Secret Service has already been alerted. Congressman Maguire has been unavailable for comment, and Senator Montgomery's office has declined to comment further, announcing that he will be holding a press conference in

Washington on Friday. It is presumed that will be the occasion for his announcement."

Kellan's telephone at the apartment was unlisted, but it was only a matter of time before reporters tracked it down. He decided to record a message on his answering machine saying that he would have no comment regarding any political rumors. That would not work for long, he knew, but it would be a start.

The women returned with packages of clothing. They also brought some Chinese takeout and two bottles of champagne. "Well, you're not going to have a bachelor party," said Alex. "But we at least have to drink to your health and Kathleen's."

Kathleen hustled into the extra bedroom with her purchases, saying to Kellan, "You don't get to see this until tomorrow." When she had deposited her new wardrobe in the bedroom, she came back, put her arms around him and kissed him. "You know," she said, "when you told me what was going to happen in the car this afternoon, just for a second I wanted you to turn around and take me back to the airport." Kellan started to protest, but she shushed him and went on. "But when I had a few moments to think about it, I decided that this is the way to do it. We could drive ourselves nuts trying to plan something fancy, but this way we'll be married and happy without a huge fuss. I couldn't have planned it better myself." She kissed him again.

It was about 8:30 when the first call came from a reporter. "Hi, Michael," said Kellan when the reporter had identified himself. It occurred to Kellan that he might well have given Michael Fraser of CNN his private number. "Did you have something you wanted to ask me about?"

Kellan smiled at the others in the room as the reporter was stating his case. "You know I'm not going to comment on that tonight, Michael. But you're just doing your job; I understand that."

There were three more phone calls that evening, and Kellan handled each one the same way. When Jordan Montgomery called, Kellan told him of the wedding plans. "I sure wish you could be here tomorrow, Jordan. It would be great to have you here when Kathleen and I get married, but I understand you have a lot going on. You'll get to meet her on Friday in any case. Will Shelley be with you for the news conference?" Kathleen, Fiona, Alex and Jean were all watching as he spoke to Jordan. "That's great. We'll see you then."

"You're going to have to make some remarks on Friday," said Alex. "You probably won't want to be thinking about that tomorrow. Shall we jot down a few ideas, or are you okay just winging it?"

"Hell, I'm not looking to make a speech," said Kellan. "It's Jordan's day, Jordan's announcement. I'm just window dressing. The interesting thing is going to be what's going to happen when they get a look at you," he said, looking at Kathleen. "All the media in this town chasing around about the election, and they've never even heard of you! Wow, are they in for a surprise!"

"You're scaring me," said Kathleen. "But at least Alex is going to take me to a hairdresser tomorrow morning. Good Lord, I can't remember the last time I had my hair done."

"Don't let them cut it," said Kellan. "I've always loved your red hair."

"I promise, I'll just get it trimmed a little bit. You don't mind if I have them turn it to blonde do you?"

"I'll throw you off the balcony if you do that," he said with a laugh. "You'll look gorgeous whatever you do."

Next morning Kellan called Jean, who assured him that there was nothing urgent for him to take care of in his office He said that while Kathleen was getting her hair done, he would probably drop by for a few minutes. He wanted to personally tell the rest of the staff that he was getting married and explain why there hadn't been time to plan a wedding and send out invitations. He would also tell them he had accepted Jordan Montgomery's invitation to run for vice president, and if asked, they should keep it quiet until after the news conference, scheduled for 10:30 on Friday at the Capitol. He assumed that one or more of them would leak it, but as it was already out there, it really didn't matter.

Kellan decided to drive to National Airport to meet Eddie and Eileen. They had been in his office before, but he suggested that they ride over to the Capitol with him to save a little time. Eileen enjoyed wandering around in the Longworth Building looking at paintings and peering into offices. When she returned to Kellan's office she commented on how quiet the building was compared to other times she had visited. "Is it like this every summer?" she asked.

"Only in a presidential election year," said Kellan. "Congress doesn't get a lot done while this is going on. Lots of people are maneuvering for positions, wondering what it's going to mean for their own elections, or maybe thinking about getting a cabinet or subcabinet post. Since it looks very likely that the White House is going to change parties, a lot of political careers will be affected."

Kellan had contacted the courthouse to make sure that everything was in order for the wedding. He was assured that the County Clerk would be available, and that the ceremony could be performed immediately after the issuance of the license. Kathleen had her birth certificate, her passport, and an official copy of Liam's death notice, though she didn't intend to use it, as she apparently had never really been married to him. Kellan just thought it wise if they covered all the bases. Kellan had a copy of Moira's death certificate just in case, although he understood that they would simply have to declare under oath that they were free to marry.

Kathleen was dressed in a silk cream-colored suit. She wore a white blouse underneath and had a pale green scarf around her neck. She had cream-colored high-heeled shoes that matched her suit. Her red hair, freshly groomed, shimmered in the sunlight as they walked toward the courthouse. They had arrived early, and they stopped on the steps for some picture taking. As Kathleen posed with Fiona and then with Fiona and Alex, Kellan was all but overwhelmed by how beautiful she looked; he could scarcely believe his good fortune. Eddie, Eileen, Alex, Jean and Fiona waited while Kathleen and Kellan finished the license application process. Following that, they were all ushered into the clerk's office, and a few minutes later Kellan and Kathleen emerged as husband and wife.

Fiona was beaming, her eyes damp with tears. Kellan was surprised to see Alex wiping away tears; she was not the crying type, he had always thought. He was aware of how much he loved Alex and how much he felt her love for him. Eddie and Eileen were delighted, and sorry that they had not been able to throw a big bash for a wedding. Kellan assured them that he would bring his bride up to Massachusetts at the first opportunity for a church wedding and they could throw as big a party as they wished.

Alex had made a reservation for the party at four o'clock at one of the District's fine dining restaurants, and had alerted the restaurant staff of the special occasion. Kellan had dined there before, and one of the owners greeted him and Kathleen, congratulated them and showed them to a large table reserved in a corner near a window. Champagne on ice was waiting for them as they sat down. Eddie and Alex each offered a toast to the bride and groom, and predictably each one was filled with a bit of humor and spice. Eddie told a rather naughty story about an Irish wedding, and Alex suggested that Kathleen had merely married Kellan in order to get her hand on the American political system and shake it up a bit.

Jean stood and made a few humorous remarks about how her duties had expanded to include wedding preparations, not that she minded, of course! Fiona stood and made a lovely toast to her father and his bride, and with tears in her eyes made a passing reference to her mother, being sure, she said that Moira was looking favorably upon the union. She loved them both, Fiona said, and was surely happy for them. Fiona's toast brought tears to Kathleen's eyes. It was a warm, happy gathering; for a few hours they were able to put politics aside and enjoy the occasion. The restaurant management provided a handsome wedding cake with their compliments to round out the wedding dinner. Kellan and Kathleen were clearly well loved by everyone in the party.

Kellan had invited Eddie and Eileen to stay at the apartment that evening. He had made a reservation for himself and Kathleen at a nice hotel on Connecticut Avenue for both Thursday and Friday night. "We're going to enjoy little privacy while we can," he told everyone. "By this time Friday, we're not likely to have any privacy at all." Kellan had arranged rooms at an Arlington Hotel for Eddie and Eileen and Tom and Mary for Saturday and Sunday nights. Despite the political doings, he would make sure that his newly expanded family would have some time together.

Kellan and Kathleen made love slowly that night, taking their time to let the sensations of pleasure build gradually. As their passion deepened, their rhythms grew stronger, and they finally lay breathless side by side, holding each other, saying little. Later, as they relaxed, they talked of things past, present and future. Although the past, for both of them, was filled with moments of anguish, frustration and longing, especially for Kathleen, they still found much in which to rejoice: warm memories of their brief moments together; the common love they had for Moira's family, especially including Fiona; their shared feeling for the long, tragic history of Ireland and its people, who through it all had managed to hold onto their pride and dignity, with their ever-present sense of humor. Most of all they reminded one another that they had remembered each other, and that their love had endured.

The present moment was, for both of them, full of wonder and pleasure. "Can you believe we are really here?" Kathleen said. "Together like this, after all this time."

"Believe it," Kellan said. "Hold onto it." He kissed her. "We don't know what's coming, but it's going to be a wild ride." He laughed.

"What?" she asked.

"I'm just thinking, Jordan may come to think he made the biggest mistake of his political career."

"What do you mean?"

He pulled her close and stroked her hair. "The press is going to have a field day with us. I hope you're ready for it."

"Bring 'em on," she said. "Isn't that one of your Yankee expressions?"

"You're a Yankee now," he said, and they laughed.

The future lay before them; what it might bring, they would soon find out.

Kellan had asked for a wake-up call at seven am. He woke up just after six and cancelled the call. Kathleen stirred and said, "What time is it?"

"You can go back to sleep," he said. "It's just a little after six." She padded off to the bathroom, and he called room service for coffee, juice and toast.

She came back and stretched out on the bed. "Come here," she said, and pulled him down next to her.

"I just ordered room service," he said.

"I heard you. Just give me a kiss." A few moments later she said, "We are going to have a proper wedding, aren't we?"

"Of course, if that's what you want."

She moved over and laid her head on his chest. "As far as I'm concerned, we're married in the eyes of God. But we should still do it before a priest. Fiona would want that—she's very religious. And your family, aren't they good Catholics?"

"Eileen and Mary sure are. Eddie, sort of. And Tom converted when he married Mary. He's pretty good about it."

"So we should definitely do it," she said. In a moment she added, "Not that I need some priest saying a couple of prayers over us to make it real."

"We'll do it as soon as we can. I think at the family's home parish in Massachusetts would be good. They'd like that. Moira and I used to go to mass there also. Seems like it would be fitting."

"Yes," she said.

There was a knock on the door—their breakfast had arrived.

Media Frenzy: Round 1

Kellan and Kathleen arrived at his office around 9:30. His whole staff was there, as well as Fiona, Eddie and Eileen. After hugs and kisses had been exchanged, Jean said, "Jordan would like to have you come over to his office."

"When?" Kellan asked.

"He said as soon as you got here. It would probably be a good idea to go right now. Everything's under control here," said Jean.

As Kellan and Kathleen walked into Jordan's outer office, a number of the people assembled, mostly members of the Republican National Committee, he assumed, looked at Kellan in a way that didn't seem altogether friendly. Kellan was aware that there had been some significant objection to his being placed on the ticket. Well, he had thought to himself, that's something they'll have to deal with. He shook hands with a few people he recognized, but didn't bother to introduce Kathleen; it would have been superfluous at that moment. As he was shaking hands, however, he glanced around and noticed that Kathleen was getting her share of attention, accompanied by a few whispers.

"Jordan's been waiting for you," said Bob Reynolds. Bob was an experienced Republican operative who chaired the Republican National Committee; he would be running Jordan's campaign. Kellan knew and respected Bob, and he knew that he would not be on the ticket without Bob Reynolds's approval.

Jordan had a look on his face that Kellan hadn't seen before, or at least did not recall seeing. He knew Jordan well enough to know that down inside he was still the same person he had always been. Kellan wasn't sure what the look said—confidence, perhaps, probably combined with something else. In any case Jordan walked over, shook hands with Kellan and grasped his shoulder. "Glad to see you," he said. "I really feel good about this."

Jordan turned to Kathleen, and whatever look he had been wearing changed. "So you're Mrs. Kellan Maguire," he said. The tone of his voice was anything but casual. Jordan glanced at Kellan, smiled and nodded.

"Kathleen, please," she said. "And may I call you Jordan?"

"Absolutely," he said. "Shelley has just stepped out for a moment, but she's dying to meet you."

At that moment Shelley Montgomery came back in to the room, walked up to Kellan, took both his hands and kissed him on the cheek. Then she turned to Kathleen and said, "Kathleen. It's so wonderful to finally meet you. May I give you a hug?"

Kathleen opened her arms and embraced Shelley Montgomery. Jordan, standing behind Shelley, said, "Hey, I didn't even get to kiss the bride."

Kathleen turned, took his hands, and Jordan kissed her on the cheek. "Kellan, I can see why you made me wait," he said.

"Okay, can we get this show on the road?" said Bob Reynolds. "We're fortunate that the weather isn't going to be too hot. Low humidity, a bit of a breeze, so we'll be outside on the East Front steps. Jordan will be in the center, with Shelley on his left. Kellan will be on Jordan's right, and Mrs. Maguire on his right. Jordan will make a few remarks, introduce Kellan, and Kellan will say how happy he is to be on the ticket, blah, blah, blah, and that will be it."

"May I interrupt you Bob?" said Kellan.

"Sure, what is it?"

"I'd like to have my daughter with me as well. Could she stand between me and Kathleen?"

Bob Reynolds stared at him for a moment, and Kellan was certain that he didn't know Kellan had a daughter. "Sure, that'll be fine," he said. He glanced at Jordan, and Jordan nodded.

"Okay," said Bob. "There's going to be a Q&A whether we want one or not, so we're going to go ahead with it. As we all know, there's been a ton of stuff in the press about this so-called split ticket, and Jordan is more than prepared to deal with that. I assume Kellan is also." He glanced at Kellan, and Kellan nodded.

"Now," Bob continued,—he glanced at Kathleen and smiled—"as for any additional questions, and I assume there will be some more questions of, shall we say, a more personal nature, we'll play that by ear." Bob looked at Kellan, smiled and shook his head. "Man, I've got to say, you have exquisite timing!" Almost everyone laughed, but Kellan detected a little grumbling in the background.

"Okay, we've got a few more things to discuss, but the main party will assemble out there at 10:25. Are we good to go?"

Another of Jordan's aides sidled up to Kellan. "Congressman, I assume you know what you want to say?"

"Yes, I think I've got it figured out. I don't have anything written down, if that's what you're asking."

"We just like to be sure that you mention Jordan more than once. After all, if it weren't for him, you wouldn't be here."

Kellan was tempted to say, 'tell me something I don't know.' Instead he just nodded and said, "Of course."

Shelley Montgomery had pulled Kathleen aside and engaged her in what was obviously a friendly conversation. Kellan noticed that Kathleen was smiling, that she occasionally reached out and touched Shelley's hand, and they were obviously sharing a bit of laughter. The room was still quite crowded, and he couldn't hear what they were saying, but he was sure that Shelley was reassuring Kathleen that everything was going to be fine. Shelley was going to make a wonderful first lady; he was sure of that.

Back in his office Kellan took Fiona aside. "Listen, Honey, you're going to be standing up there with Kathleen and me during the ceremony. You think you can handle that?" he asked with a smile.

"Sure, Dad. Is it okay if I call you that? Or should I call you Kelly?"

"Whatever you're comfortable with," he said. "Very few people in the media know anything about you, so you may get a few questions. Just answer them honestly and don't worry about it. There's nothing you can possibly say that would embarrass me or Jordan. If you get a question you don't feel like answering, just say that. Just say, 'I'd rather not answer that right now.'"

"Would they mind if I do that?"

"Just smile when you say it, and you'll be fine—your smile could stop a train!" He kissed her on the cheek. "You look wonderful, and I'm so glad you're here with me."

Kathleen had been listening to Kellan's conversation with Fiona. "Do you think I'll get any questions?" she said.

"I'd be surprised if you didn't," said Kellan. "Same thing goes. Say anything you like; you've got enough sense to know when they start trying to dig too deep. Today's just the introduction. Believe me, whatever comes up today, is going to come up again and again between now and the election." He put his arms around the two women's shoulders. "Damn," he said, "with you two standing next to me, they won't even know I'm alive."

"I heard that," said Alex, who had been standing nearby. "Kellan's right; you two are going to get a lot of attention. I've got five bucks that says both your pictures will be in the papers tomorrow."

"Are you sure?" asked Fiona. "Will they really do that?"

"Actually, make that a hundred bucks," said Alex. "Yeah, you two are both camera ready."

A buzz of conversation preceded Jordan Montgomery's statement to the assembled press and guests. As Kellan glanced to the crowd he could not help noticing that a great deal of attention was directed at the women standing to his right. Jordan Montgomery began to speak, however, and the focus shifted to its proper place for the occasion. "Thank you for coming," he began.

"It is a great pleasure to introduce the man I have selected as my running mate for the election ahead. I am perfectly aware of the discussions in the media and elsewhere when news of my choice was revealed. I was aware of some of the speculation involved, and would like to set the record straight: Here is why I selected Democratic Congressman Kellan Maguire.

"First, Kellan Maguire and I have known each other since before many of you were born; we grew up together, attended the same schools, shared many childhood experiences, and both attended Boston College. Then our paths diverged for a few years as Kellan went off to study in Ireland while I attended Harvard Law School. Our paths re-converged when we both began practicing law in the same arena. Our interests coincided, and although we occasionally found ourselves on opposite sides of a legal issue, our friendship transcended those differences, and we respected each other's positions implicitly. It was I who first entered into politics, but Kellan eventually chose the same course. Because of our legal backgrounds, our political goals were similar, even though we joined different parties.

"As you all are aware, we have worked on and cosponsored a considerable amount of legislation aimed at improving America's economic position in the world. In my campaign for the Republican nomination, I emphasized economic matters, and I fully intend to conduct the coming campaign along the same lines. So the first reason I selected Congressman Maguire was that we have shared goals.

"The second reason, which in my judgment is equally important, is that there has been a great deal of talk in this town about the need for a more bipartisan approach to solving our nation's problems. Those who have followed both of our careers understand that we are not very far apart on most important issues. But more important, for our agenda to move forward, we will need support from both parties. I firmly believe that with Congressman Kellan Maguire's name on the ballot, we will be making a significant step in that direction.

"Finally, and this is by far the most important reason why I have selected Congressman Kellan Maguire for my running mate. I have absolute confidence in his integrity, his honesty, and his fundamental decency. I have been proud to call him my friend, and I am proud to run for office with him."

Jordan turned to Kellan, nodded, and Kellan stepped to the microphone. "Thank you very much, Senator Montgomery." He turned to face the audience. "Ladies and gentlemen, I am humbled by Senator Montgomery's decision to ask me to run with him as he seeks the presidency. As he has mentioned, we belong to different political parties. Nevertheless, we share the same goals; we want America to prosper, to be stronger, and to be more efficient at solving the challenges facing us in these difficult times. As the people go to the polls this November, it is my sincere hope that they will focus on what Senator Montgomery and I have in common, rather than on ways in which we differ."

He turned back and faced Jordan. "Thank you again, Senator. I am honored to be here."

Jordan shook Kellan's hand, then raised both their hands together as many in the audience applauded.

Bob Reynolds stepped to the microphone. "Senator Montgomery and Congressman Maguire will take a few questions."

Dozens of hands went up immediately. Kellan understood that the first to be recognized were reporters known for their fairness and objectivity. They had probably been told in advance that they would be the first to be called on.

"Senator Montgomery," the first questioner began, "How many votes do you expect to lose in the election, given that you have selected a Democrat to run with you?"

"I'm sure there will be Republicans who will find it difficult to vote for me, and that's their choice. But I'm also confident that at least as many Democratic voters will find the ticket to their liking."

Another reporter directed her question to Kellan. "Congressman, how difficult was it for you to accept the invitation to run on a Republican Party ticket?"

"My only hesitation," Kellan said, "was that it might damage Senator Montgomery's candidacy. But after discussing it with him, I quickly became confident that there was as much to gain as there might be to lose. In the end, it wasn't difficult at all."

There were several more questions in the general political vein. After half a dozen or so more questions, the one that they had been expecting was finally posed. "Congressman Maguire, as you are known to be perhaps the most eligible bachelor on Capitol Hill, would you mind telling us who the two women next to you are?"

Bob Reynolds stepped back from the microphone, and Kellan glanced at him. Bob mouthed the words, "Go ahead."

"Certainly," he said. "This young lady next to me is my daughter, Fiona Connolly. And next to her is Kathleen Morrissey Maguire, my wife."

A dozen more hands went up, but Bob Reynolds held up his hands and said, "Thank you, ladies and gentlemen. Thank you very much for coming." He stepped away from the microphone as the buzzing in the crowd reached a new level. He smiled at Kellan, held out his hand and said, "Well, it's out there. We'll see what happens next."

The group retreated inside the capital and quickly made their way back to Jordan Montgomery's Senate office. Alex had been standing behind Kellan and Jordan along with the rest of the aides during the ceremony, and she and Fiona made their way back to Kellan's office, followed by reporters and guests. The mood in Jordan's office was considerably more upbeat than it had been earlier; the joint announcement seemed to have been well received.

Shelley Montgomery took Kathleen aside. "You and I need to get acquainted," she said, smiling. "I know things are very hectic right now, but we will certainly be able to find some time. You and Kellan and Jordan and I need to go off by ourselves for a while and just get comfortable."

"I will welcome that, Shelley. I truly appreciate your graciousness."

Kellan shook hands with a number of Jordan's aides. "We'll get together later," said Jordan as Kellan prepared to leave. "Good job. We're off and running!"

When Kellan and Kathleen got back to his office, Jean looked somewhat frazzled as did a couple of the other staffers. "The goddam phone hasn't stopped ringing," she said. "Guess what they all want to know about." She didn't wait for an answer from Kellan. "They all want to know who that gorgeous redhead standing next to you was, when did you get married, how long has this been going on, and how come nobody knew you had a daughter? Jesus Christ, I guess I was prepared for this, but wow!"

Kellan laughed. "It will all calm down in a month or two," he said. "But there's one thing you and I and Alex need to talk over right away. And that is, whether I'm still going to run for reelection from the Nineteenth District. The answer almost has to be no, so we'll just have to inform the folks in New York. That's probably our first order of business.

"The second thing is that Jordan has told me to go ahead and think about assembling my own campaign staff. Jean, I know you'll need to stay here for a while to keep the office running because my term doesn't end until January. But I'm sure going to need your advice and counsel at the same time. Alex, the same goes for you. You guys have been with me since day one, and I need you. Agreed?"

"Anything we can do, boss," said Jean. "We're here for you."

"You got it," said Alex. "We're with you all the way."

"The first thing we've got to do is deal with all these phone messages," said Jean. "When you have a few moments, we need to sit down and sort through them, see which ones you want to return personally. Alex and I can probably handle the rest." Even in the few minutes since they had returned to the office, the phones had continued ringing, and the staffers were busy jotting down messages. Carlos Gutierrez was overseeing the handling of phone calls.

Kellan clapped his hands. "Okay, everybody, things are going to stay lively around here. I know some of you may be nervous about what the future holds for you, but believe me, we're going to do everything we can to see that you land on your feet one way or another. For the time being, and by that I mean between now and Monday, feel free to say that we have no comment to make about the presidential election at this time. You can say that questions for Congressman Montgomery that deal directly with his office will be handled as usual. Does that work for everybody?"

The staffers nodded or voiced their assent. Each of them was pleased to have been working for a person who was about to have a chance at an even higher office.

Kellan, Kathleen, Fiona and Alex retreated into Kellan's private office. When they were alone, Kathleen held out a business card to him. "Well, the fun has begun," she said. "That was quite interesting." Kellan glanced at the card. Kathleen continued, "A woman gave it to me as we were walking back to the office. She said she'd like to talk to me and asked if I would please call her."

Kellan looked at the card. "Doris Robinson," he said. "She's a reporter for the Washington American. She's one of the good guys." He looked at Alex.

"She is," said Alex. "I've spoken with her on a number of occasions, and she's always fair."

"What do you think, Alex?" Kellan said.

Alex looked at Kathleen. "I think you should call her," said Alex. "You're going to have to deal with the media sooner or later. You might as well start with somebody you don't really need to worry about. She can get some good stuff out there, and that might take a little bit of the pressure off." Alex smiled. "I was watching the crowd out there, gorgeous, and you were getting a hell of a lot of attention whether you realized it or not. You too, Fiona. It was definitely ladies' day out there."

"I noticed that," said Kellan. "For all some of them cared, I could've been reading out of a telephone book." Everyone chuckled at Kellan's observation. Then he looked at Kathleen. "Jordan wants us to join them for lunch in the Senate dining room." He looked at Fiona. "You should come too, Sweetheart."

"Are you sure?" she said.

"Are you kidding? You used to call him Uncle Jordan, remember? I'm sure he and Shelley will be delighted."

The luncheon in the Senate dining room was pleasant and relaxed, despite all the bustle that the day had generated. Bob Reynolds was also seated with them; Kellan had pointed out to Kathleen and Fiona that they were going to be seeing a lot of him in the coming weeks, and the better Bob got to know the Maguire family, the smoother things were likely to go.

When everyone had greeted each other and they were seated, Bob looked at Kathleen with a smile. "So the mystery lady is a mystery no more," he said. "Kellan tells me you're no stranger to politics."

"To be sure, I've seen my share," Kathleen said. "It hasn't always been pretty, but politics in Ireland have never been pretty for very long at a time—a lot of it has been pretty ugly."

"Well, unfortunately, I'm sure you're going to discover that American politics can be pretty ugly also. But we're going to do everything we can to avoid that. The problem is going to be that the other party has a weak candidate, despite the fact that he's the incumbent. They're going to look for any chink in our armor, and they'll consider everything fair game."

"I'll take that as fair warning," said Kathleen. "I hope I can call on you when I get in a jam, Bob." She looked at her husband. "I'm sure Kellan will provide proper guidance when I need it."

"Whether you need it or not," said Jordan, and everyone laughed.

"Jordan, don't be mean," said Shelley. "After all, they're newlyweds. We have to treat them gently!"

"When exactly did you get married?" said Bob, "I really haven't been paying close attention."

Kellan smiled. "It seems like it was a long time ago," he said. "Actually, we were just married yesterday."

"Jesus," said Bob. "You just got in under the wire!"

"What do you mean?" said Kathleen.

Bob smiled. "Well, I'm not sure I'd be too happy if my candidate had a partner who was living in sin."

Everyone laughed again, but Kellan glanced at Fiona. She was smiling and didn't seem at all bothered by the conversation.

Perhaps sensing what Kellan was thinking, Shelley Montgomery glanced toward Fiona and said, "Shall we talk about something else."

By the end of the meal it was clear that Shelley and Kathleen had already begun to form a warm friendship. Shelley had talked about her great-great-grandmother and grandfather who had come over from Ireland during the famine years. She had visited her family's historical roots in Birr, and she clearly had a feel for Irish history, something that Kathleen immediately appreciated. And as for Fiona, it was clear that Jordan and Shelley were already extremely fond of her. Kellan was pleased that within the two families there were likely to be no signs of even the mildest discontent.

It was also very clear to Kellan that Bob Reynolds had come to the same conclusion, and that any remaining doubts he might've had about Kellan's candidacy seemed to be dissipating. He did not doubt for a moment, however, that there were plenty of 'Important Republicans' who resented his presence on the ticket. As of this day, they would have to deal with it; there was no chance that Jordan would bump him because of disgruntlement among the faithful.

"We're having a gathering up in Pittsfield on Sunday," said Jordan as the meal concluded. "Perhaps you all could make it up there?"

"I don't see why not," said Kellan. "We'll do our best."

When they were back in Kellan's office, Kathleen asked Kellan, "When should I call that reporter?" She glanced at the business card. "Doris, I guess it is?"

"How about if I call her and set up an appointment for you next week?" said Alex.

"That's a good idea," said Kellan. "Why don't you arrange a lunch somewhere?" he said. "And Alex, you should plan to go along with her."

Kathleen looked a bit miffed. "Don't you think I can handle myself?" she asked, only half mockingly.

"I know damn well you can handle yourself," he said. "That's what I'm worried about."

As Kathleen smiled, Alex added, "You and I will have to sit down and talk a little about our political media. Doris is decent, but they won't all be. I just want to see how they're going to treat you. As nice as Doris can be, she can also be very tough."

"You probably already know that my wife is very much up on American politics," said Kellan.

"I am, Dearie," Kathleen said, "but only from a distance. This is going to be—what is it that you say—up close and personal?"

"Up very close and very personal, if you let them," said Alex. "But we'll handle it."

"So I'm to be handled, am I?"

Alex looked at Kellan. "You've got one tough lady here!" she said. They all smiled, but Kellan saw that Kathleen had gotten her back up a bit. That was to be expected, he thought. After all, she's been thrown to the wolves pretty fast. He was confident she would indeed handle whatever came her way.

Paper Trail

Kellan and Kathleen spent their second honeymoon night at the hotel in the District. Their lovemaking was warm and passionate, tempered perhaps by the knowledge that they would be spending many nights together for the rest of their lives. As they lay awake, Kathleen began asking questions about the road ahead.

"What will you do if Jordan doesn't win the election?" she said. She was lying on her side facing him, and he had his hands behind his head on the pillow.

"I haven't really thought about that," he said. "My first thought would be to go back to Phillips, Shannon in New York. I've kept in touch with a couple of the partners there, and I'm confident they would be happy to take me back. Or I could go back to the home office in Boston where I started."

"You don't sound all that enthusiastic about either one of those options," she said.

He turned and looked at her and smiled. "That's probably because I don't think Jordan's going to lose."

"What makes you so sure?" Kathleen asked.

"Well, for one thing, he never would've asked me to run with him unless he was pretty sure. He knew from the start that I might cost him some votes, but the polls are showing him with a comfortable lead, so he has a bit of a cushion."

"Okay, but I'm still curious. If you didn't go back to your old firm, what would you do?"

"I don't know. There might be a place at a think tank or a consulting firm. But I don't think I'd enjoy that. I might just go back to New York or Massachusetts and hang out a shingle. Maybe take on Alex as a partner. She's a hell of a fine lawyer."

"That sounds interesting—it would be a big change for you." She paused for a moment. "I like Alex a lot. Doesn't she have a family? She doesn't seem to be married."

"She's gay; I thought you knew that. But she doesn't have a partner."

"That's right—I had forgotten that. Silly of me."

"Actually, she spends a lot of time with me," said Kellan. "I really enjoy her company."

"And she obviously enjoys yours. I can understand why you like her—I'd like to get to know her better myself."

"I'm sure she's ready to show you the ropes of Washington. She really knows her way around, and she's made a lot of friends. I hope she'll stay close to us, and I think she will. She seems to like you. "

"Anything I need to worry about there?"

"Not a chance. Of course, if you gave off some vibes, who knows? But as long as you're married to me, I don't think she would ever try anything funny."

She leaned back on the pillow and closed her eyes, reached out and took his hand. "I'm kind of scared, you know? I thought I was a big girl, but standing on the steps of the Capitol yesterday, I felt pretty small."

"It can do that to anybody." Kathleen closed her eyes, and Kellan watched her as she drifted off to sleep. He kissed her gently, rolled over and closed his eyes. Sleep came quickly.

Kellan woke up early and picked up the copy of the Washington American that had been delivered to their door. He glanced at the first headline: MONTGOMERY CHOOSES MAGUIRE FOR RUNNING MATE! A second headline said: MAGUIRE INTRODUCES FAMILY. Sure enough, a photo on page two showed Fiona and Kathleen standing next to Kellan: Alex was right. He decided not to read the articles, but would wait until he met with the staff for a general conversation about the media coverage. Normally the staff wouldn't come in on a weekend, but he had asked Alex, Jean and Carlos to come in late Saturday morning so they could think about next steps. He showed the photo to Kathleen, and she looked at it with what appeared to him to be amusement.

"Well, Fiona looks fine," she said.

"So do you!"

She smiled and shook her head. "Jesus, Mary and Joseph."

After having breakfast in their room, they checked out of the hotel at 10 o'clock. A reporter approached him in the lobby and asked if Kellan would mind answering a couple of questions. "Not right now," he said with a smile. He didn't recognize the man, and he wondered whether it was an accidental encounter, or whether he had been told to camp out in the lobby following somebody's hunch. He shrugged it off and drove Kathleen back to his apartment. Fiona was there and greeted them both warmly. "I'm going over to the office for a couple of hours," he said. "Give me a call whenever you feel like it, and we'll do something later."

Carlos was in the office when Kellan walked in. "Good morning, Congressman," he said. "Jean and Alex are across the hall in the meeting room. They've got about a thousand newspapers over there." He grinned. "I'm minding the fort."

Kellan laughed. "I wonder what that's about," he said. He checked for messages on his desk, then went across the hall to join the women. "Okay, what have we got?" he said as he walked in.

"Well, it's all over the map," said Jean. "Some of the pundits think Jordan has committed political suicide; that's mostly conservatives. Others think it's a brilliant move—I'm quoting here—a thoughtful attempt to cure the problems of the distressing lack of bipartisanship in Washington these days. Unquote."

"Who was that?" said Kellan.

"Charles Mitchell of the Times," she said, and Kellan nodded. "There are more in that vein, mostly from the solid citizens in the press. I would say the consensus seems to be that for every vote Jordan loses, he'll gain two."

"That would be nice," said Kellan. "What about Kathleen? Anything interesting there?"

"That's where it gets to be fun," said Alex. "In the looks department, it's unanimous: you picked a winner. A few of them must have heard her Irish accent, because that came up here and there. Several of them followed her back into the building after the announcement. The people who know your background are aware that you studied in Ireland, so it's no huge surprise. Once that gets around, people won't be so curious about where she came from. One article—and she picked up a newspaper and glanced at it—in a New York paper wondered if Fiona was Kathleen's daughter. They'll be running around all weekend trying to put that all together, so it would probably be good to invite a few people in and talk to them informally. I could probably get half the Washington press corps here in about fifteen minutes."

"That sounds good," he said. He looked at his watch. "It's 10:25 now. Why don't we set it up for 11:30?"

"Okay, who do you want us to call?" Jean said.

"Gather this stuff up and let's go into my office; bring your Rolodexes."

They made eight phone calls, and five of the people they talked to said they would be at Kellan's office at the appointed time. Four were print reporters, and one covered Capitol Hill for a local news radio station, WPOL. Kellan knew all of them and was confident that it would be a productive meeting. When they were assembled in the outer office, Kellan buzzed for Jean to bring them in. He greeted each one by name as he shook their hands: "Marge, Charlie, Spencer, Betty, Marty—good to see you all. Have a seat. Why don't I start by just giving you the basics and I'll be glad to answer some questions."

"Can we quote you directly?" said Marge Wellborn, a senior columnist at the Washington American.

"Let's just call it background. You can let them know you got it straight from the horse's mouth."

"Good enough," said Marge. Each one of them had a notebook and pen at the ready.

"Okay, I don't know how much all of you know about my background, but let me give you the basics. I got married when I was studying in Ireland a long time ago. My wife Moira came back to the states with me and died in childbirth about a year later. The young lady you saw next to me yesterday was my daughter from that marriage, Fiona. Since I was young and single and stupid, I let my wife's family in Ireland raise her. It seemed like a good idea at the time, but I have sometimes regretted it.

"While I was still in Ireland, I became friends with my wife's roommate in Dublin. She was very close to my wife and my wife's family, and we kept in touch over the years. I visited my daughter often, and on many of those occasions I saw my wife's friend, whose name is Kathleen. She was married for a brief time, but her husband was killed. On subsequent visits to Ireland our friendship grew, and I eventually asked her to marry me, which she has done. She was Kathleen Morrissey until a few days ago, and now she's Kathleen Maguire. I'm sure you figured out who she was yesterday, perhaps not by name."

Marty started to raise his hand, but Kellan cut him off. "I'll give you guys a shot in just a minute but there's one more thing I'd like to put out there. If you all agree, this part will be off the record. I assure you that there's nothing in it that's damaging to me or my family, but in the wrong hands it might be misunderstood. Are we okay with that?"

The reporters shared a few glances with each other, but they all nodded. "Okay, here it is. My wife's husband was a member of the IRA. Although Kathleen shared many of his views when she was much younger—I became aware of that when I was still studying in Dublin—, before long she became disgusted with the violence, and she and her husband became estranged. Her husband's uncle had been killed by the British, and he was eventually killed by the RUC. Now here's the part of that's complicated.

"Kathleen's husband was apparently married once before, and his wife had been badly hurt in some kind of IRA incident, and he thought she was dead. However, she managed to survive, though she was in the hands of British authorities. Her husband couldn't find out for sure what had become of her because of the politics in Belfast. I don't know the whole story on that, and I'm not sure anyone does. Anyway, it later turned out that she apparently was not dead, and that he might have still been married to her. In any case, whether Kathleen was legally married to him or not, he's dead. That's not in question. But what I want to emphasize is that Kathleen never had any direct involvement with the IRA or Sinn Féin or any of those outfits. My wife's family, with whom I'm still in close touch, has confirmed that for me, not that I had any doubt." He paused and looked around at each member of the group. "Okay, that's pretty much it. Any questions about this part of it, and we're still off the record, okay?"

"Just one, Congressman," said Marge. "Can you give us her former husband's name?"

"I'm afraid I can't," said Kellan. "This may sound a bit strange, but I only know him by his first name. If I had his last name, I probably wouldn't give it to you anyway. There's no sense whatsoever in dragging that part of Kathleen's life into this. None of you probably remember that far back, but during my first campaign for Congress, my opponent tried to dig around in that stuff because he somehow knew that I had sent money to Ireland, which was true. I gave financial support to the family that raised my daughter and to my daughter herself when she was older. But I am absolutely sure that none of that ever left the family."

Kellan looked at each of them and they nodded in tacit agreement to the terms that he had laid out.

"Okay, now, anything else you want to know on the subject of my family?"

"What did your wife die of?" said Betty.

"She had a very difficult pregnancy. In fact, her mother came over from Ireland for the last month or so to help out. During and right after the birth she suffered a great deal of hemorrhaging, and that's what killed her."

"Where is she buried?" Marge asked.

"Moira's mother, Libby Connolly, stayed with me until the baby was old enough to travel. Then we shipped Moira's body back to Ireland, and I flew back there with Libby and the baby for the funeral. Moira is buried in the cemetery of St. Mary's Church in Mallow. It's about twenty miles north of Cork."

"Can we ask why you never married again?" said Betty.

"Sure you can," said Kellan. "But I'm not sure I can give you a good answer. I guess the best answer is that I never met a woman that I felt like marrying after Moira. I should also say that the more I saw of Kathleen, especially after Moira's death, the closer we became. Looking back, I'm sure she was worth waiting for."

"Did you ever come close with anyone else?" Spencer wanted to know.

"Not really. I took my career as a lawyer very seriously, and I traveled a lot. As you probably know from my political stuff, I was very active in the import export trade business from a legal aspect. When I was still at the law firm, some of my friends tried to nudge me in the direction of getting married again, but it didn't take. I won't deny that I had some women friends, some close friends, in fact, and you can read into that anything you like. But I was never close to proposing to anyone. I didn't really mind life as a bachelor, especially once I began to realize my feelings for Kathleen had never really gone away. I guess you could say I was waiting for her. And now we're married."

"What do you think you're going to bring to Jordan Montgomery's campaign for president?" asked Marge.

"Guys, I don't really want to go into that today. There will be plenty of opportunity for all that in the coming weeks. I just really wanted to settle this family stuff to avoid it being a distraction. Of course I know that's not going to work, but I decided to at least give it a shot."

The five reporters all stood up, chatted with Kellan for a few moments, and he shook their hands and thanked them for coming.

As the reporters were leaving, Jean came in and asked, "How did it go?"

"Okay, I guess. We'll see what shows up in the papers tomorrow. I expect that Spencer will go on the air on WPOL within the hour and give a summary. No need to listen for it—he's a decent guy and won't put any spin on it."

"You know this isn't going to go away," Jean said.

"No reason this can't be fun," said Kellan. Jean just shook her head.

Tom and Mary had showed up and joined Eddie and Eileen at their hotel later that Saturday afternoon. They all gathered at Kellan's apartment to relax and enjoy catching up on family matters. Mary and Eileen were anxious to know how Kathleen was adjusting to her sudden new life in America.

"I'm doing fine," said Kathleen. "It's going pretty much the way I expected when I left Ireland. Except, of course, for the part where my husband, whom I've acquired since I got here, is suddenly about to run for vice president of the United States. Other than that, there's nothing particularly new." Everyone laughed.

"Yeah, just the usual Maguire family stuff. Right, Fiona?" said Mary.

"Absolutely," said Fiona. "I'm actually thinking about going back to Ireland, everything is so dull here!"

"You can take me with you," said Eddie.

"Eddie's in a terrible state because his brother's running for office on the same ticket with a Republican. Next thing you know they'll be substituting The Internationale for the Star spangled Banner," said Eileen.

"Aw, hell, I wouldn't have voted for Mayhew anyway, that crooked son of a bitch," said Eddie.

"How about if we set you up with an interview with the Boston Globe?" said Tom. "I'm sure they would benefit greatly from your political wisdom."

"Hey, I'm all for that," said Eileen. "Then he can quit his day job and run for mayor of Boston."

"Aunt Kathleen, are you glad to have become part of such an interesting family?" Fiona asked.

"Come on, now, Sweetie, you know this could just as well be the Connollys over in Mallow. Eddie, you should get together with Brendan; I think you're both cut from the same cloth."

And so it went for much of the afternoon. Kellan made a reservation for all of them as well as Alex and Jean in a private room at the Capital Grille in Tysons Corner for Saturday evening. Kellan and Kathleen were again the center of attention, and as the party served as a follow-on wedding celebration, there were more toasts to the future happiness of the bride and groom.

Mary made a nice toast to her brother and her new sister-in-law. "I always knew my big brother was smart and would be successful, but this week has exceeded all our expectations. Kathleen, we not only want to welcome you to the family; we want you to know that Kellan has been waiting for this for a long time. And I'm not talking about running for vice president—we all knew he was going to do something like that sooner or later. With all the rush, we haven't had time to go shopping for gifts for you two, which I'm sure will dismay you no end, as that's obviously the reason why you got married—to cash in on the loot." She paused while everyone laughed. "We are looking forward to another ceremony up our way when we can put it all together. We realize that it's going to be a challenge with Kellan having other business to attend to, but we promise you it's going to happen."

Jordan Montgomery's party was scheduled in Pittsfield from three to six on Sunday afternoon. As it was obviously going to be a meeting with political overtones, they decided that Fiona would fly back to Boston with Eddie, Eileen, Tom and Mary. Kellan and Kathleen would fly to Albany and drive from there to Pittsfield, which was only about an hour from Albany International Airport. Following Jordan's party, it would only be a two-hour drive to Eddie and Eileen's home, where they would be staying.

Jordan and Shelley Montgomery welcomed Kellan and Kathleen in the hallway to their spacious home and introduced them to some of Jordan's family members. The Montgomery family home was located on the northwest side of Pittsfield on ten acres of land with a view of the mountains off to the west. A tent had been set up in the backyard; food and drink were plentiful, and servers were assisting guests. Jordan ushered Kellan and Kathleen through a wide middle hallway leading to the rear of the house.

Before they reached the door, Shelley said to Kathleen, "Why don't we sit in here for a while so we can chat." She led Kathleen into a small side parlor while Jordan and Kellan continued outside. Kellan assumed that Shelley's invitation to Kathleen had been prearranged; they were now being managed. That didn't bother Kellan—it went with the territory.

"You will know a lot of folks here," said Jordan. "A lot of them are supporters—the deep-pocket sort, if you know what I mean. I've got to do a lot of meet and greet stuff, but Bob can show you around. He'll fill you in on some of what's been going on in the past couple of days."

"Is there a problem?" Kellan asked.

"Hell, Kell, you knew there were going to be problems when I nominated you." He slapped Kellan on the shoulder and grinned. "My big contributors—and there are probably a dozen of them here—want to be sure their money is going to guarantee victory. I have to be honest, my friend; you make them nervous, not because of who you are for God's sake, but merely because you're a Democrat. They understand that I'm trying to make a statement; they just don't want me to finance it with their money."

"Anything I can do to help, just let me know."

"You know what our message is: it's the same thing we've been working on ever since you came to Congress. Just stick with that, and you'll be fine. If you are introduced to any of these cats, just be yourself, act as if you belong on the ticket—which you do, dammit—and don't apologize for anything. Just remember what it was like when you and I were in court back in the old days with a reluctant witness. All you have to do is convince the jury out there that the guilty son of a bitch you're defending is innocent. That would be me." They both laughed.

"I'll do my best."

"I know you will. Here comes Bob—he'll show you around."

Bob Reynolds and Kellan shook hands, and Bob seemed pleased to see him. "Jordan tells me that some of the natives are restless about me," Kellan said. "Can you add anything to that?"

"The good news is that I think most of the Republican Committee is on board. If there are any who just can't get with the program, we'll ease them out the door. The problem, as you clearly understand, is money. Elections are won with money, and anybody who does not understand that in this day and age is living in a dream world. I'm going to introduce you to some of the RNC whom you may not have met, and then I'll try to steer you to a couple of the fat cats.

"Hell, Kellan, you're a damn good campaigner and I know that. You buried a couple of our guys more than once, and I don't know anyone who would want to run against you for anything. That's why Jordan has you on the ticket; he sees you as an asset, and so do I. But we still have our work cut out for us."

"I'm raring to go," said Kellan. "On that note, I'm planning to use the people I already have with me for most of my campaign stuff. I'm sure you know Jean Slater—she's more than capable of running a campaign. She was trained by Lynn Patterson and has run everything for me since then. You've also met Alex Crowley. She's been with me since we were at Phillips, Shannon. I'd trust her with my life and my bank account."

"How about with your wife?" Bob was smiling, but Kellan was fully aware that he had raised an issue that might be of concern.

"I know what you're talking about," said Kellan. "There's nothing to worry about there, believe me. If she has an agenda, I've never seen any evidence of it. No, I trust her completely. In fact, she and Kathleen have already hit it off pretty well. I have already told her that Kathleen is going to be her project during the campaign."

"Your wife sure is a stunner," said Bob. "You're a lucky man. I understand she's quite well tuned in to politics."

"Yeah, Irish politics for sure. And of all the people I met in Ireland when I was in school there and since then as well, I have never met anyone who knows more about the American political system than she does. Ireland and America have always had—what would you call it?—a blood relationship? When I first met her she was ready to take on the Brits single-handed. Then when she was married, she got a pretty close-up view of the troubles, as they call them. It's kind of dampened her enthusiasm for conflict."

"What was her husband doing?" Bob wanted to know.

"Okay, I knew this was going to come up sooner or later. He was in the IRA."

"Holy shit!" Bob shook his head.

"Bob, there's nothing there to worry about. She was married to him only for a short time, and she never got into any of that; in fact, she had already walked away from the marriage pretty well by the time he got killed."

"Got killed?"

"Yeah, the RUC tracked him down from Belfast to Londonderry and lured him into a gunfight, where he got shot. People can bring this out all they want, but I'm positive they won't discover anything where Kathleen is concerned. I guarantee you that. And just so you know, I met with some of the press folks on Saturday, and told them the story in confidence. They're all good people—Marge, Spencer, Charlie and a couple of others. They have the real story, which is pretty much what I just told you, so if anybody starts digging around, they're in a position to respond."

"Yeah, I heard you had met with some reporters; I just didn't know what it was about. Thanks for telling me, Kellan. I'm sure you've got it under control."

"I'll tell you something else that I'm absolutely sure of. If the media— any of those hotshots who are always trying to stir up crap—try to get to Kathleen, they are going to have their hands full. Not only is she smart, but she worked for a time as a journalist in Ireland. She's published some really good stuff—none of it probably ever reached our shores, but it's solid."

Bob looked at Kellan for a few moments, then nodded several times. "Good. Good. Okay, let me show you around a bit."

As Bob had suggested, all the political people present greeted Kellan in a friendly manner. There were some good-natured jokes about his Democratic credentials, but no one seemed ill at ease with the subject. The same was not quite true of some of the other guests.

"Kellan Maguire, I'd like to introduce you to Wayne Morrow." The Morrow-Childress Company, whose headquarters were located in Erie, Pennsylvania, manufactured equipment for mining and oil drilling. Wayne Morrow's father had founded the company.

"Congressman, I'm very pleased to meet you." Kellan didn't think he looked all that pleased.

"My pleasure, Mister Morrow."

"Please call me Wayne. I was very interested in Jordan's decision to put you on the ticket. Seems like a bit of a risk to me, to be frank."

"I wouldn't doubt that, Wayne. But Jordan obviously thought it was a risk worth taking, and I assure you, I wouldn't have accepted his offer if I didn't think we could overcome any drawbacks."

"Well, that's fine. But let me ask you, how do you plan to conduct yourself as vice president, assuming that you two are elected?"

"This has been pretty sudden, Wayne, and I really haven't had much time to think it over. But Jordan and I spoke just a little while ago, and we definitely intend to follow the path we've already carved out in Congress. As you may know, economic issues have been my focus ever since I decided to run for office, and even before, for that matter. As a Democrat, I am naturally concerned with the welfare of the American worker. At the same time, I have no doubt that what will benefit American business will also help American workers. We have some problems, of course, in that the standard of living of the average American worker—men and women like the ones who build your equipment—is generally far higher than the of their overseas counterparts. I'm sure that American workers must be conscious of that fact. People in other countries often do the same jobs for much less money. I'm sure you're aware of that problem, and so am I."

"So how is Jordan going to use you?" Wayne Morrow asked. "I assume you'll be his attack dog."

"Jordan and I have not yet had time to sit down and figure out exactly what he's going to have me doing during the campaign, but he knows I'll be on message. As for later, besides kicking a little butt over on the Hill, we haven't gotten that far yet. But I'm sure we'll figure it out when the time comes, and I fully believe that people like yourself can be confident that I will be true to Jordan's message."

Wayne Morrow stroked his chin and nodded. He seemed pleased, and Bob Reynolds, standing off to the side, was also nodding. "Very good, Congressman," Wayne said. "Kind of you to be so candid with me." He held out his hand. "Best of luck to you in your campaign."

"Thank you, sir."

"And I understand you've had a wedding. I must say, my friend, that you sure picked one hell of a way to start a marriage." He laughed, and Kellan smiled.

As Wayne Morrow walked away, Kellan said to Bob, "Jesus Christ, news travels fast around here, doesn't it?"

"You bet your ass, my friend. You're in a whole new ballgame now."

Although there were a few women present at the gathering, Kellan thought they were mostly political people. He did recognize one woman who he knew was head of an advertising firm in New York. But it was apparent that Shelley Montgomery felt no need to make her presence felt and was apparently still chatting with Kathleen. That's good, Kellan thought. If Shelley is behind her, so will everybody else be.

Satisfied that he had made the rounds sufficiently, Kellan sought out Jordan and told him he and Kathleen were going to be on their way.

"Give my regards to the family," Jordan said. "I'm sorry you didn't bring Fiona."

Kellan smiled. "I didn't think this was her kind of party."

"You're probably right. Take care, my friend. I'll be in touch."

Women's World

Kellan and Kathleen spent Sunday and Monday nights with Eddie and Eileen and decided to fly back to Washington early Tuesday. Over breakfast on Monday morning, Fiona informed Kellan that she had decided to stay in Massachusetts for a while. She was going to end her job search in Washington for the time being because she had developed another plan. On Sunday afternoon she had driven over to the hospital in Worcester where Eileen worked. "Just out of curiosity," Fiona had said.

As they sat down that morning, Eileen surprised her brother-in-law with an announcement. "I've been talking to your daughter," Eileen said.

"Yeah, I know you have," said Kellan with a smile. "You stole her all yesterday afternoon and evening."

"I wouldn't say I stole her; in fact, it was her idea to come over and see what I do for a living."

"That's right, Dad, it was my idea. I've been thinking about doing something in the medical profession."

"Aha," said Kellan. "I knew you two were up to something."

"Why don't you tell your pop what you were thinking, Honey?" said Eileen.

"I don't know, Dad, I've been watching all that stuff going on in Washington, and I think it's wonderful what you and Jordan are doing. I'm really proud of you. But I just couldn't find anything that seemed to interest me, and I've always thought about maybe nursing school or something like that."

"I think she should think about medical school," said Eileen. "She's a little old to start that, perhaps, but many people have started at even older ages. We have an excellent teaching program at St. Vincent Hospital in Worcester, and I'd be more than happy to help her along. If that seems like too big a mountain to climb, I suggested to her that she might train as a nurse practitioner. They perform many of the same functions as doctors, they just focus on one particular aspect of medicine—like my specialty, for example. They become damn good at what they do, and patients seem to love them. They have most of the skills of a doctor, though limited in

310

scope, as I said, but they seem to adopt the more caring approach of nurses."

"Dad, this is really something I want to do," said Fiona. "Aunt Eileen said I can live here and for the time being just work at the hospital as a volunteer. You're going to be busy as heck with the election anyway, and you don't need me cluttering up the place. I'm so happy for you and Kathleen, and although I love both of you very much, and I know that you both love me, I really believe that you deserve some time together by yourselves."

Kathleen smiled at Fiona, reached across the table and squeezed her hand. "Sweetheart, you are definitely your mother's daughter. I never knew a kinder person in my whole life, and you have all the same instincts as she had. Your dad will tell you that while he was finishing up his work at Trinity, she went out of her way to help him, and it wasn't just because she was falling in love with him!"

"That was a two-way street," said Kellan. "But she helped everybody that way. Many of my friends often spoke of your mother as someone who made their work a lot easier. She was amazing; sometimes she knew what we were looking for before we even asked for it. I can remember time after time that she would come over to where I was working, hand me a book and say, 'you might want to take a look at this,' or something like that. And nine times out of ten, it was something I really needed to see. She was uncanny that way."

"She was," said Kathleen. "I don't know what would have become of me without her as a friend."

Eddie had been following the conversation closely. "Fiona, Darling, one of the saddest days in all of our lives was when your mother passed. God, we wished we could have had more time together with her—she left us far too soon. And as Kathleen said, you're cut from the same cloth."

"Well I guess it's decided," said Kellan. "That sounds wonderful. And since you won't have the use of my car up here, we'll have to think about getting you some wheels."

"Ah, we can manage for a while," said Eddie. "Right, sweetheart?" he said to Eileen.

"No problem," said Eileen. "We're not that far away, and we can do fine with the two cars we have."

Fiona stood up and walked around the table and hugged her Aunt Eileen, then hugged Kellan. "This is what I really want to do, Dad."

"I'm happy for you, Sweetheart." He looked at Eileen. "For both of you!"

On Monday evening Kellan, Kathleen and Fiona had dinner with Charlie and Cynthia Wright, who were thrilled with all the things that had happened in the Maguire family since the last time they had been together. Fiona told them of her plans to stay in the area and work as a volunteer under Eileen's guidance. Cynthia was delighted with the idea and offered Fiona her encouragement.

Charlie, now a senior partner at the firm, was just a tad skeptical about his old friend being on a Republican Party ticket. "I remember when you and Jordan were going at it in the courtroom," he said. "I never expected to see you two on the same side of things. I hope you win!"

"Well, if I don't, I may come back looking for a job at Phillips, Shannon."

"Any time," said Charlie. "We would love to have you back."

On Tuesday morning Kellan dropped his rental car off at the airport and he and Kathleen boarded a flight for Washington. Once they were airborne, they pushed their seats back and relaxed. "I'm really delighted for Fiona," said Kathleen. "That will be a wonderful profession for her. Every time I look at her, I see Moira. She has that same look in her eyes, full of wonder and expectation."

"I know," Kellan said. "I really missed her a lot during all those years when she was in Mallow. But I'm still sure it was the right thing to do."

"You would have raised her just as well," said Kathleen.

"I'm not so sure about that," he said. "I tend to get pretty focused on what I'm doing when I'm working. I hope you'll be able to deal with that."

She took his hand and squeezed it. "Trust me, Darling, you'll always know I'm there with you!"

Alex met them at National Airport in Washington. She planned to drop Kathleen at Kellan's apartment and then drive Kellan to Capitol Hill. On the way back to the apartment, Alex told Kathleen that they had a luncheon date with Doris Robinson on Thursday. "She was very pleased," said Alex.

"I'm looking forward to it," said Kathleen.

Back in his office, after Jean had briefed him on what was on the agenda, Kellan assembled his staff in the meeting room across the hall. "Okay guys," he said. "We're going to run my campaign from here. There will probably be more focus on me than there usually is on a vice presidential candidate, but there's nothing you need to worry about. Technically we can't do any campaign stuff here, but the Republican folks have given me some space in their office over on K Street. We can't use the franking privilege for any partisan political stuff, as you know, but I probably won't be sending out anything anyway.

"Jordan will have me out doing some speaking, and there will probably be a debate with their VP candidate down the road somewhere. There won't be a heck of a lot to do until after Labor Day in any case, so for the time being our job is just to keep the folks in New York happy and assist me with finishing out my term as a congressman. As I said before, you've all done superb work, and I am going to do my best to make sure you are well positioned after the election, one way or another.

"As I told you before, I have decided not to run for reelection, but I'm not going to resign my seat before the official end of my term. Whatever happens, I intend to finish this job before I start a new one. Jean tells me that the Secret Service guys have stopped by again, but they won't have any presence here in this building. They will probably have someone with me when I'm out on the stump, but that's all.

"Fran, I'm going to have Jean and Alex working with me on campaign stuff from time to time, but you and Carlos are more than capable of running the show here in case we're out of the office. I assume everybody else is good with that. Any questions?" There were none.

"Okay, we go into recess next week and won't be back until right after Labor Day, as you all know. So relax, take some beach time or mountain time or whatever you do when you're not hanging around bothering me. Jean and Alex will always know where I am in case you need anything. Have fun!"

Kellan was aware that his staff was divided in their feelings. On the one hand, they were pleased for his prospects; on the other hand, all of the staff had made it clear that they enjoyed working for him, and that they would be sorry to see his tenure as a congressman come to an end. A couple of them had hinted that they would certainly like to work for him in the vice president's office if that were possible, and he promised to keep them in mind.

On the evening before Kathleen's lunch date with Doris Robinson, Alex came to Kellan's apartment and helped him prepare dinner for the three of them. Kathleen sat on a stool in the corner and watched as the two busied themselves in the kitchen. "You seem to know your way around," said Kathleen as she watched Alex get dishes and spices out of various closets.

Alex smiled. "I've done this before. Your husband would have starved to death seven times over if it weren't for me."

"She's lying," Kellan said. "I'm a pretty good cook."

"Is that true?" Kathleen asked Alex.

"He's good at boiled eggs and toast," she said. Then she laughed. "Naw, he's actually pretty good. He makes a mean lasagna."

After dinner they sat in the living room and talked about the coming interview. "What do you think I should be prepared for?" said Kathleen.

"Doris is a pretty straight shooter," said Kellan. "She probably won't come up with anything off the wall."

"But if she does, what would it most probably be?"

Kellan looked at Alex. "It's too bad Doris wasn't in on our meeting last Saturday," he said. He turned to Kathleen. "But if necessary, you can say whatever you like about your personal history. The straight story is out there, and Doris has probably heard about it."

"Maybe not yet," said Alex, "at least the confidential part. But she will—it's only a matter of time. Hell, she and Marge are both at the American. I'd bet a dollar Marge has already spilled it all."

"They agreed that that part of the conversation was off limits," said Kellan.

"Hmmm," said Alex, "that might be useful. If Doris wanders off in that direction, it will be obvious that Marge blabbed. Of course, she can play dumb and ask about it anyway. 'What, me, talked to Marge? I don't know what you mean!'" she mimicked.

"Look," said Kellan, "nobody's going to give a rat's ass about any of this until the campaign gets rolling anyway. So let's not get all worked up."

"Who's all worked up?" said Kathleen. "I'm kind of looking forward to it. I've been in the United States barely a week and already my picture has been in the papers. I must be doing something right."

"There's only one thing I've been thinking about," said Alex. "And that's citizenship."

"What about it?" Kathleen asked. "Does the wife of a congressman or a vice president have to be a citizen?"

"Of course not. But in a campaign, anything is fair game, and it just might come up."

Kellan said, "Alex, why don't you go ahead and make that trip over to the Department of Justice and check with the people in INS. Let's find out what might be possible."

"I have a friend over there from law school," she said. "All I know is that there is a waiting period—it's shorter if you're married to a citizen but still a couple of years. But there are some weird little legal exceptions and who knows, we might be able to come up with something." She paused and smiled. "Of course, you could always go over there and throw your weight around."

"No, that would make it worse. Anything that smacks of favoritism gets people all riled up." His voice had a bit of an edge.

"Kellan, I was only kidding, for Christ's sake."

"Are you two always like this?" said Kathleen.

"Yeah, but he still loves me," said Alex. "Don't you, boss?" She walked over and kissed him on the cheek.

Kathleen looked at each of them in turn with a curious smile. "I told you," said Kellan to Kathleen. "She's an acquired taste."

Alex brought Kathleen back to Capitol Hill after their lunch with Doris Robinson. Jean joined them in Kellan's office, and Kellan asked, "How did it go?"

'Fine," said Kathleen."

"Fine," echoed Alex. "She did real well."

"No bumps in the road?" asked Jean.

"She got into my family background a bit," said Kathleen, "but Liam never came up. I told her that in my younger days I was sort of a radical on the Union question, but she acknowledged that you had a lot of that kind of thing going on here during Vietnam. Of course I already knew that—we had some antiwar protests even in Ireland, though nothing like here.

"She asked if you and I were planning to have children, and I said we hadn't discussed it." She looked at Kellan. "We haven't, have we?"

"Not seriously," he said. "You said once that you wondered if you might be pregnant, as I recall."

'Yeah, and then I had to peel you off the ceiling," Kathleen said, and Alex and Jean laughed.

After a brief, awkward silence, Kathleen said, "At my age, I don't think I'm ready to start being a mother." She looked at Kellan. "But you never know."

Another pause. "Moving right along," said Alex, changing the subject "I was surprised when you said your grandfather was in the States for a time."

"Yes, he was what you called a bird of passage. Lots of Irish immigrants did that. They came over here to make some money and then went back home when they had saved up enough to put a down payment on some property, or maybe just help their families. In fact, he met my grandmother over here, though I'm not sure whether they got married here or back in Ireland. I think he was over here twice, in fact. Because my father died young, before I really cared about such things, I never really learned as much as I should have about my family."

"Is there anyone still alive who could fill you in on some details?" Kellan asked.

"My Aunt Michaela in Belfast is still alive. She was always nice to me. We write to each other every so often." She thought for a moment. "I went up to see her while I was back there, just to tell here I was moving here permanently—sort of saying goodbye. I took the train from Dublin; it's only a couple of hours. While I was there she said to me, 'You're just like your grandfather—back and forth, back and forth, except that he stayed in Ireland, down in Cork where we lived when we were growing up.'" She paused again, thinking.

"Aunt Mikki's husband is dead, and I'm her closest relative. She was kind of sad when I left, but I promised I'd write. I did send her a note saying we were married, but I haven't heard anything back."

"Good to know," said Alex. "That might be useful later on. How old is she?"

"In her seventies," said Kathleen. "She's in pretty good health—she'll probably live to be a hundred."

Kellan stood and walked to the window, looking out over Southeast Washington. After a while he said, "Tomorrow's the last day before recess. We have a few weeks to take it easy." He came back and sat down.

"Maybe I should go back and see Aunt Michaela," Kathleen said. "Could you go with me?"

"Let's think about that," said Kellan. He went back and stared out the window again. Alex and Jean began to chat with Kathleen, but Kellan suddenly turned and said, "Hey, who's up for baseball? The Red Sox are in Baltimore."

Jean and Alex raised their hands; Kathleen said, "I've never been to a baseball game."

"Might as well start now," muttered Jean. "Jesus, ten years in New York and he's still a Red Sox fan." She looked around. "Who's driving?" No one answered; Alex grinned at Jean. "Screw it, I'll drive. Boss, you get the tickets."

Later that evening, back in Kellan's apartment, he and Kathleen relaxed with a glass of wine. "You know, I've been thinking about what you said," Kellan mused. "We've got some time. That might not be a bad idea."

"What?"

"Going to see your Aunt Michaela—you said she might have some documents about your father or grandfather. We could see her and then go down and see the Connollys as well. Might be fun."

Kathleen sat up and smiled. "Aunt Mikki would love to meet you, I know. And the Connollys would be thrilled. Can we really do that?"

"Sure. I'll clear it with Jordan's people, but he won't have any problem." He thought for a moment. "Your Irish passport will always be good. Once we get your citizenship taken care of here, you'll have dual citizenship."

She stood, walked over and put her arms around him. "It can be our honeymoon."

A week later Kellan and Kathleen boarded a direct flight from New York to Belfast International Airport. Kellan had dressed casually, not wanting to draw attention. He wore jeans, a light pullover shirt, a baseball cap, windbreaker and dark glasses. Kathleen was also dressed casually; they looked like a typical middle-aged couple going on vacation. They had purchased tickets in Kathleen's name and paid for them with travelers' checks, which she signed. Kellan's decision to travel more or less incognito was not because he was afraid for their safety, but merely because he didn't want any annoying interruptions.

He had run the trip plan by the Secret Service, and they offered to have an agent go with them. "I don't think that's necessary," said Kellan. "Everything's arranged under my wife's name. If you insist, you can see us onto the plane, but once we're in Northern Ireland, nobody's going to recognize me. I'm sure we'll be safe." The Service agreed that the danger was minimal.

During the flight over Kathleen filled Kellan in on her Aunt Michaela, or Aunt Mikki, as she called her. She had received a response from her aunt about the marriage, so Kathleen was confident that she was still at the same address. Michaela was her father's younger sister. When Michaela Morrissey was twelve, she had won first place in an Irish dance competition. As a teenager she joined a dance troupe that traveled around the British Isles and even to Scandinavia and Germany. When the dancers were in Belfast for an extended stay, she met John Sears, who introduced himself by saying he loved her dancing. Michaela got to know him, and eventually they married after she had given up dancing. They settled in a Protestant section of Belfast.

Uncle John, as Kathleen remembered him, was a gregarious, friendly man who worked at a variety of jobs. He drove a city bus for a time, worked in the building trades, and was in demand as a handyman who could repair virtually anything in a house, from electricity to plumbing to woodwork. He loved music and dancing, which was how he had first become attracted to Michaela. Because Michaela had held onto her Catholic faith, tensions arose between her and her husband from time to time, and Kathleen remembered that when she visited her aunt, her Uncle John wasn't always around. Since he had passed away a few years earlier, Aunt Mikki now lived alone.

They arrived in Belfast early in the morning and checked into the Tara Lodge hotel. That afternoon after they had rested, Kathleen called Michaela and said that she and her new husband were in Belfast and would love to visit her. When she hung up, she was smiling. "She told us to come over right now!" Kathleen said. "I told her we'd come tomorrow morning. She'll spend the rest of the day running around spiffing up the place."

"There's no need for that," said Kellan.

"Oh, I know, but she's a little messy—she'll just rearrange some of the junk she has. It will be fun; I'm sure you're going to love her."

Michaela Sears looked to Kellan as if she could still do a lively dance. She was small in stature but looked very fit; her eyes sparkled, and she seemed to wear a perpetual grin. She hugged Kathleen, kissed her several times, took Kellan by both hands looked up at him and said, "Well aren't you a fine big fellow!" She turned to Kathleen. "Katie, you done yourself proud."

Michaela put on a pot of tea and brought out a plate of biscuits. She had them sit down in the living room, a small but attractive space that was cluttered with knickknacks of all kinds. Kathleen had told Kellan that Aunt Mikki was a collector, and the evidence was everywhere. "So, Katie, you told me you were off to America, and of course I thought that was wonderful, but here you are back again so soon! Not for good, I'm guessing."

Kathleen laughed. "No, Aunt Mikki, Kellan and I are just taking a short vacation. You've got to keep this a secret until we leave, but Kellan's running for vice president of the United States."

"Ah, now, Sweetie, sure you don't have to be filling me with such nonsense. I don't expect you to stay, though sure I'm glad to see you."

"Aunt Mikki, I'm serious! Kellan is a United States Congressman, and he's been asked to run for vice president in the November election. We sort of snuck out of the country to visit you before the campaign starts."

Michaela's mouth dropped open and she put both hands on her cheeks; she looked at Kellan, then back at Kathleen, and said, "By the saints, you're telling me true, you're serious about this?" She looked at Kellan. "Now, young man, you just tell me that your wife is not pulling my leg," she said.

Kellan laughed. "I'm afraid she's right," he said.

"My lord, Katie, what have you done, married a politician? And a handsome one at that! I guess I'll have to get out the fine china and silverware to entertain you properly," she said. Then she laughed and clapped her hands together. "Ah, Katie, my love, I knew you was going to marry royalty!"

"Not exactly, Aunt Mikki, they don't have that in America. But he's actually a pretty famous guy."

"Lordy, Lordy, what would your mother and father say if they could see you now!"

"Actually, I'm here to talk to you about Dad, if it's okay with you."

"Sure, Sweetheart, you know my sainted brother and I didn't always see eye to eye. He was ready to disown me when I married John Sears, but he eventually got over it. The two of them could eventually share a pint without bashing each other, but he never spent much time with us. Of course he died when you were so young."

"Yes, and you probably know about some of the things I should've asked him before he died, but I was young and foolish and never even thought of it. So now I have to ask you."

"Sure, sure, anything you want to know, Darlin'—I'll do my best to remember. But first tell me, how did you get married so fast? You were here, what, a little over a month ago, and you still hadn't quite made up your mind."

Kathleen looked at Kellan, but he was smiling. "Of course I had," she said. "I just wasn't quite ready to say goodbye to Ireland."

"Ah, well, Ireland will always be here," she said. "But you and your husband won't, so make the best of it while you've still got time. I always worried that you were going to die an old maid, beautiful girl like you, what a shame that would've been!"

Kathleen stood up, walked over and kissed her aunt. "I think the tea's ready. Shall I go fix it while you get acquainted with that politician over there?"

"Now there's a love."

"So where do you hail from?" Michaela asked Kellan.

"Originally from Boston, but now I live in Washington. I also lived in New York State for about ten years."

"So you've been all over the country. What a fine thing!"

"Not exactly, but I've been around."

"And is this your first trip to Ireland? No, I guess it can't be because Katie was never in America."

"Actually, I studied at Trinity College, Dublin for four years. That's where I met Kathleen."

"Jesus, Mary and Joseph, that must have been a long time ago! What took you so long to ask her to marry you? Or did she turn you down a few times. Wouldn't surprise me, wild thing that she was."

Kathleen returned from the kitchen with a pot of tea and cups on a tray. "Now Aunt Mikki, don't be bothering him about ancient history. He was married to my friend Moira, whom you never met."

Michaela looked back and forth at Kellan and Kathleen. "Ah, I guess I understand, then," she said. "There's no marrying two women at the same time, is there? One's more than enough trouble for any man!" She laughed at her own joke. Kellan and Kathleen laughed with her. He could see why Kathleen loved her aunt.

Kellan sat back and relaxed as Michaela and Kathleen talked about old times, and family, and how quickly the years had passed. Michaela described for Kellan her memories of her young Katie, who always seem to be bent on getting into some kind of trouble. "I'm telling you true, Kellan, I was ready to ship her back home more than once! I'm not kidding you too!"

"Oh, come on, Aunt Mikki, I wasn't that bad, was I?"

"Ah, sure, you were bad enough, young lady, but I always loved you as if you were my own daughter. I was always sorry that you had such a difficult life. And then your friend Moira went off to America and married that chap. What a shame that was."

"That chap she went off and married is sitting right over there," Kathleen said.

Michaela looked startled, and then she seemed to put it all together. She looked at Kellan, back at Kathleen, and said, "Well I never!" She looked at Kellan. "So you must have known Kathleen way back then? Oh, I guess you just said that."

"That's right," said Kellan. "Moira was my first wife, and now Kathleen's my second. I'm a very lucky man."

Michaela just shook her head. Then she looked at Kathleen. "Did you tell me that before?" she said.

"Yes, Aunt Mikki, I did. You just didn't remember."

"Ah, fiddle, half the time I forget me own name. It's terrible getting old."

"You're not that old, Aunt Mikki. You still look as spry as a teenager."

They took Michaela out to dinner at a Belfast pub and enjoyed the pleasant evening. Kellan and Kathleen had decided to leave the subject of Kathleen's father until the next day. Kathleen said she didn't want to leave the impression that the only reason they had come to visit her aunt was for information. "After all," she had said, "she's really my only relative. I've got some cousins somewhere, but I haven't seen them in years. And I've always loved her, I always did."

"I can surely understand why," said Kellan. "She's really a sweetheart."

They came back the next morning, and after more friendly talk, Kathleen began asking Michaela about her father.

"What do you want to know, Katie?" Michaela said.

"Well, I'm also interested in your father. Can you just tell me what you can remember about where he lived and when you and my dad were born?"

Michaela sat and thought for a few moments, deep in concentration. Then she looked up and smiled.

"You've told me why this is so important, so I'm doing my best to get it right. You said you wanted to know if my father was in America when your father was born. I'll start with what I remember and maybe it'll come back to me. As far as I know, my father went to America when he was about sixteen. I'm pretty sure he was in Baltimore—as I recall there were lots of Irish in Baltimore. He worked on the docks there for a time, made pretty good money, I guess, and then he came back home. That would have been somewhere around 1890, I'm guessing. A few years later he decided to go back to America, as he wanted to make a bit more money. My grandfather—your great grandfather—was not very successful, as was true for a lot of Irish in those days.

"So off he went, back to Baltimore, only it didn't go so well, so he went up to New York, just outside the city somewhere. I think it might have been Jersey City."

"How do you remember all this, Aunt Mikki? You weren't even around then."

"Come here, Sweetie," she said. She walked into the dining room, reached down under a sideboard and pulled out a cardboard box. She took out several large, folded sheets of paper, found the one she wanted and opened it on the dining room table. Kellan and Kathleen were watching and saw that it was a map of the United States. Patched with tape in a few places, it was worn but intact. "I always loved maps," she said. "John and I never traveled much, but we loved thinking about it. Look at that bookshelf over there—it's full of books about places."

Kellan and Kathleen looked over the books saw that it was filled with travel guides, two atlases and other works about places in Europe and America. "I remember that," said Kathleen.

"Well, anyway, that was where he met my mother, your grandmother, that would be." She pointed at northern New Jersey on the map. "A pity you never knew her, she was a lovely woman. Anyway, they got married there. They also had their first child there, but she died right after being born. Then they had a second child, and that was your father."

"He was born in America?" Kathleen was stunned.

"Well, I'm not sure, Sweetheart. I know they came back to Cork either right before or right after he was born. There was some talk in the family that maybe they hadn't bothered to get married before the first child was born, and since she died, they weren't in any hurry to tie the knot, as they say. So either they got married in New Jersey before your father was born, or he was born and then they got married, or maybe they came back here to Cork and got married and then your father was born. Whatever they did, the family was all kind of, you know, hush-hush about it; it was never discussed very much."

She stopped and thought for a moment. "You know, I've got some stuff around here somewhere that might tell us. She led them to a small room just behind the kitchen—not much more than a large closet. There were shelves in the room with boxes piled everywhere. She poked around and looked at the writing on the boxes and then pointed to one that sat on a top shelf. "Here, Kellan," she said. "There's a good lad; pull that one down for me."

Kellan retrieved the rather large box and carried it back to the dining room. Michaela opened the box and began taking out sheaves of papers bound with string. At the bottom of the box was a smaller box made of thin wood. She laid it on the table and opened it carefully. She took out several folded pieces of paper and opened each one. She broke into a broad smile and handed one of them to Kathleen. "Here you go, Darlin'. This might be what you're looking for."

"My God!" said Kathleen. "Do you know what this is?" She looked at Michaela and then at Kellan, an expression of wonder on her face. "It's my father's birth certificate. Sean Edward Morrissey, born August 2, 1908, Hoboken, New Jersey! My God, do you know what this means?"

"And that's not all, Dearie," said Michaela. "It's beginning to come back to me. Lord, I haven't rummaged around in this stuff for years. Look here." She handed Kathleen another piece of paper.

"A marriage license!" said Kathleen. "Patrick Morrissey—that's my grandfather—and Elizabeth Kearney. Wow! Look at the date—August 10, 1908."

"Amazing," said Kellan.

"And there's one more here. It's a letter from your grandfather to his father dated September 1910. The writing's pretty bad, but you can read it."

It was in pencil, printed, apparently written with some difficulty. She showed it to Kellan. 'Dear Da,' it said. 'I just wont you to know I have got my papers to becom a citizen of the united states of america. I thout you wud want to know. Love, Pat.'

The box contained a few more letters and legal papers, and Kathleen pored over each one. But she kept picking up the birth and wedding papers and shaking her head over them. At one point, tears came to her eyes and she walked over and hugged her Aunt Mikki. "You don't know what this means, Aunt Mikki," she said.

"Ah, Lassie, I surely think I do, from the look on our face since you saw them. Good Lord, if you two had not come nosing around, those would have all disappeared when I died."

"Could I take them? Borrow them, I mean."

323

"Darlin', you can keep them. They must've been sitting in the box for twenty years. I'd plumb forgot about them until you asked. I'm glad I remembered."

"When we get back to the hotel, I'll see if I can get ahold of Alex and tell her what you've found. It will make her job a lot easier," said Kellan.

"I might be a citizen already, right?" Kathleen said. "I'm dumbfounded!"

"I'm not one hundred percent clear on the law—it has changed a few times—but we'll find out soon."

Kellan and Kathleen spent the rest of the day visiting with Michaela. That evening they went to one of her favorite pubs, where she said she might see a few friends. "Let's keep the political stuff quiet, okay, Aunt Mikki?"

"Why, what for? Aren't you proud of him? Saints preserve us, I wouldn't blame you if you were!" She looked at Kellan and laughed. He grinned at her. 'What a piece of work,' he said to himself.

Before getting their train to Dublin the next morning they stopped by Michaela's home once more. "It was wonderful to see you, Aunt Mikki. Maybe you could come and visit us some time."

"Ah, I'm getting a bit old to be gallivanting around," she said. She looked at Kellan and shook her finger at him. "Now you be nice to this lass or I'll be over there and beat your socks off!"

"Don't worry, Aunt Mikki." He hugged her, and she kissed his cheek. "It was wonderful to meet you."

As they were getting into the taxi, they turned and waved. Michaela stood on her porch, smiling and waving back, but her cheeks were wet with tears.

They rented a car in Dublin and drove to Mallow. Their stop in Belfast had more than satisfied what they had hoped for.

When they got to the Connolly house in Mallow, Patrick and Libby were delighted to see them. Brendan and Deirdre had gone down to Cork to do some shopping, and Libby said they would be back soon. Patrick had indeed read about the vice presidential nomination in the *Irish Times*, and he congratulated Kellan enthusiastically on his nomination. "Sure, you've come a long way, worked hard, and now you're getting your reward. I'm guessing that down the road you'll be running for president," he said.

"Not necessarily," said Kellan. "There's a long way to go yet."

Libby was thrilled as well. "That's just wonderful. Patrick read everything he could find about it, and I gather that the man you're running with is someone you have worked with before. We also heard about it on the news."

"That's right, Libby. Jordan Montgomery is an old friend."

Kathleen had taken some of their things up to Moira's old room, where they would be staying. She had been freshening up and came back down into the living room. "And you two!" Libby said. "We were more than thrilled to hear about the wedding," she said.

"We saw that one coming a long time ago," said Patrick. "The only thing that surprised us was that it took you so long to get around to it."

"It was a bit complicated," Kellan said, though he might easily have agreed with Patrick.

Kathleen just smiled at Kellan and said, "We were just waiting for the right moment, and we found it. Of course we had a bit of help finding it."

"Well, at least you got it done—not living in sin anymore."

"Patrick, for Jesus' sake, hold your tongue!"

"That's all right, Libby," said Kathleen. "We've said our prayers."

More than anything else, Libby wanted to know about Fiona. When they had finally settled in the living room, and Libby had served them tea, she said, "Now tell me about Fiona. We got a letter saying that she was going to study medicine. Is that right?

"Yes, that's right," said Kellan. "She's working with my sister-in-law at a hospital in Massachusetts. I'm sure you remember her."

"That we do," said Patrick. "A fine woman, she is. And Fiona is very good about writing—at least once a week we hear from her."

"Eileen is a very fine doctor, and she has many medical students under her supervision. She's going to get Fiona familiar with the whole idea of studying medicine and guide her through the process. She has not yet been admitted to medical school, but that will come in time. Meanwhile, she has a wonderful opportunity to decide whether she wants to start on that path. It's a pretty long process, as I'm sure you both know. But I am very proud that she has decided to do that; she seems to have a real desire to go into medicine. Kathleen and I both think she will be excellent at it."

"That's wonderful," said Libby. "We were a bit worried about her; she didn't seem altogether focused on what she wanted to do. We know that she wanted to go over and spend some time with you, and we understood that, even though we missed her. She seemed to be looking for something."

"Just wanted to follow her mother's footsteps," said Patrick.

"Instead of mine," said Kellan, but he was smiling. "I don't think she really wanted to be a lawyer."

Libby continued. "We thought that maybe with a different perspective she might find something that interested her. And I guess that's what happened."

Brendan and Deirdre arrived back from their shopping, and the round of greetings was repeated, with congratulations to Kellan and Kathleen on their wedding as well as to Kellan on his coming prospects. "We're so excited," said Deirdre. "Brendan actually thinks we may be able to come to Washington for the inauguration. Fiona wrote and told us all about it; we're so excited for you!"

"Kellan was just telling me about Fiona's plans," said Libby. "I think it sounds wonderful."

"She's written to us all about that too," said Brendan. "Of course we remember your sister Eileen, and Fiona says she really loves working with her. To tell the truth, we were getting a little nervous about her as she didn't seem very settled on what she wanted to do with her life. We just thought that with that fine education she had, she could do better than working as a clerk in a bank."

"Well, she seems to have found it now," said Kathleen. "When we last saw her with Edward and Eileen, she was bubbling all over with the idea. And living right there with the two of them will be good for her. She was all set to find a job in Washington, and she probably would have done well, but I think this will make her much happier."

"And now you two are finally married," said Deirdre. She smiled at Kathleen. "Fiona told us all about it; she said you sort of had to do it in a hurry."

"That's right," said Brendan. With a smile he added, "We thought it might be one of those, what do you Yanks call it, shotgun weddings?"

"Brendan, for God's sake! Jesus Mary and Joseph, don't insult these lovely people."

"That's okay, Libby," Kathleen said. "It didn't work out that way, but it wasn't for lack of trying." Everyone laughed.

"Saints preserve us, such talk!" said Libby.

"Ah, well, they're together now, and that's what matters," said Patrick. He had fetched himself a glass of his favorite Kinsale Irish Lager, and he raised it toward them. "Here's to you both," he said. "May the roof over your heads be as well thatched, as those inside are well matched."

"Well thatched, indeed!" Brendan said. "Next thing you know they'll be living in the bloody White House." Everyone laughed.

"As you know," said Kellan, "We were married in a courthouse in Arlington, Virginia. But we're planning to have a church wedding in Massachusetts sometime this fall. It would be wonderful if you could come over and join us."

"Yes," said Kathleen, "we'd be thrilled to have you."

"You could always come back here and get married," said Patrick. "Father O'Brien would be happy to oblige."

Kellan looked at Kathleen, and she nodded. "That might not be a bad idea," he said. "We'll keep it in mind."

Libby blessed herself with the sign of the cross. "Heavens be praised," she said. "Weddings, elections, medical school, good Lord, what a wagon load of news you've brought!"

"Yes," said Kathleen, "and we got some wonderful news from my Aunt Mikki up in Belfast. It seems that I might be able to claim American citizenship."

"And how will ye be doing that?" Patrick asked.

"Well, it turns out that my grandfather, who spent some time in America, may have become an American citizen. Not only that, my father seems to have been born there. At least we have a birth certificate that says so."

"Well that's a wonder," said Libby. "So your grandfather was one of those who went back and forth, then?"

"Apparently so. It seems that he went to America twice before he finally settled back in Cork. Aunt Mikki gave us the evidence we need. We'll see how it goes once we're back there."

Kathleen and Kellan stayed with the Connollys that night and one more. The family had wanted them to stay longer, but Kellan seemed uncomfortable. They were getting ready for bed on the second night in Mallow when Kathleen asked, "What's the matter, Kellan? Are you feeling all right? You've been very quiet."

"It's wonderful to see everybody, but I can't help feeling that I should be getting back. I know we still have about two weeks before the campaign gets into high gear, but there's a lot of planning to do. Jordan has been very generous in not making demands of me, but Bob and the rest of the guys will be itching to sit me down and tell me what's what."

"But how much are you actually going to have to do? Will you be making a lot of speeches?"

"I'm sure I'll be traveling around a lot and talking to people. You know the way campaigns have become lately. It's not good enough just to put your own ideas out there; you have to try to discredit the other side also. Traditionally, that's the vice president's job, to be the attack dog, as they call it."

He was sitting on the edge of the bed, and she came over and sat down next to him and took his hand. "That's not your style at all," she said. "Alex and I were talking about it just before we left, and she said the same thing. But she also said that you would hate that, and that's what I'm talking about."

"To my way of thinking, Mayhew will hang himself. He was lucky to get the nomination, and he's got a lot of political baggage. I think it's pretty clear that the country is ready for a change. He's going to come out swinging, and it seems to me our best strategy is simply to turn his own arguments back on him. What are they going to challenge Jordan and me about? Our economic policy? That's been our bread and butter ever since we both came to Washington. If they want to get into that area, they'll find themselves in trouble. Of course politicians who are fighting to survive usually look for trouble. We'll see; I'm just ready to get going."

"I know you are, Darling. I think the Connollys will understand; we can leave tomorrow and drive up to Shannon. Our reservation isn't for a couple of days, but I'm sure you can move it up. We'll have to figure out a way to get together with them sometime before all this is over. If Jordan wins and they can come to the inauguration, that would be wonderful. We'll just have to wait and see."

In the morning Kellan called Aer Lingus and was able to move their reservation up to early the following morning. They decided to drive to Shannon and spend the night at Kells Country House, an old castle-hotel near the airport. They bid goodbye to the family that afternoon, and as usual, Libby was in tears. Their parting had a different feel for Kellan; much had changed, and he sensed the unhappiness in the Connolly family, a feeling so familiar to the Irish that they were practically born with it. Moira was gone; Fiona was gone; and now Kathleen, another daughter in almost every sense of the word, was also leaving for good.

With modern travel, the leave taking was not quite like the old traditional American wake. But there was still something poignant about a tiny country of four million people so dominated by the huge nation across the Atlantic, with millions of her sons and daughters having been born and raised there. Connections were still there and still strong, and in ways it was as sad as it had been a century earlier, when Kathleen's grandfather had made his way across the ocean in hopes of finding a measure of prosperity. The Celtic Tiger had arrived, however, and with it new prosperity for thousands of Irish people. And for the first time in anyone's memory, many of Ireland's children were beginning to return home. It was a new world.

Off and Running

Kellan returned his rental car at Shannon Airport and they took a cab for the ten minute ride to the Kells Country House. As the cab pulled around the circle and up to the magnificent old building with its pointed corner tower, parapets and steep roof, Kathleen looked out at the white stone building. "I've never been here before," she said. "Quite something, isn't it?"

"Beautiful," said Kellan.

The owners greeted them cordially as they strolled into the spacious common room off of the entrance with its comfortable looking furniture, fireplace and even a piano. They found their room to be spacious and well appointed, with a window looking out toward the River Shannon where it flowed into the Shannon Estuary and on out into the North Atlantic.

That evening, after a sumptuous dinner, Kathleen was standing in the window watching the sun go down. She had on a sheer nightgown, and Kellan could see the outline of her lovely figure. He got up and walked over to her and put his arms around her, resting his chin on her shoulder and looking out at the same view. She leaned back into him and turned her head and kissed his cheek. "You seem kind of sad," he said.

"Not really. It took me a long time to get used to the idea of leaving Ireland for good, but that's passed now. There are just so many things that have happened to me recently, almost all of them good, that it makes me think of how lucky I am to get here. Every morning I wake up and wonder if my life is real, or if I might be dreaming."

"You're not dreaming," he said. He took her hand and led her over to the bed and sat down beside her. She turned and looked at him, and he placed his hands on the side of her face and stroked her eyebrows gently with his thumbs. He softly massaged her forehead, then rubbed his fingers across her cheeks and her lips. She opened her mouth and caught his finger between her teeth and pressed down gently. He moved his hands to her neck and shoulders, continuing to massage gently. "You are always beautiful," he said, "but you are especially gorgeous when your face is relaxed. I wish I could smooth away all those troubles that I sometimes see. I wish …"

"Shhh," she said. "I know what you wish, and so do I; oh God, so do I. But just think how long we had waited, and how much more time we still have before us. We are so lucky, my love. This could all have passed us by. You might have turned into a grumpy old bachelor, and I could've died an old maid." They both laughed. "And now, oh my God, I can't help but think of the things that could go wrong. I try not to, but I'm afraid I know too much. I've spent too much of my life thinking about the bad things that happen to good people."

"I know what you mean. In the past few days I've thought a few times about how nice it would be if I could just end my term in Congress, and you and I could go off to the shore or into the mountains somewhere and just grow old together."

"There's no turning back," she said. "No matter how much we want to, we can't erase the past."

"And we can't control the future, either," he said. "As much as we might like to."

"We can't even control our feelings for each other; all we can do is protect them by holding on to each other no matter what happens. I want you to promise me that when you go out on your campaign, I can be with you all the time. I never want to be back in that place where I was for so long, wondering when I would see you again, or whether I would ever see you again."

He stood up and pulled her to her feet. She raised her arms as he pulled the nightgown over her head, then she helped him take off the rest of his clothes and they lay down side by side. The sun was setting, and its orange glow touched her skin so that it glowed in turn. He thought she looked so beautiful that he could barely breathe. She pressed her body into him and whispered, "I wish we could stay just like this forever."

"We can always remember moments like this. That moment we had together, years ago, has never left me, even when I should've let it go."

"I know," she said. "I know."

Their plane was scheduled to leave at 10:45, and they had a leisurely Irish breakfast prepared by the superb staff. "We'll have to come back here again," he said. "We'll be visiting Mallow from time to time, and from now on I always want to fly in and out of Shannon."

"No reason we can't," she said.

331

When their taxi arrived, they thanked their hosts, stowed their luggage, waved once more and in a moment were on their way back to the airport.

Kathleen closed the book she was reading and stuffed it into the pocket of the seat in front of her; their flight was about halfway across the Atlantic Ocean. "I think I'd like to start writing again," she said. "Everything has been so hectic that I haven't really thought about what I want to do with myself from day to day. You're going to be busy with campaigning, and who knows after that? I've been working since I was about fourteen and I can't imagine sitting around and doing nothing."

Kellan thought for a few moments before answering. "We've never talked about kids," he said. "I've sort of assumed that it was a discussion we might get around to, but it was unlikely that we would want to think about that seriously."

She didn't answer right away either. "I don't think so. I kind of think of Fiona as my daughter, but beyond that … When I was with Liam, there was no way I was going to even think about having a child. But I have thought about it from time to time—I assume that every woman does. But I've never felt that it was something I needed to make my life complete."

"I've thought about it from time to time, but not recently. I guess I always assumed that Moira and I would have two or three." After a few more moments he said, "I think you should start writing again. Maybe you should write a book. Or once we get settled, there are a lot of think tanks and other organizations in Washington that might be real interested in anything you would have to say. You have your own very detached view of the United States, but you know a great deal about the country. I know some people you could talk to."

She leaned her seat back and closed her eyes. Then she looked at him, opened one eye and said with a smile, "Maybe tomorrow, or the day after. Not right now." She closed her eyes again, and Kellan picked up the recent political biography he had been reading and opened it.

From the airport in New York City they took a cab to Penn Station and boarded a train for Washington. From Union Station they taxied back to their apartment; it was past dinnertime when they arrived. "Do you want get something to eat?" he said as they relaxed in the living room.

She yawned and stretched and shook her head. "We must have something edible somewhere. Let's just relax."

"It's too late to call Alex or Jean, but I should probably think about getting together with them tomorrow morning. I also need to let Jordan know we're back; I expect he'll have something going on this coming weekend since it's Labor Day. Before I left he was talking about some kind of a kickoff, maybe right here in DC, or maybe up in Pittsfield."

"The House is back in session next week, right?" He nodded. "I expect your time will be split between that and the campaign. You're going to be busy, my friend!"

He stood up and reached for her hand. "Let's think about that tomorrow." She took his hand, stood up and followed him to the bedroom.

Early next morning Kellan got a call from Bob Reynolds. "I'm glad you're back," said Bob "We were wondering when you would make it."

"How did you find out I was back?" said Kellan.

"We had spies at Dulles Airport," said Bob.

"That's fine, but we didn't come in to Dulles," said Kellan. "So how'd you find out?"

"Well you answered the phone, so that's how I knew," said Bob. "I tell you, we got some real smart people at this end of the game."

"Yeah, I can see that," said Kellan, and he chuckled. "So, what's up?"

"Well, we would like to get you on one of the news shows this coming Sunday morning," said Bob. "The People Today would like to have you, and you can do it at their Washington studio. Are you okay with that?"

"Who's going to be on the panel, do you know?"

"Well your friend Marge from the *American* will be on, and that guy from your WPOL radio, what's his name?"

"Spencer Turner."

"Oh, yeah. Is he okay?"

"He's fine. He's here on the Hill doing radio spots just about every day. He won't ask anything crazy."

"Okay, and there's one other, some guy from Atlantis Radio named Amar Daryan. You know him?"

"I've heard the name. They're kind of out there, but if People Today has him on, he can't be too bad."

"Okay, then you know the drill; you get there an hour early, let them put that stuff all over your face, and all that. You've done these things before so I'm sure you'll handle yourself just fine. But you have a tendency to be kind of a wise guy when you're talking to the press, so be careful with that."

"Me, a wise guy? Where'd you get that?"

"Hell, even in committee meetings you're always being a comedian. That might go over real well on C-SPAN, but it won't play so well out on the campaign trail. You're in a whole new ballgame now, and anything you say will be fair game for everybody from here to China. I guess I don't need to tell you that."

"I get the message," said Kellan. "What time?"

"Show's at ten. Be there at nine."

"Good. What else is going on?"

"We're doing a kickoff rally on Monday in Pittsfield. I'm assuming you can make that."

"Sure, no problem. Anything else?"

"Yeah, we're sending one of our writers down to work with you. We know you speak the King's English fairly well, but it's just to nail down any points between you and Jordan that might be up in the air. Her name is Christina Valentine. She's very good."

"Yeah, I know her name. She's written some pretty good stuff for magazines like *The Atlantic* and a couple of others. She's been with Jordan for a while now, as I recall."

"That's the one. Jordan will probably be calling you sometime later today. Will you be home?"

"Either here or in the office. I'm done traveling for a while."

"How did that go, by the way?"

"Better than expected. Kathleen got some very good news; I'll get back to you with that later."

"She's not pregnant, is she?"

"You never quit, do you? And you call me a comedian?"

"Talk to you later." Kellan hung up the phone.

Spencer Turner opened the broadcast. "Good morning, ladies and gentlemen and welcome to People Today. With us this morning is Congressman Kellan Maguire of New York, now the candidate for vice president of the United States on the Republican Party ticket. That puts him in an unusual situation, since he is well known as a leading Democratic member of Congress. More about that in a moment.

"First, my co-panelists are Amar Daryan of Atlantis broadcasting and Marge Wellborn of the Washington American. Good morning to both of you." The two panelists nodded. "We'll begin the questioning with Marge."

"Good morning, Congressman. Let's get right to the point: How did a dyed-in-the-wool Democratic congressman wind up on the ballot with a Republican senator in the race for president of the United States?"

"I thought you'd never ask, Marge," said Kellan. The panelists all chuckled politely—except for Amar Daryan. "Actually, there's a long history of bipartisan cooperation in the United States. I would start by mentioning both Theodore and Franklin Roosevelt, each of whom was able to work comfortably with members of the other party. And, I might add, each of them had difficulty with members of his own party when it came to some of the tough issues of their times. For example, even in his own autobiography, Teddy Roosevelt mentions the fact that his most difficult opponents were conservatives in his own party. And, as I'm sure you are aware, during his second term Franklin Roosevelt had considerable difficulty with conservative Democrats, mostly from the southern states. So it seems to me that party affiliation isn't the last word in political cooperation. I agree completely that that has not been the norm recently, but maybe if Senator Montgomery and I are successful, we can turn that around a little bit."

"But surely you must agree that your history as a Democrat might hinder Senator Montgomery's chances of getting elected, am I correct?"

"I'm certain that there will be some who can't see themselves voting for a split ticket. But consider their choices: they can vote to support a Democratic administration which has not done the job that the American people expected of them, or they can vote for a Republican candidate whose vice presidential nominee shares many of his political views. I think Senator Montgomery and I have made that abundantly clear during our time together on the Hill. We have co-sponsored several important pieces of legislation, and have worked together on two joint committees to achieve important economic goals. I think our record speaks for itself."

The questioning continued in a political vein until time for the first commercial break. When the cameras came back on, moderator Spencer Turner turned to his other panelist. "We'll continue the questioning with Amar Daryan. Amar?"

"Mister Congressman, you are quite well known for your economic policy agenda, which is presumably why you are running with Senator Montgomery. But it seems to me that your economic policies have focused almost exclusively on Western Europe and East Asia. As you are no doubt well aware, a number of countries in the Middle East have faced serious economic challenges. I would like you to explain to me why the American people should think you have any intention of offering economic assistance to those areas."

"That's a good question, Mister Daryan. I think it's absolutely vital that United States develop solid economic relationships all over the world, not only with Europe and Asia, but with the Asian subcontinent, the Middle East and Africa. We have lived in a global economy for some time, and I think it's safe to say that a strong international economy can only continue to grow stronger if all its parts are successful economically. As you no doubt know, the United States is trying to forge better economic relationships with many Middle Eastern and African nations, but sometimes reaching suitable accommodations has been difficult."

"So you're blaming Middle Eastern problems on the countries of that region themselves, and the United States has no responsibility for their economic circumstances?"

"Most Middle Eastern countries have vital resources which could make them extremely successful in international trade if their policies were adjusted to take advantage of those resources. But in order to do that, they must adopt a reasonable approach to trade agreements with Western nations. That has sometimes posed a significant challenge to us, despite our best efforts."

"So you are blaming it all on the nations in that region."

"I didn't say that, nor did I intend to imply that."

"I think your answer was quite clear in that regard. I have another, related question."

Amar Daryan continued in that vein until the next commercial break, and Kellan did his best to control or at least moderate the exchange of ideas. He was pleased when Spencer interrupted the discussion for the commercial timeout. Daryan continued to question Kellan when the cameras were turned off, but Kellan poured himself a glass of water from the table next to him and avoided answering. Amar Daryan did not look particularly happy, but he asked no more questions.

When they started again, Spencer turned back to Marge Wellborn. She continued in the same vein that she and Kellan and the others had carried out in his office several weeks earlier. She touched on Kellan's family issues, but did not overstep the bounds that he had created during that previous meeting. "I understand you just returned from a visit to Ireland," she said as the segment neared an end. "May I ask how that went?"

"It went very well, Marge. My wife was able to meet with her closest relative, an aunt who lives in Belfast, with whom she lived for a time when she was younger. It was a very warm reunion, and Kathleen learned some interesting things about her family."

"Will those things she learned have any bearing on her situation here in the United States?"

"They may. Her aunt was able to provide her with some documents that have helped to clarify her family background. She will be investigating further just exactly what that might mean, but for now, we're very happy to have had an opportunity to visit her family as well as my former wife's family, with whom I have kept very close touch over the years, as you know."

"Thank you Congressman," said Spencer. "We wish you luck in your campaign."

An hour later back in his apartment, Bob Reynolds was again on the phone. "Well, that didn't go too bad, did it? Except for that jerk from Atlantis. He sure had a bug up his ass."

"Well, he's got a point. There's some stuff we really need to tighten up in that part of the world. I'll talk to Jordan about it and maybe we can come up with something to use as we go down the road. How's Jordan doing?"

"He's on two of the networks this morning; we're taping them both and will do a postmortem later. From what I've seen so far, he's doing fine. Anyway, we'll see you up here tomorrow and we'll take it from there. You're bringing that gorgeous wife with you aren't you?"

"I never go anywhere without her," said Kellan. "She'll be there."

"By the way, Jordan hopes you two can stay over; we're going to have a strategy meeting on Tuesday morning."

"Sure, no problem."

"Looking forward to seeing you both."

Jordan Montgomery's campaign staff had pulled out all the stops for his opening rally. They had four large tents set up on the broad back lawn of the Montgomery estate, which covered more than ten acres. They had contacted all the chairs of the Republican committees in the surrounding states and invited them to bring a bus load or two of loyal supporters to Pittsfield, where they would be well entertained. A speaker's platform and several rows of chairs to accommodate those who couldn't stand for long had been set up. A popular band was engaged, and three caterers would handle feeding the guests. They had made arrangements with three

Pittsfield hotels to accommodate any guests for whom a one-day round trip in would be too much.

As it turned out, Labor Day in the Berkshire Hills was warm and pleasant. The music would start at two o'clock, and food would be served beginning shortly thereafter. Jordan, Kellan and several of Jordan's colleagues from Congress would mingle with the crowd, and speeches by Kellan, Jordan, and Republican Senator Alan Hallowell of Pennsylvania would be offered at about four. Bob Reynolds, who was well known by many of the visitors who would be attending, would serve as master of ceremonies.

Kellan and Kathleen had arrived early and were shown a room where they would spend the night. They stood on a balcony overlooking the long driveway onto the estate as buses began rolling in about noon. There were groups planning to attend from all the New England states, as well as people from New York, Pennsylvania, and New Jersey. Bob Reynolds reported that there would even be some party faithful coming from as far away as West Virginia or Ohio. They had hoped to be able to accommodate about 500 people, but it soon began to look as though at least that number would be comfortably reached. The early arrivals were free to wander about the Montgomery property, including the stable area and large corral where half a dozen of the Montgomery family horses could be seen.

As the yard filled with people, Shelley Montgomery, Kathleen, Sally Reynolds, Phyllis Hallowell and other prominent Republican wives were seated comfortably on the porch, which stretched all the way across the back of the house. Jordan, Kellan and Bob began to circulate in the crowd greeting the guests, many of whom were known by Jordan. Kellan knew several of them by name, and Jordan introduced him to a number of those he didn't know. Since these were party loyalists, all but one or two of them seemed completely comfortable with the idea of a Democrat on the ballot. Bob Reynolds had apparently been busy reassuring party leaders that Jordan's choice for vice president was a wise one that in the end would help lead to victory in November.

As they strolled around shaking hands, the band began playing popular songs, and the caterers set about preparing hot dogs, hamburgers, coleslaw, and other fixings. The tents provided tables and chairs for those who preferred to eat while seated. There was plenty of iced tea, soft drinks and bottled water; no alcohol would be served—close colleagues of Jordan's who felt the need for a stimulant could be quietly accommodated inside the house. It was understood that when the buses began to load their passengers for the trip home around six o'clock, a number of important party regulars, who had arrived in their own cars, would gather around the house to exchange ideas for the campaign. Several of them planned to remain overnight for the meeting on Tuesday morning.

As Kellan moved around the broad expanse of lawn, he glanced at the porch from time to time to see how Kathleen, seated on the porch with the prominent Republican women, was faring. She was sitting next to Shelley, who was talking animatedly with the other women. Kathleen did not seem to be talking much; she was watching the conversation closely with a hint of a smile on her face. After a while she stood up, whispered something to Shelley, then came down on the grass and walked toward Kellan.

"How are you holding up?" he said as she approached.

She hooked her arm in his and said, "Let's walk." She guided him gently toward the edge of the crowd where they would be out of hearing range of the guests. "Jesus Christ, Kellan," she said. "Am I ever a fish out of water! Shelley is nice enough, and Sally Reynolds seems pretty down to earth. But a couple of the others, my God, they come across like they're the center of their own little orbits and the rest of us are satellites."

He smiled. "There's an old saying in American politics. For a long time Episcopalians dominated American public life. According to the saying, when someone asked who the Episcopalians were, the answer was, 'Why my dear, the Episcopal Church is the Republican Party at prayer.'"

"Just like the god damn British, right?"

"Well, the Episcopal Church in America was once the Church of England. Many of them still consider themselves Anglicans."

"So how did Jordan wind up in that party? He doesn't seem quite so, I don't know, conservative really isn't the right word; full of himself is I guess what I mean."

"I don't know when Jordan's family became Republican, but it's been a while, I can assure you of that. It's interesting that the General Montgomery who is famous from his service in the American Revolution was born in Ireland. I think Jordan's family are distant relatives of that branch. And Shelley has Irish roots, as you know. Of course there's more to being a Democrat than just being Irish; Italians, Jews, Poles have all traditionally been Democratic. A long time ago, when we were still lawyers in Boston, Jordan and I had a conversation about which party we intended to join. With me, there was no doubt; my family were Democrats. Jordan always seemed kind of conflicted, but I'm guessing that he decided to run for office as a Republican the first time to keep his family happy.

His father is a very decent chap, but his mother would have disowned him if he had become a Democrat."

"They live here, right? I mean that house could accommodate half a dozen families. But they don't seem to be around."

"They have a summer home on the coast of Maine. I imagine that's where they are—steering clear of this mob. Jordan's mom would be fussing over them stomping on her flowers, and I'm sure she wouldn't be all that happy with the band playing in her backyard. You'll get to meet them sooner or later; they're really pretty decent folks."

As they continued to walk, Kathleen was quiet for a few moments. Then she said, "I know you and Jordan are friends, and I understand your political connections with him. But you don't seem to fit in very well here either. I know enough about American politics to know that you're considered a conservative Democrat. And Jordan is obviously a liberal Republican. But I've been reading your newspapers and trying to follow what's going on here from the Irish and British press, and it seems to me that you two—you and Jordan—are the last two holdouts in the center between the far ends of each party. It's amazing to me that the two of you are actually running for president and vice president together. You represent a dying breed."

"Jordan is one hell of a politician. He can walk into an office on Capitol Hill of either party and have a friendly conversation. You know the old saying, keep your friends close to you, and keep your enemies even closer; Jordan does that. Every time we try to get some legislation passed, he finds the sticking points and goes and talks to the people who are going to be the hardest to convince. That's kind of rare these days. But the best politicians have always been able to do that. Those are the guys who get to be Senate Majority Leader, Speaker of the House, and so on. They're the ones who become important committee chairs and pretty much run things on the Hill."

"You have the same kind of reputation, don't you?"

"I had a lot of talks with Jordan when I first decided to run. He kept an eye on me and steered me in the right direction. The other place where I was lucky was when I had Carmen Montefiore as my Chief of Staff; I'm really sorry you didn't get to know him better before he died. In a way, you're exactly right—Jordan and I may be the last of a dying breed. The way things are going in both parties, I can't imagine the two of us being where we are, say, eight years from now."

"But here you are!"

"Yeah, here we are." He looked at her and smiled. "Look, in every election, forty percent are going to vote for their party candidate, no matter who he or she is. Elections are decided by the twenty percent in the middle. That's who we have to convince."

"And the group here today? Hardly the middle, I'd say."

"Well, you have to keep your base happy in any case. Which reminds me, I'd better get back to doing my job, which is walking around, pressing flesh, and convincing all these Republican stalwarts that I'm not the devil incarnate."

"Okay, I'll go back up there with the ladies, and I'll hold my tongue. But be warned, lover, I'm not going to do that forever. Some of these people need to be shaken up a little bit. They've had it too good for too long."

"Just keep it under control until after the election and we'll be fine."

"I'll try." She kissed him on the cheek, turned and headed back for the porch. He smiled, shook his head and walked back towards the crowd.

Bob Reynolds approached Kellan. "How's she doing?" he said.

"She'll be okay. It's all new, and she's trying to figure out where she belongs, if you know what I mean."

"Sally was talking to her. She's real impressed; she said Kathleen knows a hell of a lot about us for someone who's only been here, what?—a week?"

"She was here earlier, but not that long. She's a journalist; she picks stuff up. And she's smart as hell."

"She can wind up being a real asset for you. With that brogue of hers, she'll charm a lot of people. Not to mention her looks. But that accent—it doesn't sound like some of the Irish folks I've heard."

"She has a bit of the Ulster accent. The people in the North have that, and she spent a lot of time in Belfast. She really speaks like a Dubliner, which for much of her life, she was."

"That's where you spent all your time."

"Just about."

Bob glanced at his watch. "It's about time for the commercials," he said. "Better limber up your voice."

Since the crowd was all friendly, Bob's introductory remarks, spiced with a few jokes at the hands of the opposition party, drew laughs and applause. As the crowd was in a mellow mood, there was no need for long-winded oratory. Senator Hallowell spoke first, promising that loyal Republicans from the keystone state would give fine support to the ticket.

Kellan spoke next, briefly thanking Jordan once again for the opportunity to share the ballot with him and promising to convert doubting Democrats to the cause. Jordan spoke longer, as expected. He thanked the people for coming, asked them to go back home and spread the message, volunteer to assist the campaign—acknowledging that all of them were no doubt prepared to do that in any case—and be ready to help get out the vote when the time came.

Bob wrapped things up, reminding everyone of available accommodations nearby and wishing them a safe journey home. Following enthusiastic applause punctuated by whistles and cheers, the crowd began to disperse and head for the buses. The day was declared a success and the select group of insiders retired to the spacious Montgomery mansion.

Gearing Up

When the buses had departed and the other guests had retired to their local accommodations, the remaining members of the gathering were offered a light meal by one of the catering services still on hand. Floodlights under the ceiling of the porch area provided illumination for the tables and chairs that had been set up on the porch and the adjacent patio. A bar had been set up near the rear entrance to the house for those so inclined. It was an informal gathering; the business meeting would take place the following morning. It was generally agreed that the afternoon's kickoff had been effective and well worth the expense involved, a substantial portion of which had been borne by Jordan Montgomery himself.

Kellan and Kathleen were seated around a large table on the patio with Jordan, Shelley, Bob and Sally Reynolds and Alan and Phyllis Hallowell. As they sat down, Alan Hallowell offered his hand to Kathleen. "I'm Al Hallowell," he said. "I don't believe I've had the pleasure."

Kathleen took his hand and smiled. "I'm Kathleen Maguire. It's an honor to meet you, Senator."

"Please call me Al," he said. He looked at her for a moment. "Ah, so you are the heretofore mysterious lady from Dublin. Your fame precedes you, Madam."

"Don't you mean my notoriety, Al?" Kathleen said.

The senator laughed. "Oh, I wouldn't say so. Everything I've heard so far, and I confess it hasn't been all that much, has been quite favorable. I'm sure Kellan will be pleased to have you at his side during the coming festivities."

"If that's what you can call a campaign," she said.

"Oh, indeed they are festive. If we didn't enjoy campaigning, I doubt any of us would be in this business. I grant you, the travel can be a bore, and one's hand does indeed get sore from greeting so many people, but I generally find that the positives outweigh the negatives. In Pennsylvania, at least, the voters do seem pleased to have an opportunity to meet face to face with their elected representatives. Wouldn't you say so, Kellan?"

"For the most part, I would agree with you, Al, though you do have your share of nuisances. But you're right; most of my constituents have always struck me as being pretty decent people. Though you certainly hear from them when you do something they don't like."

Senator Hallowell nodded. "I'm sure you get more of your share of that sort of thing than we do on the Senate side, but I know exactly what you mean. Still, why would we be here if it weren't to serve the people?" He turned to Kathleen. "Wouldn't you say so, Mrs. Maguire?"

"Please call me Kathleen." She smiled. "I think our politics in Ireland differ somewhat from yours. There was a long time in our history when the people who supposedly represented us did everything they could to make our lives miserable." She shook her head. "I guess this is not the time to go in to the long sad history of Ireland," she said.

"That's quite all right," said Senator Hallowell. "I am somewhat familiar with your history, though not as familiar as Kellan, I'm sure."

Kathleen nodded and smiled. "Actually our Taoiseach and the members of the Seanad Éireann and the Dáil Éireann are for the most part fairly personable, though I've only met one or two. I haven't had much opportunity to observe the proceedings in your Congress, but I'm quite sure that those in our Oireachtas are likely to be more lively than yours. I think part of that comes from the fact that your president is not a member of your Congress, whereas our Prime Minister, or Taoiseach, is a member of our Parliament. There's much less sense of separation there."

"You speak Irish, then?"

"No, it's spoken mostly in the province of Munster in the south of Ireland—County Clare, Tipperary, Kerry, and so on. Cork, where I grew up, is part of Munster, but my family spoke mostly English. Irish is an official language, and you hear it everywhere, even in Dublin. Most people know a lot of words in Irish, like parts of government, and so on. I'm sure Kellan knows a few." She smiled at him.

"It's an interesting language," Kellan said. "A bit difficult to pronounce, but it has a nice lilt to it."

"I'd be willing to bet there are people in Pennsylvania who can still speak Irish," Kathleen said. "After all, many of the Irish who came to this country didn't speak English, though I doubt that's still true."

"Fascinating, Kathleen," said the Senator. "Thank you for the lesson in Irish culture."

"*Sláinte agus saol agaibh*," said Kathleen, and she added, "*Tá sé go deas bualadh leat.*"

Senator Hallowell looked at Kellan. "I think she just said, 'To your health, and pleased to meet you.'"

Kathleen smiled at Kellan. "Wonderful, Darling, you remember! I'm impressed."

"So am I," said Senator Hallowell. "Kathleen, I assure you, the pleasure has been all mine. You and Kellan must come to visit us when you're in Pennsylvania."

Phyllis Hallowell, who had been speaking with others, came up to the table. "What's going on here, Alan?" she said. "What am I missing?"

"Well, we've just had a fascinating lesson in Irish history," he said. "I was just telling Kellan and Kathleen that they must visit us in Pennsylvania some time."

"That would be most charming," said Phyllis. "I enjoyed speaking with Kathleen earlier this afternoon."

Later that evening, when Kellan and Kathleen were back in their room after a pleasant evening of relaxed conversation, Kellan said, "You're making friends very rapidly, my dear. Half a dozen people must've said to me how charming you are. Al Hallowell was eating out of your hand. You sure wowed him!"

"I'm not sure how far I got with Phyllis Hallowell," she said. "She must be another one of those old money people."

"Those are the people who finance political campaigns," he said with a smile. "You have to be nice to them."

"Oh, that's fine; I don't mind mixing with people. I've never been antisocial; I've always tried to choose my friends carefully. Now that I'm married to you, it seems a lot of my friends are going to be chosen for me."

"You may be right. But I promise you, everything you saw this afternoon and this evening is surface stuff. When you get settled into a position, you can bring in your own friends, like Jean and Alex."

"How come Alex didn't come?" Kathleen asked. "I would've thought she would be right at home here."

"I'm not sure. I was going to ask Bob about that, but I decided to let it alone. I was afraid he might tell me something I didn't want to hear."

"You mean about her being gay?"

"She can also be kind of abrasive. Once you get to know her, she's one of the warmest, nicest people I know. But she definitely has an edge to her, and her sense of humor can often be downright raunchy. I might add that she's already very fond of you."

345

"She's wonderful. If she weren't gay, I might be scared to death that she'd take you away from me."

He put his arms around her and kissed her. She put her arms around him as she returned his kiss; and she reached up and slipped his jacket off and tossed it onto a chair. She started unbuttoning his shirt, kissing him warmly as she did. He pulled his undershirt off, then pulled her blouse up over her head. He held her close again, reached around and unfastened her bra, and she shrugged and let it fall to the floor. Then she unbuckled his belt and loosened his trousers. She had a smoky look in her eyes as she unfastened her skirt and let it fall.

They continued to kiss, and Kellan reached down and pulled down the covers on the bed. He ran his hands up and down her back and slipped them inside her panties and gently squeezed her buttocks. She put her hands inside the band of his shorts and slowly slipped them down as he tugged at her panties. She fell onto the bed and pulled him down beside her. His hands roamed all over her body, and she gasped as his hand found its way between her legs. She reached down for him and he eased himself over on top of her as she guided him inside her body. She pulled him down on top of her and whispered, "Don't move for a while. Let's enjoy the wanting." They held each other close and kissed for a few moments. He pushed himself up so that he could look down on her and see most of her body. She smiled and began moving slowly under him. He began to join her motion and she pulled him down again as their passion rose slowly to a fever pitch. "Oh my God," she said. "How good you are. How very good you are."

"God, how I love you," he said. "I will never, ever stop loving you."

"You're with me now, Darling. Come with me, just come with me."

Moments later, when they had reached and passed their peak, he rolled over on his back and pulled her over on top of him, still inside her. "Let's go to sleep like this," he said. She reached down and pulled the light covers up over them and rested her head on his shoulder. They breathed gently together, so close that Kellan was sure he could feel her heart beating against his chest. Sometime later, when it had grown very dark, he awakened to the sensation of her body still resting on top of him. He could feel her warm breath on his neck as she slept. He lay like that for a long time, gently stroking her back under the covers, touching her hair and kissing her gently on the cheek. At that moment he didn't care if he didn't ever fall asleep again.

On Tuesday morning one of the Montgomery family staff told Kellan that there was a phone call for him. It was Jean.

"What's up?" he asked her.

"The White House has called—some guy named Hamlin. You know him?"

"Yeah. What's he want?"

"He wants you to call him. I told him you were out of town, and he said to have you call him when you get back. He left a number."

"Okay, thanks, Jean. I'll call him tomorrow."

The morning strategy session was devoted to dividing up the country into areas in which Kellan and Jordan would be concentrating their pre-election efforts. Bob Reynolds was the organizer of the meeting, and he laid out the agenda. They talked about preparing radio spots, television spots, interviews with newspapers and magazine writers, public appearances in various parts of the country. They also discussed other sources for campaign exposure that might come up from time to time.

After some discussion, they decided that Kellan, as a Democrat, would concentrate his efforts in the South. They agreed that the once solid South was no longer as solid as it had been, but was beginning to drift from the Democratic to the Republican camp. Nevertheless, the political wisdom around the table settled on the idea that there were enough voters with Democratic roots in the south that Kellan's appeal might go over very well there.

In traditionally Republican parts of the country, campaign efforts would not have to be extraordinary. States like Kansas and the rest of the upper Midwest tended to be conservative, and efforts there would be modest. The important states with many electoral votes such as New York, California, Texas, Illinois, Ohio, New Jersey, Pennsylvania and a few others would be divided among the two candidates, each of whom would be concentrating in areas where they were most likely to do the most good. Two statisticians from the Republican national committee gave a brief presentation on voting patterns in areas where the most likely source of gaining votes in those important states would be.

Media consultants who had been invited, and who had arrived along with the statisticians early that morning, talked about the effectiveness of television and radio spots. A lively and largely indecisive discussion among the parties present ensued concerning the value of negative ads. It was agreed that they had to be designed to counter charges by the other side as a minimum. It was also understood that the current Democratic administration had created sufficient doubt about its integrity that attack ads would not need to be particularly vicious; they could merely point out what most of the American people already knew, namely, that the Walter Mayhew administration had not lived up to the expectations of most American voters.

Following their presentations, Bob Reynolds opened up the floor to questions and comments, and a lively discussion ensued. The meeting ended on a note of high expectations and confidence. Throughout the morning, there had not been the slightest mention of the risk involved with a Democrat on the ballot. Kellan had been wholeheartedly accepted, and he was prepared to contribute all he could to the campaign. If some of his Democratic colleagues took issue with that, well, that was their problem. Likewise, if Republicans objected to his presence on the ballot, they could vote for the other party, certainly not an attractive alternative. At worst, it was concluded, Kellan's presence might cause a few loyal Republicans as well as Democrats to stay home. It was generally felt that abstentions of that sort would not be decisive.

"Well, for those who want to stick around a bit longer, there's a light buffet set up out on the porch," said Bob. "For those of you who need to make tracks, thank you all for coming, and we'll be in touch soon. We'll go back and put together a schedule of campaign stops for Jordan and Kellan and get it to you as soon as possible. Meanwhile, you all know what you're doing. Good luck, safe trip, and we'll see you soon."

Kellan and Kathleen had scheduled a midafternoon flight back to Washington, where he planned to meet with Alex, Jean, and the rest of the staff to firm up their plans for the coming campaign season. Kellan shook hands with Senator Hallowell, several of the consultants and other figures, then took his leave from Bob and Jordan. Kathleen said goodbye to Shelley, thanking her for her hospitality, and to Sally Reynolds. "We girls have got to stick together," said Sally. "It was great to meet you, Kathleen. I'm sure we'll be seeing you soon." Kellan kissed Shelley on the cheek and thanked her "for everything."

Back in their apartment, Kellan changed into a suit to wear before going over to the Hill. Kathleen was relaxing on the couch as he was leaving. "Do you want to go over to the office with me?"

She smiled, stretched and yawned. "I think I'll stay here," she said. "I'm going to start making some notes on the meeting we just came from. I think I might keep a journal during the entire campaign; it might be interesting to have later, don't you think?"

"Sounds like a good idea," he said. "Maybe you'll want to publish it someday."

"Or maybe I'll just want to burn it in the fireplace," she said. "Sometimes those things wind up being less interesting than one might hope. We'll see. But I need to go somewhere and get a good typewriter."

"That reminds me. We also need to see about getting you a driver's license."

"That would be nice to have while you're gallivanting around."

"I thought you were going with me."

"I am. But I'm serious about the writing. I might stay here when you're not gone too long." She stood up, came over and kissed him. "Anyway, I'll see you later."

Back on the Hill Kellan summoned Alex and Jean into his office, and they began going over the details of what had happened in Pittsfield. "It looks as if we're going to spend a lot of time down south," he said. "Bob Reynolds seems to think that a Democrat will play well down there. I have my doubts about that, but Bob's a pretty smart guy, and maybe he's onto something. In any case, we'll need to put together some ideas for points that I want to press while I'm traveling down there."

"We'll get right on it," said Jean.

"I also want you guys to think about which one of you wants to go with me, or maybe both of you, and how we can divide up this campaign to make it as painless as possible. Look, I know it's going to be a drag on all of us, but this is what we do for a living."

"I thought you enjoyed getting out among the people," said Jean.

"I do, but this is going to be a real heavy dose of it among people that I'm not very familiar with. I actually know very little about our Southern culture, except that it's different from where I come from. But we'll see; they're all Americans, after all, although some of them may think they're more American than others."

"Well I'm pretty familiar with the South," said Alex. "Duke University isn't exactly the heart of the Deep South, but there were a lot of students from the South that I got to know, and I did travel a bit while I was there. I spent a week in New Orleans once, and I've been to Florida a few times. I hiked the Natchez Trace from the Ridgeland Indian mounds in Mississippi to Natchez with some friends during one summer break."

"Wow, how far is that?" said Jean.

349

"About a hundred miles; we took about a week, camped out and made a few stops along the way," she said. "Of course we didn't see a whole lot of people, but the ones we did see were real old Southern types, pretty much like I imagine the backcountry still is in Georgia, Alabama and Mississippi. Those people tend to have their minds made up and don't want to be confused by the facts. The mountain folks in East Tennessee and Kentucky tend to be that way, too."

"Yeah, a lot of them are sort of locked in concrete," said Jean. "You could beat them with a two by four and it wouldn't change any of their ideas. I guess that can be a good thing or a bad thing, depending on what it is they believe in. I just sense the feeling that we'll have to skirt some issues down there, even though they may come up from time to time."

"Right," said Alex. "We'll have to figure out a standard response for questions that have to do with race, for example. It's not something you really have to worry about that much in New England or New York or most of the Northeast, but down there it can still be a hot button issue. It's unfortunate, but that's the way it is."

"Well, I agree with you guys in principle," said Kellan. "On the other hand, South Boston isn't exactly racially friendly turf. There have been some pretty bad scenes in that part of town, and there was a famous black athlete in Boston who really was treated despicably by some of the Boston faithful."

"I didn't know that," said Alex.

"Well, it's not exactly advertised. And a lot of people don't know that one of the worst race riots in American history was in New York City during the Civil War. And I'm sorry to say that a lot of Irish were behind that."

"How do you know all this stuff?" asked Jean.

"Books. You know, those little things made out of paper and cardboard? I think we've got some lying around here somewhere."

"Okay, smart ass, so you read a lot. We already knew that," said Jean. "But I suppose it's a different sort of thing up there, compared to what you might find in rural Mississippi. But Alex is right; we'll have to think it through and come up with some sort of standard response. It will have to be along the lines of, 'at this point in our nation's history, we need to move beyond our—I don't want to say prejudices, that's too strong—beyond our attitudes of the past and accept the fact that our culture is truly a diverse one."

"That sounds about right," said Alex. She looked at Kellan. "It might not be a bad idea for you to spend a few minutes with some of your colleagues from the South. You know, an informal chat about, hey, I'm going to be in your home district for a while, any suggestions you might have that could keep me from sounding stupid?"

"Yeah, that's a good idea," said Jean.

"I can do a little poking around myself and see who it might be good to talk to," said Alex. "A lot of those folks are really pretty enlightened, or they wouldn't be here in Congress. We can't write off the whole area as being monolithic; I bet we'll be surprised at what we discover if we really start investigating down there."

"Right," said Kellan. "Well in the meantime, we have to think about a schedule. Bob Reynolds and Jordan pretty much left it up to me to decide when I want to go, where I want to go, as long as I cover the ground that we laid out during the campaign. We'll also have to do some work up North in places like New York, Chicago, Pittsburgh and some of the other states that have a lot of votes. In California we're going to have to cover both the Los Angeles and San Francisco areas."

"Talk about cultural divides," said Alex. "That's about as sharp as it can get. California is definitely schizophrenic when it comes to its state culture. I remember reading somewhere that there was a move some years ago for Northern and Southern California to separate into two states. That would have been novel, but it didn't happen."

"What was that all about?" said Jean.

"I think it had something to do with water rights," said Alex. "I lived next to a person from California when I was at Duke Law School, and she had some pretty interesting ideas about the makeup of her home state."

"Are you still in touch with her?" Jean asked.

"No, she was going back home to get married before she started practicing law, and I don't even remember the name of the guy she was engaged to. I think she planned to practice on the West Coast somewhere, San Francisco, I think, but there's no way I could track her down. I guess I could go into the alumni records and find out but at this point I don't think it would be worth the effort."

"I tell you what, guys. I have to play Congressman at least part of the time. Let's get Carlos in here and see what's up. We can continue this discussion later at my place."

"What about that guy from the White House?" asked Jean.

"I'll call him tomorrow."

Alex and Jean arrived at Kellan and Kathleen's apartment with a six pack of Bud and two bottles of wine. Kellan was puttering in the kitchen, and Alex started lifting the lids off of pots. "Smells good," she said. She helped Kathleen get out silver, plates and napkins while Jean opened the wine and poured glasses for everyone. During dinner they discussed the campaign plans they had been working on that afternoon.

"I hope we're not boring you with all this shop talk," said Jean to Kathleen.

"Oh, no, it's fascinating," she said. "Listening to a presidential campaign being planned is a new experience." Everyone laughed. "No, I'm serious!" she insisted. "You all must know how new this all is to me." Kellan smiled as he realized again how different his life was with Kathleen at the center of it. He couldn't help feeling blessed.

"I hear you got some interesting material when you were in Belfast," said Alex.

"I sure did," said Kathleen. "I'll get it for you after dinner."

When they had cleared the dining room table, Kathleen brought the papers she had collected from Aunt Michaela and spread them out. Alex looked each one over carefully then looked back at Kathleen and said, "I think we're in real good shape here. Let me check out a few things." She opened what appeared to be a manual and began thumbing through it looking for pages she had marked. "These are all the relevant regulations," she said. "I think everything we need is in here. All we have to do is figure out what the next step is, and then you and I go over to the Immigration and Naturalization Service in the Justice Department to sort it all out. I'm pretty sure we can get you a certificate of citizenship fairly rapidly, which will be a good thing to have just in case."

"Just in case of what?" Kathleen asked.

Alex smiled at her. "Oh, I don't know. You might wind up on some talk show somewhere and somebody starts poking around in your status. You can haul it out, wave it around, jump up and down and embarrass the host. That would be all kinds of fun, wouldn't it?"

Kathleen laughed. "Not that I'm likely to wind up on any talk show, but it would be fun, I'll grant you."

"Don't be too sure about that," said Jean. "You're already beginning to gain a lot of attention. I even saw a newspaper report from Springfield, Massachusetts, about your presence at the big meeting. And you even got a little notice in one of the Boston papers. You're a celebrity already!"

"Damn right," said Alex. "All those Hollywood starlets will be wondering where the hell you came from. They love to get their noses into the political game, and here you are right in the thick of it, and you've never been in a movie."

"Not yet, anyway," said Jean. "But I bet when this campaign's over, you'll get some offers."

Kathleen looked at Kellan, who had been following the conversation with amusement. "I'll have to check with the boss here," she said. "Darling, what do you think? If I get an offer to be in the movies, would you be okay with that?"

"As long as they let you keep your clothes on," Kellan said, and he smiled. "And I don't want you getting too close to any of those handsome young actors."

"I don't go for actors," said Kathleen. "Most of them strike me as kind of empty headed pretty boys. Not all of them, of course. I understand there are some people in the movie business with some intellectual capacity. But I suspect that's more common for British Shakespearean actors than your typical Hollywood stud. But you never know, there might be one or two out there. But I assure you, I'm not the least bit interested in finding out any more about Hollywood than I already know."

Later that evening when they were alone, Kellan said to Kathleen, "We need to think about getting you a Virginia driver's license."

"Why, do I need one?"

"I just want you to be comfortable driving around the streets of Washington and here in Virginia. When I'm out of town you might want to be going here and there, and I think it would be good for you to have a license."

"Well, I thought of that before I left, and I applied for an international license. I understand that along with my Irish license, it's valid here in the states. I should think that all I would have to do would be to take it in and apply for a Virginia license."

"Now that I think of it, you're right. You and Alex can do that when you're going to check on your citizenship papers." He sat down next to her and put his arms around her. "You're going to fit in as if you are right at home here. I know you will always be Irish down in your soul, and I love that. But you should feel free to come and go as you please here without having to apologize to anyone."

"When is the last time you heard me apologize to anybody about anything?" Kathleen said.

Kellan laughed. "I guess you're right. If we win this election, you're going to be the most interesting person in the administration. Maybe Jordan will give you a job at the White House."

"Hey, that would be a fine idea! I could start shipping arms to the IRA."

He laughed again. "Don't even joke about that," he said.

She reached up and turned his face toward her and kissed him on the mouth. He looked into her eyes and saw that look that told him that she was tired of conversation. Then she backed away for a moment. "Who said I was joking?" she said. Then she kissed him again and whispered, "Don't worry, Darling, the only arms I want are yours."

The next morning Kellan called the White House and was told by an operator that his call would be returned right away. A few moments later Jean stuck her head in the door and said, "White House."

Kellan picked up the phone. "Kellan Maguire here."

"Kellan, this is Howard Hamlin over at the White House."

"Hi, Howie, what's up?"

"Nothing really urgent. The president would like to have a word or two about your decision to run on the other ticket. He understands your position and is not really upset about it, but he'd just like to have a chat with you. If it works for you, could you come over, say, about four o'clock this afternoon?"

"I can manage that."

"Good. I'll send a car for you and they'll bring you around to the side entrance. Pat will meet you there." Patricia Lundy was a high-level White House aide.

"Sounds good."

"Great. See you then."

Jean came into the office. "What did they want?"

"Well, I'm guessing that the boss is pissed off that I let myself get put on the Republican ticket. Of course he's upset, but that's not my problem. In any case, they want me to come over and talk to him."

Jean said, "You think they'll try to get you to change your mind?"

"I doubt it. If they did talk me into it and it came out—which it would—they would look real bad, so that's not going to happen."

"Then why does he want to talk you?"

"Well, I guess I'll find out when I get there."

Alex wandered in and said, "What's going on?"

"Kellan's going over to the White House to get his ass chewed out," said Jean.

Alex grinned. "That sounds like fun. Can I come and watch?"

"Get outta here!" he said.

Minutes later Jean came back into the office. "She's here," she said. Christina Valentine, the woman that Bob Reynolds had sent to assist Kellan with the campaign, had arrived at the Capitol and was ushered to Kellan's office by a Capitol guide.

"Okay, bring her in."

Christina Valentine appeared to be in her mid-thirties, dark-haired with an olive complexion that suggested a Mediterranean heritage. She was single, quite attractive, and was wearing an expensive looking suit, but her jacket was unbuttoned, and the blouse underneath it was cut very low. She was also, as it turned out, very vocal. She introduced herself to Kellan, explained exactly what her role would be, which was to be sure that Kellan's speaking points were on message and consistent with Jordan's campaign. Kellan was surprised; he had every intention of following Jordan's lead for the direction of the campaign. He wondered why she felt it necessary to make that point. He was sure it hadn't come from Jordan or Bob Reynolds.

Alex and Jean were in Kellan's office while Christina Valentine introduced herself, and they listened with interest as she laid out her agenda. Kellan noticed that Jean and Alex glanced at each other from time to time, but he couldn't pick up exactly what it was that passed between them—he made a note to himself to ask them later. He thanked Chris and asked her to get herself acquainted with the other members of the staff. "Jean will find you a place to park and provide you anything you need. We'll get together and go over the travel schedule when you get settled."

"That shouldn't take long," she said, rather sharply, he thought. On their way out, Jean looked back at Kellan and rolled her eyes.

Patricia Lundy met Kellan at the side entrance to the White House and accompanied him up to the Chief of Staff's office. "Kellan, how are you?" said the Chief, Jackson Gunther. They shook hands. "Glad you could come over. Nice of you to find the time."

Kellan didn't miss the sarcastic tone, but he smiled. "Not at all, Jack. Good to see you."

Pat Lundy came back out of the president's office. "He's ready to see you," she said to Kellan. She held the door for him and Jackson Gunther.

Kellan thought that President Mayhew didn't quite look the part. As a former three-time Mayor of New York City, who then served a single term as governor of the state but failed to get reelected, he had found his way into the United States Senate where he served two terms. His nomination for president by the Democratic Party was made possible by a logjam between two powerful governors from Illinois and California. When neither of the two obvious choices could get over the top, Walter Mayhew, who had run a close third in the primaries, held his ground as the convention neared. The party faithful gradually grew more and more frustrated when the neither of the leading candidates seemed able to win the nomination. Somewhere around the eighth ballot, operatives from the three campaigns gathered in smoke-filled rooms in the hotel near the convention center and began to discuss alternatives. Walter Mayhew emerged as a compromise solution to the deadlock. He was nominated on the ninth ballot.

Although the two governors who had waged the bitter campaign promised their support for the candidate, it was at best lukewarm. In the end, Walter Mayhew was elected president, but it seemed foreordained that he would serve only one term. And now Jordan Montgomery, Kellan's friend, had challenged him and was clearly a much stronger candidate than the man who had lost to Mayhew four years before.

"Have a seat, Kellan," the president said as he shook Kellan's hand. Kellan sat down, and the president resumed his seat behind his Oval Office desk. Kellan had the impression that Walter Mayhew was trying to make the point that he was president, something that Kellan could hardly forget. The atmosphere in the Oval Office was famous for making people feel uncomfortable, and Kellan tried to keep his nerves from getting the best of him. He took a couple of deep breaths.

The president pressed his fingers together and smiled. "Well, I see that your friend Jordan has placed you on the ticket. I was a bit surprised to hear that; we have never had a loyal Democrat join a Republican on the ballot for president before. It's rather unprecedented, and people are wondering why you chose to do that."

"Well, Mr. President, as you probably know, Jordan Montgomery and I have co-sponsored a lot of legislation, we've been friends since before either of us ran for public office, and we seem to have the same kinds of goals for the country. Our policies are rooted in the economic structure and future of the country, and we both see very much eye to eye on that. Other issues we may differ on, but that's the focus of our platform, and that's what we intend to push."

"So you think my economic policies are inadequate?" said the president. He was still smiling, but Kellan could see it was a strain. The president's voice was just a trifle testy; he was obviously trying to avoid appearing overbearing, which would have been difficult in any case.

"No sir, not necessarily. We think more that there are certain options it haven't been tried, certain ideas that might be—shall we say—ground breaking, and we want to try some new approaches to trade policy and other economic issues. I would say that it's not so much that we think the policies of this administration have been wrong as much as we might say that they—to put it kindly—have lacked imagination." He paused as the president frowned. "As you know, I spent four years in Ireland, and when you look at a system from outside, sometimes you see things that others, closer to the situation, might miss. Anyway, that's our point, and that's why I chose to run with Senator Montgomery."

The president leaned back in his chair, and his expression turned to something that looked like smug. "I guess it's safe to say that your mind is made up?"

"Yes sir, I think it is." He corrected himself. "I know it is."

President Mayhew leaned forward again. "So, I imagine you'd like me to bless this union? There's nothing I can say that would convince you of the error of your ways?"

"Well sir, I'm not quite sure how to answer that. The fact that I'm over here will certainly become known one way or another. And if it looks as though I changed my mind and turned down Senator Montgomery's offer following the visit over here, I'm not sure that would do you any good, with all due respect."

The president stood up from behind his desk and walked around and sat on the front edge of it. "You're probably right about that, Kellan. I have to say, I am disappointed in your decision, but I respect it, and I expect that you two will make a good team. But god dammit, you might have shown me the courtesy of a heads up before you accepted."

"Well, sir, I apologize for that, but Senator Montgomery's offer was quite unexpected. He was in a hurry for an answer, and I had a couple of issues of my own to resolve before I could agree."

"Involving some Irish woman, I hear."

From his tone, Kellan thought, he might as well have said 'some Irish bimbo.' He felt his cheeks grow hot but took a breath. He smiled at the president. "If you mean my wife, yes, sir, she was part of the equation."

Walter Mayhew looked startled, and Kellan immediately realized that the president did not know as much as he thought he knew. He started to speak, but stopped. Then he said, "Well, I hope you will treat this office with the respect it deserves when you're out on the trail."

Kellan smiled. "I'll do that, sir. Thank you for having me over." He stood up and held out his hand, and the president took it.

Back in the Chief's office Jackson Gunther said, "Jesus Christ, Kellan, I'm sorry about that. When did you get married?"

"The day after I accepted Jordan's offer," he said. "I guess the word didn't get around fast enough."

Jackson shook his head. 'Don't worry, Jack,' Kellan wanted to say 'you'll be out of this job soon enough.' They shook hands, and Pat accompanied Kellan out.

"Congratulations on your wedding, Congressman," said Patricia as they were walking toward the entrance. "I hear she's lovely."

Surprised, Kellan smiled at her. "Why, thank you, Pat." Interesting, he thought, that Pat knew about his marriage but the big boys didn't.

Jean and Alex followed Kellan into his office as he returned from the White House. "How was your court appearance?" asked Alex.

"Well, he didn't call me over to offer me Secretary of State in his next administration," he said.

"No shit. Did he try to talk you out of it?" said Jean.

"He knows better than that," he said. "But he didn't know as much as he thought he did."

"What do you mean?" asked Alex.

"Look, he did what he had to do. Let's forget about it, okay?" He paused. "Go get what's her name and let's discuss the campaign trip."

"Christina?"

"If that's what she answers to," he grumbled.

"Damn, you really did get your ass chewed out, didn't you?" muttered Alex.

A moment later Alex came back in accompanied by Christina and the four of them began discussing the first leg of Kellan's campaign travel. He would leave on Friday for South Carolina and contact the state Republican committee beforehand to arrange a number of political gatherings over the weekend. Realizing that most voters were working people, the campaign planned the majority of its public outings for weekends and evenings. Toward the end of the campaign they might expand into daytime rallies. Kellan and the three aides discussed the schedule for television debates between the candidates. Jordan would have two debates with president Mayhew, Kellan would have one with Vice President Prichard of Ohio, and then Jordan and President Mayhew would participate in the final debate. In deference to the incumbent vice president, the debate between Kellan and the vice president would be held at Ohio State University.

They then went over a checklist of talking points that Kellan would use, including answers to possible questions. As a Roman Catholic, Kellan was aware that the issue of religion might have some residual impact, even though it had been decided more or less permanently during the election of 1960 by Jack Kennedy. Kellan had studied the replies Kennedy had made to persistent questions about his faith, but he was sure that he would not be probed in depth as the Senator from Massachusetts had been.

It was agreed that Kellan's first stop would be in Charleston, followed by visits to Columbia, Savannah and Atlanta with some brief stops in between. They also agreed that he would generally begin his travels on Friday, work the crowds during the weekend and wrap up with meetings on Monday evening. He would be back in the Capitol for the Tuesday through Thursday workweek, which was common during an election cycle. Not only was the presidential election going on, but one third of the United States Senate and the entire House would face elections in November. Although a number of representatives were either assured of reelection or were running unopposed, the schedule was based on the assumption that both senators and representatives were working toward the elections.

Finally, Kellan would visit Jordan's headquarters perhaps every ten days, and he would keep in close touch with Bob Reynolds by phone. Face-to-face meetings would be scheduled as needed. It was clear that no sense of urgency existed at the Montgomery campaign headquarters concerning Kellan's part in the campaign. He was grateful for that, as he was comfortable running his own show.

That evening Kellan went over his travel plans with Kathleen. "What do you think?" he said. "Do you want to go along on this first trip?"

"I know I said I wanted to go with you every time," she said. "But since that big Labor Day party I've been thinking that I might just be in the way. Besides, I've really been thinking a lot about wanting to get back into writing, and when you're gone would be a good time for me to get started.

I've been thinking about some things I want to say, and I'm sort of like you. When I get my mind on something I get very focused." She leaned over and kissed him. "I know I'm going to miss you, but you're always with me. Believe me, every morning when I wake up, I'm sort of lost for a few moments, and then I remember that you're right next to me, or right near me, and I get a very warm feeling."

"It's the same for me," he said.

"When my mind has been somewhere else," she said, "and I suddenly think of you, it's like a sip of warm whiskey. It goes right down to my belly, and I get tingly all over. Jesus, you excite me even when you're not touching me. I never knew it could be like this."

"Come on," he said. He took her hand and led her toward the bedroom.

Kellan had decided that Jean would accompany him on the first trip to South Carolina. She was an experienced campaigner and had already contacted some of the Republican operatives in the places they would visit. The trip went well, and Kellan was satisfied that his place on the ticket was not going to be a significant drawback. He connected well with people, spoke eloquently even in brief conversations, and had answers to virtually every question that was asked. Jean did some wandering through the audiences and reported that she had detected very little discontent. As they flew from Atlanta back to Washington late Monday evening, both Kellan and Jean were satisfied that his first outing had been a success. He spoke later with Bob Reynolds, who reported that Jordan's first round had also gone well. They were off to a good start.

Kellan was in his office early Tuesday morning when Alex came in. "We need to talk," she said.

"Oh, what's up?"

"Let's get out of here; I don't want anyone to overhear."

They found a corner in one of the cafeterias and sat down over coffee. "Okay, what's bugging you?" Kellan said.

"That bitch is bugging me!" she said. "From the moment she got here, Miss Funny Valentine has been telling us how the world works. Jesus Christ, she must think that Jean and I are idiots. It was a good thing that Jean went with you this past weekend or we might have had a fist fight in the office. Jean can't stand her either; feel free to check with her on that point."

"I believe you," he said. "I picked up exactly what you're talking about even in that first meeting. I'm not sure what we should do about it; you think you can live with her in the office, at least for a while?"

"God dammit, Kellan, she tried to hit on me!"

"You're kidding."

"And she's not even gay. Listen, Kellan, she came over to my apartment on Saturday evening, and we had a few drinks and things were not going too bad. I was sitting on the couch and all of a sudden she walked over and sat down next to me and kissed me."

"What did you do?"

"Well, I didn't kiss her back, I can tell you that. And don't ask me if I was tempted to start something. Like I said, I'm sure she's not gay. I think she was just trying to feel me out, see what she could get away with. I kind of got the impression that she was jealous of my relationship with you, which is stupid to begin with. Of course I have a good relationship with you, for Christ's sake. Everybody who knows both of us knows that, and nobody thinks twice about it. I'll bet my ass she did some asking around to find out if you and I were shacking up."

"Doesn't she know I'm married? Not only that, but recently married?"

"If she does, she doesn't give a shit. She's a hustler, Kellan, she's looking for a way to move up in the pecking order, and somehow she must've thought she could use me to get closer to you."

"That doesn't make any sense, does it?"

"Look, I said she wasn't gay. Maybe she goes both ways; women can do that, I'm not so sure about guys, and I don't really want to know. But I'm telling you, there was something that didn't sit right with me concerning her from the get go."

"Have you talked to Jean about this?"

"I haven't told her everything I just told you, but Jean knows she's a pain in the ass; she just didn't have to put up with her all weekend like I did. Kellan, you've got to get her out of here. If not right away, then soon. I don't want to get arrested for assault, but I came pretty god damn close to beating that bitch up when she pulled that crap in my apartment."

Kellan reached across the table and took her hand. "Okay, listen, I'll see what I can do. I'll try to get a sense of what Bob Reynolds thinks about her and we'll go from there. Okay?"

"I'm sorry to get so upset," Alex said. "I usually brush that stuff off pretty easily, like when a guy tries to hit on me. Unless they're being really obnoxious, I just tell him I'm gay, and that scares the crap out of them. If they get persistent, or if they're drunk, I can get mean real fast. Usually I don't have to."

"There's nothing mean about you," he said. "You know how I feel about you. I'll see what I can do."

That evening Kellan told Kathleen about his conversation with Alex. "I've never seen her that pissed off," he said. "Something about that woman really bugged her. I'm not quite sure why."

"But you said that she made an advance on Alex; wouldn't that be enough?"

"I'm sure that happens to her from time to time; she mentioned how she sometimes gets hit on by guys. But this one really got her riled up. The strangest thing was, she said that Christina is not gay. I wonder how she knew that."

Kathleen thought for a few moments. "You know, of all the people I've met since I've been here, there are two whose judgment I would trust implicitly. Alex is one, and Bob Reynolds is the other. I guess I would add Jean to that list also—she's no dummy. But both Bob and Alex strike me as being people who understand it."

"Understand what?"

"Everything. Life. What makes people tick." She paused for a moment. "What are you going to do about that woman?"

"I'll talk to Bob. I'm just not sure I can run her out of town all that quickly."

"Does Bob know Alex?"

"They've met. I'm sure he understands that she's pretty important to me. I know that he and Jean have hit it off just fine, and I think the reason that he and Jordan decided to give me a free hand is because they trust Jean and Alex."

"You're going to keep them once you become vice president, right?"

"Assuming that I do, yes that's my plan."

"In other words, they're going to be working in the vice president's office a few months from now."

Kellan did his best to keep Christina away from Alex for the next couple of days. He dispatched Alex to take Kathleen over to the Department of Justice. After meeting with the Immigration and Naturalization Service, Kathleen was informed that she was entitled to a certificate of citizenship, which would be forthcoming. Alex then took her to the Department of Motor Vehicles, and Kathleen soon had her Virginia driver's license. Later she told Kellan that she had asked Alex how it was going with the new campaign worker, and Alex had tossed it off, saying, "Kellan's going to get rid of her."

"You are, aren't you?" said Kathleen.

"I talked to Bob Reynolds last night," he said. "He's aware of the problem."

"So what's going to happen?"

"We'll see, won't we?"

The next afternoon Alex walked into Kellan's office and sat down. "She hasn't been in all day," Alex said.

"I haven't the foggiest notion whom you are talking about," said Kellan.

"Oh screw you, you know damn well who I'm talking about!"

Kellan laughed. "Well where do you suppose she's gone?"

Alex looked at him quizzically. "I don't have a clue; I called her apartment and there was no answer. I left a couple of messages this morning but got no return calls." Then a smile came over Alex's face. "You got rid of her, didn't you?"

"I just told Bob Reynolds I thought we had everything under control," he said. "Actually he brought up the subject of Christina Valentine. I sort of got the impression that they had shipped her down here to get her out of the home office."

"Where do you suppose she is now?" Alex asked.

"I'm guessing she'll have a fine career selling retail merchandise at Sears," he said. "I doubt she'll still be on Jordan's campaign staff come tomorrow. She's probably on her way back up there right now."

Alex stood up, walked around his desk and kissed him on the cheek. "Thanks, boss!" she said.

"Any time."

The presidential campaign of Jordan Montgomery and Kellan Maguire proceeded as the principles, their staffs, and the majority of the political pundits of the political world had predicted. By the first of October, Jordan had built a comfortable lead over President Mayhew. The president recovered slightly following the second debate, in which he seemed to have scored a few points against his challenger. But Jordan's lead continued to grow, and Kellan's debate with the vice president at Ohio State did nothing to slow his progress. By the end of the third debate, the issue was all but decided. It looked like a landslide in the making, unusual for a challenger against an incumbent president, but it spoke well for the reputation and abilities of both Jordan and his vice presidential running mate, Kellan Maguire.

On Election Day Kellan went to the polls in White Plains, where he had maintained an address in order to keep his New York State residence current. Jordan voted in Pittsfield, covered by a media swarm that had already concluded that the election was decided. President Mayhew and Vice President Prichard both voted in their home precincts, expressing confidence that the election would return them to the offices they held. They put on a brave face, but the media covering them were not convinced, and peppered them with questions about what went wrong. The president bristled at such questions and insisted, "Nothing went wrong! We're going to win!"

By ten pm on election night the results were clear. Jordan had taken five of six New England states, New York, Pennsylvania and New Jersey. Votes were closely divided in the southern states, but it was clear that Jordan would not lose any significant ground in that area. As results from the Midwest began to roll in, the verdict was sealed. The incumbents would be ousted, and a new administration would take over on January 20.

Kellan and Kathleen, Jean and Alex, along with a few others who had helped with the campaign, gathered in the same hotel in White Plains where Kellan had celebrated his first election to Congress. He even invited Lynn Patterson to attend, and she was pleased to be included. She had married again, a Wall Street analyst five years her junior, and made it very clear that she didn't miss George Patterson in the least.

"Kellan, wonderful to see you." She kissed him lightly on the lips. "And you must be Kathleen!"

"That I am," said Kathleen.

"Well, you couldn't have done better than this guy!" She smiled at Kellan. "The way he talked about you, I knew I didn't have a shot."

Kathleen looked at Kellan curiously. "She's right," he said. "I did tell her about you."

Kathleen looked at Lynn, then back at Kellan; she had obviously put two and two together, but she smiled at Lynn and said, "Lovely to meet you."

"Lucky man," said Lynn.

Later in the evening Kellan was startled to see Fiona suddenly appear—she rushed up to him and threw her arms around him. ""Wow, I didn't expect you to come," he said. "How did you get here?"

"A friend of mine decided to drive home to vote. He lives in Stamford. After he voted, we had dinner at his home, and he drove me over here. He's going to pick me up early in the morning so we can get back for my afternoon classes. I assume I can stay with you here?"

"Sure you can, Honey. Gee it's great to see you, but you didn't have to come all this way."

"I just wanted to congratulate you in person." She hugged him again. "I'm so proud of you!"

Although Kellan had decided that he would remain in office until the end of his term, once the election results were clear, he decided to resign his office in order to begin planning for his vice presidential staff and to assist Jordan in the selection of his cabinet. Jean was going to remain as Kellan's Chief of Staff in the office of the vice president, and Alex would be a key member of his staff as a political advisor. He also brought in several members of his office staff, now that the 19th district representative's office was being vacated. Since Kellan had not run for reelection, the Democratic victor in the November election was named to fill Kellan's seat until the new Congress convened in January.

Kellan and Kathleen traveled to Pittsfield on the day after the election to celebrate with Jordan, Shelley, Bob and Sally Reynolds, and a few others. During the course of the day Kellan became mildly disturbed by what he saw as a faintly triumphant attitude in Jordan, a posture that struck him as very uncharacteristic of his friend. Jordan had never been one to gloat; he had often exhibited the same sort of humility that Kellan felt was an appropriate posture for an elected official. In a democratic society, they were the servants of the people, not the masters. He recalled the story of a previous team of victors who had sat around on election night drinking champagne and smoking cigars. One of them had said, "This is what it's all about!" An older, wiser colleague had corrected him quickly, saying, "No this is not what's it all about; this is the beginning. What it's all about is what's going to happen over the next four years."

That was the sentiment that Kellan embraced. The victory was less important than what would be done with it. Their agenda was clear; they knew where they wanted to go, and they had a reasonable idea of how to get there. Building strong relationships with Congress would be both a challenge and a top priority, but with a former Republican senator and a former Democratic congressman in the administration, both sides of the aisle could be courted successfully. In addition to their economic agenda, they had to consider defense, agriculture, tax reform, immigration and a variety of other areas that had come up during the course of the campaign.

As the day wore on, Jordan, Kellan and Bob discussed plans and strategies, testing, proposing, adopting or abandoning myriad ideas as the women listened in. Sally, a veteran political operator herself, added her thoughts from time to time. Finally Shelley said, "All right, gentlemen, enough is enough. Can we just drop politics for a while and talk about something interesting?"

Kellan noticed that while Shelley's tone was light, she had appeared to be worn out from campaigning and was more than ready for a break.

In any case, the die was cast, the Rubicon had been crossed, and the government of the people had taken another step forward in the direction that the practitioners and their staffs had planned, and that the majority of the political pundits of the country had predicted.

Part 4

The End Game

The electors of President and Vice President of each State shall meet and give their votes on the first Monday after the second Wednesday in December next following their appointment at such place in each State as the legislature of such State shall direct.
—Twenty Fifth Amendment

"Is there anything we can do for you? For you are the one in trouble now."
—First Lady Eleanor Roosevelt to Harry S. Truman, April 12, 1945

First Daughter

As directed by law, the presidential electors met in their respective states on the first Monday after the second Wednesday in December and cast their ballots for the candidates chosen by the voters. A total of 432 electors cast their ballots for Jordan Montgomery and Kellan Maguire. The electoral vote margin was larger than that of the popular vote, but the results were a landslide by any definition. It was the fourth worst defeat of an incumbent president in the 20th century. Once the vote was official, President-elect Montgomery stepped up efforts to select members of his cabinet, his White House staff, and to decide other necessary details prior to assuming office on January 20.

Jordan decided to hold a meeting of his top advisers on December 27 at Mount Snow, a mountaintop resort in southern Vermont. A large conference room was reserved, and it was understood that the Secret Service would do a thorough investigation of the facility prior to the arrival of the President-elect and his party. In addition to the president and vice president-elect, attendees would include Bob Reynolds, five of the cabinet members who had already been selected—the Attorney General and Secretaries of State, Defense, Treasury and Interior—and several top White House aides. The president, vice president, chief of staff and a top political advisor would leave Pittsfield on the afternoon of December 26. The remaining attendees would arrive before noon on the 27th. Arrangements were made, menus selected, and accommodations assigned to the guests, including the Secret Service detail that would accompany the expedition. It would be the final gathering prior to the president taking up office space in Washington prior to his inauguration, several days after the new Congress had convened on January 3rd.

Jordan had invited Kellan and Kathleen to spend Christmas with them at the Montgomery home in Pittsfield, and Kellan had been pleased to accept. Fiona would drive over from Eddie and Eileen's home to join them, and Jordan's parents, siblings and other close relatives would be there, along with Bob and Sally Reynolds. It promised to be a festive occasion. Shelley had invited Kathleen and Sally to stay at the Montgomery home in Pittsfield during the conference. Jordan, Kellan and Bob would rejoin them following the meeting and spend New Year's Eve together, along with other relatives and friends.

Following the election, Kellan had decided to give up his apartment in Arlington at the end of December. After talking with Eddie, Eileen, Tom and Mary he decided to purchase a home in Massachusetts to which he could retire after leaving office. Although it was a long way off, he felt that he and Kathleen should have a home to which they could retreat when not busy in Washington. Fiona could live there while she completed her medical studies at the University of Massachusetts Medical School in Worcester, and one or two friends also in training would no doubt be happy to move in with her. Eddie and Eileen put Kellan in touch with a realtor in their area, who promised to find a suitable home as soon as practicable.

The days between the election and the coming Christmas gathering in Massachusetts moved rapidly. Kellan familiarized himself with the vice president's office in the Senate area of the Capitol, which he would occupy upon taking office. Outgoing Vice President Prichard had generously offered Kellan space in which to meet with aides during the weeks prior to inauguration. Alex and Jean were frequent visitors to Kellan's apartment as they worked on the transition to their new positions. Kellan arranged for them to take a tour of the vice presidential office spaces, which they would be occupying. It was a busy time, and the days flew by.

"I'm really looking forward to the holidays," said Kathleen one evening as she and Kellan relaxed with a glass of wine. "We need to figure out when the family should come over from Mallow so that we can make sure we have reservations for them."

Patrick and Libby had decided to forgo the trip, saying that someone had to stay behind and keep an eye on the farm. Kellan was disappointed, but he promised that he would arrange for them to come over to the United States not long afterward so they could get a glimpse of America. Brendan and Deirdre, on the other hand, were thrilled about the opportunity to attend the inauguration festivities. Fiona's sister Caitlin and her husband would also be coming, along with their brother Michael and his wife. They would be in the country for about two weeks.

Following the vote of the Electoral College, when his position was official, Kellan was accompanied by a Secret Service detail wherever he went. Kathleen was also assigned an agent who would be with her whenever she went out by herself. As she and Kellan went shopping for Christmas gifts for family members and friends, they gradually got used to being accompanied by young men and women in dark suits whose job it was to make sure that they remained safe. Kathleen insisted on getting to know their detail by name, and did her best to engage them in conversation. As the Secret Service agents slowly warmed to her engaging personality, she told Kellan that she felt that having a bodyguard with her for many of her waking hours would not be all that bad.

Shortly after Kellan and Kathleen arrived at the Montgomery house on the day before Christmas, Shelley approached Kellan. "You have a phone call," she said, smiling. "It's your daughter."

"Hi, Kelly, I'm glad you're there," Fiona said. "I need to ask you something."

"Sure, Honey, what is it?"

"Do you think the Montgomerys would mind if I bring a friend?"

"No, of course not. I'll be glad to meet her."

"It's not a her, Dad, it's a him."

"Aha, that's even more interesting. Is it someone I've already met?"

"Not yet, but you will. You might be seeing a lot of him."

"In that case I'd better ask you something. I assume he'll be staying here?"

"Of course."

"Then my next question is, will he need a separate room? I'm sure there's plenty of space here."

"No, we can stay in the same room, unless you have a problem with it."

Kellan laughed. "You're a big girl now, Sweetheart, and no, I won't have any problem with it. It sounds as if just maybe this could be something serious."

"I'm not quite sure yet, but I do want to know what you and Kathleen think of him. Eileen and Eddie have already met him, and they seem to like him. But I really care about your opinion."

"Well, Honey, the only opinion that really matters is yours, but as I said, I look forward to meeting him. I'm sure Kathleen will also. You know how to get here?"

"I've been there before, Dad, and even though it was a long time ago, I still remember."

"Great, we'll see you soon then. Before you hang up, are Eddie and Eileen there?"

"Sure. Do you want to talk one of them?"

"Whoever is handy."

Eileen came on the line. "What can I do for you, Mister Vice?" she said. Eileen enjoyed having fun with Kellan's new lofty perch.

"Speaking of vice, Fiona tells me she's bringing a friend, and she says you guys have already met him. Is there anything you'd like to share?"

"Kellan, she's a grown woman for Christ's sake! Anyway, we're really happy for her. He's a young intern here at the hospital, nice looking, good head on his shoulders. I'm sure you're going to like him."

"Do you think it's serious?"

Eileen laughed. "Well, since she decided to drag him along for you and Kathleen to give him a once-over, I guess you could say this is more than just casual. I'm guessing that if all goes well, and I assume it will, he may be moving in with her. As you know, the house they're getting right after the first of the year has plenty of room. One of her friends from her medical class is already going to move in with her. She's a very nice young lady, and even if he does move in with them, that's not saying they'll be sharing a room. Or should I say, sharing a bed? Anyway, I don't think you have anything to worry about."

"I'm not worried," he said. "I just wanted to get your opinion. I assume Eddie pretty much feels the same way."

"Well, since Eddie and I don't have any kids, he's not sure what he supposed to think. Maybe you can help him out with that. But he likes Mike, and I guess that's all you need to know."

"Mike, huh? Does he have a last name?"

"It's Michael Hanrahan. That shouldn't surprise you. Doctor Michael Hanrahan, to be exact."

"Sounds good to me. Thanks for the info, Eileen. I can't wait to see them."

"I hear you guys are heading up to Mount Snow the day after Christmas," said Eileen. "You know there are storms in the Midwest, and they'll be heading this way I'm sure. I hope you get up there safely."

"You weren't supposed to know that, but yes, that's where we're going. The ladies are staying here, of course, as it will be a business meeting. I'm sure the Secret Service will keep an eye on things."

"Let me know how it goes with you and Fiona and young Michael," Eileen said. "And you take care of yourself!"

"Thanks, Eileen. Best to Eddie."

Fiona and Michael Hanrahan arrived before dinner that afternoon. Kellan, Kathleen, the Montgomerys and a few other people were seated in the large living room when Fiona was shown in by a maid who had answered the door. She threw her arms around Kellan, then hugged Kathleen and Shelley Montgomery. She stopped and looked at Jordan and smiled. "Can I still call you Uncle Jordan?" Fiona said.

"Of course you can, Sweetie." He held out his arms for a hug. Then he looked at Fiona's friend. "And this must be Doctor Hanrahan, am I correct?" He held out his hand.

The young doctor look flustered. "It's an honor to meet you Sir, Mister President," he said.

Jordan laughed. "You don't have to call me that until January twenty," he said.

Michael looked at Fiona for help. "You can call him Senator," she said, smiling.

Shelley greeted Michael and introduced him to Bob and Sally Reynolds and Jordan's parents. Fiona, of course, knew the elder Montgomerys and had already greeted them with a hug and a kiss. Kellan smiled as he recalled how fond they had become of Fiona the first time she visited, back when she was still ten years old. They had watched her grow from a distance, and had always asked Kellan how she was faring. They had been very pleased to hear that she was in medical school in the United States, and would likely be staying in the country at least for the next few years.

"You're beginning to lose your brogue," Shelley said. Fiona smiled and answered, "*Tá an-áthas orm a bheith anseo. Nollaig shona duit*," and everyone looked at Kellan or Kathleen.

Kathleen said to Fiona, "*Agus a thabhairt duit freisin,*" and smiled. Fiona hugged her.

Then Kellan looked around at the group, "Fiona just said she's glad to be here, and happy Christmas to all," he said. "She just wants you to know she still speaks Irish."

"Very good, Dad! You remember!" said Fiona, as everyone applauded.

"And what did you say, Kathleen?" asked Shelley.

"Same to you!" And everyone laughed.

The Christmas Eve dinner was a lavish affair, and the mood was buoyant. Kellan was pleased to note that Jordan seem to be his old self; the slight triumphant attitude was gone, at least for the evening. Dinner conversation was animated and friendly, and surprisingly free of political talk. Even Bob Reynolds got into the spirit by talking about things he remembered from his childhood Christmases. Sally, who had known Bob and his family for most of her life, insisted that he was making things up, bringing a round of laughter to the table. Kathleen and Fiona talked about their Christmas experiences in Ireland, which they had shared at the Connolly home in Mallow.

Kellan was aware that it was a good thing that those present could see that Kathleen and Fiona treated each other as family, which, for all practical purposes, they were. Kathleen's sudden arrival on the scene had startled people, but Fiona's familiarity with her reinforced the fact that Kathleen had been Moira Connolly Maguire's best friend. It was as if a touchy area, at least from the perspective of the political crowd, had been ameliorated. As for Michael Hanrahan, from everything Kellan could tell, the young man was besotted with his daughter. Later that evening Kathleen said, "I think this one's for real."

"You may be right," Kellan said. "They definitely seem to be in love."

"With them both being in the medical profession, they're going to have to work hard at making a life for themselves. But I'm convinced that Fiona can do anything she sets her mind to, and young Doctor Hanrahan certainly seems to have his head on straight. I think we can relax and watch this grow. God, I'm happy for her. I just wish her mother could see her now."

"I know what you mean," said Kellan. "I think of her every time I see Fiona. She has that same determined look that Moira had. I can see Fiona going through a hospital ward just the way Moira went through the library, helping this person, fixing that problem, taking care of things with grace and efficiency. She had a way about her."

"Sure she did. And I know you will always love her, and that's a good thing. It makes me love you more." They were quiet for a while, stretched on the bed next to each other, half dressed and sleepy. Kathleen said, "It's all so different now, don't you feel it? I wonder if the royals feel like this—everybody sort of treats you as if you are not the same person you used to be." She kissed him on the lips. "I know you're the same person, at least you better be! I damn sure don't want to be sleeping with a stranger at this point in my life."

"I guess it hasn't started to sink in with me yet. Being a Congressman isn't quite the same thing as being the vice president-elect, but so far it doesn't seem that different. Jesus, I hope I can keep my wits about me. I can't imagine what it must be like for Jordan; he's changed, and that was to be expected. People used to go up to him, slap him on the back and say,

'Jordan, you old son of a bitch, how are you doing?' They can't do that anymore. Now they have to address him as 'Mister President.'"

"You won't have to do that, will you?" Kathleen asked.

"Out in public, if we're in earshot of the public or the media, I'll have to be formal. But behind closed doors, nothing should change. I just have the feeling that it's going to be difficult for Jordan. When his mother and father are fawning over him, I imagine he can't help feeling more important than he used to be. Of course he's done a remarkable thing, getting elected president. I doubt anybody has ever held the office who hasn't been changed by it. During the first hundred years, the office was nothing like it is today. And a man like Abraham Lincoln wouldn't have let the office change him very much. In this century, General Eisenhower was a pretty big cheese before he got elected president, so he took it fairly well. But even he had to learn the political ropes, and that took some time. He made some mistakes until he figured out that being a president wasn't quite the same thing as being a general."

"But you are feeling okay about it, aren't you?"

"Jesus, I don't know—I hadn't really planned on this."

"You never thought about running for president?" Kathleen looked at him in a way that made him understand that it was a very serious question.

"Oh, I guess every politician lets that thought cross his or her mind from time to time, just like every kid who ever played baseball thinks about playing center field for the Boston Red Sox. That's a little different; athletic skill is something you can measure. You can judge yourself by how well you do against competitors. But politics is nothing like that—I'm not sure I ever really figured out what makes us tick."

"There's no doubt that you got into it because you felt that you wanted to do something to help your country. That's who you are; you were never in it for the glory."

"I hope not." He walked over and looked out the window at the broad Montgomery estate. "I don't think Jordan was in it for the glory either, but I can't help feeling that he's really enjoying it. I guess we'll find out how it's going to affect him."

In accordance with the Montgomery family tradition, a Christmas breakfast was served, complete with mimosas and a wonderful assortment of breakfast delicacies. Following breakfast, gifts were exchanged, and also in keeping with Montgomery tradition, the gifts within the Montgomery family tended to be modest rather than lavishly expensive. Kellan remembered Jordan saying that his parents felt that aside from their sumptuous home, it was rather vulgar to display wealth ostentatiously. Kellan's response had been that when you've had money for a long time in your family, it's easy to feel that way. But now that Kellan had prospered financially from his law business, and from the unexpected royalties from the book, which were still coming in, he considered himself quite well to do.

In addition, Kathleen had made a reasonably good living as a journalist in Ireland, had lived modestly, and had saved what she could. With the vice president's salary and his savings, Kellan would be able to continue paying for Fiona's medical training, in addition to providing her with a home. Eileen had graciously offered to help with Fiona's expenses, and Kellan appreciated the offer. Although he told Eileen he could manage, she created what she called a 'Fiona fund,' which would be available in case of emergency.

By the time Fiona and Michael left for Worcester early on the morning after Christmas, Kellan and Kathleen were sure that they had met Kellan's future son-in-law. He obviously adored Fiona, and she just as obviously returned his affection. He was respectful of Kellan, but not intimidated by the fact that Fiona's father was about to become vice president of the United States. Kellan noticed that Michael had quickly become fond of Kathleen, and she enjoyed hearing stories of the trials and tribulations of his medical internship. He was very serious about his chosen profession, but he was just as serious about his intentions with regard to Fiona. Kellan and Kathleen were sad to see them go, but were happy for what the two young people had revealed.

"Ah, to be that young again!" said Kathleen as she and Kellan watched them drive off.

Other members of the Montgomery clan departed on the same morning, and the focus of conversation shifted back towards the political, as Jordan, Kellan, Bob and the women discussed the events that were about to unfold, the changes that would affect each one of their lives. In midafternoon the Secret Service agents and the cars that would drive the party to Mount Snow arrived from the nearby hotel where the agents had been staying. Four vehicles would be involved: the lead car, a "heavy" four-wheel-drive sport vehicle, would contain a skilled driver and agents who would scan for any possible trouble ahead. The president and his agents would be in the second vehicle, Bob Reynolds and an additional staff member in the third, and Kellan and another advisor would be in the trailing vehicle. The Secret Service had arranged for Massachusetts State

Police to accompany them to the Vermont border, where they would be picked up by Vermont police cars for the rest of the journey. The trip would take about an hour and a half.

At about 4:30 the caravan set out for Vermont. The sky was heavily overcast, the temperature slightly below freezing. A gusty wind was blowing, though not too hard. The Secret Service agent-in-charge reported that a storm was approaching, but he felt that they could reach their destination before it hit hard enough to cause them any problems. On the radio in his bedroom, Kellan had picked up an Albany radio station report that it was already snowing there.

The four vehicles were equipped with radios for communication among the agents, and as they made their way northward, they updated each other on the conditions ahead, according to what they were hearing on the broadcast networks. The agent driving Kellan's vehicle was Sam West, the man who had inspected his apartment during the summer. In less than half an hour after their departure, it began to snow, and within a few minutes it grew heavy. By the time they reached the Vermont border, the roads were covered, and the vehicles slowed their progress. By the time they turned onto the road leading up to the resort where they would be meeting, the Secret Service radios continued to report the worsening conditions. A suggestion was made that they might think about turning back, but President-elect Montgomery made it clear that he preferred going forward. The vehicles they had were heavy and sturdy enough that with their four-wheel-drive, they were making suitable progress. The sky had grown dark, and as the wind grew stronger, blowing the thickly falling snow across the road, visibility became limited. Even with their headlights on, each driver slowed in order to allow the distance in front to widen.

Near the top of the mountain, one of the agents in the first vehicle alerted the other three cars to a problem that had suddenly emerged. Kellan heard the voice from the first car say, "Look out! There's a semi coming down the hill toward us." In a moment the same voice said, "God dammit, he's out of control." And then, "He's jackknifed! Jesus Christ, his trailer just bounced off us. Look out, God dammit, he's heading right for you!" The state police vehicle that had been leading the procession had his lights flashing, and as Kellan peered through the windshield, he saw chaos develop ahead. He could just barely make out the tractor-trailer moving sideways in the direction of the second vehicle carrying Jordan. The driver tried to steer the rig, but the trailer slammed into the president-elect's vehicle and swung back across the road as the cab sideswiped the third vehicle on its way by. The right wheels of the tractor-trailer went off the road to the right and plowed into the trees directly opposite Kellan's vehicle. The state police vehicle behind Kellan also had its lights flashing, and the officers jumped out and began lighting flares and placing them in the roadway to block any following traffic, though none was in sight.

The agents shouted excitedly among themselves on their radios, and several were already out of the vehicles shouting at each other. The car carrying Jordan had been knocked off the road and had rolled over twice and crashed into a tree about fifty yards from the highway. Kellan got out and ran up to join Bob Reynolds, who was hurrying toward the scene of the disaster. The agents were busy, and the state police officer from the lead car shouted that he had contacted emergency services, and that a helicopter was on the way. The officer reported that the Mount Snow airport was only about a mile ahead. There was an emergency vehicle standing by at the lodge and the police officer announced that he had summoned it to start down to their location.

The car in which Jordan had been riding was standing upside down against a tree, the roof partially crushed and the vehicle badly smashed. The driving snow stung Kellan's face, and it was difficult to see anything, but it was clear instantly that the damage was severe and injuries were more than likely. Bob Reynolds was muttering, "Jesus Christ, what do we do now?"

For the Secret Service agents, decorum was abandoned. One of them shouted at Kellan and Bob, "Stay back, god dammit, that fucking thing could blow." Even with the wind blowing the other way, Kellan could detect the smell of gasoline—some of it must have spilled as the vehicle flipped over. Two agents were peering into the damaged vehicle with flashlights, and one of them shouted, "We're going to need a god damn crowbar! We've got to get those guys out of there!"

A few minutes later Kellan heard a siren and looked up to see red flashing lights approaching. The police officers and agents stood in the road and guided it to a stop next to the place where the damaged vehicle lay upside down. Emergency medical technicians rushed toward the vehicle to do a quick assessment of what was necessary.

"Bring those crowbars! We've got to get a door open," an agent shouted.

One of the state troopers had produced a large flash lantern, and he brought it down and shined it on the vehicle. Kellan and Bob were standing close enough that they could see the outline of bodies inside, and Kellan was relieved to see that there was some movement. But it was also clear that at least some of the occupants of the vehicle must have been injured, probably seriously.

As the agents worked feverishly, one of them approached Kellan. "Congressman, so far all we can tell is that the president has been injured. We're not sure how badly, but it doesn't look good. Sir, I need you to go back to your vehicle; Agent West is going to go back with you. Until we know what's wrong with the president, you are our top priority."

"I understand," said Kellan. "Just keep me informed."

"I'll do that, sir. I'll send Mister Reynolds back as soon as we know anything. A helicopter is on its way and should be here within a matter of minutes. If we can get the president out of there and into that ambulance, that will be a good thing. We'll do our best, sir."

Kellan thanked the agent, and Agent Sam West accompanied Kellan back to the last vehicle, which sat undamaged in the roadway. The state police had completely cordoned off the road, but there were no other vehicles in sight. He wondered how long it would take for news of the tragedy to be broadcast, and he wondered how the Secret Service would go about informing Shelley of her husband's condition. He knew Kathleen would also be worried as soon as she heard about the accident, but he could do nothing about that. He asked the agent who joined them in the car how they would communicate their situation to others.

"We can contact people by radio, sir, and they can pass information along. We have all the telephone numbers we need, but we hesitate to put anything out until we know the president's condition. Except for the agents in the car with him, everyone seems to be all right. I guess the driver of that semi is pretty badly banged up, but his injuries are not life threatening." The agent thought for a moment. "God damn, I'd sure hate to be in that guy's shoes. He's in a world of shit."

Everybody's in a world of shit, thought Kellan. He began to go through his mind, trying to assess the possibilities of whatever the outcome of the accident would turn out to be. He knew that since the Electoral College had already voted, he and Jordan were the heirs apparent of the offices to which they had been elected. Exactly what would happen depended on Jordan's condition. Kellan would simply have to wait to find out what that was.

He asked Sam West to move the vehicle forward and keep the lights on so he could see some of what was going on at the accident scene. Before long he noticed two emergency technicians taking a stretcher down the hill to the car, which meant that they had managed to extricate at least one body from the wreckage. A few minutes later Bob Reynolds came toward Kellan's car, and Kellan rolled down the window.

"They got the president out, but it doesn't look good," said Bob. "He's unconscious, and he's covered with blood. He got banged around pretty bad in there. The agent said they're going to put him in that ambulance and take him up to the helicopter, and the helicopter will take him to Boston to a trauma unit at Mass General, assuming they can stabilize him. The driver of Jordan's car may not make it. The other two are pretty banged up, but they're stable and can wait for the ambulance to come back."

"And if they can't get Jordan stable, what then?" Kellan said.

"They've got some kind of a dispensary up there somewhere," Bob said, looking up the hill toward the resort. "They will do their best with whatever they have here and fly in a team with anything else they need. Jesus Christ, this looks bad." Bob reached out for Kellan's hand, and Kellan gripped it through the window. "Keep your wits about you, my friend," said Bob. "You may wind up running the show, at least for the time being."

Kellan took a deep breath. "I'll do my best, Bob. I'm going to need all the help you can give me."

"You've got it, my friend."

Tragedy

It was close to midnight when the car bearing Kellan and Bob Reynolds got back to the Montgomery home. Sally and Kathleen rushed out as the car pulled up. Both women were crying as they hugged their husbands. "Are you okay?" Kathleen said.

"Bob and I were in other cars. We pretty much saw the whole thing, but we weren't hurt. The truck sideswiped Bob's car and he got a little shaken up, but it missed the one I was in. How's Shelley?"

"A helicopter landed on the back lawn and flew her to Boston where they took Jordan. Do you know how he is?"

"He was unconscious at the scene. Bob saw him when they got him out of the wrecked car and said he didn't look good. The agent who drove us back told us that Jordan's in surgery. We probably won't know anything for a while."

Jordan's father and mother were standing on the front steps. His mother had her hands over her face and was crying. Mr. Montgomery had his arm around her and looked stricken. The agent who had been driving approached the senior Montgomery and they exchanged a few words. Snow was still swirling around in the porch lights, but not as heavily as before. On his way back to the car Agent West stopped and said to Kellan, "We'll be staying here in the house tonight, sir. Just a precaution until we know more. We'll take care of your luggage."

"Thanks, Sam." Kellan took Kathleen's arm and they followed Bob and Sally into the house. Kellan hugged Mrs. Montgomery as they went in. Mr. Montgomery patted Kellan on the shoulder and said, "It's on you now, my boy." Then he broke down, weeping.

Kellan, Kathleen, Bob and Sally sat down in the living room. A maid approached Kellan and said, "We have some fresh coffee if you'd like it, Mr. Maguire." Kellan looked around and everyone nodded. "I'll bring it in," she said.

There was not much to say, and the two women whispered questions to their husbands, but everyone knew all they needed to know for the moment. In a while two agents appeared, and Sam West said to Kellan, "Is there anything you need, sir?"

"Not right now, Sam. They're bringing us some coffee. Why don't you guys just have a seat with us while we try to put this all together. I assume you still have your radios going."

"Yes, sir, we're in constant contact with the agents in Boston. The president-elect is still in surgery. They expect it will be some time before we know any more."

"His condition?"

"They said critical, sir, but they always say that at first; we'll know for sure when he comes out of surgery."

"But it doesn't look good."

"No, sir, it doesn't look good."

The maid arrived with a tray of cups and soon returned with a pot of coffee and some snacks. Sally stood up and poured the coffee, offering it to the agents first. As she handed a cup to Kathleen, whose cheeks were still damp with tears, she said, "It's going to be okay, Sweetie."

After a while Bob spoke. "It's a good thing the electors have already voted. If they hadn't, we'd be in unknown territory. In this situation, we're covered by the Twenty-Fifth Amendment."

"Yeah, but nobody has been sworn in yet," said Kellan.

"What's does that mean?" asked Kathleen. It was slowly dawning on her that she might suddenly be about to become the First Lady of the United States. The idea was almost overwhelming.

"The fact that they haven't been sworn in yet doesn't really matter," Bob said to Kathleen. "They have been confirmed by the electors. Depending on what happens, Jordan will be sworn in if he's conscious and rational, and assuming that he will still be hospitalized, Kellan will be sworn in as vice president and will immediately become acting under the Twenty-fifth Amendment."

"And if he ... you know, if he doesn't survive the accident, what then?"

"If he were to die before the twentieth of January, Kellan would be sworn in as president and would then have to name a new vice president. The problem will be if Jordon is alive but unconscious. Cabinet officers are supposed to affirm that the president is incapable of carrying out his office, but there won't be any new cabinet officers yet, and I'm not sure what the old cabinet officers would do. I assume they would make the affirmation, but that's not clear under the amendment. It could get messy."

"It's going to be messy no matter what happens," said Kellan. "Can you imagine the uproar—'hey, we elected a Republican, and now we've got a Democrat; how is that fair?' If this had happened down the road a couple of years, people might have gotten used to it; but now?"

"Gotten used to what?" asked Kathleen.

"Having a Democrat for vice president. The last time we had a president and vice president from different parties, it was Adams and Jefferson," said Bob. "And that didn't go so well."

"But Kellan is well qualified," said Sally. "You've been saying that all along."

"Yeah, I know that, but a lot of people don't. Nobody pays a whole lot of attention to the vice president until something like this happens. It's just that it doesn't usually happen this soon."

Kellan said, "Bob, if Jordan does pull through, I'm wondering. There's something I've been wanting to ask you, and this is surely a bad time. But it's the only time we have right now. Have you noticed anything different in Jordan since the election?"

"Why do you ask?" Bob didn't seem put off by Kellan's question, but he wanted to be clear what Kellan was getting at.

"Do you really want to go into this right now?" said Kathleen to Kellan. "I know you and I have talked about it, but are you sure?"

"Hell, we're among friends here." He glanced at the agents, who had been talking quietly between themselves. "I'm sure we can speak freely."

"Don't mind us," said Agent West. "We're just part of the furniture." He glanced at Kathleen. "Mrs. Maguire, we hear all kinds of stuff we're probably not supposed to hear, but it stays in here." He pointed to his head. "We can keep secrets."

Kathleen nodded and turned back to Kellan, who went on. "I don't know, Bob. I've known him for a long time, and he's always been, I'm not sure what the best word is, humble, maybe. That's not quite right, but I think you know what I mean. He's never been full of himself, he's never put himself out there as the most important person in the room. But I sense that a little bit of that has gone away during the last few weeks."

Bob nodded and Sally said, "Tell Kellan what you told me about that."

"When?"

"Back when this all started right after the convention."

Bob thought for a few moments. "Kellan, he's not the first guy I have taken to the White House, and every one of them goes through this. I'll tell you something though: Jordan is the best one I've taken this far, ever. And I'll tell you something else, my friend, and you keep this under your hat or

I'll clock you. You're just as good; I know that what's happened is a catastrophe, and there's going to be hell to pay with the media and all that. But I'm not the least bit concerned about the fact that you may wind up behind the president's desk. I've watched you closely, and I am absolutely convinced that you're up for the job."

"That's very generous of you," said Kellan.

"He means it," said Sally.

"I tell you," Bob went on, "it was one hell of a job selling you as Jordan's running mate. When he first brought it up, it was as if he had taken a dump on the table. Nobody could understand why he would want to do that."

"Lovely image, Bob," said Sally, and she rolled her eyes. Kathleen smiled.

"But you have friends; you have a reputation, and there were a few who were willing to listen to the idea. Now I want to tell you this here and now because I want you to know how I feel if this all goes south. I want you to know what you can expect of me. I fought like hell to get you that position, not because I had any concerns about Jordan, and not because I was in a sweat to advance your political career. I fought for it because there was nobody else whose name came up who I thought could do the job better. I just want you to know that, and I want you to know that if this goes the way it looks like it's going to go.

"There's no other way to put it; the shit is going to hit the fan. There are a lot of people who were willing to accept you as second-place, who assumed that's where you would stay for the next four years, or maybe eight. But if it goes the other way, God help us. I have no idea how this is going to play out. Oh, you'll get the office all right, but getting there may be a really bumpy road. We'll have to just wait and see what happens."

"I appreciate your saying all that," said Kellan. "I'll be leaning on you."

Bob smiled. "I'll tell you something else. Way back when it all started, I thought you might take on Mayhew in the primaries. You'd have cleaned his clock. Scared the shit out of me because I didn't want to run a campaign against you."

"I never would have run against Jordan."

"I know that now, but I didn't then. In the first place, I wasn't one hundred percent sure that Jordan would get the nomination, and besides, I didn't know how close you two were. Once I figured that out, I was all for you being his running mate."

Kathleen covered her face to stifle a yawn. "Why don't you go up and lie down," Kellan said. "It's probably going to be a long night."

Sally stood up. "I'll go up with you, Sweetie," she said to Kathleen. The two women kissed their husbands, said good night to the agents and headed for the stairs. Sally put her arm around Kathleen's shoulders as they walked down the hallway.

"You gentlemen can retire if you like," said Sam. "We'll let you know if anything happens."

"We're good for now," said Kellan. He kicked his shoes off, leaned back in his chair and closed his eyes.

After a few moments, Bob said. "It's probably kind of shitty to bring this up, but if the worst does happen, who would you be thinking of?"

"To …?"

"To replace yourself."

Kellan thought for a moment. "Hallowell," he said.

"Good," said Bob. "That's what I was thinking."

Media Frenzy: Round 2

Newspaper headlines across the country on the morning of December 27 blared:

PRESIDENT-ELECT INJURED IN AUTO CRASH
MONTGOMERY IN CRITICAL CONDITION
MAGUIRE NEXT IN LINE

A typical story began:

Boston, December 27. President elect Jordan Montgomery was injured in a serious automobile crash in Vermont during a snowstorm at approximately 6 PM on the evening of December 26. The president's party was on its way to a retreat at the Mount Snow resort in southern Vermont approximately 55 miles from the president-elect's home in Pittsfield, Massachusetts. His chief campaign adviser Bob Reynolds, vice president-elect Kellan Maguire and a number of potential cabinet officials and other advisors were scheduled to attend the two-day strategy session at the resort. The president was lifted by helicopter to the trauma center at the Massachusetts General Hospital in Boston where he remained in critical condition early this morning.

Doctors said that the President-elect had suffered severe head injuries with internal bleeding inside the cranium and would likely remain in a coma for at least several days. Surgeons worked on Jordan Montgomery throughout the night and said they had controlled the bleeding for the time being. The president-elect suffered no other injuries except severe bruising to one shoulder and a twisted leg that apparently has muscular damage.

The Secret Service agent who was driving the vehicle in which President-elect Montgomery was riding was killed when the vehicle was struck by a tractor-trailer that had lost control coming downhill from the resort area in the opposite direction from the president's party. The driver of the truck, who was badly bruised in the crash, apparently lost control during snowy conditions. The driver's name is being withheld pending investigation and notification of next of kin. He was not charged with an offense at the time of the accident. The other Secret Service agent riding in the automobile with the president was also badly injured, though not critically. He was treated at the hospital where the president was taken and was released early this morning. The other members of the party, including Vice President-elect Maguire and senior advisor Bob Reynolds were not injured, although the car in which Reynolds was riding was sideswiped by the truck as it skidded down the hill in the snowy conditions. The truck ended up in a ditch on the opposite side of the road.

The president's car rolled over twice and came to rest upside down against a tree and was badly damaged by the impact with the truck and with the tree. Mrs. Montgomery, who had remained at the Montgomery home, was flown by helicopter to the hospital as soon as she was informed of the accident. Vice President-elect Maguire is reported to have returned to the Montgomery home in Pittsfield where he and the rest of the Montgomery family are awaiting further news from the hospital in Boston.

Kellan had decided to call Jean and Alex early in the morning, before they were likely to see the morning news shows. The accident report had made the late news, and some stations had interrupted regular programs for bulletins about the crash, but Alex didn't watch television very much. Jean, on the other hand, was probably already aware of the story and would be anxious to hear from him. He called her first, told her that he and Kathleen were okay and that he would be back in Washington later that day. Jean took the updated news with aplomb and said she would be ready to take on any additional responsibilities that might be necessary, depending on the president-elect's status. "Just let me know when you'll be back," she said. "God, what a mess—I'm so sorry."

"Yeah, me too."

He then called Alex, apparently waking her. "Hey, what's up?" she said.

"There's been an accident," he said.

"When? Who?"

"Last night on the way to Vermont. A truck crashed into Jordan's car. He's in a hospital in Boston."

"Oh, my god! Wait a minute while I turn on the news." After a few moments she said, "Are you okay?"

"I'm fine. I was in another car." He went on to tell her that he was still at the Montgomery residence and would let her and Jean know exactly when he would be back.

"Jesus, Kellan, what happens now?"

"I've been talking with Bob most of the night. Everything is under control for now. We'll have to see how it goes between now and the inauguration, but at the moment there's nothing urgent. I mean, everything is urgent, but we have time to adjust. Sam West is on my detail and he's in touch with Boston. I'll let you know if I hear anything."

Sam West was up early as well, and told Kellan that he had checked with the other agents during the night and that they would like to have him flown back to Washington sometime later in the day. They were trying to arrange for one of the presidential helicopters from Quantico to come up and get him, rather than having to book a commercial flight. With the tensions that had been raised by the accident, it was best to keep him out of the public eye until things settled down a bit.

It was likely that during an emergency of the kind that had just occurred, people might feel that there was more going on than simply a random accident. Nervous media people would speculate on the air that the country might be under some sort of attack. More responsible media outlets would do their best to squelch unfounded rumors, but once they got started, they were very difficult to contain. The safest bet from the perspective of the Secret Service was simply to keep a close eye on Kellan and move him about as surreptitiously as possible.

Later in the morning, as they were looking over the newspapers—Sam had sent the other agent into town to get all the papers he could find—and watching television reports, Sam West informed Kellan that a Marine helicopter from HMX-1 at Quantico, the helicopter squadron that provided transportation for the president and other top officials, would be coming to fly him, Kathleen and Bob and Sally Reynolds back to Washington. They would land at Andrews Air Force Base, and Kellan would be taken to the vice president's office on Capitol Hill where security was easy to maintain. The helicopter would land in the spacious back lawn of the Montgomery home, as was done for Shelley Montgomery the evening before, when a state police helicopter had flown her to Boston.

After speaking with agents in Boston, Sam reported that Jordan Montgomery's condition had stabilized, but his condition was still "guarded," meaning critical. Kellan wanted to talk to Shelley, but they said that she had been taken to an empty room and was resting, so he decided not to disturb her. She would have news sooner than anyone else, but he was confident that the Secret Service would keep him well informed. As they waited for the helicopter to arrive, Bob and Kellan discussed things that might have to be done in the interim as they waited to hear more about Jordan's condition.

Bob reminded Kellan that Jordan had already named five cabinet officers and suggested that Kellan might be thinking about his choices for the positions that had not yet been named. Bob assumed, and Kellan concurred with his assumption, that Kellan would keep the selections that Jordan had already made and would simply supplement those with the remaining positions. Bob Reynolds gave him the names of those who were under consideration for presidential appointments—cabinet members and other top officials. "I know there might be some in your party that you might want to consider, but that might not play too well in Peoria," Bob said. "Republicans are probably already thinking that they've been screwed. Christ, before you know it, some asshole will claim you hired the fucking truck driver. Jesus, this is going to be a mess!"

"Are you sorry now that you pushed for me?" Kellan said, trying to keep it light.

"Well, if I'd known this was going to happen, I might have thought twice," Bob said. Then he smiled. "No, god no, I'm glad it's you. As I said last night, you're the best man for the job."

From what they knew so far, Jordan might remain in a coma for days or even weeks. The doctors at the trauma center had also pointed out that once Jordan came out of the coma, he might still be severely handicapped and be facing a long period of rehabilitation before he could assume the functions of president.

Kellan also needed to think about the staff that he would assemble if in fact he were to assume the highest office. "Bob, I know you were set to be Jordan's Chief of Staff. Regardless of what happens, I would like you to stay in that position. I think it would make everybody breathe a little easier."

"I'll be glad to, Kellan," said Bob "We need to stick together."

The senior Montgomerys left for Boston with one of Jordan's brothers just before noon. By the time Kellan was back in Washington, medical reports suggested that all concerned had best prepare for a long period of Jordan Montgomery's recovery, and that indeed, his recovery was not a certainty.

Jean and Alex and several others were in the vice president's office when Kellan arrived. Kellan thanked Sam West for his assistance, and Sam said he would be nearby. He gave Kellan a pager in case he needed to get in touch quickly.

The mood among Kellan's staff people was somber. On the one hand, Kellan understood, everybody in the room knew that a White House job might materialize, but that was hardly something they could openly acknowledge. A couple of the staffers tried to make jokes about it, but they fell flat.

Bob Reynolds sat on a desk and addressed the group. "Look," he said, "it's been one hell of a long night, and Kellan and I are tired. So please bear with me. Folks, we are in uncharted waters here. It's very clear that the provisions of the 25th Amendment will be in force, which means that either Jordan and Kellan or Kellan alone will be sworn in on January 20. The office of president will continue to function, whether it's under Jordan Montgomery, or Kellan as acting, or Kellan in fact as president. We are not likely to know that for several days, unless the President-elect dies, which, you need to understand, could happen at any moment, down the road somewhere, or not at all.

"If Jordan is still in a coma at the time of the inauguration, Kellan will most likely be sworn in as vice president and immediately assume the position of acting president. That's going to be a little dicey because of the wording of the amendment. Senior administration officials and cabinet officers need to affirm the president's incapacity, and we're not sure exactly how that's going to work, since none of the new cabinet will yet be in place. We'll worry about that later.

"What Kellan needs now, and what I need as his advisor, is for you to keep your wits about you and start planning as if all of you will be working in the office of the president. That means we have to get jobs sorted out, start screening names for important positions, and thinking about some sort of an agenda for legislation, travel, and so on. There will also be a state of the union address to think about, but we obviously can't plan for that until we know more about what's going to happen with Jordan Montgomery.

"Now, Kellan and I have discussed a great deal since the time of the accident. He has asked me to continue in the position of Chief of Staff, which is what I would be doing for Jordan Montgomery, assuming that he was not where he is now. Kellan has assured me, and I concur one hundred percent with his thinking, that there is plenty of talent in this room and that one of you might well have been chosen for that position." He nodded at Jean, and she smiled and gave him a thumbs up. "But here's what you need to keep an eye on. Kellan is a Democrat, and that was fine with Jordan and it's fine with me. But it's not going to be fine with a whole lot of people out there, and all of you are savvy enough to understand that.

"So what we're going to have to do is try to make this administration, even if it winds up being the Kellan Maguire administration, have the look and feel of a Republican administration. On the surface, that might not look so hard, because Jordan and Kellan were both centrists—after all, that's how the ticket was put together—but in reality, folks on both ends of the spectrum are going to be looking for something that's not there. As close confidants of Kellan, you all are going to take your lumps, perhaps not personally, but certainly collectively. Everything that Kellan decides to do, should he be acting as president, will be seen as some sort of a plot to smuggle leftist ideas into the system.

"Okay, I've blathered on long enough. You all know what's at stake here, and you're all grown-ups. You know that we're in the middle of a shit sandwich, and we're going to have to fight our way through it as best we can. I'm going to be here every step of the way, and I'll be counting on you for your help. In return, you have every right to expect that Kellan will have my absolute loyalty, which he will. To be blunt about it, and false modesty aside, I'm pretty much the man who got him on the ballot in the first place. I'm not sorry I did it, and given where we are right now, I'm glad he's the one who's waiting in the wings." Bob looked around the room. His face was drawn and lined with evidence of the strain he was under. Many in the room nodded and murmured words of appreciation and support.

"Okay," he said, "I'm going to get my ass out of here and let Kellan and you guys talk over where you want to go. But I need some rest, and he needs some rest, so give him a break. We are not going to solve a god damn thing today. I'll be here tomorrow, and every day after that, and we'll sort this thing out."

A couple of people on the staff began to applaud, and in a moment everybody had picked up the idea. Bob Reynolds had successfully won the hearts and minds of Kellan's staff, not just with his speech, but in everything that Kellan had said about him since he had been put on the ballot. Bob shook hands with Kellan and made his departure.

"We all ought to be damn glad that Bob Reynolds is with us," Kellan said. "He's been down this road before—not the exact one we're on, of course, but you know what I mean. As Bob said, I'm pretty tired; we hardly slept at all last night. So I don't want to go making any decisions today because they would probably come up stupid. But I'm going to hang around for a while in case you all have questions or suggestions, and we'll plan to get the ball rolling tomorrow."

Kellan went into the vice president's personal office and signaled for Jean and Alex to come with him. Kellan opened the conversation. "It was crazy. It was snowing like hell, the wind was blowing, and maybe we should have stopped. But turning around halfway up that mountain wouldn't have been any picnic either. And we were moving okay—four wheel drive cars, excellent drivers. The worst that could have happened if it hadn't been for that truck was that we got stuck. Nobody saw it coming. The state cop out in front said he was blowing his horn, but nothing could have stopped that semi."

"What's done is done," said Jean. "We can't change what happened."

"From everything I've heard so far," said Alex, "we won't know anything for days. The last report from Boston said that they're going to keep him in an induced coma until the swelling inside his head has gone down. That's probably weeks away, and when he comes out of it, who knows?"

"So here we are," said Kellan. "I think we'd better proceed on the assumption that I'm going to be sworn in as vice president on January 20 and will immediately take over as acting president. So what the hell do we do to get ready for that?"

"Okay, here's where we start," said Jean, "Jordan had already named, what—five cabinet members?"

"Yup," said Kellan. "Attorney General, State, Interior, Treasury and Defense. Bob is going to meet with them tomorrow and basically tell them to hang loose. If it goes as we assume, the first thing I'll do is submit their names for confirmation. There shouldn't be any problem with that; the Senate will know that these were Jordan's nominees, and there's no way they can turn them down.

"So item one on the agenda is probably to come up with the remaining top posts. I'm thinking maybe I should ask the other incumbents to remain in their posts for, say, thirty days, until the president's situation becomes clearer. A couple of them might have a problem with that because of other plans, but in that case we'll just ask them to have their deputies step up for the time being.

"Item two is my staff, and with one exception I'm going to proceed pretty much as they would have anyway, except that there are going to be more slots to fill. As Bob said, I have asked him to stay with me as Chief of Staff. Jean, I know you can understand why I'm doing this, and believe me, it has no reflection on you. Bob will stay for as long as I need him. He knows you and respects your work, and I'm sure he'll be sensitive to your expectations."

"I know he will, Kellan, and I know why you're doing it," said Jean. "I'm fine."

"It's politics, plain and simple. His job one is going to be to defend me against those who are outraged that a Democrat has somehow or other stolen the election. I can just imagine the kind of crap that's going to come out before this thing is over."

"It's already started," said Alex. "Some reporters have gotten through to us on the phone, and they're reporting that people have said that this is somehow not really an accident. Of course we ask them who those people are, and they just mutter something and dodge the question. They're just making it up to see how we're going to react."

"Okay," said Kellan, "I'm going to have to face the media, and probably the sooner the better. I think the best thing to do is to just open it up and let them have at me. Bob will be there—we talked about it on the way back from Massachusetts—and we'll probably do it at noon tomorrow. Once we announce the time, they won't be bugging us so much about granting interviews. Before we start we'll get the latest from Boston, and I'll announce that at the beginning. When they start badgering me with questions about that, I'll just refer them to the medical people."

"I gather there are crowds of media in the street outside Mass General," said Alex. "They'll be hounding the medical staff around the clock."

"Those folks know how to handle that—they've been there before, as you know. And the Secret Service is right there on the spot, and they've instructed the lead surgeon to let them know first of any developments and have promised that I'll be the first to know except for the family."

"How's Shelley holding up?" Alex asked. "I know you haven't seen her, but have you heard anything?"

"She's a strong woman. To tell the truth I'm more worried about Kellan's parents than I am about Shelley. Both of them were a wreck on the night of the accident, and I only saw them briefly when they left the next morning. I'm sure the rest of Jordan's family is gathered at the hospital, and they'll help each other. I gave the Secret Service a number that Shelley can call me on if she wants to, but I don't expect to hear from her."

"Probably not," said Jean.

"Anyway, back to business. Alex, I'm going to appoint you Counselor to the President. It will be similar to what you've done here in Congress. Jean, I think for the time being I'm going to have to stick with Jordan's senior advisor; I'm just going to have to keep some of his people close so it won't look like a coup. I think the best bet is for you to be Deputy Chief of Staff, so you can work closely with Bob Reynolds. If you wind up staying in the job, working with him will be the best training possible."

"That's fine, Kellan. We're all a little antsy, so having people in there who've at least been thinking about the job for a few weeks will help. I honestly don't think the problems are going to come from within the people who wind up in the White House. They're going to come from outside."

"I'm sure you're right," said Kellan. "I've got a list here of the offices that will need to be filled. It's pretty daunting. There are fourteen cabinet positions, with nine yet to be named. Bob has a short list for each position that he'll share with us. Then there are about twenty other top-level offices that have to be filled. We'll have to prioritize them, and again, I'll have to bring some of Jordan's people in to talk about who he had in mind for those spots. We don't necessarily have to stick with all of his choices, but I'm going to be real careful about appointing anybody who wasn't already under consideration."

"What about a few Democrats?" asked Jean.

"I'm sure some of Jordan's choices would have been Democrats. I already know about a few of them, and they were predictable. No president would be wise to try to fill up every position from his own party, and Jordan had no intention of doing that."

Alex said, "Kellan, you know it's going to be really tough if Jordan's situation isn't settled by the time you take office, no matter which one it may be. Let's assume that Jordan's still in a coma. That's one condition in which you won't be able to get any direct input from him on any of these choices. That's obvious. If he's out of his coma but is not able to speak, or something like that, you're pretty much in the same boat. If he's conscious and functioning, then you can get direct input from him."

"The other scenario is, suppose he doesn't make it at all?" Jean said.

None of them spoke for a moment or two; then Alex offered, "In a way that might be the worst situation of all. In that case you would be free to do whatever you want, but you'd get a lot of flak from Jordan's people unless you stuck with his agenda, and the Republicans in the Senate would fight you on every appointment."

"Well here's the one thing we know for sure right now," said Kellan. "The three of us are not going to come close to being able to handle this, even with help from Bob and a couple more of Jordan's people. So let's talk over who we want to use from our own staff, and where we'll go to get other people. Think about everyone you know on committee staffs who might be looking for a new job, or other people you know, even people outside, like Ray up in New York. He's out of a job when my term ends and he might want to come to Washington."

"I think the thing for us to do is start making lists of names," said Jean. "One for appointees, one for people we know will be on your staff, and one for people we just want to keep in mind when spots come up."

"Okay," said Kellan. "I'm going to go home and unwind for a while. The Secret Service will be keeping an eye on my place, but I've given them the names of folks who should have immediate access. Be sure to bring some ID with you. Before I leave, tell me who else you think ought to come over."

"Kellan, until you meet with the press tomorrow, I think everybody knows that Washington is on hold right now. Nobody's going to expect anything dramatic at least for a day or two. We have a tentative plan, and I think we ought to just let it percolate until tomorrow afternoon. Then we can get down to business."

"I think you're right, Alex."

Kellan met with Alex, Jean and a few more of the staff in his apartment later that evening. Bob Reynolds dropped in for a while, but for the most part they just talked casually and tried to relax. When Bob left, Jean said that she was going to retire as well, and all but Alex said goodnight. Alex asked if she might spend the night in Kellan and Kathleen's apartment in case any news came in. Kellan and Kathleen were happy to have her stay. Kellan left instructions with the Secret Service to notify him immediately of any change in the president's condition, and they had promised to do so. The agents told Kellan that they would keep an eye on his residence, and that he could expect their full protection as long as the situation remained as it was.

Later that night Kellan was lying on his back with his head on the pillow, hands behind his head staring at the ceiling. Light from the streets outside shined faintly through the window. Kathleen was next to him, facing toward him with her elbow on her pillow and her head resting on her hand. She was rubbing his chest with her other hand and watching him. "You're totally lost right now, aren't you?" she said. He grunted a response. "Look, I know that this is a terribly intense time for you, but please don't forget that I'm here, okay?"

He looked at her. "How could I forget?"

"We were talking the other day about how intense we both get once we're involved in things. I can't imagine what you're going through right now and how it must feel. But please remember that I'm going through it too; good Lord, I'm about to be in a position that I have never dreamed about in my whole life, and it's all come about so quickly. Six months ago I was a single woman in Ireland wondering what I was going to do with the rest of my life, and now here I am in a position that's totally unfathomable to me. I guess we'll get through it, but please, please don't forget me. Don't leave me hanging out here. I need you to need me because you're everything in my life. I also know that at this point I'm only going to be a piece of your life—you have so much else to worry about that I'm afraid that I might get lost in the shuffle."

"You're never going to get lost in the shuffle," he said. "I'm just trying to adjust to everything that happened; but believe me, I know you are here. I'm counting on you to be my anchor—my connection with reality. I'm living in some sort of a weird, surreal dream world right now; it's somewhere I never intended to be. I keep thinking about poor old Harry Truman, who never wanted to be anything but a senator, and Franklin Roosevelt cajoled him into being vice president, kicking and screaming all the way. Well, Harry adjusted and made it work, but it was an ordeal for him. Do you know that he didn't even know that the atomic bomb was being built when he took over as president? The Secretary of War had to tell him what was going on. Jesus, at least I don't have anything like that facing me. We're not in any national crisis right now, and the outgoing administration has sort of left everything up in the air. So at least I can start from scratch, or Jordan can start from scratch if he's back. But from everything I'm hearing, he won't be back soon, if at all, so here we are. We're in the same boat as Harry was, and I guess it's sink or swim."

"You're lucky to have Bob Reynolds working for you. When I first met him I didn't care too much for him—he seemed like a typical crusty old politician. But I realize that he's a very wise man, and I also have to add that Sally is a lovely person."

"Sally's an old political operator herself. I think she and Bob met when they were working on their first campaign; she was a volunteer and he was running the staff of some local election in Ohio or someplace, and they took to each other, fell in love, got married and have never looked back. He's extremely loyal to her, and she is his alter ego." He looked at Kathleen. "That's what I need you to be—I need you to be my anchor, my rock. You have to be the place where I go when it looks like the wheels are all coming off. You have a wonderful mind, and you're very much attuned to how politics work. After all, you've seen politics at its worst up there in Belfast. While this isn't Belfast, it's not going to be any picnic either. Please tell me that you'll be patient until I can sort everything out."

Kathleen leaned over and kissed him on the cheek. She said, "I will always be here with you, believe me." She pulled up his shirt and started kissing his chest. She put her arms on his shoulders and pulled herself up on top of him. She laid her head on his chest and said, "Look, I know you're too distracted for romance. But just let me lie here and be close to you. I can live with that right now, okay?"

He kissed the top of her head. "I hope I'll always be in the mood for romance with you," he said. "It's just that right now I can't quite get focused on it."

"I understand, Darling, honestly I do." She lay her head down on his chest and closed her eyes.

The crowd of reporters assembled for Kellan's remarks at noon was the largest he had ever seen. Every network was present, including representatives of several foreign news services. All the major dailies in the United States had reporters on hand, as did the major radio networks. Because of space limitations, Bob had used Art Fowler, designated to be Jordan's press secretary, to help finalize the list of those who would be admitted. The Secret Service, of course, had participated in the process and would screen access to the briefing, which would be held in a large meeting room.

Kellan decided not to have anyone introduce him; after all, he did not yet hold any office. After offering words of condolence for the Montgomery family, Kellan began his remarks.

"Ladies and gentlemen, thank you for coming. We spoke with the medical staff at Massachusetts General Hospital a few minutes ago, and nothing in the president-elect's condition has changed. He is still in a coma, and no further surgery is scheduled at this time. The operations they performed immediately after the accident have helped control the pressure on the president's brain, and his condition has remained relatively stable. Your best source of information in that regard is the regular briefings offered by the medical staff, which I'm sure your organizations have covered.

"The United States has never been in this situation before. But presidents have been injured before, and some of them have lingered for a time after being shot. Since the Twenty-Fifth Amendment was enacted, we have a clear course laid out, which we will follow. An inauguration will take place on January 20, and depending on President-elect Montgomery's condition, that may take one of several forms. But the office of president will transition to a new administration on that date regardless of what happens between now and then.

"With the assistance of those who have served Jordan Montgomery, who, I might add for those of you who may not be aware, has been a close friend of mine for all of our adult lives—with their assistance, and with members of my staff, we will take all possible steps to ensure that when a new administration assumes office in January, the business of the United States will go forward without interruption."

Kellan provided a few more details about how the planning would proceed, and told the assembled media representatives that a spokesperson would be named later that afternoon. He then turned the microphone over to Bob Reynolds, who offered some strong remarks about the need to support the vice president-elect, adding that he had full faith and confidence in Kellan Maguire's ability to handle the difficult situation in which he found himself. Knowing that it probably would not be forthcoming, he nevertheless asked the media to be patient, and promised that they would be kept aware of developments pertaining to the coming administration.

Bob and Kellan then opened the floor to questions, and the barrage began. As was common in many such press briefings, many of the questions answered themselves. Since very few decisions had been made since the accident, many of their questions could not be answered. That didn't prevent the most routine questions, such as, "When will you name your cabinet appointees?" from being asked repeatedly, though perhaps in slightly different formats. Most of the questions invited some sort of speculation, and Kellan declined each time to speculate or offer answers to hypothetical situations. The most common of those was, "What do you plan to do in case the president does not recover?" His consistent answer was that he would proceed under the guidelines of the Twenty-Fifth Amendment.

As Kellan concluded the session, questions continued to be shouted at him as he left the room. As he did not yet officially hold an office, the courtesy and decorum that normally attended presidential press conferences was conspicuously absent. As he discussed the briefing with Jean, Alex and the others, they concluded that the ladies and gentlemen of the press were delighted to be free to conduct themselves without restraint. It wasn't going to end soon.

Kellan agreed to meet with a special edition of the most popular question-and-answer program on television the following Sunday. The session would last an hour and would not be interrupted by commercials. The network announced that as long as conditions remained as they were, the program would be held. In case of other developments, the implication being the death of Jordan Montgomery, they would adjust their plans accordingly.

When the press had worn itself out trying to wring every last bit of drama out of the accident and its unfortunate results, they began to dig for other fruitful areas of investigation. It did not take them long to hit on the subject of Kathleen Morrissey Maguire, the possible next first lady of the United States. Kathleen was interested and a bit startled to learn that there was an official office of the first lady within the White House executive structure. There was no such provision for the wife of the vice president; if Kellan were to become acting president, it was unclear what his wife's position would be. As long as Jordan Montgomery remained alive, most social functions of the office of president would be curtailed in any case. If he were to die, a period of mourning would naturally follow.

Kellan arranged for himself and Kathleen to be quietly flown to Boston so that they could visit with Shelley and the rest of Jordan's family. If Jordan were to be communicative, which was unlikely, Kellan might be able to have a brief conversation with him. The visit would be kept secret, although the press would be informed after it had taken place. It was quite likely that the media would discover what was going on in any case, and they would probably try to intercept the party on its way to Boston, either before he left Washington or after the aircraft arrived at Logan Airport. Kellan's party would deal with that by offering as many 'no comments' as necessary.

Kellan was stunned at Jordan's appearance. His head was covered with dressings, and there were tubes everywhere. Kellan also noted bruises on one of Jordan's arms. Shelley took Kellan's hand as they stood by the bed, and he put his arm around her. Jordan's breathing was shallow, but there were no other signs of life from his friend. As Kellan left the room, Shelley hugged him and said, "I'm going to stay here for a while."

By the time the new Congress convened on January 3, little had changed. The somber mood that had hung over the nation since the accident continued, and new members of Congress were sworn in with less than the usual fanfare. What was generally a pleasant if not joyous occasion took on something closer to the character of a wake.

Turmoil

The news announcer began his broadcast: "Good evening, ladies and gentlemen, here's the news.

A joint statement issued by the Republican and Democratic National Committees late this afternoon tells us that the men and women gathered to fulfill the mission of organizing the administration that will commence operation on January 20th will sequester themselves in a secret location while they work out the details of their plan. The statement adds that covering the various contingencies that face the nation will require their full concentration. Those contingencies are first, that President-elect Jordan Montgomery recovers quickly; second, that he continues in a coma, incapable of carrying out his office; or, third, that he might pass away as a result of his accident.

The joint statement was delivered by former chairman of the Republican National Committee, Bob Reynolds, soon to become, if the speculation is correct, the new White House Chief of Staff. He did not take any questions.

The last time government tried to operate in secret to reorganize itself was at the Constitutional Convention in 1787. It worked then, but will it work now? These are, after all different times, and people like me and other media personalities were not hovering around the edges of the Constitution Hall in Philadelphia, waiting to grasp at every bit of information that might leak out. As far as is known, nothing did leak until the founding fathers concluded their deliberations some four months after convening.

Here in the late twentieth century, reporters from all media will do their best to take us behind the scenes and tell you what's going on. By the time the new administration takes office on January 20th, we will know whether secrecy in that environment is possible.

The sequestered location was in suburban Maryland, a few miles outside the District of Columbia. A new office building in a business area was almost ready for full occupation. The two upper floors, with phone lines, electrical outlets and all other necessary paraphernalia, including plumbing, were fully operational. An elevator in the lobby served the upper floors and was in full working condition. The bottom two floors were still being finished off, and although from the outside they seemed to be ready for occupants, some of the final pieces were still in progress.

The site was ideal—off the beaten path in a new shopping and business development with little but construction traffic. The top floor had a central conference room not visible from outside. The third floor had interior offices available for smaller groups. The people involved would be aides and assistants to President-elect Montgomery, Vice President-elect Maguire, and others selected by Bob Reynolds and his immediate advisors. Representatives of the Democratic National Committee had been quietly invited to participate, on the grounds that the purpose of the divided ballot had been to unite the country politically in contrast to the divisive politics that had stalled the government during the previous administration. The point was to get both sides working together, and organizing the new administration needed input from both sides.

Bob Reynolds had pointed out that the plan at work was conceived largely by President-elect Montgomery, and he leaked evidence of that fact to selected media persons. In a joint statement issued by the Republican and Democratic National Committees, the two parties vowed to improve their relations and to try to proceed on a more cooperative basis.

Kellan's people formed one core group of the task force, and Bob Reynolds chaired the other. Jean, Alex and other aides of Kellan's quickly made themselves known as competent advisers with a breadth of political knowledge that seemed surprising to their colleagues. Having served a congressman from New York for the past several years, they were not well known outside the Hill.

The plan was a good one, but it didn't quite work. The media, with little to do but await further developments from Mass General or news from the principals at work in their hideaway, indulged in speculation that ranged from the reasonable to the outer fringes of reality, with the latter gaining purchase as the days progressed. The cause of the accident, the creation of a bipartisan ballot, and other notions, mostly fanciful, worked their way upward. The lack of hard news fed the desire for soft news, less than half a step removed from idle gossip.

The floors of the House and Senate had witnessed a spate of lofty oratory concerning the accidents, the unfortunate victims, including the president and the deceased Secret Service agent. Speakers praised the actions of the emergency crews on the scene who extricated the president from his damaged vehicle and the brave pilots who flew him to Boston in a blinding snowstorm. The oratory was also full of promises of cooperation from both sides as the country tried to sort out the unprecedented situation in which it found itself. It all broke loose on the second Monday following the opening of the new Congress. The prior weekend was relatively quiet, with guest positions on the talk shows dominated by those with some level of knowledge of the ongoing process. On Monday afternoon everything changed.

Radio talk show host Phil Paynter was an equal opportunity complainer. Whereas a tendency had evolved for talk show hosts in the political arena to vigorously defend one party or the other while criticizing their opponents, Phil Paynter's base position was, "A pox on both your houses." Whatever administration had been in office for the previous twelve years of Mister Paynter's dominance of his network, they were victims of his nonstop assaults on their policies, their processes, their people, and their ideas. Nothing satisfied him; no attempt at making progress in government failed to attract his vitriol. When his stories would be uncovered as little more than outright lies at the worst, or idle speculation at best, he ignored the criticism and simply moved on. One newspaper columnist reviewing his show claimed that he provided a vehicle for every harebrained idiot and crank in the country to vent his wrath against something, anything, whoever or whatever was available for criticism.

Phil Paynter opened his broadcast on that Monday as follows:

Good afternoon, ladies and gentlemen, this is Phil Paynter, your voice of reason.

As we approach the coming inauguration, it has occurred to me that the rather bizarre chain of events that has led us to this juncture might suggest a few questions. Now, I'm not here to point fingers, nor make accusations, nor to challenge the integrity of the man who is about to assume our highest office, whoever that turns out to be. But it seems to me that with the extraordinary chain of events that has led to this point, the American people are entitled to some explanations. Let's start at the beginning.

We now know that our presumptive president-in-waiting completed his education in Ireland. He spent four years there, more than enough time to pursue a course of graduate studies. As far as we know, he spent most of his time at Trinity College in Dublin, certainly a fine institution. But we wonder if his contacts at that august University led him down paths that might raise a few questions. Our research team has uncovered the fact that his advisor and mentor was Doctor Sean Levinson, the son of a German Jewish refugee to Ireland who was well known for his rather leftist political views. Doctor Levinson published several works, among which was one entitled, "The Capitalist Dilemma: Confronting Social Problems." In that work Doctor Levinson questions the ability of a modern capitalist economy to adequately meet the needs of the lower echelons of a society.

Now Doctor Levinson published this book long after Kellan Maguire left Dublin, but we wonder how much of his thinking was infused into our American scholar.

Also while in Ireland, Congressman Maguire—and we should keep in mind that until he is inaugurated, he is still only a former member of the House of Representatives—became acquainted with two women, both of whom he eventually married. His first wife died shortly after he returned to the United States. Despite having a child, who was raised in Ireland by his wife's family, he never married again, but he kept up his relationships with his acquaintances in Ireland and sent considerable sums of money to that country. Now Congressman Maguire has claimed in the past that all of that money went to the raising and education of his daughter, but we have only his word for that claim. One of those acquaintances was the woman he recently married, and we'll get back to her in a moment.

While practicing at the law firm of Phillips, Shannon and Steinberg in Boston, Mister Maguire forged a friendship with Jordan Montgomery and engaged him in many courtroom battles, where they frequently found themselves adversaries. Subsequently, Jordan Montgomery went into politics, first as a Congressman and then as a senator from Massachusetts. Kellan Maguire soon followed in Senator Montgomery's footsteps, although he joined a different political party. Moving to New York, where his activities in Massachusetts would not necessarily follow him, he continued to maintain his relationship with Senator Montgomery, as he himself sought a seat in Congress, which he won.

He brought with him to Congress as his top aides two women who had worked on his campaign. One of them, Jean Slater, was mentored by Lynn Patterson, whose former husband George was recently indicted for securities fraud, a charge made possible in part by legislation co-sponsored by Congressman Maguire and Senator Montgomery. Lynn Patterson of course was the manager of Congressman Maguire's first campaign. Also on his staff was a former colleague from Phillips, Shannon and Steinberg, a lesbian who so far has managed to keep any possible radical agenda well hidden. Our presumptive president has already announced that she would be appointed to his White House staff as a top advisor. Those two women, whose relationships with Congressman Maguire go back to the very beginning of his political activities, have been with him all the way, and have no doubt helped to shape his thinking.

Then, shortly before he joined Senator Montgomery on the ticket, his Chief of Staff Carmen Montefiore died of a heart attack. We are told that he had suffered heart disease for some time, and that his death was just a coincidence. Well, perhaps it was. But need I point out that Carmen Montefiore was well known for having served members of Congress from both parties. Might he possibly have gotten wind of a plot afoot to throw a wrench into the political apparatus which, if it were uncovered, might derail plans for a joint administration? We may never know, my friends.

That brings us to the extraordinary chain of events that occurred once this presidential campaign just completed began. On the day after Congressman Maguire was invited by Jordan Montgomery to be his vice presidential candidate, despite his being a member of the opposite party, Congressman Maguire married the woman we mentioned before, whom he first met in Ireland while he was still a student. Our investigators have learned that she spent a considerable amount of time in Northern Ireland in the company of people known to have IRA connections. Although she has very eloquently proclaimed her innocence from any significant connections with that radical group, again, we have only her word for it.

We have also recently learned that when he was already the nominee selected by Jordan Montgomery to run for vice president, he and his new wife made a secret visit to Belfast. Now he and his wife have both claimed that the only purpose of their trip was to visit her aunt in order to gain some information about her family. Her investigation into that topic has led to her claiming United States citizenship, even though she has only been in the United States for a very brief time. And we know very little about the man she was alleged to have been married to, except that he was very likely an IRA member who fought against British authorities in the Belfast area.

Now those are all things that we're familiar with, but ladies and gentlemen, don't they raise other, more troubling questions? What was it that prompted Jordan Montgomery to place Kellan Maguire on the ticket with him? Did the Congressman from New York have something on his old friend, or were they merely cooperating in a common venture? And what *else is there to know about the truck driver who allegedly lost control of his vehicle by accident, just as the presidential party was ascending that mountain in Vermont. And who was on the other end of the driver's CB radio, which was still activated after the accident scene was cleared? The driver had apparently been speaking with someone shortly before the accident, but the identity of that person has not been revealed. Just to make things more interesting, the driver responsible for the accident has apparently disappeared without a trace.*

And finally, we are told that Kellan Maguire visited President-elect Montgomery at the hospital sometime after the accident, and that a conversation between them may have taken place. Just how did that alleged conversation between the comatose Jordan Montgomery and Kellan Maguire come about, and what was really said? We were told that it was a private conversation, and that we have no right to know its contents. But with all the other questions that have been raised, ladies and gentlemen, don't you think we are entitled to something more? Don't you think there are other questions that might be posed about the real agenda of the man who is going to take office next week? It seems unlikely that Jordan Montgomery will survive his accident; if he does, what will happen next? Will Air Force One mysteriously crash? Or if he doesn't survive, can we be sure that everything possible will have been done to save his life?

Questions, my friends, are all we have at this point. Just what is Kellan Maguire's Irish connection? We'll take your calls following the break, but meanwhile this is Phil Paynter, your voice of reason on VRR, the Voice of Reason Radio Network.

Kellan, Jean, Alex, Bob Reynolds and a few others, forewarned about Paynter's broadcast, had gathered in one of the rooms in the Maryland hideaway where they had almost completed their work to listen. When Phil Paynter's program went to its commercial break, they turned the volume all the way down.

"Jesus Christ, Kellan, they ought to lock that son of a bitch up," said Alex. "How does he get away with that shit?"

"Everybody knows him for what he is," said Bob. "He's an asshole with the power of the microphone, and the more outrageous he becomes, the bigger his following, and therefore the more power he has. I can tell you right now that phones are lighting up over on the Hill with callers, especially the ones who want to know when their representatives are going to start impeachment proceedings, and for Christ sake, we're not even in office yet!"

"I'll bet Preston Fuller fed him a bunch of that crap," said Jean.

"What's that all about?" asked Bob.

"It was when Kellan was first running for Congress," said Jean. "Kellan had him on the ropes, and in their last debate he came up with that Irish stuff. Kellan shoved it all back down his throat, but Fuller would've lost anyway. If Fuller didn't give it to Paynter, how would he have known to mention it?"

"Interesting, but irrelevant," said Bob. "Let's take a trip down a list of possibilities. First, we ignore it, and it dies of its own weight. How likely is that?" He looked around the room.

Alex shook her head. "There's enough smoke there that somebody's going to think there's a fire. I mean, that kind of crap never dies. Judas priest, there are still people walking around who think Franklin Roosevelt engineered Pearl Harbor."

"Yeah, but what can they do about it?" Jean asked. "Sure enough, there will be some dork in Congress who will float an impeachment resolution, but that'll never get off the ground."

Bob looked at Kellan. "You're probably going to have to address it," he said. "Even though you will be dignifying his lunacy by even responding to it, if you don't, people will wonder why."

"Yeah, I suppose you're right. So the only question is, how do we go about it? The last god damn thing I want at this point is a news conference with questions coming from everywhere."

"No, that's out of the question," said Bob. "A full press conference will give weight to the accusations and make it look like you really have something to hide. We'll have to find a venue that will put you with some responsible person or a small group, and let them grill you up one side and down the other."

Alex said, "That same group you met two Sundays ago would be appropriate. The problem with that is, people will think somehow or other you got to them and that's why you agreed to meet them again."

"Alex is right," said Bob. "We might include one of them, but we'll have to find a couple of other good people."

"They were the cream of the crop, though," said Jean. "We'll have to come up with some others who are equally credible. Shouldn't be that hard—there are a lot of fine people in the business."

Nobody said anything for a few minutes as they pondered the possibilities. Then Alex said, "Kellan, do you have any contacts at the *Irish Times*, or anybody you will know over there who might be able to lend some dignity to what otherwise will surely be a vulgar brawl?"

Bob Reynolds laughed. "That's an old line from the artillery people. Where the hell did you come up with that?" Bob had done a tour in the army right after high school.

Alex smiled. "My brother Frank is a major in the Marines. I got it from him."

"It's a good point, though," said Jean. "What do you think, Kellan?"

Kellan thought for a few moments. "I think we need to get Kathleen in on this conversation. They'll start focusing on her right away anyway; in fact, I'm sure they've already begun. I wonder if anyone is listening to the callers on that show."

Bob said, "A couple of the guys upstairs are listening to it. Let me give them a call." Bob went over to a corner and picked up one of the telephones. In a few minutes he came back. "Right as rain," he said. "Charlie said that several of the listeners had wanted to know more about the IRA lady. I think you're right; we're going to have to bring her in."

"She was a journalist," said Alex. "Surely she must have some contacts over there that she could get in touch with."

"That's a possibility," said Kellan. "But a lot of her more recent work was in a publishing house." He thought for a moment. "In fact, the house she was with was the one that published Sean Levinson's book. There might be something there we can use."

"You're still in touch with him, right?" said Alex. Kellan nodded. "You think you could get him over here?"

"What would he be likely to say?" Bob asked.

"Well, if he's heard about this, which he may well have, the first thing he would do is laugh his ass off. No, he'd be good if we could get him, but I think he's retired now and I don't know whether he'd want to travel. Maybe we could get somebody from the *Irish Times* to talk to him."

After another half an hour or so of discussion, Bob Reynolds announced, "Okay, here's the plan. We get Kellan before a panel of respectable journalists. He denies everything. Then we get some kind of a public appearance arranged for Kathleen. We'll have to think about how we go about that after we talk to her. There are lots of possibilities there, but I'm sure she can handle anything we ask of her."

Alex laughed. "Man, I can't wait to see her take on this stuff. She'll bury anyone who tries to lay any of that nonsense on her."

"You sound like you know her pretty well," said Bob.

"The first time I met her in London, she blew me away," said Alex. "She's amazing."

"She ain't bad looking either," said Bob. "That won't hurt."

"I don't know," said Jean. "Beautiful women sometimes piss people off just because of their looks. There are some women who say they want to be admired for their brains and not for their looks, but half the time the only reason anybody is interested in them is because of their looks."

"What movie was that in?" said Alex, and everyone laughed.

"Here's what I suggest," said Bob. "You two guys"—he looked at Alex and Jean—"go with Kellan and talk to Kathleen. When you figure out what to do, give me a call and I'll help set it up."

"We're about done with this building, aren't we?" Kellan asked. "It seems to me we've got everything just about wrapped up."

"That's right," said Bob. "I'm going to have them start gathering up the papers and other stuff, and we should be out of here by noon tomorrow. You guys don't need to come back after today, though."

The Countess Kathleen

In the aftermath of the accident, Kellan requested the manager of his apartment building to extend his lease for thirty days. The uncertainty regarding his assumption of office made it wise to keep his options open. For the time being, Kellan had an additional line with an unlisted number installed for family and colleagues to use, but he felt it advisable to keep his regular number in service as a way of drawing phone calls that could be controlled.

Kellan, Alex and Jean arrived back at the apartment following their discussion with Bob and their reactions to the Phil Paynter broadcast. Kellan had asked Carlos to remain with Kathleen in the apartment to help answer phone calls, which had been coming in with irritating regularity. Kathleen and Carlos had also listened to the Paynter program, and soon after it ended, the phone had started ringing. "You can't believe some of the wackos who tried to get Kathleen on the line," said Carlos. "It was a real circus."

Kathleen of course recognized the seriousness of the charges, but at the same time she was amused by what she referred to as Paynter's ridiculous exaggerations. "I know you value freedom of the press," she said, "but somebody ought to muzzle that guy."

Kellan, Carlos and the women shared their impressions of the program, and Jean filled Kathleen in on the history of the Irish component going back to the Preston Fuller debate.

"So this isn't something new?" Kathleen said.

"Nope," said Jean, "we've been down this road before. This clown has upped the ante a little bit, but it's the same old garbage. The difference is that now it's probably going to go viral, and we're going to have to deal with it."

"And you're part of the deal," said Alex to Kathleen. "We just had a strategy meeting with Bob, and it's pretty clear that you're going to have to respond to some of that stuff one way or another." Kathleen looked at Alex and the others and was smiling. Alex returned the smile and asked, "Okay what are you thinking about now? I have the feeling you're going to enjoy this."

Kellan and Jean looked at each other, initially with apparent skepticism, but then it began to become clear that Kathleen was indeed more than ready to go to war. Kellan reflected on how much she had seen of political ugliness, violence, and all the other bits and pieces of the phenomenon known as 'the troubles' in Ireland. He started to speak, but Kathleen spoke first. She was looking at Kellan. "I know what you're thinking," she said. "Look, I know that we're in the midst of a tragedy with Jordan. I know how much he means to you, and how his loss will affect you personally.

"But that aside, and I know how hard it is to put that aside, this whole business with conspiracies and the Irish stuff strikes me as being nothing short of preposterous. I'll say this for the Irish, at least we know what we're fighting for. But the political bickering that's been going on here in this country is very often amusing to the rest of the world. I've been reading the British and European press for years, and sometimes they just don't understand how a country with everything that the United States has going for it can get itself in such an uproar over things that aren't really that important."

"Oh, I think they're important all right," said Jean. "But you're right in a way. It's true that we have our ridiculous side, but we've fought over some pretty important stuff, too. We had a million casualties in our war over slavery, and there was a lot of blood in the streets over our last war. But it's true that we can get just as fractious over the petty stuff as over the important stuff. And now here we are with a little bit of both going on. A president dying before he even gets to take office is pretty damn important. But crackpots taking advantage of tragedy to foist some wacko agenda on the people is at the other end of the spectrum. So were going to have to sit down and sort it out. We've got to pay respect to Jordan while we take on the others. Do you think you're up for it?" She looked at Kathleen.

"You're absolutely right, Jean," Kathleen said. "And believe me, I'm up for it. I think it's wonderful that I had a legitimate claim to American citizenship. For most of my life I had no idea that my grandfather had spent time here and that my father may even have been born here. But now I'm one of you, and just like my Irish ancestors, I'm ready to do battle for what is right. Where do we start?"

Carlos spoke up. "Well, one place we might think about starting is with Zelda Brewer. We got a call from her about an hour ago, and I took it. She wanted to know if Kathleen was available to go on her show. I had to cover up the phone to keep from laughing at her, but I was polite and said I would take a message. I actually did write down her number, but I wasn't even going to bother to give it to Kathleen. I just thought it might be something to have in case we needed it."

"Jesus Christ, Zelda Brewer!" Alex said. "She almost makes Phil Paynter look like a philosophy professor. Let me correct that; I don't think she's stupid. I just think she has a very weird idea of what people think is interesting."

"A couple of weeks ago she had on that woman who tried to stuff her husband into a fireplace and set him on fire," said Jean.

Kathleen said, "You're kidding, right?"

"Nope. I guess the guy had beat her up a bit, passed out drunk, and she was sick of it. She doused him with lighter fluid or something, then thought better of it and called the fire department in case he went up in flames. She didn't get arrested because they decided that no actual crime had been committed, although the husband's relatives wanted to have her committed."

"Not everything Zelda does on her shows is that crazy," said Alex. "You know the old saying, even a blind pig finds an acorn once in a while. She manages to get a serious guest with a serious topic on there from time to time, but a lot of people are afraid to go on her show because she's liable to spring anything on them."

"I don't think we want to go there," said Kellan.

"Why not?" said Kathleen. "If she's the worst of the lot, then I'm all for it. It seems to me that if I put myself up against the toughest possible adversary, I'll do better than if I try to get somebody who's going to treat me with kid gloves."

"I think Kathleen has a point," said Alex. "But if we decide to go that route, we're going to have to set up some parameters of our own."

"She's not going to like that," said Kellan.

"Kathleen is the hottest ticket in town right now," said Alex, "and I'm guessing Zelda will do anything to get her on her program. It will be a huge feather in her cap, and she'll probably have the biggest audience she's ever had. That will be good, because Kathleen will be able to put her message out to a very broad base."

"How do we go about that?" asked Kathleen.

"Okay, one of the things that those shows do to trip people up is to tape the session and then edit it in their favor. They don't necessarily distort what people say, but they arrange it in such a way that it seems to mean something different than what the speaker intended."

"How do we get around that?" Kathleen asked.

Alex seemed to be getting excited about the idea. "Okay, here's what might work. We tell her that you'll only go on her show for a given period of time, say half an hour. And you agree to do it only if she does it live. That way she can't edit it for viewing later. No tapes will be made or kept once it's over. They'll ignore that, but they won't be able to use it. You'll have to be damn sure you're ready for anything, but if you can get her to agree to that, you can beat her at her own game."

"Can I get to see how she works before I'm tossed onto the fire?" said Kathleen, but she was smiling.

"I tell you what. I'll scratch around and see if I can get some tapes of her old shows, and we can go over them together to get an idea of her tactics. Then we can have our own plan on how to deal with her. What do you say, Kellan? Do you think this is worth a shot?"

"Bob Reynolds will shit a brick," he said. He thought for a moment. "But he just might go along with it." He looked at Kathleen and smiled. "He thinks very highly of you, and he knows you're nobody's fool."

"Why would he have to approve of something like that? Don't I have freedom of speech, or is that just something you Yanks preach but don't practice? We Yanks, I should say!"

"Sweetheart, you can say anything you want, but this is a lot bigger than just you and me and my so-called Irish connection. Let's face it, if the thing backfires, then we're in worse trouble, and not only that, but it might reflect on Jordan."

"Well, we have to do something," said Alex.

"You know what they say," said Kellan. "When you find yourself in a hole, the best thing to do is stop digging."

Everyone chuckled. "I don't think we're in a hole," said Kathleen. "It seems to me that the guy who has dug himself his own grave is that other guy, Pinter or Painter or whatever his fucking name is. Why don't we grab a shovel and hand it to that Zelda Brewer character. I'm ready to have a go." She smiled. "I've got my Irish up!"

Everyone laughed. Kellan said, "Let's let Carlos handle it. Carlos, you're friends with Spencer Turner, right?"

"Yeah, we hang out together sometimes. I tell him where all the bodies are buried, and he gives me a heads up on what's coming up on the evening news."

"Really?" said Jean.

"Yeah, but he's a good guy. I could ask him about Zelda; I think he knows her."

"Let's think it over for a bit, and I'll call Bob and see what he thinks," said Kellan. "Now who's ready for dinner? Will it be Chinese or pizza?"

The next morning, everyone reassembled in Kellan and Kathleen's apartment. Bob was skeptical, but went along with the plan. "From what I've seen of her, there will be no keeping her quiet anyway," he said.

They decided that Carlos, who had taken the original call, would return Zelda Brewer's call and set out the parameters. Carlos dialed the number, which was answered by an assistant, and after a wait, Miss Brewer came on the line. Carlos explained that Kathleen Maguire would be willing to go on to her show but only under certain conditions. He laid out what the group had agreed on, namely, a live broadcast, time-limited, no editing to be done, and any replays or rebroadcasts would have to be approved by Kathleen.

Zelda Brewer told Carlos that those terms were completely unacceptable. Carlos said, "Thank you Miss Brewer, but those terms are non-negotiable. You have our number." Carlos smiled as he hung up the phone. "Okay," he said, "I'm collecting bets for how long it takes her to call back. Anybody who thinks it will be more than half an hour, raise your hand."

Zelda Brewer called back in about thirty-five minutes, time enough, the group concluded, to have had a lengthy conversation with her network attorneys. She requested a slight modification in the terms, but Carlos reiterated that they were non-negotiable, and she offered to call back again. The second time it took about ten minutes. Carlos gave a thumbs-up sign as he put down the phone.

"You're on, baby!" said Alex. As the group exchanged high fives, Kellan smiled, and tried not to wonder whether this was indeed a wise idea. Then he watched Kathleen, who was enjoying the moment, but was clearly not yet ready to celebrate a victory that had not yet won; she knew better, but she was ready for battle.

It was finally agreed that Kellan would do a special edition of the Sunday morning program, and that Kathleen would go on live at nine pm the same day with Zelda Brewer. As she and Kathleen reviewed Zelda's old shows, Alex pointed out the predictable pattern. Zelda was going to start out all sweetness and light, trying to set Kathleen up for the kill. They decided that Kathleen would use the same tactic, pretending that she was thrilled to be on the show. "I'll play the dumb Irish immigrant," Kathleen said.

Kathleen and Alex also made note of some of the tactics that Zelda Brewer had used on others, people who had been unable to defend themselves, either because Brewer overpowered them or because the tape was edited before being shown. Alex identified episodes with public figures that had apparently been distorted, and she called and spoke with three of them on a confidential basis to get a bit more insight. Alex and Kathleen concluded that although Zelda Brewer could be tough, many of her guests more or less asked for it because they had done something less than admirable to get them on the show, as in the case of the women who had thought about roasting her husband in the fireplace.

Kathleen and Alex were waiting at the apartment when Kellan returned from his Sunday morning show "You did very well," Kathleen said. "I was quite proud of you, I think you hit all the right points, and you left no doubt that everything that happened was just as reported."

"One thing I'd like to know," said Alex. "Why didn't they make any attempt to dismiss the Paynter stuff? It seems to me that responsible journalists ought to take it upon themselves to counter that sort of nonsense. After all, they're part of the same profession, and to some extent they're responsible for everything that they all say. If one of them lacks total credibility, doesn't that imply that the others could be at least partially suspect?"

"You have a point, but before the show, they assured me that they were not going to mention the Paynter broadcast. They knew about it, knew it was a bunch of crap, but I guess their position was that they didn't want to dignify it, even by merely mentioning it. I think I answered all the issues that were raised without referring to him, but of course that won't shut him up. On the other hand, if I had responded to him through that group, I would just have given him more ammunition. You know the old saying: Never wrestle with a pig; there's no way you can win, you wind up with mud all over you, and besides, the pig likes it."

"But shouldn't somebody in the media come out and condemn that guy?" Alex insisted.

"I'm not so sure about that" said Kellan. "In any profession you're going to have people who abuse their license, abuse the public trust to which they think they're entitled. But I don't think we can condemn the whole media for the rotten eggs who spread the rumors and phony stories to the public."

"That may be," said Kathleen, "but in a free society like this one, especially in a democracy where the people are supposed to be sovereign, they have to have access to the truth. They have to know what's really going on, and for an individual who has a license to use the public airwaves, which after all, belong to the public, don't they have some responsibility to adhere to certain minimal standards of truth?"

"Of course they do, but policing that is very difficult. The FCC has responsibility to monitor the airwaves, but they can't run down every crazy story put out by the Paynters of the world to find out what's really true. It would take more manpower that they have just to discover what the real story was. And most of those people are smart enough to hide behind words like 'alleged' and 'possible' and 'it has been rumored that,' and all sorts of crap like that. I mean, all Paynter did was pose questions; he didn't offer any answers, even though they were implied."

Kathleen said, "Well anyway, Darling, you did very well. You put most of it to rest. Now it's up to me to deal with the Irish stuff. We'll see what happens this evening. Alex says she's going to go with me, and I think that's a great idea. It will be nice to have her standing by just for support. She won't be out there on camera with me, but I'll know she's there. What about you?"

"I don't think I need to go," said Kellan. "If things go badly, I might be tempted to jump in, which would not be good. I would just embarrass you, embarrass myself, or make things worse. So I think the best thing for me to do is to just stay here with Jean. I'll ask Bob and Sally to come over and we can watch the show together. We can talk about it when it's all over. I'm sure you'll do well, and I know Alex has helped you figure out how to deal with her. She might even wind up taking your side. As we were saying a few minutes ago, if one journalist stinks up the joint, the odor will waft over the whole business. If she can stick a pin in Paynter's balloon, it will only help her ratings. Just keep your guard up."

"She's ready," said Alex. "It's going to be a lot of fun."

"We'll be cheering you on," said Kellan.

Zelda Brewer opened the show with Kathleen already seated in the chair opposite her. As predicted, she began effusively. "Welcome, Mrs. Maguire, it's just wonderful to have you on the show! I have been looking forward to this conversation for some time, as you have certainly caught the public's imagination in this town, and presumably all across the country."

Kathleen gave the host a big smile. "Thank you, Miss Brewer, I'm very pleased to be here. It was very kind of you to invite me."

"The pleasure is all mine," said Zelda.

"There she goes, lovey, dovey," said Jean. "Just as advertised." They were seated in Kellan's living room watching the show. Sally Reynolds harrumphed.

"As you know, of course," Zelda continued, "your name has been brought up in connection with the situation we have with our president-elect. By now everyone is surely aware that President-elect Montgomery is in a coma in a Boston hospital, and if he does not recover from his accident before January 20, your husband will be sworn in as vice president and will then immediately become acting president under the 25th amendment."

"Yes, that's right, and although my husband was stunned at the accident, as we all were, I know him well enough to know that he will be able to do the job before him, however it may turn out."

"Questions have been raised about how your husband was selected for vice president. Can you tell us anything about that? I understand that you were in Ireland at the time."

"She's setting the bait," said Jean, back in the apartment.

"Yes, I was. I had gone back to Ireland briefly to take care of some personal business, but I arrived back in Washington just after my husband Kellan met with Jordan Montgomery. I had no prior knowledge of what was decided. In fact, I was stunned when I heard about it."

"Have you ever met Jordan Montgomery?"

"Yes. As everybody knows, Kellan and Jordan have been close friends for most of their lives. They went to college together, practiced law together and have kept in close touch ever since. I have known Jordan Montgomery for only a short time, but I have been quite impressed by his judgment, his wisdom, and his political sophistication. I think his choice of my husband for his vice president was a measure of the character of both men."

"You mentioned that you are impressed with Jordan Montgomery's political acumen. That suggests that you have a political background of your own."

"Here it comes," said Jean. Kellan said nothing, but leaned forward in his chair.

"That subject of course has come up recently in conjunction with your husband's time spent in Ireland, both when he was a student and in later times when he kept up connections with friends and relatives in Ireland.

Now I hate to have to ask this, but I must. Could you tell us straight out whether you have any connection whatsoever with the Irish Republican Army, commonly known as the IRA?"

Kellan noted that Kathleen did not answer immediately, but she did not appear to be bothered by the question. In fact, Kellan thought, she seemed to have a trace of a smile on her face. "I hope Alex can see this," said Jean.

"You say you must ask the question. May I ask why you 'must' do that? Doesn't your posing the question imply that there may be something to it? I mean, if your intention is to perpetuate the same nonsense that has been put out by a colleague of yours, I wonder why you feel it's necessary to do that. Frankly, I don't think it's necessary at all."

"First off, Phil Paynter is no colleague of mine," Zelda snapped.

"I apologize. I thought he was also in the news business."

"All right, but that aside, you're refusing to answer my question?" said Zelda Brewer.

"No, I am not refusing to answer your question," said Kathleen calmly. "I am challenging the fact that you said you had to ask the question, implying that I must therefore answer it. I want to know before I give you an answer why you say it's necessary. To me that suggests that you believe the charges and think that I have something to hide."

"Mrs. Maguire—may I call you Kathleen?"

"Sure, Zelda, why not?"

"All right, I brought you on the program to give you an opportunity to set things straight. I had no prior agenda, I assure you."

"What a load of crap!" muttered Jean.

"I said I must ask the question because the question has been raised and it's out there. If you have a problem with that, perhaps you are holding something back, perhaps you do have something to hide; is that not a reasonable inference?"

"Fair enough, but let me put something on the table first, before we go any further. I was for a brief time married to a man whom I met when I was very young and very impressionable. I had a sense that he might be engaged with activities involving the IRA or Sinn Féin, the Irish political group. If you know anything about the history of Ireland, you should understand that the Irish relationship with the British governance of Ireland going back hundreds of years has been one of constant struggle.

"The British for all practical purposes held the Irish people in slavery for several centuries. In fact, most of your listeners may not be aware that slavery still existed among the Irish people after the end of your American Civil War. I should add at this point that it's also my American Civil War, because I am after all also an American citizen, in addition to being Irish. So the struggles that have been going on in Ireland for generations are legitimate struggles of the Irish people to maintain the freedom which they deserve—the right to govern themselves without interference from the British, or anyone else, for that matter."

Zelda started to speak, but Kathleen said, "Let me finish, please."

"All right."

"Now, it is true that in Northern Ireland there are two sides who have different opinions about what is right and what is wrong. But the man that I was married to happened to have a close relative killed by British authorities, and he was rightfully indignant that such a thing had happened. It occurred after we met, and it colored his political views quite sharply."

"So you were involved with the IRA, am I correct?"

"No, I was not. In fact, although I married the man out of a sense of sympathy, among other things, as soon as I became fully aware that he was involved in violent activity, I left him, and fully intended to end the marriage. Before I could accomplish that, however, my husband was killed in Londonderry by British troops who tracked him down, lured him into a gunfight and shot him dead. The extent of my involvement with any of that was simply that I was married to a man who I later discovered was deeply involved with the IRA, and whom I left once I found that out. I have never in any way involved myself in political activity or violence or anything else, not only against the law, but against human decency. I will admit to having written about Irish rights during my career as a journalist."

"Good that she got that in," said Jean. "Puts her on the same level with Zelda."

"I'd say it puts her a cut above," said Sally.

"All right," said Zelda, "let me go on to another point. You said a few moments ago that it was your Civil War, that you are also an American citizen. Let me ask you point blank, Kathleen. How can you possibly be an American citizen when you have been in this country less than a year? In fact, when you allegedly achieved your American citizenship, you had only been in this country for a matter of days, and had been married for less than a month. By what stretch of the imagination does that possibly entitle you to claim to be an American citizen?"

"Well I'm glad you asked that, Zelda. I have a right to American citizenship on two grounds. First my grandfather achieved his citizenship papers when he worked for a time here in the United States. I have in my possession his certificate of citizenship that was granted to him by the United States government in 1891. A provision of American immigration law entitles me to citizenship for that reason—it's obscure, but it's there. My grandfather also got married while he was here in the states to another woman of Irish background, and they had a child who was born in the United States. I have a birth certificate showing that my father was born in New Jersey. On either of those grounds I have a legitimate claim to United States citizenship, and I have in my possession a certificate to that effect issued to me by the Immigration and Naturalization Service several months ago."

"Do you have those items in your possession right now?"

"I did bring with them with me but I do not have them on my person at this moment. My attorney is here in the dressing room where I left my personal belongings; she has them in her possession."

"Would you be willing to have your possessions brought out so that you might show me those certificates which you claim you have?"

"No, I will not do that."

"Why are you refusing to show me those documents?"

"Because your request to see them implies that you think I may be lying. In other words, you don't trust me to be telling the truth, even though I have no reason to lie. If I were lying, it would eventually come out, and that would have a very detrimental effect on other people."

"Meaning your husband, I presume?"

"Yes, and it would not only be a reflection upon my husband, but also on the man who asked him to run on the ballot with him, Jordan Montgomery, who as we speak, lies in a coma in a hospital in Boston. As I said, I have had the pleasure of meeting Jordan Montgomery, and I find him to be an extraordinarily decent and honorable man, and since he is also a close personal friend of my husband, I would never under any circumstances do anything that might reflect upon his character or judgment.

"So my answer once more is no, I will not show you those documents, because I am telling the truth and I have no need to prove it. My certificate of citizenship was given to me by the Immigration and Naturalization Service. If you want proof, you'll have to ask them for it. But I have no need to prove my honesty in this environment."

"Well, don't you think the American people have a right to see the evidence?"

"Evidence of what? That I'm telling the truth? You accept as unvarnished truth the word of a man whose charges are truly outrageous, but you question my veracity based upon absolutely no evidence. How can I assume that you're even trying to be fair during this interview?"

Zelda Brewer said, "Excuse me Mrs. Maguire, but I'm the one who is supposed to be asking the questions here."

"So much for Kathleen and Zelda," said Jean.

"Oh?" Said Kathleen. "I don't remember anything like that being in the agreement we made before I came on this program. Would you care to discuss that further?"

"I don't know what agreement you're talking about," Zelda Brewer said. "Guests who are lucky enough to be on this show are not given any agreements."

"Gotcha!" said Jean.

"Well I have several witnesses who would be happy to tell the world that you agreed that this program would be done live, that there would be no taping, and that if a tape were made, it could never be put on the air. I recall that you were reluctant to accept those conditions, but you finally did. I congratulate you for that; it was a very honest thing to do."

"Well, thank you, but … "

"But now you're claiming that there is no such agreement, when in fact three phone calls were made between my representative and you in which the agreements were reached. I don't recall anything ever being mentioned about who got to do the questioning and who was supposed to do the answering. You have made some claims, you have bought in claims which are one hundred percent outrageous, and I am challenging you to either defend or disavow a person who is a well-known fabricator of facts. If you're willing to do that, we can continue this interview. If not, then I will terminate it."

"Well, you're certainly entitled to your opinion," said Zelda Brewer. "But let's move on. Shortly after your husband was placed on the ballot with Jordan Montgomery, you and your husband made a trip to Belfast. Would you care to tell me what you were doing there?"

"I'd be interested to know how you found out about that trip," said Kathleen, "but I'll let that pass. I was in Belfast to visit my aunt, with whom I lived as a young woman."

"Has your aunt lived in Belfast all her life?" Zelda said.

"She's fishing now," said Jean. "She has no idea where she's going with this."

"She moved to Belfast when she married her husband. My aunt was a dancer, and her dance group was performing in Belfast when she met her future husband. When they married, they settled in Belfast."

"Did your aunt's husband ever have any connections with the IRA?"

Kathleen smiled and shook her head. "He was a Protestant. He's dead now, but that was his faith. My aunt happened to be Catholic, but that's not uncommon for people in Belfast."

"Well, there might be Protestants in the IRA, I should think," said Zelda.

"Well if they are, they're probably spies," said Kathleen. "I think if you investigate that a little bit further you'll see that your question makes no sense at all."

Zelda ignored the dig. "So you had nothing to do with the IRA during that trip to Belfast?"

"No, I went to visit my aunt, and that's where I was able to locate the documents regarding my father's birth."

"You mean you didn't even know where your father was born?" said Zelda, with a touch of enthusiasm. She seemed to have stumbled upon new territory to explore, and she was determined to take advantage of it.

"No, I didn't know where my father was born. He died when I was young, and because my mother had difficulty raising me, I went to live with my aunt. She was my father's sister. She was very kind to me and took good care of me. But as I was a rather troubled young woman, I never took much interest in my father's heritage. As I grew older, it became more interesting to me, and that's why I visited her, in order to close the file, so to speak."

"Had your husband ever met your aunt before?"

Kathleen looked down and smiled and shook her head briefly, then looked back at Zelda. "No, he had never met her before."

"Well, that's all very interesting," said Zelda. "I'm not sure all the questions are answered, but it seems to me that we've covered quite a bit of ground. One more thing. When did you meet your husband?"

"When he was studying at Trinity in Dublin. He was engaged to my best friend."

"And you're married to him now. What happened to their marriage?"

"That's really no one's business," said Kathleen. "But just to set the record straight, she died in childbirth about a year after they were married."

"And where was all that? What happened to the child?"

"I'm sorry, Zelda, but you're way off base here. I'm not going to answer any more questions about that. All I will say is that Kellan's first wife was my best friend, and I mourned her death, just as he did."

"But ... "

"You have covered all the ground you need to cover, in my opinion," said Kathleen. "Again, I thank you for inviting me on the show. It was a pleasure to meet you and to discuss these matters." She stood up and offered Zelda her hand.

"We'll be right back," said Zelda, and the program went to a commercial break.

Back in Kellan and Kathleen's apartment, everyone was smiling. "She did a good job," said Bob.

"She sure did," said Sally. "I've never seen Zelda so flustered."

"You mean you actually watch her?" said Jean, but she was smiling.

"Oh, sure," said Sally. "You know, a little comic relief never hurt anyone."

"They'll be back pretty soon," said Kellan. "I think this calls for a bit of champagne." He started for the kitchen.

"Let me get it, Kellan" said Jean. "Sit down and relax. You need a break!"

The studio announcer on radio station WPOL in Washington was doing an hourly news update. It was the third Monday in January. At the end of the session he said, "Now we'll turn to some commentary by Spencer Turner on the Hill. Spencer?"

Good morning, Jack.

Well, I'm over here on the Hill standing outside the office of the vice president where Vice President-elect Kellan Maguire has spent the past few days preparing for the coming inauguration. It has been a busy time for the former Congressman from New York. Following allegations leveled by talk-show host Phil Paynter, Congressman Maguire appeared on a special session of People Today yesterday, where he cleared up a number of, shall we say, misunderstandings—and I'm being generous here, Jack. Last evening, Kathleen Morrissey Maguire appeared with Zelda Brewer in an attempt to further clear the air concerning the vice president-elect's alleged Irish connections.

The consensus here on the Hill, and across much of the country as far as we can tell, is that none of the allegations about some secret agenda concerning the IRA have any merit. It is true that the former Congressman has a strong Irish background, that he has spent considerable time in Ireland, and that his roots there are not only deep, but current. At the same time, any possible controversy concerning his Irish connections seems to have evaporated.

As you know, Jack, it looks almost certain that Congressman Kellan Maguire will be sworn in as vice president this coming Friday, and that he will immediately assume the position of acting president, given that President-elect Jordan Montgomery is very unlikely to be capable of assuming office. As you just pointed out, medical reports indicate that he is still in a coma, and although his condition remains stable, doctors seem to be skeptical about the possibility for his recovery.

Having covered Congressman Maguire for the past several years, I can attest to his standing among his colleagues here on the Hill, not only among Democrats but also with Republican colleagues with whom he has worked closely on legislation and committee work. As we have discussed before, there is bound to be disgruntlement over the fact that the people elected a Republican president of the United States, but will soon see that office occupied by a Democrat. But there are those here on the Hill who think that's not necessarily a bad thing.

It is clear to anyone who has been following politics recently that the country has become divided, and that cooperation between the two parties has become difficult. The country's economic troubles, which have continued unabated for months, have apparently been exacerbated by the lack of political unity. Given that Senator Montgomery and Congressman Maguire ran on a platform with strong economic focus, it is assumed that whichever one of them winds up atop the new administration, the economic future of the nation should brighten. Movement of the stock market since the first of the year seems to reflect that optimism.

"I think it's safe to say that for the first time since the tragic accident that injured the president-elect, the country is returning to a mood of optimism, something which, quite frankly, we have been missing for some time. That's it from Capitol Hill. Back to you, Jack.

Kellan had met with the five Cabinet members already named by Jordan Montgomery and assured them that he intended to go forward with their nominations. The working group organized by Bob Reynolds had settled on names for most of the remaining top posts for the administration, and he and his aides along with Kellan were in the process of contacting them to inform them of their coming selection.

Bob had also helped Kellan select key personnel to man White House positions, leaning heavily towards those whom Jordan Montgomery would have selected, but allowing for Kellan to include aides who were close to him, since it would likely be some time before Jordan Montgomery could return to the office, if indeed he ever would.

Following the inauguration, which would be very low key, given the circumstances, Vice President and Mrs. Maguire would move into the vice president's personal quarters on Massachusetts Avenue pending further developments.

They would, however, for as long as the vice president served in an acting capacity, be permitted to occupy temporary living quarters in the White House. It had been decided to suspend the normal inauguration festivities, including the inaugural parade and the inauguration balls. Celebrating the transition while the president-elect lay comatose would have been seen as unseemly at best. As Kellan and Bob Reynolds had discussed, proceeding as though things were normal would create a crushing emotional burden for Shelley Montgomery and the rest of the Montgomery family.

Kellan and Bob planned to fly to Boston on Tuesday to visit briefly with Shelley Montgomery, who had taken up residence in a hotel near the hospital, to discuss the plans for a very low key inauguration day. If and when Jordan were to recover, a proper celebration could be scheduled in his honor. Should the death of the president-elect occur, appropriate ceremonies would be arranged. The remainder of the week would be devoted to final preparations for the assumption of office of the new administration.

Epilogue

Kellan Maguire was sworn in as the Vice President of the United States in a large room in the Senate side of the Capitol. The ceremony was attended by Kellan's wife Kathleen, his brother and sister and their spouses and children, members of his staff, his designated Chief of Staff Bob Reynolds and his wife Sally, his daughter Fiona, and Brendan and Deirdre Connolly, who had arrived from Ireland a few days earlier.

Brendan and Deirdre Connolly had been planning to come for months, had purchased their tickets, and were not deterred by the fact that the inauguration would be low key. They would spend time in Washington, be shown the sights of the National Capital, then would travel to New England to spend time with the Maguire family, including with their adoptive daughter, Fiona, who was in medical school in Worcester, Massachusetts. The Connollys and the Maguires had met before when members of the vice president's family had traveled to Ireland.

As a matter of courtesy Kellan had invited Shelley Montgomery to come to the ceremony, and he was surprised when she accepted. She had arrived the night before, and Kellan and Kathleen had visited her at the hotel near the Capitol where she was staying. They had a long warm but sad meeting where they discussed the things that had happened to all of them during the past few weeks. On the day of the inauguration Shelley Montgomery stood by quietly as the ceremony progressed.

Vice President Kellan Maguire didn't make a speech, but he did thank everyone for coming, and promised to do his best to uphold the spirit of the team that he had been invited to join right after the Republican National Convention. As soon as he had concluded his brief remarks, the first person he greeted was Shelley. He embraced her warmly and whispered that he was glad she was there but understood how difficult it was for her to be away from her recovering husband. "I was surprised that you came," said Kellan, "but it means a lot. Not only to me, but for the country."

"It wasn't a difficult decision," said Shelley. "He's already gone. The doctors won't say that, but he has gone deeper into the coma. For a while he was recognizing me; he would squeeze my fingers when I touched him and he seemed to react to my voice. But over the last few days there has been no reaction whatsoever. The doctors say it could end soon, or it could go on for weeks, or even longer. Kellan, one way or the other, I don't think he's coming back—I think the end is in sight, and you should prepare yourself for whatever is ahead."

"I'll do that, Shelley. God, I can't tell you how sorry I am for all of this. But you're being here is just wonderful, and means a great deal to me. And I'm sure that Jordan, if he understands, is also glad that you are here."

"Yes, he would have wanted that."

"If you don't mind, I'd like to let it be known that you were able to attend."

"Do you think that's necessary?" Shelley asked.

"No, but it might lay to rest any lingering doubts about the conspiracy theories that have been floated."

"Oh, of course. I guess I did hear something about that."

"We can use Carlos to get it out. He has some friends in the media."

Fiona was standing next to them, and Kellan turned and embraced his daughter. She was thrilled for Kellan, but also sad for the man whom she had called Uncle Jordan. "I'm glad you could get some time off from your studies," he said. "Eileen tells me you've been working really hard."

"I am, Dad, but I wouldn't have missed this for anything. I can't believe you're actually now the acting president of the United States. And I talked to Aunt Shelley. It doesn't sound too good, does it?"

"No, it doesn't, Sweetheart, but we'll just roll with the punches and see what happens."

The group retired to the Senate dining room for a light lunch. The mood was somber, but not depressed. There was an air of anticipation, as was always the case with the new administration, and everyone gathered in the room, from Bob Reynolds to the least member of the incoming staff, recognized that the man who was about to don the mantle of president of the United States, if not the actual title, was more than capable of carrying out his duties. They were relieved that Kellan seemed so well prepared, and those who knew him were more than ready to parry attacks of those who might be frustrated that their party had apparently lost the highest office in the land. Kellan had plans to relieve them of their frustration, possibly by declaring himself an independent for the duration of his time in the White House. But all that would come later; for today was a day of quiet anticipation, if not celebration. The rest would follow in due course.

Toward the end of the meal an aide came into the dining room, walked over and whispered in Shelley Montgomery's ear. She stood up, her face was drawn, and Kellan knew instantly what had happened. He got up and went over to her and put his arms around her.

"He's gone," she said. "He died a few minutes ago."

"I'm so sorry, Shelley, truly I am. We'll do everything we can to see to it that he is given a proper farewell. Please stay close, and we will give you as much support as possible."

Kathleen had picked up what had happened, and she too embraced Shelley and offered her condolences, as did Fiona. The four of them stood huddled in a group, their arms all around each other, as the rest of the room went silent, rapidly perceiving what news had been brought. After a while Kellan turned and faced the quiet room.

"President Jordan Montgomery has died," he said. "All of us here mourn and pray for him, and our sympathies are with Shelley and the rest of the Montgomery family. I would ask you all to take a few moments to reflect on the man we have lost, a man without whom many of us would not be here today. It is truly a sad day for America."

Moments later, the Chief Justice of the United States, who was present, swore in Kellan Maguire as President of the United States. Later that afternoon Kellan and Kathleen Morrissey Maguire and Fiona Connolly were driven to the White House and given a tour of the mansion.

Six Months Later

On a lovely Saturday afternoon in June, Fiona Connolly and Doctor Michael Hanrahan were married in the White House Rose Garden. The bride was given away by her father, President Kellan Maguire, jointly with her adoptive father and mother, Brendan and Deirdre Connolly. The maid of honor was Alexandra Crowley; the chief usher was Lieutenant Colonel Frank Crowley, USMC, the president's military aide. Also in attendance along with members of both families were Mrs. Shelley Montgomery, Mrs. Stella Montefiore, Charles and Cynthia Wright, Mrs. Lynn Patterson, Martin and Diana Downey, and Bob Reynolds, Jean Slater and Carlos Gutierrez, members of the president's staff. Sally Reynolds, the First Lady's press secretary, and columnist Marjorie Wellborn of the *Washington American* also attended. Among the family members were Patrick and Elizabeth Connolly, the bride's grandparents. It was Patrick Connolly's first visit to America; Elizabeth—"Libby" to her family—had been in America briefly several decades earlier. The reception, with music by a United States Marine Band chamber ensemble and the Irish rock group, The Shamrocks, was held in the East Room of the White House.

A pool reporter seated in the back row during the ceremony noted that as the president accompanied his daughter down the aisle, he had tears in his eyes.

About the Author

H.J. Sage is a retired Marine Corps officer who spent much of his career as a teacher and writer. He wrote speeches and articles for top ranking military officials and published articles under his own name in several journals. As a history teacher for forty years he has specialized in American political and military history. He has published two American history textbooks which are widely used as Open Educational Resources. He holds the rank of associate professor emeritus at Northern Virginia Community College. He has also taught at Holy Cross, George Mason University, and the University of Maryland both in College Park and in Japan. His has also worked as a ghostwriter, and has taught American literature and writing as well as history. In his spare time he enjoys music, baseball and wrestling with his two dogs. He lives in Northern Virginia with his wife, Nancy, a retired teacher.

Also by H.J. Sage

From Colonies to Free Nation: United States History 1607-1865

Freedom and Responsibility: United States History 1865-2000

The United States in World War II

www.sageamericanhistory.net